THE POLYGLOTS

WILLIAM GERHARDIE was born in St Petersburg in 1895. He was educated in Russia and later at Worcester College, Oxford, where he wrote his first novel, *Futility*. During the First World War he was posted to the staff of the British Military Attaché at Petrograd, and in 1918 he went with the British Military Mission to Siberia. After two years there, he left the army with an OBE, sailing home by way of Singapore, Colombo and Port Said—a journey that forms the closing chapters of *The Polyglots*. Gerhardie wrote much of the novel at Innsbruck, completing it under difficult conditions while his father was dying.

In addition to his novels, which include *Resurrection* (1934) and *Of Mortal Love* (1936), William Gerhardie wrote several non-fiction works, among them *Anton Chekhov* (1923), written during his time at Oxford; *Memoirs of a Polyglot* (1931) and the posthumously published biographical history *God's Fifth Column* (1981). He died in London in 1977.

MICHAEL HOLROYD is well known as an author and biographer, notably of Lytton Strachey and Augustus John. He was editor, with Robert Skidelsky, of Gerhardie's *God's Fifth Column* (1981).

Prion Lost Treasures

The Bourbons of Naples • Harold Acton

Disraeli • Robert Blake

Dylan Thomas in America • John Malcolm Brinnin

The River War • Winston S. Churchill

Doom • William Gerhardie

Poets in a Landscape • Gilbert Highet

The Dilessi Murders • Romilly Jenkins

Mozart • Annette Kolb

Sardinian Brigade • Emilio Lussu

Napoleon and his Marshals • A G Macdonell

Byron—The Last Journey • Harold Nicolson

Verdun • Jules Romains

Conversations with Wellington • Earl Stanhope

Napoleon's Letters • J M Thompson

A King's Story • H. R. H. the Duke of Windsor

Memoirs Vol I • Duc de Saint-Simon

Memoirs Vol II• Duc de Saint-Simon

Memoirs Vol III• Duc de Saint-Simon

The Dukays • Lajos Zilahy

Two Prisoners • Lajos Zilahy

Century in Scarlet • Lajos Zilahy

The Case of Sergeant Grischa • Arnold Zweig

William Gerhardie

The Polyglots

with a Preface by
Michael Holroyd

This edition published in 2001 by
Prion Books Limited, Imperial Works,
Perren Street, London NW5 3ED
www.prionbooks.com

First published in 1925

ISBN 1-85375-445-5

Printed and bound in Great Britain
by Bookmarque, Croydon, Surrey

Preface

Michael Holroyd

William Gerhardie was twenty-nine when *The Polyglots* was first published in 1925. Like his first novel *Futility*, it draws largely on personal experiences. The son of a successful British industrialist living in St Petersburg, and his Yorkshire wife, Gerhardie had been considered the dunce of the family and was sent to England in his late teens to be trained for what was loosely called 'a commercial career'—that is, to acquire some financial acumen or, in default, marry a rich bride. But he detested commerce and dreamed only of the dramatic triumphs with which he hoped to take the London theatres by storm. To improve his English style he was studying Wilde; and an elegant cane, long locks and a languid expression were parts of his literary make-up at this time.

During the war he was posted to the staff of the British Military Attaché at Petrograd and, arriving there with an enormous sword bought second-hand in the Charing Cross Road ('*le sabre de mon père*—a long clumsy thing in a leather scabbard' that makes a momentary appearance in Uncle Lucy's funeral procession in *The Polyglots*), he was welcomed as an old campaigner. The Russian Revolution (which ruined his father who owed his life to having been mistaken for the British socialist Keir Hardie) sent Gerhardie back to England. But in 1918 he set out again, and after crossing America and Japan reached Vladivostok, where the British Military Mission had established itself. After two years in Siberia, mostly in the company of generals, he left the army with an OBE and two foreign decorations, sailing home by way of Singapore, Colombo and Port Said—a journey that forms the closing chapters of *The Polyglots*.

The Polyglots is the narrative of a high-spirited egocentric young officer who comes across a Belgian family, rich in eccentrics, to whom he is related and with whom he lives while on a military mission to the Far East. There are obvious parallels here with Gerhardie's own life. His impressions of the First and Second Revolution in Petrograd and the Allied Intervention in Russia of 1918–20, of the whole business of interfering on an international scale in other people's affairs, are recorded here and in *Futility*. He draws, too, upon his own family. His aunt Mary is the prototype for the extraordinary Aunt Teresa; his uncle Willy was the model for Uncle Lucy, that unfortunate gentleman who hangs himself in his sister's knickers; while the beautiful nincompoop Sylvia is based on a girl Gerhardie met in Westbourne Grove. Gerhardie makes them not into comic Russian stereotypes but universal characters, each in his or her way a corrective to the other. They are ourselves and the people we meet every day. 'There, but for the grace of God, goes H. G. Wells,' remarked H. G. Wells of that amorous knight of the bedchamber, Uncle Emmanuel.

On returning to England, Gerhardie went to Worcester College, Oxford. Though he was responsive to the beauty of Oxford, his opinion of academic life was not high and is probably reflected in the Johnsonian statement of the narrator in this novel: 'There are as many fools at a university as elsewhere...but their folly, I admit, has a certain stamp—the stamp of university training, if you like. It is trained folly.'

On leaving Oxford, Gerhardie wrote much of *The Polyglots* at Innsbruck. He completed it under difficult conditions while his father was dying. His mother would read out pages from the manuscript to the old man 'to kill time', and for the most part he listened uncomplainingly and without comment, though occasionally pronouncing some passage to be 'instructive'. But when she came to the sea-burial of Natàsha, she began to cry, and this bothered him. 'Don't cry,' he urged. 'It's not real. Willy has invented it.'

The narrator in *The Polyglots* has by the end of the novel decided to write the novel we are reading. 'I have already written the title-page,' he announces in answer to his Aunt Teresa's query as to what they are going to do for money. ' "Is it going to sell well?" ' she demands; and the narrator notes, 'I was silent.'

On *The Polyglots* were pinned the family's hopes of remaking the family fortune, but Gerhardie's father died a few months before publication. The book did make Gerhardie's name as a novelist; but as to fortune, he later calculated that, contrary to expectation, it had brought in 'something equivalent, in terms of royalties, to nothing'.

In later years Gerhardie was to adopt as his colophon the ampersand. None of his novels display with more dazzling skill and vitality than *The Polyglots* the peculiar inclusiveness of his philosophy, and no happier narrator ever adopted the first person singular. Captain Georges Hamlet Alexander Diabologh is a young man with literary aspirations. He labours intermittently at a work whose title, *Record of the Stages in the Evolution of an Attitude*, suggests the theme ('the central thing round which the world revolved') of *The Polyglots*. Our attitude to life, Gerhardie implies, is the same as our attitude to fiction which is born of our experience of life. When Sylvia, on board the *Rhinoceros* as it moves through the Red Sea, wants to know what will happen after they get back to Europe, the narrator replies that he has noticed, with regret, 'the same morbid and unhealthy appetite in the readers of novels'. And later, now the author of this novel, he asks us to co-operate with him—financially (by buying several copies to help the fortunes of the characters about whom we have been reading) and imaginatively 'in a spirit of good will'. The book stands, the readers evolve.

Our emotions in relation to time past, present and future are seen to guide our method of making the most of life—which itself, in ironic counterpoint, keeps interrupting the philosophical discussions which chart the evolution of the characters' attitude to it. After listening to Wagner, the narrator reflects that music understands what words and thoughts cannot analyse. Inanimate Nature behaves as if we were not here and life exists irrespective of our reasoning about it. Therefore life is wiser than reason which, being only the partial discovery of life, is merely inquisitive. By the same token Gerhardie believed that no intellectual credo was demanded of the poet-novelist whose stereoscopic vision saw through everyday happenings to a world of dreams, mystery and immortality. Here the comic and the tragic are not alternative or successive attitudes but deeply intermingled, so that every event—Uncle Lucy's suicide, Sylvia's unexpected wedding night, the Russian Revolution itself with its consequences, after the cherry orchard has been cut down, on this miscellany of unwilling refugees moving westwards—contains both sadness and humour.

It is in the orchestration of contradictory moods and attitudes that *The Polyglots* excels. Though it owes something to Chekhov (about whom Gerhardie wrote a brilliant little book at Oxford), the tone is original and unmistakable: 'personal, light and glancing, often lyrical but always self-deflating' as Walter Allen described it. Believing that the invention of psychologically convincing characters and artful well-balanced plots was a mistaken ambition for the novelist in that it cut across the grain of his natural material and ignored the plots that already exist in life, Gerhardie introduces his people and lets them, as it were, carry the event-plot along for him. In *Futility* and *The Polyglots* he brought something new to fiction. The characters, or at least the social personalities they have developed, are suggested very simply with recurring patterns of words: Uncle Emmanuel's '*Que voulez-vous?*' '*C'est la vie*' and '*Courage! Courage!*'; Gustave's cough and adjustment of his Adam's apple; Georges Diabologh's repeated admission, unintelligible to the others, that 'I'm good-looking... You think I'm conceited? I think not'; Sylvia's quotations from the *Daily Mail*; the 'stinks' of Major Beastly, the insensitive man with the sensitive skin; Captain Negodyaev whose attitude to life was a dark smile; and overseeing them all the indomitable hypochondriac Aunt Teresa, who can stand anything except disagreement and whose presidential attitude to everyone successfully moves her family and its dependants round the world in the midst of 'the greatest war the world has ever seen'. As Georges Diabologh comments: 'All is in the Hands of God—and Aunt Teresa.'

Living alongside this amorphous agglutinated mass of helpless humanity that trails back and forth across Gerhardie's pages, are the children. They are handled with extraordinary dexterity and in a manner for which it is difficult to find a parallel in other novels. They are observed with passion yet without sentimentality, accurately yet with the dimension of pathos in that they are surrounded by a ludicrous world into which they must grow up.

Except Natàsha. Her burial at sea is an anguish of the heart, an involvement in grief chronicled with rigorous detachment. We see the yellow moustache of her father ceaselessly twitching; the curiosity of the passengers on the upper deck; the Captain's awareness of his gala uniform and the ship's inflexible routine; the obsolete Russian tricolour; the surgeon puffing at his cigarette; everywhere the atmosphere of unreality surrounding the blunt fact of death that must be faced yet may not be understood, Natàsha having gone unharmed through two revolutions, five sieges, two seasons of famine and pestilence to die in plenty and quietude on the tropical ocean.

'It was a cloudless morning of extreme heat and stuffiness and damp, and the decks were crowded, noisy and indifferent, and I thought that suffering and death should be in the wind and cold of winter, in the slough and drowsiness of autumn, but not in summer—oh, not in summer...The sea went out in large ripples. The gulls flew screaming and wheeling above them...The ship had been brought to as near standstill as possible; barely perceptibly she slid along on the deep, deep, flapping sea. The plank was on ropes, like a swing: a seaman on each side—Uncle Tom and a young one. Below loomed the Indian Ocean, stretching out its white paws of froth—like a big cat...The mother was held up by her husband and Berthe. She looked pale, pasty, she looked awful. Swiftly the flag was pulled off. Then they swung it—once our way, once to the sea. Natàsha slid off, and describing a curve in the air splashed into the water. A few seconds—and she disappeared beneath the foam...the liner, stealthily, relentlessly, like life itself, went on.'

Gerhardie's writing at its best is simple but suggests a widening circle of lyrical and ironic possibilities. He used increasingly the delaying phrase and clause within a sentence, measuring the length of procrastination while declaring the power of time regained. It is this tension that helps to hold in equilibrium the incongruity of life as he presents it to us. 'To maintain a position is to maintain a false position,' he writes. In *The Polyglots* the search for an attitude excludes no attitude: the lies we tell ourselves are part of the truth we live. Gerhardie's success, as in an artistic conjuring trick, is convincingly to maintain what is intellectually the untenable position.

Beneath the compulsory conviviality of wartime party-going runs a current of melancholy, and this, together with many farcical episodes and philosophical speculations, is interwoven with a number of powerful anti-war passages. 'No one wanted the war,' he writes; 'no one with the exception of a score of imbeciles, and suddenly all those who did not want a war turned imbecile and obeyed the score of imbeciles who had made it...' The eccentrics and lunatics who surround the narrator are, we see, no madder than those who run the world and make its wars. There is a strong parallel here, as Anthony Powell has pointed out, between *The Polyglots* and *The Enormous Room*, e. e. cummings's account of being incarcerated for 'careless talk' by the French authorities, which was published in 1922.

Anthony Powell has written of *The Polyglots* as 'a classic', adding that he put off reading it for several years because so many people had recommended it. This was a trick in the English character that Gerhardie really never understood. *Futility*, he once said, which had stunned the world of letters, had left it silent with admiration. With *The Polyglots* he came to town. He was taken up by Arnold Bennett and H. G. Wells, and promoted by Lord Beaverbrook. At Oxford the book became the young man's bible. Bernard Miles, Isaiah Berlin and Emlyn Williams proclaimed Gerhardie their literary hero; Evelyn Waugh wrote that he had 'learned a great deal of my trade' from it; Graham Greene, who was leaving Oxford when *The Polyglots* appeared, wrote that 'to those of my generation he [Gerhardie] was the most important new novelist to appear in our young life'. As the narrator remarks in this novel: 'Oxford is best in retrospect.'

The book reads as freshly now as it did nearly sixty years ago and has continued to influence a wide variety of novelists from C. P. Snow to Olivia Manning. 'The humour of life, the poetry of death and the release of the spirit—these things William Gerhardie describes as no prose writer has done before him,' wrote Olivia Manning. '...He is our Gogol's *Overcoat*. We all come out of him.' But if such recommendations deter you, ignore them. Gerhardie died in some poverty and without recognition: you may safely discover him now for yourselves.

1

I stood on board the liner halted in midstream and looked upon Japan, my native land. But let me say at once that I am not a Japanese. I am very much a European. Yet when I woke that morning, and, looking through the porthole, found the boat had halted in midstream, and Japan, a coral reef, lay glittering in the morning sun before me, I was touched and spellbound, and my thoughts went back to my birth, twenty-one years before, in the land of the cherry blossoms. I dressed quickly and ran up on deck. A faint breeze ruffled my hair and rippled the water. Like a dream, Japan loomed before me.

All last night I had watched for the approach of the enchanted island. Like sea-shells, islets began to bob up to right and left of us as we stood watching, heedless of time, as in a trance, the liner stealing her way on in the warm nocturnal breeze of July. They came and swam by and were like queer apparitions in the charmed light, and the boat, lulled to sleep, seemed to have yielded to dreams. And waking in the morning I looked and saw the cliffs—and gladness filled my heart.

Even as we stood on board at Yokohama, waiting to be taken alongside, we saw two little statuettes standing in the middle of the road, it would seem with no conceivable object in their heads, each holding a parasol and fanning herself gently. The colours of the fans and parasols seemed too marvellous to be real.

2

And here we lolled in midstream. How nice, and for the most part how strange. Barely four weeks ago we had left England, crossed the Atlantic in the *Aquitania*, and spending only a day in New York, hurried across the United States to Vancouver. Yes, I had watched for that 'advent of New York,' that 'magnificent crescendo of approach' of which I had read in one of H. G. Wells's novels, and true, New York 'rode out of the sea'. The day was one of the brightest kind; the sky was full of buzzing aircraft; troop-laden transports and warships big and small steamed steadily out of the harbour, passing us as, with ineffable splendour and majesty, in steamed the *Aquitania*. The approach of New York indeed had been heralded earlier by a crescendo amiability on the part of the stewards. For days the Atlantic had been severe, defiant, and the stewards harsh, indifferent. Now they had changed, as if with the weather. We just missed the famous Statue of Liberty, going through an elaborate passport formality in the saloon, pledging on a printed form that we were verily neither anarchists nor atheists nor believers in bigamy nor yet in leading a double life. The War Office agent who was to meet us at the docks and arrange our passage to Vancouver no sooner came on board than he began drinking—prohibition had just then been proclaimed in the United States—and was not seen again.

Then followed a small disappointment. I had expected some sort of super-automobile, seeing that it was New York, to convey us, in a flash, to our hotel. Instead, there was a clumsy 'growler' of the oldest pattern with an antique coachman with a red nose and an ancient-looking horse—straight out of Dickens. 'Well, how are things across the water?' he enquired in a nasal intonation as a preliminary to discussing the fare. And in a flash the Dickens illusion was shattered to the ground. I drove through the warm, brightly lit streets of New York, wondrous, incurring as I did a curious sensation. 'Me in America!' I seemed to be saying to myself. 'Me in New York!' For up to the present the United States had been to me an inanimate idea connected with the map of the new hemisphere. Now the towering buildings and the teeming streets were a living reality. And the midsummer aspect of Broadway, in all its newness, juvenility, and brightness, probed to the springs of life.

My companion, who prided himself on knowing New York inside out, determined next morning to show me Fifth Avenue; accordingly we took the subway and found ourselves, upon enquiry, in Brooklyn. As the train steamed out of the lofty precincts of Pennsylvania Station we had our first glimpse of the victorious Alliance. A Japanese gentleman had occupied the lower berth of the sleeper, to the unspeakable wrath and disgust of a citizen of the United States, who prevailed upon him to surrender this privilege to himself, as a member of the superior white race. 'I'm American,' he was explaining. 'You go up—up—up you go, understand? I'm American.'

The Japanese gentleman either knew no English or very wisely pretended that he did not. He bowed politely and sucked his breath in and showed his teeth and wreathed his face in smiles. 'Ha!—zzz—Iz zas so?' he kept asking. 'Ha! Iz zas so?—zzz——?'

'I'm American, you son of a gun. You—Jap; I—American, understand?'

'Ha!—zzz—Iz zas so?' asked the Japanese gentleman, bowing and sucking his breath in. 'Ha! Iz zas so?—zzz——?'

They seemed destined to go on like this for ever. I took up a book—and fell asleep.

I sprang up in my sleep, for somebody had slapped me hard on the knee as I was sleeping. I opened my eyes and beheld the American citizen who now took his seat beside me, and, inspecting my British uniform, said:

'Well, I guess you'll be glad as hell to feel you're in a free country at last?'

I rubbed my eyes.

'No kings and princes here to lock you up in prison. No priests and courtiers intriguing against your liberty. Ah, this is a free country, my friend. We are a pure-minded simple people. Our home life is a clean, simple, healthy and straightforward life! Ah, you've got to be an American to understand it!' He paused. 'See that bridge?' he said. 'Cost 11,000,000 dollars to build; 6,600 feet long, 108 feet wide, 123 feet high, with a distance of 1,464 feet between the pillars; is made entirely of steel; holds 2 elevated railroads, 4 trolly tracks, 2 automobile streets, 2 bicycle tracks, and 2 sidewalks. Yes, God's country, we call it !'

Imperceptibly, to the lull of his voice, I fell asleep.

I was wakened up by another slap on the knee, as vigorous as the first.

'Say, how's the armistice doing? Guess our boys over there are right glad. Ah, our American boys are fine lads. Have you seen General Pershing?'

Then one morning I raised the window-blind and saw the Union Jack flying over the station building. We were in Canada.

3

And now, to their mutual astonishment, both the American citizens and the Japanese gentleman, who had followed us all the way to Yokohama, had donned uniforms. It transpired accordingly that one was Colonel Ishibaiashi, of the Imperial General Staff, while the other was Lieut. Philip Brown, of the U.S. Naval Intelligence Service, who, with the perennial secrecy of Secret Service men, had hitherto thought it incumbent on himself to masquerade in mufti, but seeing his erewhile enemy in the glamour of his uniform, probably felt he could hold out no longer. He was standing now, a little away from us, whistling through his teeth: 'Johnnie, get your gun, get your gun, get your gun; go and kill the Hun, kill the Hun, kill the Hun.' Then, coming up to the Colonel, he slapped him on the shoulder cheerily. 'Hello, Colonel, glad to see you looking so smart. I thought all along you were a blooming spy, don't you know!'

Colonel Ishibaiashi showed his teeth and drew his breath in. '——Zzz—Ha!' he said; 'ha!' And once again, 'Ha!'

The reconciliation was complete.

'We are going alongside,' said my companion. And indeed we were moving at last. Now we were going alongside. All eyes turned shoreward. On the quay—a red-banded brass hat, some assistant to the British military attaché maybe. A score of red-capped Nippons with tin swords. Now we are going alongside. The dark space of water between us and the pier grew narrower and narrower. Gangway. Coils of rope fly over on to the quay. Gangway! At long last we move: all move to the gangway. The feel of the bars on the gangway as you hang on to them by the heels—it would be merely absurd to slip at this stage—and you're on firm ground once more. What matter if that ground be Japan?

At first we drove by the side of the quay, then through queer, narrow, evil-smelling Yokohama streets. To sit with hat and stick in the spidery rickshaw, and sniff at the atmosphere of a strange place—oh, what a rare, what an exquisite pleasure! 'This is Japan,' I said to myself. And it was. Now if I had been brought up in Japan, schooled there and lived there these twenty-one years, it would be about as interesting to me now as Manchester.

The dream is more real than the substance. And thus when I travel in a strange land I get out at the station, sniff at the 'atmosphere'—and get back into the train. It is enough. So now immediately I felt that I had 'got' the atmosphere. Besides, there was one. Leaning back in the rickshaw, first I had a feeling that I was too heavy for these delicate toys, as I watched the little man, who was half my size, run before me, his shirt gradually betraying signs of perspiration as he covered mile after mile in a steady trot. I soon got used to it. Once or twice we lost our way, and when we made enquiries in English some Japanese invariably replied to all our questions, 'Ha!…' and showed his teeth and sucked his breath in, and bowed politely, and walked away.

'Hi!' cried my companion.

'I always understood that the Japanese spoke English,' I observed.

'And if they do they are the only ones to understand it,' he rejoined sardonically.

No, my companion did not like Japan. He called it a tin-kettle nation. He had been annoyed, and with his delicate digestion he could ill-afford to be annoyed in the heat. He tried to ring up Tokyo on the telephone, and was interrupted by an absurd '*Mashi, mashi*?' which he did not understand, and so shouted 'Damn!' into the receiver.

But already we were bound for Tokyo. The train raced on through green fields and pastures that might have been England or anything else. And, behold! a kimonoed gentleman reading an impossible newspaper. The whole thing was like a dream, and my impending meeting with relatives I had never seen—that too seemed like meeting unseen relations in dreamland, a place so utterly foreign and strange it might have been Mars. I sat very still, my eyes fixed on the whirling landscape—the engine whistled, the train went fast—while my thoughts went faster still, sending forth incalculable impulses of torment and delight. I thought of my aunt, of my lovely girl cousin whom I was to meet for the first time. In Tokyo I would get out, and then—what strange—what unthought-of things might begin!

4

I wondered what my aunt was really like. I had heard so much about her life that I was strangely curious to see her in the flesh. I chortled at the thought of her puny consort with a waxed moustache, whose faded photograph in Belgian uniform with a row of medals on his military chest I well remembered. They had always lived at Dixmude, uncle being a Belgian *Commandant*. In the so-called Great War, however, in the year of grace 1914, my aunt decreed that Belgium—indeed, Europe—was no fit abode for her, and together with her husband and her daughter set out in flight for the Far East. The Far East, I think, was chosen on the ground that it was far—as far at least as my aunt conceivably could get without coming back across the other side of our round globe. I shall be told, of course, that it is against all military precedent for officers to be allowed to leave their country in the midst of a great war. To that, in the light of after-knowledge, I have but one reply to make: you do not know my aunt. And let me say at once that I would not have you think my uncle other than an honourable and gallant officer. He had even been at the siege of Liège; but deciding, I suppose, that he had tempted Providence enough, he left the front of battle and acquiesced in his wife's arrangement that he should leave the country, as she was far too weak and ill to go alone, their daughter at that time being still a child. But if they all left Dixmude at the sound of the first gun, don't blame my uncle for it, rather blame my aunt who, to say the least of it, was a woman with a will. At the age of twelve she had been adopted, while in Russia, by an old Princess who brought her up with her own daughter, and no doubt because of her marvellous beauty Aunt Teresa was spoiled and treasured by them out of all proportion. They married her off to a young good-for-nothing, born in circumstances of romance. Her husband, to be sure, was the son of a young heir (of the highest in the land) and his erewhile governess, Mlle Fifi, and his arrival—the flower of spontaneous exultation—caused both parents at the time profound astonishment. Whether he took more after his father or his mother, it is hard for me to say. Nicholas (for this was his name) seemed to combine a grand-ducal recklessness with a truly Parisian gaiety. There was no end to his antics. He flourished loaded pistols into people's faces, firing at random. He took up with wild gipsy girls and drove about with them madly in *troikas*. He was at home in every kind of orgy, and thoroughly neglected my aunt. He played practical jokes on policemen, and on one occasion tied a constable to a tame bear and threw them both in the canal and held them floating on a rope. Another time, returning in the small hours of the morning, he encountered on the bridge a young giraffe which was being led from the railway station to the zoo, bought it on the spot and brought it up to Aunt Teresa's bedroom. And, in the circumstances of the case, my aunt suffered. For years she suffered silently, kept going by the hope that some day they might be raised to princely rank. And, as she had foreseen, Nicholas was about to be legitimized and granted princely status, when, following the precedent of a milliard others, he gave up his soul to God. And Aunt Teresa missed the cherished prize by the skin of her teeth. But the dignity that she had missed she somehow managed to retain, and when Uncle Emmanuel met her in Brussels he addressed his letters to 'Madame la Princesse'—although this had never been her rank. It was her beauty rather and her manner that suggested it, and all his people could not but think that Emmanuel, clever chap, had contrived to marry right into the Russian aristocracy. Her sisters, on the other hand, were not a little pained to learn that she—their pride and hope—had married an insignificant little Belgian officer, who, however satisfactory as a husband and a lover, was a poor fish (they said) as an officer and a money-maker. This was the more disappointing because all my aunts on my father's side—all singularly fascinating women—of whom, however, Aunt Teresa was incomparably the queen—had married duds. Her father, a pioneer British merchant in Siberia, beholding his new son-in-law Emmanuel for the first time, thought that he was 'no great shakes'. Beholding him the second and last time, he found no cause to alter his opinion.

And now the train was racing towards Tokyo.

5

The Vanderflints and The Vanderphants

We stepped out at Tokyo as though it were Clapham Junction, and repaired to the Imperial Hotel. Tokyo, too, seemed a weird city. The houses were weird; men, women and children moved about on weird bits of wood like some mechanical dolls. The sun was blazing hot as we stepped into our rickshaws and drove in search of my aunt's house.

As we drove up round the corner, I saw an apparition of short skirt, dark-brown curls and ruby lips, moving on seductive legs. There was a soft smiling look in her eyes which had a violet glint in the sun. Her head slightly bent, she flitted past us—with her brogues unlaced—and disappeared round the corner.

I guessed that it was Sylvia—perhaps on an errand to a shop across the way. I had seen one or two not very good snaps of her, and there was something sweet about her mouth that made me recognize her in a flash. How she had grown! What a 'find', to be sure! You read of such in novels by Miss Dell, but you did not often come across them in real life. But what had always rather stirred my blood, long before I ever saw her picture, was that she bore this lovely name—Sylvia-Ninon.

We were first received by a thin middle-aged woman, on the heels of whom followed a somewhat stouter edition of the first, who called out 'Berthe!'—the thin one turning round at this word. As we were shown into the little sitting-room, in came a girl and curtsied in the Latin way, followed by number two (*révérence*), obviously of the same brood. Here, I could clearly see, was a family—mother, sister and daughters.

'Your aunt will be down in a few moments,' said the elder of the ladies, who was called Berthe. And while we conversed in French—'*monsieur, madame*', with the usual complimentary allusions—I heard a rustle, the door opened, and a tall, slim, grey-haired lady with a greyish moustache stooped into the room, and—'Well, well, here you are, here you are at last, George!' she said in a deep drawling baritone which reminded me of my father. I kissed and was kissed by her in turn, feeling how her moustache tickled my cheek.

'My friend,' I introduced, 'Major Beastly.'

'Major *who*?' asked my aunt.

'Beastly.'

To suppress the impulse to laugh she looked round quickly. 'This is my nephew George,' she said vaguely. 'Mme Vanderphant and Mlle Berthe. Madeleine and Marie. We all came over from Dixmude together—what is it?—four years ago now.'

'Yes, we Vanderphants and Vanderflints have been getting on very well together, as though indeed we were one and the same family—*n'est-ce pas, madame*?' said Mme Vanderphant, smiling pleasantly.

Aunt Teresa at once assumed a presidential attitude towards the people in the room. When she spoke I visualized my father, but in most other particulars she differed from her brother. Aunt Teresa's eyes were large, luminous, sad, faithful, like a St. Bernard dog's. Thick on her heels was a very small gentleman in a brown suit, with a waxed moustache—plainly Uncle Emmanuel. He came up to me, somewhat shyly, and fingering the three 'pips' on my shoulder, slapped me approvingly on the back. 'Already a captain! *Ah, mon brave*!'

'I owe my recent promotion,' I said, 'to having, at a psychological moment, slapped a certain War Office Colonel on the shoulder: just as his ego had touched the height of elation. Had I slapped him a second too early or a second too late, my military career would have taken a different course altogether. I am sure of it.'

Uncle Emmanuel did not take in what I said, but generalizing the topic into a human attitude, murmured: '*Que voulez-vous*?'

'Yes, I wouldn't be here but for that.'

'After a big war there are always little wars—to clear up,' said Uncle Emmanuel, shrugging his shoulders.

'We sailed three days before the armistice.'

'We were in mid-Atlantic,' said Beastly, 'when the armistice broke out. We did have a binge!'

'*À Berlin! à Berlin!*' said my uncle.

A novel is a cumbersome medium for depicting real people. Now if you were here—or we could meet—I would convey to you the nature of Major Beastly's personality in the twinkling of an eye—by visual representation. Alas, this is not possible. At my uncle's remark, as indeed at all remarks, Beastly screwed up his eye and gave a few slow heavy nods and guffaws, as though the thing—the Germans, the Allies, my Uncle Emmanuel, nay, life itself—confirmed his worst suspicions.

Then the door opened, and Sylvia sidled towards us, with her eyes on the floor. I looked at her closely and noticed that in truth she had lips kissable to the point of delectation, asking for nothing better. She had the same St. Bernard eyes as her mother, only perhaps of a younger St. Bernard in the act of wagging his tail.

Having greeted me, she went over to the sofa and began playing dolls by herself—a little insincerely, I thought, perhaps out of shyness. Then: 'Oh, where's my *Daily Mail*?' She got up to get it, spread it out on the sofa, and began to read.

Uncle Emmanuel stood pensive as though meditating before giving utterance to his thoughts.

'Yes,' he said, 'yes.'

'To-day, after the Big War, the world is in as childish a state of mind as before,' I pursued. 'I do not even vouch for myself. If tomorrow these silly bugles went off again, calling the manhood of Britain to arms, inviting us to march against some imaginable enemy, and tender girls said "We don't want to lose you, but we feel you ought to go", and loved us and kissed us and white-feathered us, I should find it hard to overcome the fascination of donning my Sam Browne belt. I am like that. A born hero.'

Irony was not a strong point with them, I noticed. Uncle Emmanuel again did not take it all in, but, with a gesture indicating '*Que voulez-vous*?' he murmured these words.

While I spoke I was conscious all the time of Sylvia—short-skirted and long-legged, in white silk stockings—playing dolls on the sofa. For my own part I know of nothing so secretly exhilarating as the first meeting with a good-looking cousin of the opposite sex. The rapture of identifying our common relatives, of tracing the lifeblood bondship between us. When I looked at her I felt it was enchanting, amazing that this stripling girl of sixteen summers with the wide-awake lustrous hazel eyes, though with a slightly frightened look, should be my cousin, that she should call me by the second pronoun singular, be intimate with the details of my childhood. I felt that I should like to dance with her in a crowded ballroom which would throw into relief the intimacy of our movements, gestures, murmurs, looks; that I should like to float away with her down the sleepy river on a Chinese houseboat, or better still, fly away with her to some enchanted island and drink of her, to satiation. What I would ultimately do on such a desert island did not, of course, occur to me.

Aunt Teresa had just got up out of bed on purpose for me, as she explained. Great exertion! And Uncle Emmanuel enquired at intervals if it was not too much for her, if the talk was not tiring her. No, she would stay with us a little longer. In fact, we would sit out on the terrace.

It was too hot to move; so we sat still all day until evening, staring before us with a kind of semi-intelligent look, as we sat in big soft leather chairs on the open veranda, impotent after a heavy lunch, unfit for anything in the heat but day-dreaming.

And so we sat and looked into the garden, and beyond the garden into the street, and all around us seemed weird and unreal. Weirdness, an unearthly charm, cast a spell over the place. And as I dreamt I fancied that these moving statuettes and the weird-coloured landscape were merely a scene from some ballet or a Japanese screen: so unreal they seemed. Even the trees and flowers seemed artificial trees and flowers. Some strange birds or insects made a weird continuous sound. But there was not a breeze, and even the leaves on the trees were motionless, listless with enchantment, lost in unreality.

'To-day the air is soft and tender as in spring, and haunts one as in spring; but the cherry blossoms are over.' Aunt Teresa as she spoke looked at me with a long, sad, silent gaze. Let me say at once that I'm good-looking. Sleek black hair brushed back from the forehead, lips—and something about the mouth, about the eyes, something—an indefinable something—that appeals to women. You think I'm conceited? I think not.

'You're very much like Anatole,' said Aunt Teresa. 'Neither of you is good-looking, but both have pleasant faces.'

At that I am frankly astonished. I must take an early opportunity to re-examine my face in the looking-glass.

'And you're the same age. I remember so well when Anatole was born and we were thinking of a name for him, your mother writing to me and telling me they had decided to christen you Hamlet.'

'But he's called George!' said Sylvia.

'Georges Hamlet Alexander—those are my names. A certain sense of delicacy, I suppose, prevented my people from actually calling me Hamlet. Instead they call me Georges.'

'But why Georges and not George?' asked Sylvia.

'I really can't tell,' I confessed. 'Not after Georges Carpentier, I hazard, for he could not have been many years old when I was born.'

'In Tokyo!' Aunt Teresa gaily exclaimed, looking round at the Vanderphants. '*Mais voilà un Japonais*!'

'*Tiens*!' said Mme Vanderphant.

'At the Imperial Hotel. An unlooked-for diversion during my parents' pleasure trip in the Far East, I fancy.'

'But you're British-born, so you've nothing to complain of,' said my aunt.

'I suppose I am lucky.'

'Yes, names are a great trouble,' said my aunt, looking round again at the Vanderphants. 'My daughter was christened Sylvia because when she was born she was perfectly fair and looked like a fairy. Eventually her hair has turned darker and darker, and is now, as you see, almost black—with gold-brown lights in it.'

'And light brown after it has been washed,' Sylvia said.

'Is it really?' I asked with genuine interest.

'Or take the names of my brothers,' said Aunt Teresa, turning to Mme Vanderphant. 'Our mother wanted girls at the time, but the first two born happened to be boys: so she christened one of them Connie, and the other Lucy.'

'*Tiens*!' said Mme Vanderphant.

'Connie—his father'—she pointed to me—'was near-sighted, and Lucy very deaf. And how well I remember it when they took us for a trip on the Neva in a steam launch. Connie, as blind as an owl, was at the steering-wheel, and Lucy, stone-deaf, down below attending to the engine. And when Connie shouted down the speaking tube to Lucy to back engines, Lucy of course could not hear a word, and Connie, who could not see a thing, landed us right into the middle of the Liteiny Bridge. How well I remember it! And then they shouted, shouted at each other, nearly bit each other's heads off. It was awful. Your mother was on the launch'—she turned to me. 'I think they were just engaged.'

And as we plunged into reminiscence I took the opportunity of asking Aunt Teresa to enlighten me concerning my paternal ancestors. Whether what she said was fact or partly fiction I cannot truly vouch. I learnt, however, that originally, centuries ago, our fathers sprang from a Swedish knight who came to Finland to introduce Christianity and culture to the white-haired race; that subsequently he betrayed his stock and went over to the Finns and was disowned by his own clan without ever really being assimilated by the Finns, who, because of his forbidding looks, suspected him of being the devil's envoy and called him old *Saatana Perkele*, which name—von Altteuffel—he adopted as he strayed into Esthonia and joined the missionary Teuton knights, I daresay in sinister extravagance, perhaps in evil irony, a dark romantic pride—who knows?—and chose two devils with twisted interlocking tails as his new coat-of-arms. His son, a Finn, but domiciled in northern Italy, had changed his name from Altteuffel to Diabolo. *His* son, an Italian born, but persecuted on account of his Protestant faith, had fled to Scotland, where *his* son, a Shetlander by birth, to make the name appear more Scottish, added a 'gh' ending to it, after the manner of MacDonogh—'Diabologh', to give it a more native air, but only succeeded in so estranging it from its original philology that it was neither fish nor flesh nor good red herring. So much so that when I, a distant offspring (born in far Japan), was joining up a Highland regiment to fight in the World War (for the freedom of small nationalities), the recruiting sergeant looked at it, and looking at it looked at it again, and as he looked at it he looked—well—puzzled. His face began to ripple, changed into a snigger, developed into a grin. He shook his head—'*Gawddamn*,' he said. Just that—and then no more. I took the oath and the King's shilling—which then was eighteen-pence. My grandfather, who had been born in London and was of a restless disposition, after travelling in Spain, Holland, France, Denmark and Italy, settled in Siberia, where he had bought a large estate in the vicinity of Krasnoyarsk, where later he developed a successful business in exporting furs. In his diary there are curious references to the bull fights which he saw in Barcelona, where he also met his future wife, a Spanish lady who, after marriage, followed him to Manchester where, prior to settling on the Krasnoyarsk estate, she gave birth to my father, Aunt Teresa, Uncle Lucy, and half a dozen other offspring. My grandfather, who outlived his wife, provided in his will that the Krasnoyarsk estate (known by the Russian rendering of our surname 'Diavolo') should be equally divided among his many children. 'But your father could not get on with your Uncle Lucy,' Aunt Teresa told me, 'and he withdrew his share of money and set up his cotton-spinning mills in Petersburg. And of course, he has also done very well.' And as she spoke, I saw myself as a child back in the magnificent white house overlooking the Neva and contrasting strangely with the desolating quay on which it stood. Outside the snow was falling. The wind sweeping across the quay was hard, defiant. The ice-chained Neva looked cold and menacing. And looking at me, Aunt Teresa said, 'You, George, are not a business man, you're'—she made gestures with her blanched bejewelled hand towards the heavens—'you're a poet. Always in the clouds. But your father—ah, he was a business man!' And Aunt Teresa, to uphold her personal prestige among her friends from Belgium, gave it to be understood that both her brothers had been rich as mischief. 'If you went to Petersburg,' she said to Berthe, 'and asked for the works of Diavolo, why, any cabman would take you to my brother Connie's place at once.'

'*Tiens!*' said Berthe, with a very conscious look of reverence for the prestige of Connie coming on her face.

'And now we've lost everything!' she sighed, 'in the revolution!'

'*Courage! Courage!*' said Uncle Emmanuel.

My aunt was very proud of the achievements of her clan, and exaggerated a little when talking to strangers. Mme Vanderphant at this point intervened to say that an uncle on their mother's side also had big works in the vicinity of Brussels, and incidentally, a lovely house in the capital. But Aunt Teresa dismissed her lightly. That was nothing, she implied. Mme Vanderphant should have seen Connie's house in Petersburg! As if talking to me, but really to impress the audience, in a deep contralto voice she said:

'Your father's house in Petersburg. Ah, that was a palace! And now, alas, all gone, all gone.'

'*Courage! Courage!*' said Uncle Emmanuel.

While Aunt Teresa talked of the glorious past, the Vanderphants, with their own thoughts far away, assumed a polite interest: Mme Vanderphant feigned to attend, with an unconvincing smile of humility on her face. Berthe, half-closing her eyes, listened to what I said and exchanged frequent glances with Aunt Teresa—little nods of intimate reminiscence, of warm approval and understanding. She could not have shared these memories, but in this assumption lay the secret of a personality too kind and sensitive even to think of chilling us with any attitude to our memories less intimate than our own.

'Sylvia! Don't blink!' said Aunt Teresa sternly.

Sylvia made an inhuman effort—and blinked in the doing.

'Of course, your father is independent of us,' said Aunt Teresa, 'and we can't expect him to be sending us any remittances. But your Uncle Lucy has been our trustee ever since our father died, and is obliged to see that we receive our dividends as they are due to us.'

'And has he managed well?'

'Well, yes,' she said. 'I must confess that he has been very generous. Very, very generous. Only lately——'

'Lately——?'

'Lately he hasn't been sending us any dividends.'

'Oh?'

'It's very strange,' she said.

'Of course, his business is paralysed by what is going on in Krasnoyarsk.'

'Quite. But we can't be living on nothing. And in Japan where everything is so dear! Sylvia's convent alone eats up half of my money! It's over two months overdue. It's very strange,' she said. 'We've waited, waited…'

'All things come to him who waits,' said Uncle Emmanuel.

'Emmanuel,' said my aunt, 'you will go tomorrow morning to the General Post Office, and enquire if our telegram has been received by Lucy.'

'Very well, my angel.'

Aunt Teresa's way of speaking to her husband reminded me of regimental orders: 'B Company will parade——. 3rd Battalion will embark——.' It was neither hectoring nor flustered; it quietly assumed the thing done (in the future), it just did not consider the possibility of non-compliance.

'*Emmanuel, tu iras*—— *Emmanuel, tu feras*——'

'*Oui, mon ange*.' And he went. And he did.

When Aunt Teresa went up to her bedroom to lie down before dinner, Uncle Emmanuel told us that he would be able to procure the autograph of a famous French marshal for anyone who chose to contribute twenty thousand francs to the French Red Cross; and my uncle took the opportunity to ask us if we knew of any possible buyers or, perhaps, of an auction or a war charity where such a bait would prove attractive. 'Zey askèd me to do it,' he was telling Major Beastly, with propitiatory gestures, 'and I takèd it; I tellèd dem: I doèd what I can.'

'I know a chap,' said Beastly, 'an American called Brown, who knows everybody who is anybody. I'll tackle him, and I am sure he'll take it on. But'—he held out a warning forefinger—'no bunkum, you know.'

'Please?' asked my uncle, not understanding the word.

'No bunkum!' warned Beastly, who was suspicious of 'foreigners'.

My uncle did not deign to reply.

6

Aunt Teresa

Some little time after my aunt had gone up to lie down in her bedroom I was called up to her. There was an acute scent of *Mon Boudoir* aroma and of miscellaneous cosmetics in the room. She powdered herself thick—you felt you wanted to scrape it off with a penknife. On the bedside-table were medicine bottles, cosmetics, old photographs, books; and on the quilt a red-leather *buvard*, a writing-pad; behind her, soft pillows; and ensconced in all this, as in a nest, was Aunt Teresa—the incarnation of delicate health. She remembered every birthday and wrote and received a multitude of letters at Christmas and Easter, on occasions of family weddings, births, deaths, confirmations, promotions, appointments, etc., and made careful notes of the dates of all letters and postcards received and dispatched in a little red leather-bound book specially kept for the purpose. It was July—late afternoon, early evening—and melancholy.

'You look fairly comfortable,' I observed, gazing round.

'Ach! if I had *Constance*!' drawled my aunt. 'If only I had *Constance* to look after me! Alas! I had to leave her at Dixmude! and I have no trained nurse to look after me in my sad exile!'

Constance was the daughter of a great friend of Aunt Teresa, whom she had befriended after his death, and befriending her, had made a servant of her.

'They are nice friendly people, the Vanderphants,' I said after a pause.

'Yes, but Mme Vanderphant is a bit thick-headed, and doesn't quite understand about my poor miserable health!—and talks so loud. And she's terribly greedy. On the boat, four years ago, she ate so much (because she knew that food was included in the fare) that the Captain was quite disgusted, and purposely steered alongside the waves—to make her sick.'

'And was she?'

'Wasn't she!' exclaimed my aunt, with malice. 'She just was.'

'But Berthe is awfully nice, isn't she?' I said.

And Aunt Teresa, in a deep, deep baritone, in the voice of the wolf who, masquerading as the grandmother, spoke to Little Red Ridinghood from beneath the bedclothes, drawled: 'Yes, Berthe has taken pity on me in my illness and she looks after me, poor invalid that I am! She is kind and attentive, but isn't she a perfect fright to look at?'

'Well, there's something sympathetic about her face, all the same.'

'No, but isn't she ugly—that long red beak! And you know she doesn't know she is ugly. She even fancies herself. She thinks she isn't at all bad to look at.'

'Well, I've seen worse.'

'But, *non, mon Dieu*!' she laughed. 'I don't think I've ever met anyone so ludicrously ugly. But, as I say—of course, she is not *Constance*, but she's quite kind to me and attentive.' Aunt Teresa was looking all the while at my shining brown calves, where my servant Pickup had 'put on' a 'Cherry Blossom' shine. Perhaps she thought of her own youth, regretted that her pigmy husband had never had such calves as mine. For I am strong of limb, my calves especially, and my dark-brown tightly strapped cavalry boots and spurs (in which I cultivate a certain swaggering kick in my walk), polished to a high degree by Pickup, show off my legs to advantage. Women like me. My blue eyes, which I roll in a winning way when I talk to them, look well beneath my dark brows—which I daily pencil. My nose is remotely tilted, a little arched. But what disposes them to me, I think, are my delicate nostrils, which give me a naïve, tender, guileless expression, like this—'M'm'—which appeals to them.

'That's enough, George,' said my aunt.

'What?'

'Admiring yourself in the looking-glass all the time.'

'Not a bit——'

'You will dine with us.'

'Yes. Now I must go back to the hotel to change.'

'Don't be late,' she called after me.

When I descended, Beastly had already gone. At the hotel I found an invitation for me to attend next week a dinner given by the Imperial General Staff. As I drove back to dinner, full of half-apprehended anticipations, the shadows were already black under the wheels, and next to the little dwarf slave there ran another with a longer neck and legs like stilts.

7

And as I rang the bell and the boy opened the door to me, Sylvia was there, standing in the hall, bright-eyed, long-limbed, graceful as a sylph. We waited for my aunt: some moments afterwards she came down, and in her wake we all went in to dinner. Sylvia sat facing me. She bent her head, closed her eyes (while I noticed the length of the lashes), and bringing her outstretched fingers together, hurriedly mumbled grace to herself. Then took up the spoon—and once again revealed her luminous eyes. And I noticed the exquisite curve of her finely drawn black brows.

She was so strikingly beautiful that one could not get used to her face: could not rest one's eyes on her, could not make out what was the matter with it, after all. She was so beautiful that one's eye could not fix on her—and one asked oneself why the deuce she wasn't more beautiful still!

'Sylvia! Again!' said Aunt Teresa.

And, involuntarily, Sylvia blinked.

'And your friend?' Mme Vanderphant asked.

'Who? Beastly? He is dining out.'

'*Mais voilà un nom*!' laughed my aunt, and revealed her beautiful profile against the light: it was plastered up pretty considerably with powder and paste, but the outlines were intact and lovely enough, I can tell you.

'There are some funny names in the world,' I agreed, 'like that of my batman, for instance, who is called Pickup. I didn't invent them, so I can't help it.'

'*Ah, je te crois bien*!' Uncle Emmanuel agreed.

'He has perfectly vertical nostrils, that man Major Beastly,' exclaimed Aunt Teresa. 'I never saw anything like it!'

'He seems a very nice man none the less,' said Berthe.

'But—a horrible nuisance! When he wasn't seasick he suffered from acute attacks of dysentery all the way out.'

'Poor man!' she exclaimed. 'And nobody to look after him.'

'And instead of shaving in the clean manly way as he should, he used a fiendish contrivance (devised, I think, for the benefit of your sex) for burning off his facial growth, making an unholy stink in the doing—regularly on the fourth day.'

Sylvia laughed.

'The voyage across the Pacific'—I turned to her—'took us fourteen days, during which time Major Beastly made a stink in our cabin three times.'

'George!' said my aunt, calling me to order.

I raised my eyes and looked straight into hers. 'I use the word advisedly: a smell wasn't in it!'

'But, *mon Dieu*! I should have protested against this,' said Mme Vanderphant.

'To a senior officer?' My uncle turned to her sardonically, as one who knew that such things were not done in the Service.

'Impossible?'

'*Mais je le crois bien, madame*!' he said excitedly.

'As a matter of fact,' I explained, 'Beastly was my junior three days before we sailed. But he was promoted in a single day from a sub to a major because he deals in rail and steam, and is just the man they wanted to advise them on the Manchurian railway, I believe.'

'Sylvia! Again!' Aunt Teresa interrupted.

Sylvia blinked again.

'His answer when I approached him diplomatically was that he had a very delicate skin which couldn't stand the scraping of the razor blade.'

'And nothing happened?'

'I cannot say what happened. As I was about to press him more definitely, he had an acute attack of dysentery, and the question was indefinitely postponed.'

'*Pauvre homme*,' said Berthe.

The two Vanderphant girls were conspicuously well-behaved, and confined themselves to saying, '*Oui, maman*,' and '*Non, maman*,' or possibly, when passing things to Aunt Teresa, who was like a Queen amongst us, they might anticipate her wishes with a coy: '*Madame désire*?' But scarcely anything more. There they sat, side by side, the one dressed exactly like the other and wearing the same fringe across the forehead, neither plain nor yet particularly good-looking, but very well-behaved; while their mother talked to me of Guy de Maupassant and the novels of Zola.

'It is so good that your parents sent you to Oxford,' my aunt said.

I lowered my lashes at that. 'Yes, of course, it is rather an event to go up to Oxford. It's not as if you went up to Cambridge, or anything like that.'

'It had always been my ambition,' said Uncle Emmanuel, 'to go to the University. Alas! I was sent to the Military Academy instead.'

'And Anatole, too,' exclaimed my aunt, 'would rather have gone to the University, as his father also would have liked him to go. But I wouldn't let him—I don't remember why—and he, good boy that he is, would not have done anything to sadden me. His only thought, his only interest in life is his mother.'

She sighed—while I remembered how Anatole said to me one evening while on leave in England:

'Oh, you know, I get round mother easily enough.'

'Still, a university,' she mused, 'may have been better for him, now that the war's over. Like his father he is a poet, though he is his mother's boy. But I sent him to the Military College instead.'

'There are as many fools at a university as elsewhere,' I said to calm her belated qualms of conscience. 'But their folly, I admit, has a certain stamp—the stamp of university training, if you like. It is trained folly.'

'Ah!' said Mme Vanderphant, with a very conscious attempt at being intellectual, 'is it not always so: one belittles one's past opportunities if one hasn't made full use of them?'

'It's not a question of belittling anything,' I said. 'It's the attitude which Oxford breeds in you: that nothing will henceforth astonish you—Oxford included.'

And suddenly I remembered summer term: the Oxford Colleges exuding culture and inertia. And I became rhapsodical. 'Ah !' I cried, 'there's nothing like it! It's wonderful. You go down the High, let us say, to your tutor's, enter his rooms like your own, and there he stands, a grey-haired scholar with a beak that hawks would envy, in his bedroom slippers, terribly learned, jingling the money in his trouser pockets and warming his seat at the fire, smoking at you while he talks to you, like an elder brother, of literature. Or take a bump supper. There's a don nicknamed Horse, and at a bump supper, after the Master has spoken, we all cry: "Horse! Horse! Horse!" and he gets up, smiling, and makes a speech. But there is such a din of voices that not a word can be heard.'

To tell you the truth, when I was at Oxford—I was bored. My impression of Oxford is that I sat in my rooms, bored, and that it ceaselessly rained. But now, warmed by their interest, I told them how I played soccer, rowed in the Eights, sat in the president's chair at the Union. Rank lies, of course. I cannot help it. I am like that—imaginative. I have a sensitive heart. I cannot get myself to disappoint expectations. Ah! Oxford is best in retrospect. I think life is best in retrospect. When I lie in my grave and remember my life back to the time I was born, as a whole, perhaps I shall forgive my creator the sin of creating me.

There is this gift of making another feel that there is no one else of any consequence in the world. While I lied ahead, I felt

Sylvia exercise that gift—a most subtle kind of flattery this, needing no words, just a look, a touch, a tone. And as I spoke I felt this in the looks which Sylvia cast me. The stars twinkled. The night flushed, listened, as I lied on. And now I felt that my interminable talk already bored them a little.

'The war is over,' said my aunt, 'and yet there will be men, I know, who will regret it. The other day I talked to an English Captain who had been through the thick of the Gallipoli campaign, and he assured me positively that he liked fighting—and simply carried me off my feet. And I don't know whether he isn't right. He liked fighting the Turks because, he said, they are such splendid fellows. Mind you! he had nothing at all against them; on the contrary, he thought they were gentlemen and sportsmen—almost his equals. But he said he'd fight a Turk any day, with pleasure. Because they fought cleanly. After all,' my aunt continued, 'there's something splendid, say what you like—a zest of life!—in his account of fighting the Turks. The Turks rush out of the wood with glittering bayonets, chanting: "Allah! Allah! Allah!" as they advance into battle. Because, you see, they think they are already at the gates of Heaven, only waiting to be admitted. So they rush gravely and steadily into battle, chanting: "Allah! Allah! Allah!" I don't know—but it must be, as he says, exhilarating!'

'And then,' I said, continuing the picture, 'some sportsman sends a cold bayonet blade into the vulnerable parts of the man. You understand what happens?' I became cool, calculatingly suave. 'The intestines are a delicate tissue; when, for example, you eat a lump of something that your stomach cannot digest, you are conscious of pain. Now picture what happens in that human stomach at the advent of a sharp cold blade. It isn't merely that it cuts the guts; it lets them out. Picture it. And you will understand the peculiar intonation of his last "Allah!" '

'Oh, you are disgusting!'

'This is cruel! cruel!' said my aunt.

'Yes, to you, who would like your wars "respectable", conducted in good taste, outside in the yard, but please not on the drawing-room carpet! While my own feelings are that in a war soldiers should begin at home with the civilian population, particularly with the old ladies.'

'That is enough,' she said.

'No, I won't have you run away with a partial picture. Allah, indeed. What of your son in Flanders?'

'Oh, he is all right. Besides, it is all over now.'

'M-m…wait a few days.' I was excited. But I knew that to give the full effect to your sermon you must be calm, let your passion sift through your sentences. When I am righteously angry I let my righteous anger gather, and then put the brake on it, and give vent to it in cool, biting, seemingly dispassionate tones. I harness my anger to do the work of indictment. Turning ever so gently towards her, I fixed an evangelic look upon my aunt. 'What is the terrible thing in a war? In the war men's nerves gave way, and then they were court martialled for their nerves having given way—deserted them—and were shot at dawn—as deserters, for cowardice. And the sole judges of them were their superior officers who dared not know any better.

'And why is it,' I continued, avoiding momentarily the look which crept into Aunt Teresa's eyes, 'that stay-at-homes, particularly women, and more particularly old women, are the worst offenders in this stupid business of glorifying war? Why is it that they are more mischievous in mind, less generous in outlook than their youngsters in the trenches?'

Aunt Teresa closed her eyes with a faint sigh, as if to indicate that it was a strain on her delicate system to listen to my unending flow.

While, 'I remember,' I continued, 'an hotel in Brighton where I stayed two weeks before joining up in the so-called Great War. The inevitable old ladies with their pussy cats were by far the worst of all. They talked in terms of blood. They demanded the extermination of the whole of the German race; nothing less, they said, would satisfy them. They longed to behead all German babies with their own hands for the genuine pleasure, they said, that this would give them. They were not human babies, they argued, but vermin. It was a service they desired to render to their country and the human race at large. They had a right to demonstrate their patriotism. I was not a little shocked, I must confess, at this tardy display of Herodism in old, decaying women. I told them as much, politely, and they called me a pro-German. They discovered unpleasant possibilities in my name that had slipped their attention heretofore—a serious oversight. A danger to the Realm. Diabologh—but in heaven what a name to be sure! One of them went as far as to say that there was—there seemed to be—a distinct suggestion of something—well—diabolical about it that should be watched. They talked of cement grounds prepared by German spies at various vulnerable points in England to serve the purpose of future German heavy guns, ingeniously disguised as tennis courts, and of me in the same breath. "Why don't you," said one of the old ladies, a particularly antiquated specimen of her sex, "rather than make that impossible noise on the piano, go and fight for your country?" "Die?" I said, "that you may live? The thought's enough to make anyone a funk."

'Throughout the countries which had participated in the war' (I continued, because my aunt, breathless at my imputations, had nothing ready with which to interrupt my flow) 'there is still a tendency among many bereaved ones to assuage themselves by the thought that their dead have fallen for something at once noble and worth while which overtowers somehow the tragedy of their death—almost excusing it. Mischievous delusion! Their dead are victims—neither more nor less—of the folly of adults who having blundered the world into a ludicrous war, now build memorials—to square it all up with. If I were the Unknown Soldier, my ghost would refuse to lie down under that heavy piece of marble; I would arise, I would say to them: keep your blasted memorials and learn sense! Christ died 1918 years back, and you're as incredibly foolish as ever you were.'

I subsided suddenly. There was a pause.

'Thank you. We are much obliged to you for your lecture,' said Aunt Teresa.

'Welcome,' I said, 'welcome.'

8

After dinner we sauntered over into the drawing-room, and Uncle Emmanuel lit a cigar. The open piano beckoned to me as I stood in front of it, sipping my coffee.

'Do you play?' asked Mme Vanderphant.

I do not like to say that I don't, because as a child I had had innumerable piano lessons. But I could never be bothered to learn even to read music with any degree of proficiency. I therefore resent being pressed to play the piano in public. And my shy feeling is wasted, for they think it is merely false modesty, and that I like being asked. When I was at Oxford I took up music as a supplementary subject. I soon gave it up; I simply could not be bothered to learn the rudiments of its technical side, and finally, when I decided to give it up, I was told by my teacher of music that I could do so with no loss to music as a whole. Yet I am intensely musical.

'Play us something,' said Berthe.

'I don't feel in the mood.'

'Oh, do play,' Sylvia said, coming up to me; her dress touched me, her scent gave me a thrill of something delicate and beautiful and yet strangely intimate and near. How beautiful she was.

'What is this scent?'

'*Cœur de Jeanette*. Oh, do play.'

'Very well, then.'

I struck some introductory chords, and after repeating them a dozen times or so plunged into that climaxic bit of bursting passion from *Tristan* that I loved. And then stopped. I knew no further.

'Oh, go on!'

'I'm not in the mood.'

'Please, please,' they entreated.

I played the crest waves twenty times over, and then stopped.

They sighed appreciation.

'You have such feeling,' my aunt said.

Well, that's true. But I am impatient of technicalities. Once while at Oxford I played the same passionate bit from *Tristan*, and a D.Mus. rushed up to me, horror-stricken. 'Either,' he cried,

'I've lost my ear—or you are playing in the wrong key!' I was playing in the wrong key, by ear at that (because I could not tackle it in the original). But they asked me to go on playing, and all through my playing I had a feeling of warmth, as though the sun was shining on the tissues of my skin. Sylvia's warm eyes followed my every movement. And of this I was pleasurably aware.

Uncle Emmanuel who, while I was playing, looked as if he had something more urgent up his sleeve, immediately I stopped, took the opportunity of saying: 'Now that the war is over one must rejoice, one must amuse oneself a little.' And Aunt Teresa, who looked unhappy and preoccupied while I played, replied:

'The war is over, thank God. But I am anxious…about the last six weeks that I've been without news of him—I mean before the armistice was signed.'

I thought: they talk in terms of blood and fire—and then hope for safety and peace.

Nevertheless, to calm her for the sake of all of us, I said:

'Most of the suffering and pain in the world is imaginary suffering and pain—which is not there. The next story I write will be a tragedy of people who imagine that certain things will happen: they imagine, and their drama is a drama of imagining. Actually nothing happens.'

'It's you—it's you—you,' she said heatedly, 'who've upset me——'

'But, really, *ma tante*——'

'It's you—I won't sleep all night.'

'But listen, *ma tante*——'

'Oh, why get excited! Why get excited!' Uncle Emmanuel hastened between us. 'Peace! Peace in the household.'

For a while she sat silent in her big soft chair, thoughtful, bent over her fancy needlework. As her *tisane* was brought in to her by Berthe, she looked at me tragically with her large, sad, St. Bernard eyes, and her lip quivered. 'How I worry, George! Pity me. Pity me, George! George, understand, can't you, how dreadfully I worry!'

'That, believe me, is unnecessary. There's nothing either good or bad but thinking makes it so. Nearly all unhappiness in the world is caused by futile recriminations, anticipations, fears, forebodings, remembrances—that is, by the failure to control imagination.'

She sighed; then bent forward and sipped her *tisane*.

'What good is it your deliberately spoiling so many days and weeks of your short life by imagining the worst? And if the best occurs instead, you will have cheated yourself out of so many æons of your life, and the knowledge that this dim unhappiness of yours was but a phantom of your ill-controlled imagination will not retrieve a minute of your wasted life.'

She said nothing, only sipped her *tisane*.

'Then you will spend the rest of your time being miserable in retrospect for having wasted your days so unprofitably.'

'They will seem sweet then by the very contrast,' she said, with a sigh. And suddenly she expressed one of those strangely feminine views which always reassured me that Aunt Teresa was, in some ways, not as selfish as I thought, but, in the end, as egotistical as mortal man could be. 'No,' she said, 'if the best happens, and he has come out of it alive, unscathed, I will, by my utmost anxiety now, have paid, and gladly paid, the heaviest dues that may be exacted. I will have squared fate, and I shall be proud and happy to remember that I have not been ungenerous and have secured his safety by my suffering. Therefore I must be worrying now, it is dangerous to be calm and happy. I must pay the dues in advance. I feel I must—I ought to be anxious—and I have been—I don't know why—all this last month.'

She rose wearily from her arm-chair and stooped up to bed on the gallant arm of her husband. Aunt Teresa, I learnt, had an attack of nerves after that, '*une crise*', as Berthe called it, and could not sleep all night.

I looked at Sylvia. 'When I saw you in the street to-day I knew at once it was you.'

'Oh—with my shoes unlaced,' she laughed. 'I ran out just to buy some sweets.'

And later, when Sylvia and I played dominoes, I was so fascinated by her presence that I didn't care a rap about the dominoes, and Sylvia corrected practically my every move, as much as if playing by herself, while I only gazed at her in rapture. In another week her holidays would be over and she would return to Kobe to a boarding-school run by Irish nuns—the 'Convent of the Sacred Heart'.

'You are a wonderful, unique, great writer, George,' she said, and then added, in her serious way, with a perfect absence of guile: 'I must read one of your books some day.'

Then she too went to bed.

'Ah! the night life of Brussels! Ah!...' said Uncle Emmanuel over the drinks. 'It wants some beating!'

A moment later he came up to me. '*Mon ami*,' said my uncle, taking hold of me with both hands by the waist and looking up at me frankly, 'you must see Japan—life—it's amusing! The night aspect especially.'

9

Uncle Emmanuel had whispered things into my ear, and I had nodded, and now we were on our way. Our two rickshaw coolies ran smartly side by side in the abated heat of the evening. The lighted lanterns at the shaft and the side bobbed gaily through the gathering dusk. We went past endless bazaars, through endless lanes lined with shops. Uncle Emmanuel lit a cigar. He wore a brown bowler hat, yellow gloves that had been washed so often that they looked perfectly white, and with his stiff waxed moustache and his gilt-knobbed cane he looked quite a dog as he sat there, contented at last, in the feather-spring vehicle. The interminable progress through the city. Tokyo indeed was like an endless succession of villages. Night fell. The two men ran as smartly as ever. I, with my thoughts full of Sylvia, listened to those queer plaintive chants—A-a-a—y-a-a—yaw—y-o-o—that emanated from every nook and lane; shrinking aback at the touch, disinclined.

At last we drove up before a queer-looking wooden structure on long legs, and at once the hostess and attendants came down the crude wooden staircase to meet us. Our boots were removed at the foot of the stairs, and we were ushered upstairs into a low-ceilinged drawing-room, where I could not even stand up without bumping my head (though Uncle Emmanuel could do so with ease), and I had a feeling as if I had left the company of human beings and had joined that of birds or some undefined species of animals. While we were thus seated on the matted floor, fruit was served round; then a side-door opened, and a small procession of blanch-faced, short-legged women filed before us.

I was repelled by their flat blank Asiatic faces, and by the thick paint thereon. But Uncle Emmanuel smiled as he looked at them.

'*Elles sont gentilles, eh*?' he turned to me.

'M...' I demurred.

'Ah!' he retorted, provoked by my critical attitude, '*Ce n'est pas Paris, enfin*!'

He said that, say what I might, they were '*mignonnes*'. I maintained that their legs were much too short for my liking—a defect that, to me, stripped them of all feminine attraction. '*Que voulez-vous*?' he said philosophically. And we mildly fell out. The women stood before us, awaiting our choice. From outside came the din of the streets, and the plaintive whining chant of Mongol music, and the listlessness of the city stealing on us at the dead of night. I sat listless, too, on the matted floor in the low-ceilinged room, and I felt as if I had been locked up in the upper drawer of a cupboard—locked up and abandoned, in an age and place that were not mine. It was too inhumanly strange, and I longed for what I had left. Then I felt I wanted to cry, cry for what they had done to my soul....

'Rum-looking place,' I said. 'Rum-looking girls.'

'*Que voulez-vous*?' he said. '*C'est la vie*!'

At this point the hostess came up to us with a book and, pointing at it, exhorted us to register. 'Police,' she said, 'police.'

'Any name will do,' said Uncle Emmanuel lightly. But I refused emphatically, and after trying vainly to persuade me to put down my name, the hostess sent for an interpreter—a youth who presently appeared but whose command of our tongue did not appreciably extend over her own. He pointed at the register and said: 'Ha! Police—zzz—police. Ha!—zzz——'

'Ha!' said the hostess.

But I 'wouldn't have any'.

They looked at each other, and decided I was mad. But I seized the opportunity as an excuse for going, pretending I had been provoked, and, accompanied downstairs by their propitiatory smiles and bows, and restored once more into my boots, I got into the rickshaw and drove off, and waited for my uncle a few doors away, where I was immediately surrounded by a swarm of street urchins begging alms. The rickshaw coolie greeted me with a happy grin as if to say 'Ee! the young gentleman has been amusing himself!'

'Very good?' he asked, turning round in the shafts and grinning at me broadly.

I shook my head. 'No good. Girls very bad. Why so bad?'

'This bad Yoshiwara,' said the rickshaw man comprehendingly. 'No good. Good Yoshiwara very good.'

'Really good?'

'Ha! Very good.'

'Why didn't you take us to good Yoshiwara?'

'Good Yoshiwara far, far, very far—three hours far.'

At last Uncle Emmanuel was ushered down the steps. He got into his rickshaw, and we drove off. Uncle Emmanuel, as we drove home, held forth to me upon the sanctity of the family, the family hearth, '*le* 'ome', as he put it in English, and on the duty of keeping clean at home and of not mixing the two lives.

I returned to the hotel in the early hours. I had a bath in tepid water and went to bed under the white mosquito curtain. I could not sleep; all night I heard the whistling and screeching of the trains passing and halting near by. I lay sleepless, images now of Sylvia, now of the rickshaw man saying: 'Good Yoshiwara far, far, very far—three hours far' floating in and out of my brain, with the trains screeching and whizzing through in the night. In the end, sleep had taken its own. I dreamt that I was playing dominoes with Sylvia while a U.S. citizen was fighting with a Jap over the sleeper, and when the train stopped we had arrived in Oxford, which was being 'opened' by my mother and Lord Haig. Here there was much noise, like at the Palm Week bazaars to which we went as children in Russia. And suddenly I was confronted by an enormous frog. I am a trainer in a zoo. I am frightened, but they ask me: 'Can't you manage a frog better than that?'

'What must I do?' I ask.

'Shoot at it out of this.'

And I am handed a toy gun shooting cranberries.

If we are not a bit surprised at the inconsistencies, the incongruities, the rank ludicrousness of our dreams, perhaps we shall not be any more surprised if we discover that our life beyond the grave has similar surprises in store for us. It will all fall into place, and will not seem strange but inevitable, as our wakeful life of broken images, for some strange reason, even as the strangest of dreams, seems not the least strange but inevitable.

'Perhaps,' I said, on wakening with these pictures fresh but quickly fading from my memory, 'our instruments of measure are illusions, like the rest...'

I had a lavish breakfast, the pleasure of which was enhanced by the thought that the War Office was paying for it.

10

It was evening. I played that voluptuous bit from the *Liebestod* in *Tristan*, and Sylvia sat by and listened, absorbed. From the open window the moon swam out, exactly as in a romance, causing me to remember that I was not Hamlet but Romeo.

I played louder and louder till suddenly the door opened and Berthe said:

'Your aunt asks you to stop playing, as she has a *migràine*.'

'Come out on the balcony,' Sylvia said.

'Ha, ha! High-heeled shoes at last! How they show off the calves!'

She laughed—a lovely dingling laughter.

'It's dishonest to show too much of your legs. It upsets men's equilibrium. Either don't go so far, or if you do, then go the whole hog.'

'Alexander' (she called me by my third name because George, she thought, was too common and Hamlet a little ridiculous)—'Alexander, read me something.'

'What?'

'Anything. This.'

'Whose book is this?'

'*Maman's*.'

I opened and read: ' "...Besides, Dorian, don't deceive yourself. Life is not governed by will or intention. Life is a question of nerves, and fibres, and slowly built-up cells in which thought hides itself and passion has its dream. You may fancy yourself safe, and think yourself strong. But a chance tone of colour in a room or a morning sky, a particular perfume that you had once loved and that brings subtle memories with it, a line from a forgotten poem that you had come across again, a cadence from a piece of music that you had ceased to play—I tell you, Dorian, that it is on things like these that our lives depend." '

Sylvia had shut her eyes.

'Lovely,' she murmured.

Night, the patron of lovers and thieves, enwrapped us, casting upon us a thin veil of white mist. But the light was on in the corridor, and I had the feeling that every moment the door might fling open and my aunt would come in. This disconcerted me somewhat. A wicked smell, as of burning fishbones, rose from behind the backyard wall which the balcony overlooked.

'Tomorrow I'm going back to school,' she said, 'and—and we've never been out by ourselves. What cold hands you have, Alexander.'

'What is it like at your school?'

'Quite nice,' she said. 'We play hockey.'

A phenomenon of transformation! A Belgian girl, after four years in an Irish Catholic convent in Japan, came out an Irish colleen; there was even a trace of the delicious brogue in her accents. But withal there was a Latin warmth of grace in Sylvia which underlined her naturally acquired anglicism. There was a British freedom in her, but she would remember the restraints of a Latin upbringing, what was at Dixmude, and the ceremonious notions of her parents as to conduct that becomes a Belgian young girl. And there was something 'taking' in such discipline, as in a beautiful young horse submitting to the harness, or the discomfiture of ornament upon a lovely female form.

' "Play me something. Play me a nocturne, Dorian, and, as you play, tell me, in a low voice, how you kept your youth..." '

While I read aloud, Sylvia 'prepared' an expression of wonderment on her face, to show that she was sensitive to what I read. But she began to fret as I read on, absorbed, and then nestled to me closely. Her nostrils widened as she breathed in the fresh air.

' "The tragedy of old age is not that one is old, but that one is young..." ' And although neither of us had anything to do with the tragedy of old age, here we kissed. A light breeze that moment wafted the smell of the burning fishbones upon us.

'Isn't it lovely?' she purled.

I agreed.

Besides, it was.

'Lovie—dovie—cats'-eyes,' she said.

' "Why have you stopped playing, Dorian? Go back and give me the nocturne again. Look at that great honey-coloured moon that hangs in the dusky air. She is waiting for you to charm her, and if you play she will come closer to the earth..." '

We kissed.

And then we kissed again, this time independently of Dorian.

She had soft warm lips, and I held my breath back—at some considerable inconvenience to myself. Then I released her, and began breathing as if I had just climbed up a very steep hill.

'Go on, darling.'

'What lovely hair you have!'

'Wants washing,' she answered.

I stretched out my legs, my hands in my trouser pockets, and stared at the moon—and suddenly shot out: 'Art thou not Lucifer?' (causing Sylvia a little shock):

...He to whom the droves
Of stars that gild the morn in charge were given?
The noblest of the lightning-wingèd loves,
The fairest and the first-born smile of Heaven?
Look in what pomp the mistress planet moves,
Rev'rently circled by the lesser seven;
Such, and so rich, the flames that from thine eyes
Oppress'd the common people of the skies.

She stretched herself to my mouth the moment I finished, having, as it were, watched all this time till it was vacant. I kissed her, with considerable passion. 'What are all your names?' I asked.

'Sylvia Ninon Thérèse Anastathia Vanderflint.'

'Ninon,' I said, and then repeated lingeringly, sipping the flavour:

'Sylvia Ninon. Sylvia Ninon. Sylvia,' I said, and took her hand. 'Be not afear'd; the isle is full of noises, sounds and sweet airs that give delight and hurt not.

Sometimes a thousand twangling instruments
Will hum about mine ears; and sometimes voices,
That, if I then had waked after long sleep,
Will make me sleep again; and then, in dreaming,
The clouds, methought, would open and show riches
Ready to drop on me: that when I wak'd
I cried to dream again.

'Who wrote this?'

'Shakespeare.'

'It's—very lovely.'

I trotted out such quotations as I could remember—my Sunday best, so to speak. And, presently, grasping her passionately by the hand—'Adorable dreamer,' I whispered, 'whose heart has been so romantic! who has given thyself so prodigally, given thyself to sides and to heroes not mine, only never to the Philistines! home of lost causes and forsaken beliefs and unpopular names and impossible loyalties!'

'Who wrote it?'

I wanted to say that I wrote it; but I told the truth. 'Matthew Arnold wrote it. It's about Oxford.'

'Oh!' She was a little disappointed. 'And I thought it was about a woman—who'—she blushed—'who gave herself to some hero.'

'No, darling, no.'

After that I recited the passage about Mona Lisa who, like the vampire, has been dead many times, and learned the secrets of the grave; and has been a diver in deep seas, and keeps their fallen day about her; and trafficked for strange webs with Eastern merchants; and, as Leda, was the mother of Helen of Troy, and, as Saint Anne, the mother of Mary; and to whom all this has been but as the sound of lyres and flutes, that lives only in the delicacy with which it has moulded the changing lineaments, and tinged the eyelids and the hands.

'Oh, darling, let us talk of something else.'

'But I thought you liked—literature?'

'Well, darling, I *listened*—for your sake. But you are so long, you've never finished.'

'But good heavens!' I exclaimed. 'I've been trotting it out for *your* sake! I thought you liked books.'

'This is too high-brow for me, darling.'

'High-brow! What do you like, then?'

'Oh, I like something more—fruity.'

'What d'you mean?'

'Anything with a lot of killing in it.'

'Of course, my case is different, I admit. When I cease earning my living by the sword I shall commence earning it by the pen.'

'One day you will be a great author, and I shall read your story in the *Daily Mail*,' she said.

'The *Daily Mail*! Why on earth the *Daily Mail*?'

'They have serials there. Don't you read them? I always do.'

'Oh, well—yes, there are—I know there are.'

'I also write,' she said.

'You?'

'I do! Letters to the Press.' She went out and returning brought a newspaper. 'I wrote this.'

Under a rubric headed 'Questions and Answers', I read:

'Do you think it wrong for one girl and one boy to go for a picnic up on an island by themselves?'

'I wrote this,' she said.

'But why did you write it?'

'I write—because I want to know things. Besides, it's nice to see one's letter in the Press.'

'And what is their answer?'

'Here is their answer.' She showed me. 'Not necessarily.'

I read on questions from other correspondents. 'What is the proper height and weight of a boy nineteen years and one month?' asked one. 'Is he too young to be engaged?' asked another. 'If you say yes, it'll be in time to save him, as he is my friend. I'd like to persuade him to wait awhile, but what's your answer?'

'These others are silly,' she said, wrinkling her nose.

I smiled. She looked at me with a long, searching glance, as if taking stock of me as a man and a lover, while I, conscious of her scrutiny, manipulated an expression like this—M'm. There is something eminently seraphic hovering over my six foot of flesh and bone. I forgot whether I told you I'm good-looking? Sleek black hair brushed back from the forehead—and all the rest of it.

'You're so clever—and yet you're nothing much to look at,' she said.

This, I must confess, astonished me. I have no shallow vanity—but this astonished me. Sleek black hair, eyes, nose, and all that sort of thing. It astonished me.

'Never mind, darling. I don't like handsome men,' she added.

Now this sort of thing puzzles me. What am I to make of it?

'I love you all the same,' she said.

'How am I to understand it?'

'There's nothing to understand.'

'H'm. It's—strange,' I said. And then, after a pause, again: 'It's strange.'

I rose at last, for I was due that evening at the entertainment to be given us by the Imperial General Staff.

11

I found Beastly there and Philip Brown and Uncle Emmanuel and Colonel Ishibaiashi and a fair proportion of the Diplomatic Corps, in short, white, tail-less evening coats, all moving about on the matted floor in their socks, our shoes having first been removed in the hall, and I noticed that Beastly had a hole at the big toe. Not that this disturbed him at all, for he drank many cocktails and chaffed Philip Brown, guffawing loudly as he gave those ironical heavy nods with his head, as if to ask what indeed the world was coming to!

Percy Beastly was a Cockney by birth, and the years that he had spent in Canada as a youth had not contrived to polish his naturally rough-and-ready personality. He and Brown were each representative of the cruder class of their respective countries. (Brown, before the war, was a detective.) They were not individuals: they were merely samples of a type. They prided themselves on going through life with eyes open, but could only see 'graft' or 'bluff' in all human activities; they said 'they weren't born yesterday', asked if you could see 'any green in their eye', and always suspected that someone was 'pulling their leg'. The world has a strange way of 'pulling the leg' of such people! Beastly was very free and cheery, and chaffed the *geisha* girls at his side and drank much lukewarm *saké* with the officers who crouched up to each of us in turn to drink our health, and ate little pieces of shark and whale, it seemed cheerfully enough. But the unaccustomed *cuisine* had, I gather, played havoc with his sorely-tried digestion; and when a stout and cheery old Englishman came up to him in the hotel next morning and said, as men say over cocktails, 'Well, Major, what d'you think of Japan?' he answered, with some feeling:

'There's only one decent place in the whole of Japan, and that's the British Embassy.' And guffawed loudly.

A *geisha* girl perched on either of Uncle Emmanuel's knees, and he seemed very content. 'Don't look!' he said, as I turned round. And all the time he tried to press the Japanese officers at his side into taking him that very night to the 'good' Yoshiwara. But the Japanese officers only laughed and chaffed and promised gingerly. Anyway, I left without him.

When next morning I called to take Sylvia to the station, Uncle Emmanuel had not yet returned.

12

She leaned out of the train window, and I came up to say goodbye. My hat nearly came off as we kissed, and so the kiss was too slight; we barely brushed each other's lips. She stood at the window and looked at me with her large, luminous eyes. Her broad black velvet hat gave her a kind of Spanish appearance, and there was her nose faintly *retroussé*, nearly as good as her mother's—but too heavily powdered. And pink powder on her cheeks, too.

'You have a natural complexion,' I told her, 'but when you put powder on top you make it seem artificial, and that's a pity.'

She laughed, and showed a gold crown at the end of her mouth; and even that crown seemed exceedingly sympathetic.

'Back to the *Sacred Heart*!' she purled, blinking.

I looked up with something like anguish. 'What will you do there all these long months without me?'

'Well—I'll play hockey,' she said.

Then the train pulled out.

I stepped into a rickshaw and drove back to my aunt's. Gladness, like the sun-lit sea, engulfed me, choked me, but the white-winged bird in me came to the surface, saying: 'I am glad. I am glad.' So the screaming sea-gull bathes in the pearly air, its white wings glistening in the sun as it turns a *salto mortale*. And God seemed to say: 'I knew what I was doing.' When did I love her first? When last? There seemed no beginning and no end. And as I drove along the yellow sun-bespangled lane, the sun-lit verdure at both sides bowed low to me as I continued my triumphant progress in between, almost impelling me to raise my hat as if I were the Prince of Wales acknowledging the cheers of thronging crowds that lined my way.

I came back whistling. Sylvia's room being empty, I had cancelled mine at the Imperial Hotel, and at the invitation of my aunt now occupied my cousin's bedroom. I was happy, and moved, strolling about, breathing in her scent of *Cœur de Jeanette*, examining her *bric-à-brac*, when Berthe came in with a foreboding look on her face and a telegram in her hand. 'I had feared all along,' she said. 'I had a sort of feeling—why, I don't know, but I had it even when she talked of the Allahs. I had it when I opened the telegram. Your uncle has still not come back. Now what are we to do?' And she gave me the missive.

I read it—and I sat down, Berthe having done likewise.

'You're the only relative here,' she said. 'I suppose *you* had better tell her.'

'I shall wait till Uncle Emmanuel comes home. He'd better tell Aunt Thérèse.'

'Poor Anatole,' she sighed. 'To be killed on the eve of the Armistice.'

'I pity the mother most.' And I thought: with opinions like those—opinions that cause murder—what right have they to hope that *their* sons will survive? I saw Anatole but once, when he was on leave in England. Like his little father, he wrote sentimental poems à la Musset, and read them aloud to his intended as he held her white hand in his own and she dropped her fair head on his shoulder. In matters of love he had, like his father, been indefatigable. His mother spoke of him as of an angel imbued with one thought, one feeling—herself. But the only time I saw him he boasted to me that he knew how to 'get round her all right'. 'Oh!—maman; we don't take her seriously. We don't tell her things, and wink at what she says.' And winking he got off a bus at Leicester Square and went away with a young siren. He was dead.

Death is like this: you go along happy-go-lucky and suddenly somebody hits you over the head with a poker: *whack*! That is to mean that you are no more. Why do men die? To make room for others. That is all very well so far as it goes. But what are the other men for? If you think you understand death, I congratulate you.

Uncle Emmanuel was still away at the 'good' Yoshiwara. Late that night he returned. We took pity on him and did not tell him.

All next day till dusk I rickshawed about Tokyo, with the telegram in my pocket, guarding a dismal secret, wondering whether I should spare them their pain a little longer, and how much longer. The clouds had closed in, hung dark, leaden and foreboding; the weather could not make up its mind. I felt angry with humanity talking murder today only to whine on the morrow, and I felt wretched and miserable at guarding a sorrow I could not lessen. Of course, they'll make a hero of him, I thought: they will make a hero of that muddy eddy of confusion they call 'life'. But they will not apply themselves to the kindling of the divine spark in us, the feeble flame flickering in a void. Anatole too was a militarist at heart. He had the spirit of detached generosity to a cause that would have made him a valuable recruit in the fight for more life and more light. But his cause for which he had fought with a wholly admirable courage and devotion had, centuries ago, ceased to be a holy cause, was a carcass like the man who died for it. It had died centuries before the man who had just sacrificed his life for its hollow sake was born—and now he too was a carcass.

And I thought: the one thing that makes for war is just that speck, that pinpoint of weak thinking in men's minds which is the pivot of this gruesome cycle of unending war. Somehow, while nobody was looking, the idea had got into the thinking people's heads that wars were unavoidable. It would be really better at that rate if they did not think at all. But the unthinking people seem to be more interested in the shape of Winston's hat than in the contents of the brow it hides. I may be an eccentric, but somehow I can't bring myself to see that my cousin's death in Flanders is an event which is perfectly in order. The cold army missive would suggest that it was so. My aunt's own attitude to this young death would be, I knew, that it was tragically necessary. But she would not see that it was tragically necessary only because the world had men and women of her foolish outlook. Then why these tears? Oh, why these tears, good tears, falling upon ashes where they cannot thrive? I felt embittered that these tears should fall upon the barren ground of human folly and so lend it meaning. One wonders what Jesus died for.

Before I had to impart the message, I asked myself if I would willingly take on the death of a near one were I thereby to save her tribulation—and I felt I would not. Not very chivalrous? What matter, since I would not be called upon. I felt now what it was to be human: what the human heart may be called upon to endure.

I stood at the door before opening it to go in, because I said to myself: now he still lives for her; now she doesn't know and she knows no pain; but in a moment she will know and feel pain everlasting. I went away and walked about the garden and the terraces, and tarried till evening. The shadows crept up. And I thought: you aren't even being happy now while you can. The inconsequence of their conversation over lunch and tea had been painful to listen to. At dusk I entered my uncle's study, and leaving the telegram on the table went out. The lamp was burning, the curtains were drawn, the rain drummed against the window-sill.

He rose, with the telegram in his hand. 'It can't be!' he said, and came out into the corridor.

'Is it possible that they've made a mistake?' Berthe asked.

He turned hopefully to the interlocutor. 'Did you say you think it's a mistake?'

'I asked, is it possible that it's a mistake?'

He turned very red, and his little eyes behind the pince-nez glittered with unusual brilliance.

'It can't be!' he said. 'It can't be!' He walked up and down several times, and then, all of a sudden, went back into his study and shut the door behind him.

Some time afterwards he came out and knocked at Aunt Teresa's door.

'*Entrez*!' came her voice. And he went in. Berthe and I stood outside, listening, and I thought that her feeling at hearing his words must be that he and other sympathetic souls were souls assisting at a tragedy not wholly understood; that listening to warm condolences her only thought was that the son whom she had borne she would not see again. And—strange—my aunt, that woman who revelled in self-pity, now controlled herself and did not cry. There was something quiet and austere about her—like sombre music, like deep red wine. The storm had rolled over, but the rain fell quietly, steadily. And as I entered the bedroom I saw the two of them together. He was sitting on her bed, saying, 'My son! My son!' He had upset a jug of water which stood on the floor, but it took him some time to realize what he had done. The despair that had come on them with the first news had worn off a little; they were sobbing softly, quietly, timidly. 'I knew, I knew all the time,' she said, crying. 'You had better go and leave us, George; thank you, you can do nothing.'

Too late, I thought, you can't repair it now, there is no help! I went out quietly, quietly shutting the door. For a while I stood on the terrace, my thoughts circling round and round unprogressively. I noticed now that it was raining heavily.

13

On the 23rd of July, Beastly and I and Pickup, my servant, left Tokyo and crossed from Tsuruga to Vladivostok on the s.s. *Penza* of the Russian Volunteer Fleet, whose Captain, as he sat among us at the head of the table, had a meek, resigned look in his eyes, as if he didn't quite know what he was going to do next, while the ship's officers, professing disgust for the tedium of their prosaic occupations, speculated with enthusiasm on high politics, religion, literature, and metaphysics, upon which plane of thought navigation and such-like matters appeared proportionately negligible things. Meanwhile the ship somehow went on, thud after thud—and even reached its destination.

Vladivostok, as we surveyed it from the boat, struck me as a city of disgruntled individuals. Dock-labourers sat inertly on the quay, as if disgusted with Red Guards and White Guards and Green Guards alike, and the people, as they moved to and fro in the drizzle, looked tired of their work, of themselves, and of existence as a whole.

Our 'Organization', let me say at once, was something without precedent—one of the really comic sideshows of after-armistice confabulation. It was the poor old sentimental military mind, confronted with the task of saving civilization, forced to draw upon the intellect, and finding that in truth it had no such reserves to draw upon, plunging gallantly into a Russian sea of incoherence. And puzzled—daily more puzzled; coming out of it at last, with its tail between its legs, considerably bedraggled. There was really nothing to it but to enjoy the spectacle. The spectacle consisted of a number of departments whose heads amused themselves by passing buff slips one to another, the point of which lay in the art of relegating the solution of the question specified to the resources of another department. It was a kind of game of chess in which ability and wit counted for quite a great deal. The department which could not pass on the buff slip to another and in the last resort was forced to take action itself was deemed to have lost the game. From time to time new officers would be called for: specialists in embarkation, secret service, and so forth, and usually six months or more would elapse before their arrival from England, by which time the need for them would generally have passed. Unwilling to go home, they would prowl about the premises, coveting their neighbours' jobs, and usually end by establishing a new department of their own, with themselves as heads. A fat, flabby Major prowled about our offices, intriguing hard to get my job, and I (myself a master of intrigue) intrigued to keep my place by letting it be known that I would soon vacate it on my own account. Meanwhile the Major was content to work under my orders. I favour, on the whole, a mild atmosphere of Bolshevism in public affairs. Accordingly I occupied myself with writing novels and let the office work be run by the two junior clerks. And very well they ran it, I must say! Some readers at this point may feel inclined to censure me a little for my levity. Believe me, they are (if I may say so) talking through their hats. To regard a Government run by Churchills and Birkenheads seriously is not to know how to be serious. At any rate, we cultivated a certain literary spirit in our office as we pursued our silly military tasks, while our elders (after bungling us into the most ludicrous of wars) were building up that monument of foolish greed—the Treaty of Versailles!

After serving under me for some little time, the Major, nervous of being sent home, established a new department of his own—a post office of which he got himself appointed chief. I had to work under Sir Hugo (of Vladivostok fame), of whom you may have heard. My chief was a lover of 'staff work', and besides the many ordinary files he had some special files—a file called 'The Religious File', in which he kept documents supplied by metropolitans and archimandrites and other holy fathers, and another file in which he kept correspondence relative to some gramophone records which had been taken from the Mess by a Canadian officer. And much of our work consisted of sending these files backwards and forwards. And sometimes the gramophone file would be lost, and sometimes the religious file, and then Sir Hugo would be very upset. Or he would write a report, and the report—so intricate was our organization—would also be lost. Once he wrote a very exhaustive report on the local situation. He had corrected it very carefully, had, after much thought, inserted a number of additional commas, had erased some of the commas on secondary consideration, had had the report typed, and had corrected it again when it was typed, inserting long sub-paragraphs in the margins which he enclosed in large circles, and so attached them to wherever they belonged by means of long pointed arrows trespassing on each other's ground, thus giving the script the appearance of a spider's web. Then he had read it through once again, now solely from the point of view of punctuation. He inserted seven more commas and a full stop which he had previously omitted. Sir Hugo was most particular about full stops, commas and semicolons, and he was very fond of colons, which he preferred to semicolons, by way of being more pointed and incisive, by way of proving that the universe was one chain of causes and effects. In order to avoid any possible mistakes in the typing of his manuscript, Sir Hugo surrounded his full stops with little circles, and in producing commas he would turn his pen so as almost to cause a hole in the paper and then slash it down like a sabre. The colons were two dots, each surrounded by a circle; and a semicolon was a combination of an encircled full stop and a sabre slash of a comma. There could be no possible mistake about Sir Hugo's punctuation. And would you believe it? After he had dispatched the report, marking the inner envelope in red ink 'Very Secret and Personal', and placing the inner envelope in an outer envelope and sealing carefully both envelopes—the report was lost.

Sir Hugo had, of course, made enquiries. He established a chain of responsibility, and it seemed that each link had done its duty: yet the chain had failed. But Sir Hugo would not give in. He had accumulated a pile of unshapely correspondence on the subject of the prodigal report and had collected the papers in a file named 'The Lost Report of Sir Hugo Culpit', and when he collected a scrap of evidence on the subject he would scribble it down on a buff slip and then send it in to me (whom he had now entrusted to keep the file), with the words: 'Please attach this slip, by a pin, to confidential file, entitled "The Lost Report of Sir Hugo Culpit".' And in a humorous vein I had written on the slip in imitation of Sir Hugo's manner:

> Please state *what* pin:
> 1. (*a*) An ordinary pin; (*b*) a safety-pin; (*c*) a drawing-pin; (*d*) a hair-pin; (*e*) a linch-pin.
> 2. What make and size

and sent the slip back to Sir Hugo.

I thought that Sir Hugo would rejoice over this slip, it being so very much in accordance with his own methods of procedure. Not so indeed. Sir Hugo hated people like himself, because they acted as a sort of caricature of himself: served to remind him of a fact of which in his more open moments with himself he was dimly conscious—that he was to a large degree absurd.

But when I was called before Sir Hugo and reprimanded for my levity, I felt it to be my best course to maintain a sort of honest, stupid face as if in testimony of my innocence; and Sir Hugo may have believed me.

And yesterday—two months later!—the prodigal report had returned to the office. To the unspeakable horror of Sir Hugo it was found in an empty oat sack at the distant wharf of Egerscheldt, and Sir Hugo now broke his head as to how it could have possibly got there. He was determined to trace back its journey to the office, even if that should cost him his health.

He had convened a special conference comprising all the heads of departments and told us of the mysterious circumstances. 'We must begin,' he said, 'right at the beginning. There is, in fact, many a worse point to begin at. I am not entirely pessimistic. We've got the sack. That is all right. Beyond the sack we know nothing. Now here is the sack.' He stretched out the sack. 'I suggest, gentlemen,' he said, 'that you work backwards. The first thing to do is to trace the manufacturers of the sack.' The task was entrusted to me.

Is it to be wondered at that I fell ill?

14

It was winter, clean, white, crisp, impenetrable. All around me—the bay and the hillocks—was covered as with a tablecloth. I lay in bed, ill, and dreamed into the future, back into the past. Long, peaceful thoughts. In those still twilight hours when you lie on your back you float as if outside and beside life, draw from the deep well of inhibited emotion that dreamy substance which underlies our daily life, remove layer after layer of 'atmosphere', veil after veil of mood, cloud after cloud of misty oblivion, till your soul shines forth like a star on a frosty night. What is that soul of yours, and is it *you*? My *I*, as I now came to see, has always been changing, was never the same, never myself, but always looked forward—to what? Perhaps we change our souls even as the serpents are said to change their skins. There are feelings awaiting me I know nothing of yet. When I shall know them, they will have added to my ever-changing soul—towards the ultimate totality of God.

Alone, in the deep silence of the night, we steal up to the door. We pause. We press the handle. The door is locked. We die: the door is open, and we enter. The room is empty, but at the other end we see a door. We press the handle. It is locked.

And so for ever…

Sir Hugo sent a note to Major Beastly, which ran:

> Please say:
>
> 1. Have you, or have you not, as yet, taken steps to cause a doctor to be sent to see your friend?
>
> 2. If so, (*a*) what step; (*b*) what date; (*c*) what time; (*d*) what doctor?

But Major Beastly, as he was about to bestir himself on my behalf, had an attack of dysentery, and the matter was indefinitely postponed. And only my sleepy apathetic batman Pickup was here to look after me as I lay, lost in a cloud of timeless thought, in the last grips of influenza. We are like icebergs in the ocean: one-eighth part consciousness and the rest submerged beneath the surface of articulate apprehension. We are like stars passionately intent on looking at the world and loth to go out; like children resentful of being sent to bed while the party is on. Were I to die now, where would be the meaning of my having lived at all? So once I had feared to die in France away from my real 'atmosphere', while not owning my real soul. I felt that if I died then I would take away with me into eternity a soul not truly mine and leave the true one languishing behind—in Petrograd. How absurd! The house was empty. Workmen prowled about re-decorating the interior for our impending use. They came and went. Away in the kitchen the Chinese cook sang a plaintive native air, and now and then I seemed to hear the sound of Pickup's heavy Army Ordnance boots. The smell of paint sent me back some fifteen years, to the time when I was yet a child, and made the memory of it sweet, which the experience had never been. Easter eve. The advent of spring. I return home from a shop where I had bought—oh rapture!—an electric torch. The big, stupendous world enshrouds me. The ice is breaking on the Neva. A moist, languid warmth sets in. The stars in heaven twinkle through the dark. That too has gone. And I remembered suddenly the Island drive in Petersburg, when I was still a boy, how I alighted from my father's coach and stood and looked out to the Finnish Bay glowing in the evening sunlight. Mysterious light. What life it brought with it, what tortuous life! Surely this gathering gleam evolving into streaks of red, green, pink, gold, lilac, was no hallucination. It was more like a chord, soft, sad and lost. And it was then, before I knew it, that I anticipated love: 'my wife', a young woman stranger and more marvellous than anything that I had ever met: those dreams which went with her as I trudged home from school, imagining myself an artist, a great writer, an actor, a famous tenor rendering Faust's *Cavatina*, the world's champion lawn-tennis player, a conductor of orchestra, a composer of music, and withal a banker and a millionaire, living in a marble palace on the banks of the wide Neva, owning a steam yacht, horses, a wife who would desert me—and then die, and I would be pitied as I stood in a tall hat, with a broad black band on the sleeve of my astrakhan coat, at the open grave, having forgiven her. These memories—they too had gone. Where? Why? And, again, I remembered Oxford, how I strolled down Queen's Lane one evening towards New College, and the glorious twin towers of All Souls stood, wise and quiet, in the nacre-coloured air. They had stood there long before I had come into the world, and they would stand there long after I had ceased to be. And between that and now was Flanders, the war, trench-ladders and parapets, the white wooden crosses we made for ourselves before an impending attack, on a divine June night. Memories, past moods, past souls. They have been and gone. When as a boy I dreamed of love, the type of feminine beauty I cherished was so utterly different from Sylvia's that I could not have thought I would ever love one like her, who was not at all 'my type'. To have done it would have been to betray my soul. I have betrayed my soul. And there is nothing left of my former soul: we might have been acquaintances. What matter? I don't care a rap for my old soul. I have found—I will not say a real—no, a new meaning of love. Bathing in the luxuries of convalescence, I thought no longer of 'my wife', but of Sylvia as my wife, dwelling in the marble house with pillared terraces, the leaden water of the Neva lapping at the sloping granite steps. Her letter which I had on wakening was like a desirable but premature caress breaking through receding sleepiness.

> My Own Darling Prince [she wrote]. Here I am in sad, sad Trouble. My lovely brother Anatole Roland Joseph was executed in Flanders on the 22nd of last month. He had gone to sleep on watch duty which he had taken over voluntarily for some soldier who was very tired, and was caught asleep by an N.C.O. who hated him, and court-martialled.

She enclosed the letters he wrote with an indelible pencil on the night before the execution, and the tears he poured as he wrote to his mother, father and sister, each a separate letter of farewell, stained them in pale-blue blobs. Judging by the size of the blobs, he must have cried freely at the stern injustice of being pushed perforce out of this world, at the thought of never seeing them again. 'They can kill my body, but they can't kill my soul,' he wrote. 'I shall go to heaven and be with God.' They sent his clothes home, blood-stained in places, with several bullet punctures about the chest.

> Needless to tell you how Heartbroken I feel. I have waited for a letter from you: but none. Are you angry with me? Please, please write to me Princie Darling lovely Child. It will be Christmas soon. I will send you a little gift later in the week. I had a fall and hurt my Arm—better now. And here I suffer while His Grace dances gaily on the warships. I just longed for a letter from you, and of course disapp. was Sylvia.
>
> Ever yours,
>
> Sadie. New name.
>
> VERY SAD
>
> Please wire.

Aunt Teresa wrote that her poor health was in as miserable a state as ever and that she had resigned herself to spend the remainder of her days in her exile in the Far East. There was little purpose in going back to Belgium now that Anatole was dead, and they were all removing to Harbin, where Countess X., an old Russian friend of hers, who was going back to Europe, would let them have her flat practically free of rent. Uncle Lucy's remittance had still not arrived, and she was taking Sylvia home from the 'Sacred Heart' as she could not afford the fees.

15

When, after my recovery, I returned to the office, I found that the Major had usurped my job. I worked, for a little while, under his orders, and then got sick of it. The clerks (like permanent officials untroubled by a change of Minister) worked unperturbed as before. 'Chesterton,' said Sergeant Smith, from his desk. 'Ah, Chesterton, sir!'

'What about him? He says more than he knows.'

'But,' rejoined Sergeant Smith, 'how he walks down Fleet Street, stopping every few paces, lost deep in thought; then suddenly dashes across, stops dead in the middle of the thoroughfare, the buses and taxis and things all whizzing past and around him, then touches his forehead—"Got it"—and having captured the missing link in his thoughts returns to the pavement. A great character.'

'A hair-splitting dud!' rejoined Sergeant Jones.

'No!'

'Now then,' said the Major, from my former desk. 'Now then!'

Finding it impossible to evict him from my chair (now more amply occupied by his form), I accepted Sir Hugo's offer of combining a little duty with pleasure, and proceeded on a sheepskin expedition to Harbin to bring back a quantity of sheepskin coats which had been ordered for the Russian Army. As Beastly was returning to Harbin to consult the railway authorities in that city on matters locomotive, we agreed to go together, Pickup and Beastly's batman Lenaine (the latter a public school boy whose father as he came to see him off at Euston wore a top hat and looked like a lord) travelling with us. It was full winter, and bitterly cold. Two weary nights, impenetrable gloom.

A lovely morning. I stood on the open platform as the train raced between a forest and a field, both deep in snow. A harsh wind whipped me in the face, but the sky was blue and cloudless and the vast space of snow glittered in the sunshine.

Sylvia was waiting for me at the station, looked out, and seeing me went in—I suppose out of shyness. Then we met. She had grown. She was taller and more beautiful than she had been in Japan; she looked fresh and strong in her short astrakhan-bordered coat and warm overshoes. And Harbin, which I had visited one summer, seemed full of precious associations; but under the cloak of winter it had acquired an unreal, fantastic appearance. The pines and firs were covered with snow; the ground creaked agreeably under our feet as we walked to their house.

As we entered the large stone building, a door on the landing was open and a terrific row seemed in progress in one of the flats, as if someone—someone who shouldn't have been—had been killed. I looked up at Sylvia, in alarm.

'It's Berthe and Mme Vanderphant,' she said, 'talking.'

And indeed, as we ascended the steps, it transpired that Berthe and Mme Vanderphant were amicably imparting to each other their deep-felt impression that it was very cold in the flat.

'*Mais, Mathilde, c'est épouvantable ce qu'il y fait froid!*'

'*Ah, mais je te crois bien, Berthe!*'

And so on.

The flat was a little dark, but otherwise nice and comfortably furnished, and there was a bath. But when I applied for its use I created a commotion. '*Allons!*' said Berthe, 'we must send for the workmen to repair the bath.' Some hours afterwards they arrived and set to work on the geyser, which gave angry little puffs of explosion—when they all began to curse each other. While the bath was being prepared for my impending use, two homeless dressmakers who had been allowed by Aunt Teresa to use the bathroom as a room for dressmaking were enjoined by Berthe to leave it. They stood in the corridor, surprised and afraid, as if wondering what was 'up', and holding their work in their hands, while I washed, slowly, lingeringly, interminably. And I could hear their voices, amid the angry little puffs of the geyser, while in the adjoining room Uncle Emmanuel conversed politely with Mme Vanderphant:

'Monsieur is supporting the cold remarkably well.'

'Ah, madame is truly amiable.'

'Monsieur is too kind.'

'Ah, madame is flattering me!'

'Is monsieur then not afraid of the climate?'

'Ah! not at all.'

'*Enfin*, monsieur has courage!'

'Ah, madame is flattering me.'

'Monsieur is too kind.'

In the twilight of the cosy drawing-room Sylvia was playing patience and telling fortunes, talking a lot to herself, cooing like a dove—half-audibly. Having finished telling her own fortune she began telling mine—something about a fair lady, an important letter, a long journey, and so forth.

'Darling,' I said, 'you only wrote to me once all the time. I wrote three times.'

She did not answer at once because she was laying out the cards and cooing to herself the while. I thought she hadn't heard, but presently she replied: 'I wanted to know.'

'What?'

'When a man loves he writes, writes, writes—goes on writing. I wanted to know.'

'What?'

'If you would go on.'

'Oh!'

'Oh!' she mimicked. 'I did.'

'But I've no time for writing letters. I like writing for print.'

'You write something about my darling beautiful brother Anatole.'

'But, darling, what am I to write?'

'Write something. I want to have something from you. Write about his little dugout and how he joined at eighteen and—and how they killed him.' Her eyes filled.

I thought: we shall forget your sacrifices, curses, vows, and what you went through—and we shall live as though those things had never been. We shall forget the things you died for—and the peace will yet calumniate your deaths.

We arrived on a Thursday, and on Saturday, it being the fourth day since we left Vladivostok, Major Beastly made a *stink*. Uncle Emmanuel at once lit a heavy cigar. Aunt Teresa applied her lace handkerchief to her chiselled nostrils. '*Mais mon Dieu*! He wants to kill us,' she exclaimed. 'It's poison gas!'

'*Ah, je crois bien, madame*!' cried Mme Vanderphant in tones of acute anguish. And Berthe uttered: '*Oh la la*!'

Uncle Emmanuel shrugged his shoulders several times in that provoked, astonished way by which the Latin race implies that 'it's a bit much!' and said, '*Allons donc, allons donc*!'

'*Ah, mais*! he has some cheek!' echoed Mme Vanderphant.

To which Uncle Emmanuel could only answer, 'Ah! Ah——!' completing with his gestures the unspeakable.

He had a delicate skin, said Beastly, when I approached him diplomatically, which would not stand the touch of the razor-blade. I cannot say what happened. As I was about to press him more definitely to give up this evil-smelling practice, he suddenly fell ill with dysentery, and the question was again indefinitely postponed.

It fell to Berthe to nurse him. Beastly was no great beauty at the best of times. His nostrils were strictly perpendicular to the ground on which he trod—that is vertical instead of being horizontal; so that when he leaned back in a chair, or now in bed, before you, they were parallel with the incline of his body. You had a full view of them, as though they were drawn up for your inspection. Nevertheless, Berthe took a fancy to him and nursed him with especial care.

16

When, two weeks later, Beastly was leaving for Omsk, Aunt Teresa charged him with a mission to her brother Lucy, whom he was to see *en route* at Krasnoyarsk. 'Tell him, tell him,' she enjoined, 'of the awful, terrible conditions I have to suffer in my sad exile, and of my poor, miserable state of health!'

'I'll talk to him, never you fear. I'll tell 'im what I think of 'im,' said Beastly, guffawing and nodding heavily as if he thought that Uncle Lucy was a poor fish—a silly business man who didn't know his own silly business.

Meanwhile, the situation as regards the sheepskin coats was vague and obscure. Obscure and uncertain. Uncertain and hypothetical, to a quite extraordinary degree. The fact was that I could find no trace of any sheepskin coats in the neighbourhood. No one seemed to have heard of such an order. But I liked Harbin and I was in no hurry to return to Vladivostok, and so refrained from telegraphing for instructions and tarried as long as ever possible. For (I make no secret of it) it was nice enough to be with Sylvia, to breathe the same air, eat the same food, lead the same life. Meanwhile, the sheepskin coats, as I said, could not be traced.

After Anatole's death Aunt Teresa more madly than ever buried herself in medicine bottles, old photos, hot-water bottles, thermometers, books, *buvards*, writing-pads, cushions, cosmetics. At the time of Beastly's illness, Uncle Lucy's remittance still not having arrived, Aunt Teresa had asked me to speak to Uncle Lucy on the 'direct wire', for which privilege, however, special leave had to be obtained from the Commander-in-Chief, General Pshemòvich-Pshevìtski, while the telegraph operator who transmitted the message for me threw out hints that he was fond of smoking English cigarettes. And now again, there being no report from Beastly relative to his *démarches* at Krasnoyarsk, Aunt Teresa got very fidgety indeed.

'*Courage, mon amie*!' said Uncle Emmanuel.

'But, Emmanuel, it's five months overdue. I can't be borrowing all the time from Mme Vanderphant. She's beginning to look quite suspicious.'

'All things come to him who waits. Patience,' he said. 'Patience.'

' "Patience, patience, and once again patience," said General Kuropatkin,' said I, 'as he lost the Russo-Japanese War.'

'*Courage! Courage!*' said Uncle Emmanuel, lighting a cigar.

All these years he had been thriving on the dividends of Aunt Teresa, was always cheerful, and said, '*Courage, mon amie*! Life is worth living!' But one afternoon as we went out together—Uncle Emmanuel wanted a shirt and a new pair of boots—he looked sad, morose and wretchedly unhappy. His cry 'My son! My son!' uttered on that fatal day at Aunt Teresa's bedside reverberated in my brain at the sight of him, dejected and unnerved. I thought that he was thinking of his son, when he confessed to me that Uncle Lucy had written him a dreadful letter—which practically held him up to ransom, so crudely worded was the document. He showed me the missive. It was incredible. Uncle Lucy, renowned for his unselfishness, Uncle Lucy who liked to play the *grand seigneur* towards his sisters and their families, Uncle Lucy the insanely generous, had suddenly turned mean and carping, petty and dishonest! Indeed, suddenly he seemed to have turned the corner in his ethics. So far it was he and he alone to whom they looked for dividends. His present missive was as crude a way as if he said, 'Your purse or your life!' It was a blunt enough letter demanding that Emmanuel should send him £100 sterling forthwith, and threatening in default of it to send 1*s*. (one shilling) worth of roubles in settlement of all Aunt Teresa's claims against him. He signed himself: '*Ton frère qui t'aime, Lucy.*'

It was incredible. I thought: this document will scare her off her perch and send her cackling like a hen. Or she will have a stroke. And indeed my uncle said that he could never show this awful letter to his wife, for fear of a fatal *crise de nerfs*. And all through his shopping Uncle Emmanuel was very dejected and very morose. He first bought himself the boots and put them straight on, and in the new boots set out in search of the shirt. He was as tiresome and exacting about the shirt as he had been quick and conciliatory about the boots, and the lady who served us became visibly exasperated and asked us how many shirts at least we wanted (implying an expectation in proportion to the trouble we were causing her). '*Une seule*,' said my uncle. He arrived home utterly exhausted in his stiff new boots and would have done better, in my view, if instead of first buying the boots and going out in them in search of the shirt, he had first purchased the shirt and gone out in it in search of the boots. He was, as I said, utterly exhausted and did nothing more that day.

But next morning he drafted an answer, pointing out that the action which his brother-in-law had seen fit to threaten him with was not only '*peu fraternelle*', but, nay, also peculiarly '*criminelle*', and he asked my Uncle Lucy to terminate the painful correspondence. Uncle Emmanuel requested me to take this message to the General Post Office and to transmit it with all priority by 'direct wire' to Uncle Lucy at Krasnoyarsk, for which special favour I had to obtain once more the permission of the Russian General in command. Armed with a note from the Commander-in-Chief, General Pshemòvich-Pshevìtski, I proceeded to the General Post Office where a telegraph operator, reading the Commanding General's note, transmitted Uncle Emmanuel's message in my presence with a superlative degree of priority, known as 'Clear the Line'. Uncle Lucy having now arrived at the other end, six thousand versts away, the telegraph operator received Uncle Lucy's answer, which, ignoring all Uncle Emmanuel's elaborate arguments, ran as follows:

'*Pas criminelle, mais tout en ordre.*'

And once again Uncle Lucy signed himself: '*Ton frère qui t'aime.*'

I folded the message and put it away in my pocket, while the telegraph operator asked if I could let him have a box of English cigarettes.

17

Then, one day, came Uncle Lucy's letter, this time addressed to Aunt Teresa. The Bolsheviks had occupied Krasnoyarsk and seized his works and all his property. He wanted the £100. He had all his life been paying them more than he had any business to do, and had incurred thereby the grave displeasure of his family which—so they said—he had neglected for the sake of his beautiful three sisters. 'Why don't you,' he wrote, 'sell your useless jewels and cough up the money?' Anyhow, the £100 not having come his way, he enclosed 1*s.* (one shilling), the silver bob, at the present favourable exchange, being over and above Aunt Teresa's capital in roubles in the Diabologh concern which hereby he considered liquidated for all time.

What a shock to Aunt Teresa! After her son's death, it was probably the greatest shock of Aunt Teresa's life. She suffered a complete relapse. She lay prostrate and speechless, and Berthe busied herself about her slender form with hot and cold compresses, with eau-de-Cologne and pyramidon.

'How is she?'

'Ah!' said Berthe with a sarcastic mien. 'There is nothing ever the matter with your aunt. She is a *malade imaginaire*!'

But even as she spoke Berthe would rush off back to Aunt Teresa and be very kind to her. She would enjoy a malicious laugh at the expense of my poor aunt, about whose 'miserable health' she had no illusions and indeed no tears to waste, and sneer behind her back; yet even as she sneered she would suddenly get interested in her again, with a warmth, a pity, an attachment which was as genuine as her cynicism was sincere. She would delight in sharing anyone's illiberality upon the subject of my aunt; yet all the time she would be at the beck and call of her new friend who had contrived to make a servant of her. From Vladivostok I had written Aunt Teresa a sentimental letter full of *ach*'s and *och*'s, 'poors' and 'alases', a letter in which the sentiment, intended as it was for a notorious sentimentalist, was laid on with a trowel. I was therefore all the more astonished when Berthe now imparted to me that my aunt had been repelled by the odious sentimentality of my letter and looked upon me as a kind-hearted but withal a sentimental fool. 'A nice boy, George, but too much in the skies, too sentimental, a little mawkish, too. A dreamer of dreams!' she had said.

'The difference between the dreamer and your practical man, as somebody has said, is that the dreamer sees the dawn before the other fellow.'

'Why? Because he sits up all night?'

'That is one of the reasons.'

'But your aunt,' she said. 'Why, there's really nothing the matter with her. Nothing at all. It is all put on. But she is jealous of me even when I say I have caught a chill. But I've no more time to waste,' she hastened. 'I must go and change her compresses and make her her *tisane*.'

'This is remarkable!' exclaimed my aunt as I went in to her. 'Your Uncle Lucy evidently imagines that our money is his own and that he can do with it whatever he likes! He must have gone off his head! When our father died we each had 100,000 roubles. Two months later your Uncle Lucy, who continued at the head of affairs as managing director, informed us that we each possessed 400,000 roubles, and less than a year hence he wrote to tell us we possessed one million roubles. Fifteen years later he told us that we had just 30,000 each. We never knew *what* we had! And now he writes to tell me that I've nothing.'

To Uncle Lucy, I daresay, it must have seemed that all he had done was to present the case to them in a new and startling light, but to his sister he was now worse than a criminal. Uncle

Emmanuel drafted a reply in French and stood over her as she translated it hurriedly and not very efficiently into English. From long disuse Aunt Teresa's English had become very foreign; but assuredly Uncle Lucy's was no better. Opening her red-leather *buvard* and placing the writing-pad upon it, she began, without deigning to address him:

I duly received your insultent [so she spelt it] wicked and unjust letter dated 17th inst. I cannot realize that you, a gentleman, could have written in that shameful way to your poor old sister you have known enough to state she was true, *honest* and straightforward! You seem to have forgotten that when our father died we all inherited the same sum which you begged of us to leave in the business which you undertook to manage! I perfectly admit you made it prosper the first years and paid us a very good dividend, of which you profited *more* than any of us, as you lived in a palace as you may say—in the greatest luxury—spending money wholesale—this was of course your business. *We* lived plainly and spent the money on our children's education, added what Emmanuel earned, as he has never lived doing nothing as you seem to think!

My jewels are the only thing I will have to leave to my daughter after my death! Emmanuel is trying to sell my silver, as we are head over heels in debt to the Belgian lady and family who share our flat with us, but he must consider the future when no more able to work and a sick wife to support, and the comfort and care my poor miserable state of health requires. And still I cannot afford consulting a first-class specialist, nor having sufficient strengthening food in my sad exile! We live in no luxury and I have to struggle hard to make ends meet. I do all the correspondence and write to all our relations for Christmas and Easter and birthdays as I cannot on account of my poor miserable state of health do house work—you have been able to shake my poor health, which is still worse since my poor son's death!

If Major Beastly told you we live in luxury, it is not true, of course. We tried to give him a good time during his stay in Tokyo and here, in depriving ourselves—at great sacrifice to ourselves, not knowing that he was to show himself a turncoat and informer!—and at very great inconvenience, too, for this man, as you may know yourself by now, doesn't shave but—oh, makes such a smell with a hair-burning apparatus that we have been obliged to open all windows in the house, and I caught a chill in consequence, which is terribly dangerous in my miserable state of health!

If you had no wife or sons to help you, I assure you I would give anything to allow you a small sum, but as it is, and having no money of my own, I cannot do so.

Well, this is the last you will ever hear from me—you have hurt and offended me too cruelly, too unjustly! I shall *never* forget your shameful *insultent* letter I certainly *never* deserved!

Uncle Emmanuel suggested her signing it at this point. But Aunt Teresa felt that this was not really enough.

'May God forgive you!' she added, and then signed it:

'Teresa Vanderflint.'

Uncle Emmanuel, writing his letter in French, began thus:

> To my brother-in-law Lucy Diabologh.
>
> I have just read the abusive letter which you have had the audacity to write to your sister Teresa who had nothing but the tenderest feelings towards you. Allowing for your own feelings in the matter, I choose to tell you that you have surpassed the measure of decent behaviour and that your letter has completely wrecked the health of my poor wife whose precarious state impels constant care and attention, and for whom, I must warn you, such emotions may prove fatal. If my income was inferior to that derived by my wife from the money inherited from her father, it does not yet follow that I have lived on your money, as you imply. Nevertheless, your offer to settle your debt to us of 500,000 roubles by one shilling appears to me so indescribably odious that I decline to discuss the matter with you any further. I repeat that I have never had the privilege of living on you, as you imagine, but that my family benefited by an advantageous (?) investment in a Russian industry at a time of prosperity of a capital of 100,000 roubles which belonged to my wife and that you were in duty bound to do your best for all of us. The facts have proved, alas! that the too absolute confidence that we have reposed in the ability and judgment of our brother-in-law has resulted in a catastrophe which must have occurred even if the war and revolution had not intervened. It must not, therefore, be forgotten by you that *we* are your creditors and not you ours, as you erroneously suppose.
>
> I regret that for the first time that I have to correspond with a brother-in-law whom I had never had the occasion to meet I must be called to give him a lesson in *savoir vivre*. I ask him to cease all malignant polemics in regard to his brother-in-law and to spare his sister emotions so painful as those caused by his last missive.

He signed with a flourish:

'Emmanuel Vanderflint.'

Aunt Teresa's and Uncle Emmanuel's letters were so long and explicit that Uncle Lucy as he read them must have felt he wanted to dine in between.

18

The Dove

Meanwhile, the situation as regards the sheepskin coats was still uncertain. Vague and perplexing. Dubious and undetermined. Confused and unsettled. Oracular, ambiguous, equivocal. Bewildering, precarious, embarrassing and controvertible, mysterious and undefinable, inscrutable and unaccountable, impenetrable, hesitant—apparently insoluble. Incredible! Incomprehensible! My orders were to ascertain their whereabouts and to arrange for their dispatch by rail to—I didn't quite remember where. This I tried to arrange. 'But where are the coats?' the railway authorities questioned. Alas, this was more than I knew. For the sheepskin coats, as I said, could not be traced.

At last I telegraphed:

'Sheepskin coats cannot be traced. Wire instructions.' And tired out by this exertion of duty and feeling the need of wholesome recreation, I said to Sylvia:

'Come out and dine with me.'

'Oh! Oh! Really? Oh! Indeed! I see! Oh! Very nice!' she said in tones of roguish whimsicality which that moment made her irresistible.

I added: 'Without further cost to yourself, as they say in the business world.'

'Without further cost to yourself, as they say in the business world.' She learnt my expressions, I noticed, and repeated them. A very good sign.

I looked at her tenderly. 'My Irish darling! *Mein irisch Kind*!'

'Oh! Oh! Indeed,' she said. She was brimming all over with life and wanted to be naughty like a child, but didn't quite know how to set about it, and so only hopped about on tiptoe, while I wondered if I had sufficient money in my pocket-book, and if so, whether I could not spend it better than by dining out—buying a new pair of cavalry boots, for example. And my spirit clouded. Like my old grandfather on my mother's side, I was not over-fond of spending money, and now at this extravagant resolution to distract myself with Sylvia by an expensive meal, my old grandfather called to me from the grave. His motto had been: 'Bargain, bargain, bargain hard, and when you've done, beg a hank of thread.' He was never tired of warning: 'When poverty comes through the door, love flies out of the window.' Or he would buy a pennyworth of paper clips and demand a guarantee. He had spent his whole nervous force in life in seeing that he always got full value for his money, and he died unconscious of the fact that he had not received the value for the life that he had spent. But in moments of wanton extravagance, my grandfather would be calling to me from the grave.

At the big shop in the Kitaiskaya—I have forgotten the name—I bought Sylvia a bottle of scent. In another shop she bought a piece of elastic; sat down and examined the articles with a proud, competent air and sent the girl about her business. And again I noticed her astoundingly charming profile. As the elastic was being wrapped up for her she took hold of her little vanity-bag, a little insincerely, perhaps, while I was looking dreamily away; then I bestirred myself and anticipated her action with a wholly admirable gallantry. And possibly because the amount was something like tuppence, for once my grandfather did not stir.

As we entered the restaurant '*Moderne*' we were confronted by an enormous savage-looking head waiter—the sort of man of whom you tell yourself at once, 'That man's an ass.' And subsequent events confirmed our worst suspicions. The waiter looked at us with that savage dubious look, as though he were not quite certain whether Sylvia and I were human beings or some other animals. He displayed the greatest inefficiency in the seemingly simple task of finding us an empty table, of which the number, in proportion to the tables occupied, was vast. Around us stood the waiters—internationals all: a race unto themselves—with that look of theirs betraying that their minds were only set upon a share of what I had in my breast-pocket. And because I was palpably allergic to such menials as porters, waiters and the like, I talked in a loud unconcerned voice, calculated also to reassure myself, and generally assumed the attitude of a gastronomic connoisseur and a man of the world—as though I were Arnold Bennett. Sylvia was studying the menu, and the enormous head waiter bent over her chair. And I looked at him with dark hatred. Among other things, Sylvia wanted chicken. There were two kinds of chicken. A whole chicken cost 500 roubles. A wing, 100 roubles. The rate of exchange, be it remembered, at that time was only 200 roubles to £1 sterling. The enormous head waiter strongly recommended the whole chicken. 'Straight from Paris in an aeroplane,' he said. I felt cold in the feet.

Sylvia hesitated dangerously. 'I don't think I want as much as a whole chicken. I'll have a wing,' she uttered at last. I breathed freely.

'But the wing is larger than the chicken, madam,' said the fiend. I longed to ask him to explain that curious mathematical perversion, but a latent sense of gallantry deterred me. I felt like clubbing him. But civilization suffered me to go on suffering in silence. '*Go away*,' I whispered inwardly. '*Oh, go away*!' But I sat still, resigned. Only my left eyelid began to twitch a little nervously.

'All right,' she said. 'I'll have the whole chicken, then.'

Five hundred roubles! £2 10*s*. for a solitary chicken! My dead grandfather raised his bushy eyebrows. And I already pictured to myself how under the removed restraints of matrimony, probably in my braces and shirt-sleeves, I would exhort my wife to cut down her criminal expenditure.

There was a variety of ice-creams at 'popular prices', but Sylvia ordered a silly dish called 'Pêche Melba'—and proportionately more expensive.

'What wine, darling?'

'French,' she said.

'But what kind?'

'White, darling.'

The waiter bent over the wine list and pointed to the figures which were double those he did not point to.

'But what kind?'

'Sweet. The sweetest.'

And, according to the waiter, the sweetest wine concorded with the highest figure on the list.

How I hate extravagant drinks! How I hate extravagant food! What I really wanted now, if I could have my way, was eggs and bacon and hot milk.

'Yes, that will do,' she said.

The waiter, bowing, whipped his napkin under the arm and retired with the air of one who has his work cut out. The band struck up a gay waltz, but in my soul was darkness.

'Whatever is the matter, darling?' she enquired.

'This soup,' I said. 'It's damned hot. And why should I eat soup?'

'You eat soup at home.'

'At home I eat it—whether it's there or not—I mean I eat it—I don't care—because it's there. Automatically.'

'Well, eat it here as you would at home,' she said. 'Automatically.'

'But here—oh, well, never mind.'

Spreading the table-napkin on her knees, quickly she brought her fingers together and bending a little and closing her eyes, hurriedly mumbled grace to herself. Then she began to eat the soup, dreamily rolling her eyes.

Meanwhile, the waiter had returned. 'I regret, madam, but no more whole chickens left. Only the wing.' And that moment the music seemed exhilarating.

'Cheer up,' I said.

'In that case,' said she, slowly recovering from the blow, 'I'll have something else.'

In front of us were two women of twenty. 'Look at those two grannies there,' Sylvia called out aloud.

'Sylvia!'

She smiled a beautiful bashful smile: her mouth was closed, only the lips withdrew and revealed a portion of her teeth. A delicious smile.

She rolled her eyes and talked a lot to herself, cooing like a dove. I felt she wanted that I should propose marriage to her, but she was shy to ask. 'Major Beastly,' she said, and blushed, 'thought that—that—that we were—you were—my, as it were, in a word, my fiancé.' And she blushed crimson.

'He's a good man, Beastly,' I said. And she blushed again. Sylvia had brought with her to dinner a letter from a man who had proposed to her once in Japan. 'Read this,' she said. The letter, which struck a devil-me-care tone, ended with the words: 'If the price of rubber goes down by one jot, I'm a ruined man.'

'He is in the rubber trade now,' she explained, 'somewhere in Canada, some place called Congo or something——'

'You mean in Africa.'

'Yes, yes.'

'What is he? English? American?'

'A Canadian.'

'Where did you meet him?'

'At the dance in Tokyo.'

'And——?'

'He wanted to marry me.' She lowered her lashes. 'He loved me.'

'And you——?'

She did not answer at once. 'He was rather like you.'

'No excuse.'

'Only worse.'

'Still less.'

'I wanted somebody to love me. And you were away.'

'And you let him?'

'Only one kiss—one evening.'

'I am not listening! Not listening!' I cried, covering my face with the table-napkin.

'Darling, listen——'

'*No*!'

'You're not listening,' she laughed. Her laughter was a lovely thing.

'I am not.'

There was silence except for the sound I made in eating the soup. She beamed at me with her lustrous eyes. 'Tell me something.'

'You're Cressid—I mean Chaucer's, not Shakespeare's, of course.'

Like Cressida, she knew neither Chaucer nor Shakespeare.

'When did you see him last?'

'As we left Tokyo. He caught me while *maman* had turned away. We stood on the platform. He went in—and gave me a cocktail.'

'Did you like it?'

'Yes. He drank and looked at me. "Marry me, Sylvia," he said. "I will go away, make a lot of money on rubber, and then come back for you."

' "I can't," I said. "I love another." '

'Whom? Whom?' I asked in alarm.

'You. Or I liked to think so.'

'And what did he say?'

' "The blackguard!" he said.'

'Oh!'

'I said to him that you used to kiss me without being engaged to me. "The cad!" he said. "I'll punch his head for him." I said you wrote very short letters. "The rotter!" he said, "taking a mean advantage of you. The scoundrel!" '

'That will do,' I said. 'I'll punch his own silly head for him. Who is he, anyhow?'

' "I'll break him in two," he said. "The scoundrel! The blackguard! The cad!" '

'Now, that will do, that will do. What did *you* say?'

' "I love another," I said. Then I held out my hand to him, like this: "Good-bye, Harry; you will probably never see me again." And there were tears in his eyes as he turned and walked away quickly.'

'Never mind. Eat your soup, darling.'

She did not eat but stared in front of her.

'You're not thinking of him?' I asked, with suspicion.

'No.'

'H'm!... Who're you thinking of?'

'You.'

'Only me?'

'Yes.'

She took a few spoonfuls and then asked, 'Have you by any chance seen in the *Daily Mail* what the price of rubber——'

'Look here,' I said, with some ill-controlled impatience, 'never you mind about the price of rubber. Eat your soup.'

'Oh, when you were away I came across an ideal menu in the *Daily Mail*. It was supposed to be the ideal dinner for young people just engaged. And I thought then: if Alexander comes back and takes me out to dinner I must have this menu.'

'What was it, darling?'

She looked unhappy as she strained her memory. 'I can't remember,' she said.

'Well, but some of the dishes surely?'

She strained her memory and again looked as unhappy as she could be. 'I can't remember.'

'Well, then, one single dish out of the blooming lot,' I cajoled. I waited. 'Out with it!'

She strained her face again. 'No, I can't remember.'

'But this is remarkable,' I said, laying down my spoon in astonishment.

'Eat your soup, darling, or it will be cold,' she said.

I ate, and she ate, and we looked at each other as we ate.

Yet in a way it was all very nice. *Dîner à deux*. Shaded lights. Her charming profile. Her fragile young body. Her beautiful gown. Her scent of *Cœur de Jeanette*. And the music was so loud that we shouted at each other as though in a gale at sea. And she laughed. Her laughter was a lovely thing, like dingling silver bells.

After soup (consommé double) there was lobster mayonnaise; noisettes of veal with tiny carrots and sauté potatoes; omelettes en surprise; and Pêche Melba. The enormous head waiter evidently did not catch our order: the wine on being opened turned out to be red. 'Have this, it's just as good,' I advised.

'No, no. I must have white wine.'

And it had to be changed.

She drank one glass.

'Darling, some more wine?'

'No, thank you, darling, I couldn't. I must have strawberries,' she added.

I looked round. We were alone in the room. 'No, you mustn't.' A kiss. 'This is the dessert.'

In due course, I ate ice-cream, and an enormous concoction on a silver dish of Pêche Melba costing a fortune arrived for Sylvia. She tasted a little—and left it all.

'Have some more, darling,' I said, in despair.

'No, thank you, I couldn't.'

'Will you have liqueur?'

'Yes.'

'Have you ever had a liqueur before?'

'No. Only a cocktail.'

'What will you have? A crème de menthe?'

'Oh, no!' She wrinkled her nose—just like her mother. 'That's what all the flappers always have.'

I arched my eyebrows and then looked at her steadfastly

straight in the eyes. 'You're not a student of Arnold Bennett's works, surely, are you?' I asked.

She listened, blinking. 'Why, darling?'

I did not say why.

'I'll have a cherry brandy, dear.'

'All right.'

'And amber cigarettes.'

'I have cigarettes.' I opened my case.

'No, darling, I want amber ones.'

'All right,' I sighed, 'all right, all right.' And as time drew out and the courses were removed one after the other, we drew closer to each other, and I felt the warmth of her silk-stockinged leg against my own, and fleeting images flew by from that electric touch.

We ordered coffee. The enormous savage-looking head waiter arrived and said that coffee was no easy matter in these days—that coffee must be *made*. He put down everything to intervention and the blockade. And so he kept us waiting for our coffee quite three-quarters of an hour, and then when he brought it, upset it all over my lap.

And while he removed the tablecloth and dried the table he referred disgruntledly to the political situation as an excuse. 'Things are not what they used to be, sir. Everything is upset. Intervention—blockade. The country is no longer what it used to be. People are upset.'

'Thank you,' I said, wiping my soaking knees with the table-napkin, 'I can quite believe it.'

I talked eagerly while I settled the bill—partly to conceal my natural suspicion when dealing with waiters—partly to conceal my apprehension at the cost. Still, it could have been even more expensive.

'Let me see,' Sylvia said. (She would ask to see every restaurant bill when we dined out together. The heavier the bill the greater her pride, the more her enjoyment.)

She noted the figure—and seemed content.

We walked a little down the Kitaiskaya before we could hail a cab. On the way Sylvia stopped at a lighted shop window—a jeweller's. I tried to take her away.

'Wait, darling,' she said.

'How well these imitation necklaces look!' I observed dispassionately.

'I prefer these small and short ones: they are more convincing.' She stared at the glittering objects within.

'Or would you like to buy me a little bead bag instead?'

My grandfather stirred in his grave.

'Come away from there. Some day—when I am rich. Or let me send you one later. Come away now.'

'Let us go to the cinema,' she said.

We hailed a cab, and nestling to each other drove in search of a movie. The north wind blew a wet drizzling snow into my face, and it was dim and dreary out of doors: but in my heart was gladness.

We settled down in a dark cosy box, and turned our eyes on the screen. Harbin was a speck on the globe of the earth, and I was a speck in Harbin; but that moment my love circumscribed and encompassed the earth and all living creatures upon it: and I blessed them all. The orchestra was a large one for a cinema. Hebrews they were, all—dark as Spaniards, twenty-one strong: and I blessed them all, the one-and-twenty. Good old Judaea! Blessed be the Jews! What emotion. How the violins sobbed. We sat back in the box. Sylvia clung to me, but did not speak. The 'cellos wept bitterly, they wept for those who were dead, and for those who were living. And I discovered a thing utterly new to me: I discovered that they all had souls independent of mine, and I saw those souls, and I blessed them. We nestled close, close to each other, and that all this—our love—besides being ineffably glorious was also absurd did not detract from it. And I remembered my mother, saw her when she was a young girl with eyes very blue, and I blessed her dear memory and her love for my father, as fragrant as ours. And I laughed with happiness. I thought of old men who, bidding us carry on, had stepped into their graves, and I perceived that each soul asked only for a working modicum of happiness, and my mind's eye went out into the street and blessed them all. And I thought of Sylvia at my side, without passion, through a film of laughter and tears and my pure love of her, and of my uncle and aunt, of Berthe and Mme Vanderphant, of winter and summer and autumn and spring, and of the sheer joy of being alive. I wanted to do for them, build up their happiness by my overpowering strength. I wanted to harness my thoughts, to imbue the world with ideas. I wanted to preach to a multitude from street corners, from a very high hill, to bless babies; I wanted mothers to bring them to me, for if any man had *I* had, that moment, the pure power of blessing them: legitimate, illegitimate, all, I would bless them, consecrate marriages, with the holiness that was in me but which was not mine. The orchestra wept. The broad rays beat on the screen and projected a sort of gala pitch-battle. Bang! bang! Men and women were shot, turned head over heels, multitudes scrambled, pushed forward, unloading revolvers in the flesh of their brethren: bang! bang! bang! tumbling over each other—Red Indians, cowboys, tigers, leopards, horses, giraffes. The orchestra, merely twenty-one strong, played something—it didn't matter what—my own ears made up the deficiency, adding twenty bass instruments, thirty trombones: sixty fiddles sobbed in my heart. But the people who died in the pictures I had no sympathy for—a sure indictment of the screen! Had there been a real play with real actors I would have felt the same human pity for them as for all living things, and would have blessed them. I looked at Sylvia, so silent at my side, and the heart in my bosom went wild. I wanted to shout, yell at the top of my voice, aiding the orchestra, crack whips, roar with the lions and leopards, fire off maxims! Such was my love.

When it was all over, I hailed a cab and helping Sylvia to step into the vehicle, stepped into a ditch. 'Asia!' I swore. And driving home I had a very nasty feeling: a soaking sock in the left shoe, which meant, of course, that I would catch a chill. There are fifty-two weeks in the year, during thirty of which I have a sneezing cold. And, of course, so it was.

At home I found a telegram for me: 'Regret misunderstanding. No coats ordered. 50,000 fur caps instead. Arrange transportation and return forthwith with caps. Urgent.'

19

There are times when, after feeding my mind and soul upon ideas of our most hopeful evolutionists, I suddenly experience a spiritual relapse and think that after all, perhaps, human beings are a race of biped rats—that human destiny on earth doesn't greatly matter. I meditated thus as I recalled the 50,000 caps intended for 50,000 soldiers intended to restore by their commanders some of that 'law and order' in the land and so preserve the continuity of our glorious humanity. This nonsense was hatched by strong silent men, men 'with no nonsense about them'. Rats, I thought, 50,000 rats in fur caps, sacks of flesh and disease, bundles of incoherent urgings, rapacious beasts. The rats had crept out of their holes and went for each other. All out of silliness. Rats, I thought, rats.

In the drawing-room as I entered stood a Russian officer whom I had seen before, so far as I could remember, at the local censorship department. And indeed the officer looked like a rat on its hind legs—a rat in khaki. At my approach he clicked his heels, introducing himself: 'Captain Negodyaev.' What a passport for a man! The name translated into English would read Captain Scoundrelton or Blackguardson—ominous enough. Yet Captain Negodyaev was meek and servile, humble and very timid, but was said to bully his wife. He had a long narrow head with a scanty growth of yellowish hair and a small scraggy moustache with wrinkles round his mouth, and eyes as if he had stolen somebody's cuff-links and feared to be found out. His chin was shaven—I mean on days when it was shaven; on other days one could surmise that this at all events was roughly what he aimed at. He had a wooden leg which he liked to pass off as an honourable war wound. But everybody knew that he had fallen off a tram at Vladivostok while the ground was slippery and broken his left leg which later, owing to blood-poisoning that had set in, had been amputated for him. He was always spurting scent on his handkerchief, and every time he opened it to blow his nose there was an all-pervading odour in the atmosphere.

'I have two daughters,' he was telling Aunt Teresa. 'Màsha and Natàsha. Màsha is grown up and married and lives with her husband Ippolit Sergèiech Blagovèschenski. And Natàsha is only seven and lives with her mother also in Novorossiisk. I should like them to come over to Harbin. But there is a great shortage of accommodation in the town. I myself live in a railway carriage. Luckily enough it does not stand out very far from where I work—in the censorship department, you may know.'

'Look here,' said Aunt Teresa, 'when our friends the Vanderphants go back to Belgium in May, why not come here? We'll have lots of room to spare.'

Captain Negodyaev opened his handkerchief. And, automatically, I whisked out mine and applied it to my nostrils—in order not to suffocate. 'I would be very glad indeed,' he said, bowing awkwardly.

But my time came to an end. One morning as I came down, I found the entrance hall cluttered up to the ceiling with fur caps, so that Berthe grumbled and cursed at me, because she could not get to and fro.

'*Ah, que voulez-vous*?' Uncle Emmanuel calmed her. '*C'est la guerre*!'

'How am I to get them to the station? Damn these caps,' I said.

'Don't you bother,' said Captain Negodyaev who had come to see my aunt relative to his forthcoming installation in our flat. 'My man is here. He will take them to the station for you ...Vladislav!' he called out. 'This is Vladislav. He will take them and dispatch them for you and do all that's necessary.'

I had a talk with Vladislav and found him on the face of it a very capable, smart fellow who inspired confidence. Vladislav had once upon a time been batman to a Russian Colonel who took him with him on a trip to Paris; and his attitude ever since to things Russian was that nothing at home would astonish him. 'What civilization!' he was telling me. 'What education! politeness! A plain cabman, a common *izvozchik* you might say, and even he, if you please, jabbers in French! *Monsieur—madame—s'il vous plaît—comprenez-vous*—and all that sort of thing. As for Russia——' He only waved his hand—an abject gesture. 'No civilization at all! You live here like a brute—just the same as if in Australia or somewhere.'

At the hotel where I had called on business, the porter—a good soul with a kind smile—came up to me. Because he was a good soul with a kind smile he fared well at the hands of the generous who took a liking to him and his soul, and he fared badly at the hands of the unscrupulous who took advantage of his smiling good soul; and so, on the whole, he fared no better than others. 'You have a separate coupé, sir?' he said. (Harbin is a terrible place.)

'Yes. Why?'

'There's a lady here who can't get a berth in the train. Perhaps——' He paused.

'Good-looking?'

'Awful good-looking!'

I scrutinized him suspiciously.

'Has travelled with a gentleman before,' he hastened to assure me eagerly. 'Gentleman very satisfied.'

Harbin is a terrible place. Human nature is frail. Men are born in sin—and I suppose I am no exception. But I digress.

The train was due out at midnight. I paced the platform and surveyed the crowded third-class waiting-room where bundles of unwashed humanity—bearded men, young girls and women with sucking babies—slept on the naked floor in heaps, among their chattels. So insistent was the demand for space in the train that I had ordered Pickup to stand on guard outside my coupé, with fixed bayonet. The prudence of my action was vindicated a few moments later when a strange Polish doctor came up and addressed me in Polish.

'I don't speak Polish,' I said.

'Will you send for your Polish interpreter?'

'I haven't got one. Besides, I observe that you can speak Russian.'

'Oh, yes,' said the Polish doctor.

'May I ask why in that case you cannot speak to me in Russian?'

'Because I am a Pole,' he replied, and beat himself on the chest.

'What can I do for you?'

'I am a Polish doctor,' said the doctor, 'and I desire to be admitted to your coupé.'

'We haven't got any room, I fear.'

'But you *must* have room for a Polish doctor. You are Allies.'

The reiterated pertinacity of this man annoyed me. It annoyed me in particular that he should intrude on my privacy and space at a time when I expected...never mind what I expected. In short, it annoyed me. 'My dear sir,' I replied, quietly but with a subtle side-smile, conscious of a short and easy road to victory, 'it is not a question of your being a doctor, a Pole, or a Polish doctor, but a matter of there being no *room* for a man, woman or child of whatever profession or nationality or combination of both. Good evening to you.' It seemed to me that I had settled both the Polish nationality and the medical profession.

Tired of pacing the platform, I got into my coupé, took out a book and scanned the pages. I am a serious young man—an intellectual. I was plunged in thought, when Pickup interrupted me.

'Who? What?...Ah, yes.'

Then the train drew out.

20

'Have you, or have you not, an intelligible account of the present situation?' Sir Hugo asked when I reported two days later.

'Yes, sir. It is quite simple.' I shuffled. 'You see, sir, it's like this. Irkutsk is now once again in the hands of the Whites who are being driven by the Reds towards Irkutsk. The Reds at Irkutsk, you will recollect, had taken it over by a *coup de main* from the Social-Revolutionaries after these had captured the town from the Kolchakites and had later defeated Semënov. Now the Kappel Whites, I think, will join in with Semënov, but being hard pressed by the main Red forces will, I think, strive east and may possibly recapture Vladivostok from the Reds, I mean the Social-Revolutionaries, at the same time evacuating Irkutsk, should they have been compelled to seize it, which will then, I think, be recaptured by the Reds. Is that quite clear, sir?'

Sir Hugo closed his eyes and laid his fingers on the lids in order as it were to yield the maximum concentration. 'M'm!... It is at least as clear as the situation seems to be at present,' he said.

'Of course, sir, I have said nothing of the Poles, the Letts, Latvians, and Lithuanians, the Czechs, Yanks, Japs, Rumanians, French, Italians, Serbians, Slovenes, the Jugoslavians, the German, Austrian, Hungarian and Magyar war-prisoners, the Chinese, the Canadians and ourselves, and many other different nationalities, whose presence rather tends to complicate the situation in view of the several politics they follow.'

'The devil they do,' grunted Sir Hugo.

'It's a fact they do, sir.'

'I know they do.'

'Of course,' I said, 'the position of the Czechs is probably the most difficult of all.'

'Excuse me,' Sir Hugo interrupted me. 'I think I caught you saying "Letts, Latvians and Lithuanians". Now, when you say "Letts, Latvians *and* Lithuanians", do you mean...what the dickens *do* you mean?'

'They are kindred races...in a way,' I said lightly, by way of evading an embarrassing question on which, in fact, I was not very clear myself.

'Now, when you say "kindred races in a way" do you mean "kindred people"—and in *what* way?'

'Yes, sir,' I said cheerfully, as a way out of the difficulty. 'The position of the Czechs,' I continued, 'is a very difficult one——'

'Now I was inclined to ask you,' Sir Hugo interrupted, 'if you are aware of the relation between the so-called nationalities such as the Letts, Latvians, Lithuanians, and so forth, and the so-called countries as Lettland, Latvia, Lithuania, Esthonia, Livonia, Esthland, Kurland, Livland, and so forth, and whether or not, in fact, they are not all, or if not all, largely the same people. But let this drift. To return to the subject at issue, what were you going to say about the Czechs?'

'The position of the Czechs,' I proceeded happily, 'is a very difficult one. Two years ago they fought the Bolsheviks and were involuntarily driven into the camp of the reactionary old-régimists. They stuck it for a year till they could stick it no longer, being a democratically-minded people; they then, by way of atoning for their sins, helped the Social-Revolutionaries against the old-régimists. The S.-R.'s by the aid of their Czech brethren established themselves, but all too late in the season, and so lost their identity amidst the Bolsheviks.'

'Well?'

'Well, you see, sir, the Czechs had to fight the Bolsheviks.'

'Why?' said Sir Hugo, somewhat defiantly, as the smoke from his Japanese cigarette curled round his ruddy face and his eyes assumed a kind of roguish expression.

'Because the Bolsheviks fought them.'

'Why?' asked Sir Hugo with the same intonation and expression.

'As their traditional enemy of two years' duration.'

'Oh!' said Sir Hugo.

'They are pursuing the Czechs in their retreat east.'

'The devil they are,' said Sir Hugo.

'Well, sir, there were still certain reactionaries, the remnants of what used to be the Kolchak Army, under the command of General Kappel, who retreated to the east along the railway track and fought a rearguard action against the Bolsheviks who were pursuing them. The Czechs were in the same boat, so they identified themselves with that section of the whites and fought their cause against the pursuing Reds.

'But there was another section of the Whites of whom Ataman Semënov was the nucleus whom the Czechs had antagonized by their support of the Social-Revolutionaries against Semënov.'

'Well,' said Sir Hugo, with eyes closed, 'it is all perfectly clear to me. Where is the confusion?'

'The real confusion came when their friends the Social-Revolutionaries turned as red as their advancing foes the Bolsheviks, and their comrades the remnants Kappelites as white as their bitter enemy Semënov.'

'Well?'

'Well, they didn't quite know then where they stood, sir.'

'The devil they didn't,' he said.

We both sighed.

'And the caps?' he said. 'Have you got the caps?'

In truth, I hadn't thought of the caps since I had delegated the matter to Vladislav; but I presumed that they were there, nevertheless. 'Yes, sir,' I said, somewhat uncertainly.

'You *have?*' he questioned.

'Yes, sir,' I said—somewhat more certainly. For it seemed to me a rum thing indeed if the caps weren't there. Why shouldn't they be there?

The Major was still in charge of my late office as I got back; but as luck would have it, a week later when crossing a steep frozen path, he slipped and broke his leg—and once again I was in charge of the office. When, two months later, he came out of hospital he was hard put to it to regain his place, and finally gave up the struggle and went back to his post office. But the office, which by now contained a score of shell-shocked officers, my seniors in age and service, was no easy thing to run, and so insidious and powerful grew the revolt that, in the end, I found it necessary to erect a 'buffer-state' within, a sub-department, so to speak, containing the unruly officers in charge of an ambitious 'sub', who, while responsible to me, now bore directly the full pressure of their discontent: the price of his ambition. From time to time buff slips would be passed on to me from other sections and departments, which ran: 'Please state whereabouts of 50,000 fur caps dispatched by you in February from Harbin.' And according to the rules of the game, I must confess, I lost it every time, for in the nature of the case there was nowhere I could pass the buff slip on to for action. The action was unquestionably mine. And the drama of it was that I could not act on it. These are the tears of things! For the caps were not there.

'Enquiries still pending', I would reply ignominiously—and so on until the next buff slip. Enquiries had been pending for over two months; but the caps were not there.

Another thing, I waited for a letter from Sylvia—but no letter came. These are the tears of things! Once, only once, a long time ago, she had sent me a postcard—a coloured English landscape. 'Something artistic. Alexander will like it,' she must have thought to herself. Below was the printed inscription:

'Soft green pastures, gay with innocent flowers', and then in her own hand:

'Ever yours,

'Bébé (new name).

'P.S.— I've sent you a Hanky—this is a little gift.'

The 'Hanky' had arrived. But never anything since. What was the reason? What *could* be the reason? I felt I wanted to take the first train to Harbin, to send a messenger, to telegraph, at least to write; but I could not even get myself to write to her, as this simple effort was damped by the thought that at any moment the postman might stroll into the office with the long-awaited letter. And thus relieved, I was made to suffer by another thought, that, with equal justice, no letter might arrive by the next post or indeed by any after.

'What is it, Sergeant?'

He laid a buff slip on my desk.

'Oh bother!'

It ran:

'Please state whereabouts of 50,000 fur caps dispatched by you three months ago from Harbin. Urgent.' To which I answered:

'Enquiries still pending.'

I wondered: who was the most capable and energetic person in Harbin to whom I could safely entrust the task of moving heaven and earth to find the 50,000 fur caps. And suddenly my mind recalled the little red-leather book with the dates of receipt and dispatch of correspondence, and I decided that the most capable and energetic person in Harbin was Aunt Teresa. I found it quite an easy matter to write to Aunt Teresa, because I thought that Sylvia might read my letter, although I found it difficult to write to Sylvia direct. At last, unable to bear the torture of suspense any longer, I wrote a letter to her, entreating Sylvia by all that was holy in the world to write to me at once. To this I had a telegram from her. Not a word about her having written or of her going to do so now.

'Sorry. Love. Sylvia.'

That was all.

And then, one morning, came her letter. Her handwriting was like her nature: those thin, swift, naïvely, irresponsibly confident strokes seemed to say: here am I, Sylvia Ninon Thérèse Anastathia Vanderflint, a woman of the world! There was, moreover, an unconscious kittenish quality about her curves, but the exaggerated length and confidence of the fine stroke was splendid out of all proportion.

I loved her letters. What attracted me was that she did not even pretend to think that her unintellectuality could be anything but interesting to me, an intellectual. Her style was inspirational. Obviously she never troubled to read through her writing, and the capitals she used recognized no law save that of impulse. Sylvia would put a dot inconsequently after any word, just as the fancy took her; or suddenly she would put a dash with two dots beneath it. She would suddenly—for no apparent reason—insert a mark of interrogation, or more often three at a time. This freedom, this utter disregard of punctuation and the fact that I was, in a way, a man who specialized in prose, delighted me exceedingly. Enclosed was another envelope marked, '*Please read carefully*!'

Dear Alexander. Your Letter was Lovely and cheery and beautifully Long and for once you were not in a 'Temper'? and also that you are well and happy. Are you delighted to be back? It must be Perfect now. flowers etc. and so forth in full Bloom. I do want to come and see you. But what can I do if I run away my Father will run after me. Mr Brown has just come back from there and he said. 'It is perfectly glorious down there. the Harbour is a Picture.' He came to see Papa about the Marshal's autograph which he wants to sell at an American Red Cross auction. I asked about you. I said you asked me to come boating. 'Oh,' said He, 'he will drown you.' I was disapp. when you did not send me the little bead bag. If you really wanted to see me Love finds a way. Your weak excuse 'Broke' I absolutely ignore. Back of my hand to you 6 Times. There is a Porter here and he came in about 10–15 days ago to see Mr Brown and I asked him about you and he told me. I won't mention names. but he told me you had gone off with a woman on the train when you left us. and that He was sorry. Why oh why are you doing such to me. Can it be possible George Hamlet Alexander? knowing perfectly well in your heart that I would not be at the train. If such is the Case. don't you dare write me or even wish to see me again. I would write and ask your General if he knew about such. tho' on second thoughts you at Least have the Honour I hope to tell me from Your heart. Have you ever thought in your mind. how Little you study me. now just think. Very Probably the Wonderful woman you travelled with, is taking my Place now. You forbid me to write, speak or visit any of my men Friends. I must slave at Home while you enjoy yourself in the Army???? What beautiful exclamations. Admire them please. Maman is always laid up and Mme Vanderphant is also ill and my Poor Nerves. are quite scattered [she wrote] and I am so tired of sick Individuals. Mr Brown is going to Omsk and I want to run away with him I think. Seeing the interest you take in me and how you study me I had better go. I've told you once well to be correct 79,000 times my intentions towards you. 'The many times I've told you.' I can quite see you never Listen to anything I tell you just Like water on a ducks back. and you are getting more and more selfish. Words or Letters. nothing could explain how angry I am with you.

Very Disapp. with you.
Good Bye.

I had in my letter, referring to the difficulty of extracting a reply from her, said she was 'impossible'. And now she signed herself:

Sincerely yours
Sylvia the Impossible Woman.

PPPSSSS.

and I am not Kitten.

Enclosed in the outer envelope was another letter.

Alexander Darling Prince of Angels. You see how very angry I am with you and you can Prepare for Punishment. This is just a tiny note to wish you Very many happy returns of Tomorrow the 27th You Little treasure. How many years are you now? 21 Yes No. Yes. And I am writing to tell you how very disgusted I feel with the Rotten Idiots of Photo foolery People. My Photos are not finished how disapp. you will be Alexander. I simply cried with vexation and Berthe shrieked with laughing, not because Photographs were not done, but because of my delightful 'face.'

Thank you so very much for the lovely Chocolates the only disapp. was I thought I would find a beautiful Long letter inside. never mind I was happy just the same. I know you will forgive me Darling about the Photos. You will be sorry I am ill. and then my poor Brother in Flanders. And I have never written to your dear Lovely friend Major Beastly. What a dreadful Person I am. I have a Dear little Bedroom and also a sitting Room to myself tiny but sweet so I can have you to Tea. How lovely says He to himself. goo. goo hoo. I miss you awfully. I would like to be crumpled in your arms and close to your lips, but so far and yet so near. But you will be back in three months, Darling for all those kisses. and no quarrels. Are you Listening. There is such a lot I want to say. The weather is beautiful, I am not very busy. and I am not flirting hope you are the same, Princie. Depression seems to haunt me lately. I do not know why. There is certainly something making me so very unhappy. What is it Alexander. I've nobody but you to talk to. Oh yes! I have a Lovely dog called Don. You must see him. Are you listening to me. Your last letter sent my heart wild. Darling I long to see you. Alexander, your letters make me cry now. I really do hate being parted from you, still I am always and shall be .. yours. I will write again as it is awful just now, all nerves and maman stupid. Alexander bless bless bless you and Please Please do not worry I love you dearly and I am True but oh so Lonely. not seen you 3 mths and then just Two days perhaps. only time to see if you got your spurs on??? You Fairy Boy. You never mentioned your holidays did you? had nice time Yes. No. Thank you. My letter Alexander is not very interesting. so sorry. I cannot tell you anything about the Easter holidays because I had to remain in doors and amuse myself with the gramophone. How dreary it was and the wretched, awful weather was appalling. It poured cats and dogs. rats and mice and so on etc. I am so very sorry you were ill, how did you manage such you naughty naughty child and here I am waiting for you to come and see me. Your spurs and your blue eyes. 'The back of my hand to you.' Oh and your Hankie. do you really like it tell me. Yes. No. Yes. Yes. Yes. You little Fairie Princie. I will write you again this week. One of your photos has disappeared from my Room. I've made fruitless efforts for the thief. To-morrow I am going out to buy a frame for your Princie Face. I must be off to sleep now. and keep away from 'Pond' you funny child. and do not seal your letters you are horrid. Good night. I am still annoyed; they all warn me against you. Oceans of devoted love and long lingering kisses. Good night little Bébé. Accept all my beautiful Love and lots of sunshine kisses. Cheerio little cat [Whether it was cat or cad I could not quite decipher, and so felt a little disconcerted.]

Bye Bye
Ever yours
Pansy (new name).

There followed a lot of crosses, big and small and of medium size.

21

Aunt Teresa wrote that she had duly cross-examined Captain Negodyaev (who was about to move over to them when Mme Vanderphant and her two girls vacated the rooms, probably about the middle of June), that Captain Negodyaev had in her presence cross-examined his man Vladislav, who told them that in France such a thing would have been impossible, that Vladislav had cross-examined all the requisite railway officials on the subject of the lost fur caps, and that the unanimous opinion seemed to be that the caps could not be traced in Harbin, or it would seem anywhere else, and that in the circumstances of the case Uncle Emmanuel recommended courage and patience. Uncle Lucy had still not remitted the money, nor had Major Beastly yet reported the result of his *démarches*. Did I think that the British Mission might help them, seeing that they were Belgians who had suffered in the war and that the English had helped the Belgians before, as a matter of course, and seemed to have thought nothing of it then? So why not now again? This was Uncle Emmanuel's idea. She herself was, moreover, directly entitled to such aid, having, as I knew, been born in Manchester of an English father born in London.

That day Sir Hugo called me in and said:

'And where are the caps?'

I explained to him that enquiries were still pending. And he said:

'In that case you had better go back for the caps.'

I could ask for nothing better.

The very next morning I left for Harbin.

22

It was midsummer now, and Harbin looked green, fully dressed. My arrival synchronized with the departure of Mme Vanderphant and her two girls. The lady, dressed up for the journey, with a veil over her beak (it was of a somewhat smaller dimension than Berthe's and was tanned rather than red), had come into Aunt Teresa's pink bedroom to say good-bye just as I came in to greet her.

'*Adieu, madame.*'

'*Adieu, ma pauvre Mathilde*!' sighed my aunt from her pillows. 'God bless you.' They embraced. 'You won't see me again. Ah! With my poor miserable health——' She sobbed softly into her lace handkerchief, petulantly, like a child. 'Pity me! Pity me!... The money you lent us,' she said, her sobs having suddenly ceased, 'will be remitted to you direct to Dixmude as soon as Lucy sends me the dividend.'

Mme Vanderphant stood still for a moment, sad and mute. 'How strange: people meet, and then part, then write letters, grow tired of that, forget—and then die.' She looked at her sister. '*Ma pauvre Berthe*! When shall we see each other again?'

'*Adieu, Madeleine. Adieu, Marie.*'

'*Adieu, madame*!' they curtsied.

The door closed after them.

'I am quite alone in the house,' said my aunt, 'Emmanuel!' she called out.

"Yes, my darling?' He stood in the doorway.

'You will stay at home with me.'

'Yes, my angel.'

'Sylvia has gone to her piano lesson. I had to let Berthe go to the station to see them off.'

'Berthe is stopping, then?' I asked.

'Yes, she could not leave me, in my poor miserable state of

health, with no one, alas! to look after me in my sad exile! She will stay till we can arrange for *Constance* to come over from Belgium.'

'This is awfully kind of her, isn't it—stopping behind for your sake, while her people are going home to Europe? Isn't Berthe awfully good to you?'

"Yes, but she is rather abrupt and sometimes she has such a temper! *such* a temper! This morning she said to me while making my compress: "I am tired out after packing all night for them—tired out." Just like this: "Tired out!" It quite upset my poor nerves. Queer! as if I were to blame for her having to pack for them! She is very abrupt. But I never say anything. It is not my nature. Other people like Berthe and Mme Vanderphant always allow their anger to get the better of them. They let it out and are free. But I keep it all to myself, never complain, and suffer in silence!'

'I suppose she does get tired.'

'But she ought to remember that I'm a helpless poor invalid and can do nothing! This had such an effect on my poor nerves that, alas! I couldn't sleep all day after it!'

'But, after all, she is not a paid nurse.'

My aunt looked as me as if to say: What do *you* know about it? '*Ach*, if I only had *Constance* here!' she sighed.

When Berthe, with tear-stained eyes, came back from the station, Aunt Teresa called out:

'Berthe! Berthe!'

'Yes?'

'Give me a pyramidon, will you? Insufferable head-splitting *migraine*!'

'One moment.'

Berthe looked very sombre and somewhat bedraggled, perhaps unnerved at her sacrifice.

'Oh, my God! *Pyramidon*! This is aspirin, which is fatal for my heart! *Ach*! if only I had *Constance* here to look after me!'

'I am tired out to-day…tired out,' muttered Berthe. 'Packing all night, never had a wink of sleep.'

'How unkind!'

Berthe looked very sombre.

'Oh, not so much water, Berthe! I've told you!'

'Oh, please, Thérèse; really!'

'Ah... *Constance*...!' she sighed dismally.

In the dining-room I came across Berthe. She stood close to the window. She was crying.

Uncle Emmanuel, passing by, noticed her crying.

'Orphan...I feel like an orphan,' she said.

'*Ah, c'est la vie*,' said my uncle facilely.

23

In the middle of July an opera company which had been touring the Far East halted in Harbin, and we went to the theatre twice—the first time to *Faust*, and the second to *Aida*. As we listened to the recitations, explanations, vows, entreaties of the musical love-dialogue, and as the lovers' singing protestations accompanied by florid gestures were at their very strongest, Philip Brown's Anglo-Saxon sense of humour was tickled and he winked at Sylvia.

Oui, c'est toi! je t'aime!
Oui, c'est toi! je t'aime!
Les fers, la mort même
Ne me font plus peur...

Faust and Marguerite argued, argued at cross-purposes, it seemed, and with a self-sufficient detachment as though wilfully ignoring each other but competing for attention at the hands of the audience. Aunt Teresa liked the music of Gounod. It reminded her of Nice and Biarritz, Petersburg and Paris, Lucerne and Karlsbad, Geneva, Venice, Cannes, and all the places where she had heard these melodies before. She knew them, and now, as she leaned back in the red-plush box, she looked at Berthe and nodded at her with glances of sad and intimate reminiscence, and Berthe, though she could not have divined all the places that Aunt Teresa had in mind, nodded back at her with that same air of delicate and memorable experiences—for ever gone, and never to return. There was no disturbing passion, no intensity about this sort of music: Aunt Teresa had only to sit back in her chair, and the orchestra and singer combined to do the rest: *Fai—tes-lui mes aveux, portez mes vœux*!...' Aunt Teresa liked sitting out in the public parks, on the Terrasse at Monte Carlo, or on the Promenade des Anglais at Nice, surveying the passing people through her gold-rimmed *lorgnon*, and listening to just this kind of music, *pots-pourris* from Verdi and Gounod—so unstrenuous! It claimed so little of one. Really nice of the composers to acknowledge music was not *all*. Nice men they must have been. She would have liked to ask Gounod to tea had he been alive: she was sure he would not stay too long.

Next night was *Aida*. Sylvia, sitting a little to the front of me, bent forward, like a rose on a stem. Berthe had closed her eyes—lost in the vortex of familiar melody; and even Philip Brown was serious. Oh, I liked it! I felt that I was born for love—while the priests invoking the chieftain to repent and change his mind, sang:

'Rhadames! Rhadame—e—s!'

Driving home, I treated them to fragments from *Aida* in my own peculiar voice and individual intonation: 'Rhadames! Rhadame—e—s!' when Brown uttered:

'What a mess!'

Before retiring to bed, in my pyjamas, I was conducting with a brush before the looking-glass, when Sylvia entered from the back. I wanted to be a composer, a conductor of orchestra, passionately, painfully. What was I? An army officer. It was—as if it wasn't quite good enough. 'I wasn't born for the Army,' I said. 'I was born for something better—though I don't quite know what it is.'

'You are very naughty,' she said.

After that she was silent, her eyes fixed on the floor.

I sighed. There was a pause. And she sighed.

'What do maidens wait for, I wonder?'

'What does anybody wait for?' she said, her eyes still on the floor.

'I know: for the moment when, suddenly, you shoot out roots into the very source of life and taste the sap running up, as through a straw, on to your palate, and feel that there is nothing you have missed and you are glad to be alive.'

I took her up to the glass and kissed her—just to see what we looked like in the glass, kissing like that—when the door opened and Aunt Teresa surprised us.

For a moment she looked dazed. Then, coming up to us, with a curious, unfamiliar smile on her face—'I'm so glad,' she said. 'I always wished it. And your parents, too, would have been glad, I know.'

She kissed us both, as if by way of putting the seal on our intentions. 'But—do put something on top of these pyjamas, George.'

I put on my dressing-gown, and we sat together in my room long into the morning, Sylvia staring at the floor. And it somehow seemed as though Aunt Teresa had forgotten about the serious state of her health.

After they had gone, I sat on my bed in my pyjamas, my bare feet dangling down—perhaps a little stunned. I am a serious young man, an intellectual. And I wondered whether marriage in my case was wise. I had a sneaking feeling that it was not. 'Rhadames!' rang in my ears. And another voice, a small private voice in me sang: 'What a mess! Oh, what a mess!…'

24

Màsha and Natàsha

It was the crest of a truly blazing summer when I had a telegram from Vladivostok that the 50,000 fur caps had been found at the station in a disused shed. I had been interviewing Captain Negodyaev, who had just installed himself in our flat and had come up to see me in my attic, where I did my literary work, to press on me the need of Allied censorship at Harbin, when the telegram arrived: 'Caps found in disused shed Vladivostok station. Return forthwith.'

In the light of Captain Negodyaev's urgings and with an eye on my engagement, I wired stressing how essential in my view was the establishment of an inter-Allied military censorship at Harbin. Having wired, there was nothing to it but to wait for a reply.

Captain Negodyaev sat at table facing Aunt Teresa, drinking tea and dipping a rusk into his glass. 'I have two daughters,' he was saying. 'Màsha and Natàsha. Màsha is married, and lives with her husband Ippolit Sergèiech Blagovèschenski. Ah, poor Màsha, she has suffered a great deal at the hands of her husband.'

'Is he—cruel to her?' asked Aunt Teresa.

'No, not cruel. But he neglects her—for another woman——'

He stopped somewhat abruptly, a little confused. The clock ticked on uninterruptedly for a space. And Berthe said, to fill the awkward pause of silence, '*Cela arrive quelquefois.*'

'*Ah, c'est la vie,*' said Uncle Emmanuel philosophically.

'I have a letter from my wife,' said Captain Negodyaev, 'which describes the conditions in Novorossiisk. I will read it to you if I may.'

'Do,' urged Aunt Teresa.

'This was written in the spring, but I have only just received it.'

He cleared his throat and read:

Three months have passed since I received your last letter. How long the days seem without news from you. Perhaps I shall hear something about the parcel. I so longed for a letter. I hoped to have one somewhere about my birthday, but no, nothing, not a word. None reach this miserable land. Life has no joy for us. To us there seems no future, no tomorrow; today we are alive and thank God for that. Weary—yes, that we are, so tired, so worn out, so weary. To die is the only right left us. The million things one felt but could not say.

Another year has passed. I feel stronger this spring. Now the cold weather is over it will be easier, but there is still so much hard work ahead. We have kept alive, thanks to the stock of vegetables, but now there is very little left. So many of our friends have died. They have died, and no one will ever tell of them how they have suffered. But the spring is as wonderful as before, as though nothing were the matter. Natàsha has written to you several times. Write to her if you receive this letter. It will give her such pleasure and she has so little pleasure, poor little girl. You will hardly know her if you see her. She is very tall for her age, she looks ten. Her hair is quite fair. Some days she looks better than others. She is very delicate, and has a very tender skin, blue veins showing through. She is said to take entirely after my people, though some find that she resembles Alexei. You will find me quite old, I am sure, if you ever see me again; trouble does not make one beautiful. I have grown coarse. Yesterday I killed the hen, chopped off its head. An old, sick hen. I closed my eyes. So far we are still at the same house, but everything is being taken from us, and what is left us we have got to sell to keep alive. I kept the silver tankard, you know the one my godmother Aunt Jenya gave me—I kept it for Natàsha. Though it has got quite yellow, I kept it, as I have nothing else for her. We've sold everything. But they came and took it. What's to be done if our mite has such a miserable old mother? I am not to blame.

Màsha is very unhappy, but tries to bear up. Ippolit is just the same as ever and brings that dreadful woman to the house. Nothing will stop him. He says it's Love the Conquering Hero. At Easter we boiled up mother's old wedding cake, which is thirty-seven years old, and ate it. Màsha and I break up barges on the river for fuel. But Ippolit doesn't lift a finger—only sits and plays cards all day long in the café. We have one stove which we call the 'Bourgouyka'. We are trying to get a goat in exchange for furniture. If we succeed Natàsha will at least have some milk food, poor mite; she is so delicate and, I fear, consumptive too. She dreams of better days and longs to see you badly. She loves you with all her heart, and thinks Harbin 'the blessed land'. God bless and protect you. Your loving wife, Xenia.

Aunt Teresa and Berthe sighed in unison, and gave vent to condolences. Captain Negodyaev gave a nervous little cough, and blowing his nose with his scented handkerchief read Natàsha's letter. All attempts at punctuation omitted, she wrote:

Dear Papa you are probably very lonely without mammy she is often ill but we take care of her I want very much to go to you mammy has written you a letter for your birthday but has lost it we'll send it along when we find it I have rabbits two grey ones they had kiddies but the rats have eaten them probably will soon eat us too. Natàsha.

And while he read Natàsha's letter Aunt Teresa interrupted him, like a deacon in church, with exclamations of beatific wonder, and Berthe's voice came like a second fiddle in practically the same melody of acclaim. One could see that Aunt Teresa had at once taken a liking to the little girl.

'How old is Natàsha?' she asked.

'Seven,' he said.

'But don't you want to see her awfully?'

Of course he did. But how? How?

Aunt Teresa took the tenderest interest in Natàsha.

'There are ways and means,' she said. And remembering how she had contrived to bring away her husband in the midst of the greatest of all wars, I understood that indeed there must be ways and means.

Captain Negodyaev looked spiritually intoxicated. 'How strange! Only yesterday my life seemed grey and dull and hopeless, and today—it's like a dream come true. These rooms, after living for months on end in a railway coach. These rooms!—He too'—he pointed to his batman Vladislav— 'is pleased, I bet.'

'Yes, there is no doubt,' said Vladislav, 'these are good rooms. But a long way off the French!'

'Go along, that will do,' said Captain Negodyaev sternly. 'Gone dotty from too much happiness, I expect. Take no notice of him'—he turned to us with a propitiatory smile. 'Yes, I'd do anything to have Natàsha here. Anything.'

'What of your daughter Màsha? Would she also come?' It seemed as though my aunt was not too keen on Ippolit.

'Hardly. Màsha is grown up and lives with her husband. She loves her husband.'

'Anyway, we've room enough here for Natàsha and your wife. George'—she turned to me quietly— 'you will telephone General Pshemòvich-Pshevìtski and ask him for an interview tomorrow morning.'

25

The General had sent word by his aide-de-camp son that he had reserved 11 o'clock for Aunt Teresa and myself; and Aunt Teresa's carriage had been ordered for 10.30. But at a quarter to eleven Aunt Teresa, finally attired, discovered that she had mislaid her bag, and while she was looking for it Beastly had arrived from Omsk, quite unexpectedly, accentuating the general commotion.

'A letter from your brother Lucy!' he exclaimed triumphantly.

'No time till I come back from the General,' she warned him off. 'Besides, they've lost my bag for me.'

Because just before losing the bag she had had 'words' with Berthe, she now blamed Berthe for having lost it.

'But it isn't I who lost the bag!' Berthe exclaimed excitedly.

'All the same, you upset me,' retorted my aunt.

'But you've lost it yourself!'

'Ah! if *Constance* were here!'

'We had better look for it,' said Berthe appeasingly.

Beastly's Anglo-Saxon common-sense, directed towards advising other people how to manage their own silly business, was sometimes too much for Aunt Teresa. Now when she had lost her bag, he thus consoled her, 'Well, my dear lady, there's nothing to get excited about; the house isn't on fire, you know, you've only got to find the damned thing: now where the deuce have you put it?'

'*Ah, enfin*! if I knew I wouldn't be looking for it!' wailed my aunt in accents of astonishment and anguish.

Beastly only nodded his head in that crude sardonic manner of the British sergeant who tells an obviously hopeless recruit who has mislaid his kit or possibly got hold of the wrong end of the rifle: 'No wonder we're winnin'!'

At last the bag was found, hanging on the back of a chair that everybody had been gazing at. The victoria with the two meagre mares and the disreputable coachman Stepàn drew up to the porch. Aunt Teresa and I stepped inside, and we drove off to the General's train.

The General's special train stood on the viaduct, in a commanding military position, as if holding a pistol at the head of the city. Almost opposite lay the train of the Chinese High Commissioner, an amiable gentleman upon whom I had already had occasion to call, and who had treated me to excellent port on that occasion. As we mounted the train we were at once invaded by an official and military atmosphere. A personnel of experts received us—experts in *coups d'état*. The tall officer on duty escorted us to the aide-de-camp, the General's son, and the aide-de-camp conducted us into the carpeted interior of the General's private office. Behind his writing-table sat the General himself, dark, wiry, with a stiff black moustache and closely cropped hair turning grey. With the General was a gentleman whom I at once recognized as Dr. Murgatroyd, an English newspaper correspondent. The General rose with the customary precision of Russian officers, and clicking his spurs introduced himself: 'Lieutenant-General Pshemòvich-Pshevìtski,' and politely enquired of what service he could be to us. He wore very high heels, and scented his hands and handkerchief without cease with eau-de-Cologne.

'I have come,' said Aunt Teresa, sinking by his desk into an arm-chair, 'about a Russian officer who lives with us at present, whose wife and little daughter—a charming child—are starving, I'm afraid, in Novorossiisk.'

'Quite. Quite,' said General Pshemòvich-Pshevìtski.

'I so want to get them over here. The father, Captain Negodyaev, is so wretchedly unhappy.'

'Quite.'

'I know you feel as I do in the matter.' Aunt Teresa wrinkled her nose a little—how becoming!

'Quite,' said he, surveying her with interest. He stroked his stiff moustache, then sprayed some more eau-de-Cologne over his hands and martial chest bestrewn with decorations. And the oft-heard rumour flashed across my brain again that he had been a constable who had obtained a commission in the war, and had since, while nobody was looking, promoted himself to a General. He seemed much interested in Aunt Teresa's person—more so than in the subject of her call—and enquired how it was: she was not Russian—and yet, and yet?…And Aunt Teresa plunged with eagerness into her triumphant past and told him all. She was English, born of English parents (her mother was a Spaniard though)—in Manchester, it seemed. But she had been brought up in Russia, where she had also lived her youth and early married life, among the dear old Russian aristocracy, now so unhappily dislodged from their secure positions. Ah! didn't she remember the old days!

And the Galìtzins! And the Troubetzkòys! And the Yusùpov-Sumaròkov-Elstons! And the Princess Tènisheva! And the Belosèlski-Belozèrskis! And the Most Illustrious Princess Suvòrov! Ah! she knew them all! And the Viceroy of the Caucasus Count Ilaryòn Vorontzòv-Dàshkov! The Dàshkovs and the Pàshkovs—she knew them all. Aunt Teresa exchanged glances with the General, glances of intimate melancholy reminiscence. The General, who must have been a gendarme constable in those days, perhaps guarding the very street in which some of these aristocrats resided, smiled sadly, a little timidly; but the contrast must also have reminded him of his present undisputed hegemony, of his commanding military position, as he sat in his luxurious armoured train, with the town at his mercy; and so his smile, besides shyness and awkwardness, conveyed a tinge of satisfaction. And in answer to her question if he *knew* the Troubetzkòys he said (with a beatific look which was to cover such a point-blank question): 'Ah! who didn't know them!'

'And the Galìtzins?'

'Mercy! who hasn't heard of them!' And added, to consolidate the impression, 'They were worth knowing! Curious people, you don't say!'

Aunt Teresa was a beauty in her day: not merely pretty, handsome, or good-looking, but a *beauty* recognized and unmistakable. Even now, as the General looked at her, he was, I knew it with a certainty that defies all doubt, swayed by the majesty of that elusive quality which had commanded worship when she was young. He must have felt the throbbing chain of years that linked her back to her disturbing youth, now past, for looking at her he seemed perturbed and animated as if he were in love: gallant, anxious to please. Her lovely nose, though amply powdered, had survived the ruin of the years, remained intact with its delicately-chiselled nostrils; as well as the superbly-moulded forehead and the chin. Her marked moustache and little beard could not kill one's adoration!

Life is full of chip love, strewn with abortive romances, of glances exchanged in a railway carriage that must die premature deaths because at this junction or that our trains take us asunder; because we had met a little too early or else a little too late, or not perhaps in just the right place. In a future age of wireless sight it may be that we shall arrange our love affairs more efficiently. We shall send out and receive SOS calls from love-stricken, love-craving hearts, and we shall never languish alone.

'Then you agree with me, General, about Captain Negodyaev's wife and daughter?'

'Quite,' he said. 'Quite.' He pressed an electric button.

His aide-de-camp son stood in the doorway, as if he were in some mysterious way a part of this electrical contrivance.

'Communicate immediately by telephone with Captain Negodyaev at the Censorship Department. Tell him to appear here *at once*.'

'Quite so, your Excellency!' The aide-de-camp dashed out of the room.

A serious situation had arisen, so it appeared meanwhile, and the General, as we waited for Captain Negodyaev's advent, confided to us his earnest apprehension. The peasants in the Province round about Vladivostok who lived on game had shot-guns; but the General, conceiving guns to be a sign of overt Bolshevism, dispatched a squad to confiscate these guns, whereon the peasants seized the squad and took the officers prisoner. The General had since arranged for a further squad from Russian Island Training School to go forth to the rescue of the prisoners, but last night there had been a storm, and the squad was reported to have well-nigh drowned in crossing. At this point the wires had been cut and the General was still in ignorance of their fate. Yes, an uphill task, he sighed, to attempt to save your country from red ruin!

'I always say,' said Aunt Teresa, 'the only hope for Russia lies in a powerful White Army. I feel that when the Whites get the upper hand again, peace and brotherhood will be restored to this long-suffering land. And if you win the Civil War I am sure that you will justify your victory by the wise policy you will pursue after that. Have you a policy?' she asked.

Yes,' said General Pshemòvich-Pshevìtski, a look of eager determination creeping into his eyes. 'I will decorate the lamp-posts with the corpses of the bandits. That's my policy—I give you my word of honour, you can count on me to keep my word.' He held out his hand. 'And,' he added tenderly, 'you may deny your friendship to me if I fail to keep my promise.'

Aunt Teresa proffered a reluctant hand. It was not quite what she had meant by 'saving Russia'. However, she had not the heart to disappoint the sincerity of his emotion.

'Things have gone far,' he sighed. 'They have been allowed to drift. You won't retrieve them now! What I regret,' he said, 'is not so much the revolution (too late to lock the stable door after the horse has run away), but the liberation of the serfs in 1861 that caused all the mischief. Yes—but what's happened about Captain Negodyaev?' He pressed the button.

His aide-de-camp stood in the doorway.

'Well? Have you telephoned to Captain Negodyaev?'

'The telephone, your Excellency, is out of order.'

'Repair the telephone!' the General snapped savagely.

'Very well, your Excellency!'

'Yes,' said the General, turning round to us again as the aide-de-camp retired with the air of one who had his work cut out. 'Yes. The Bolsheviks are scoundrels and murderers, and have acquired power by force; they are, in fact, anti-democratic, having thrown over, as you know, the All-Russia Constituent Assembly.'

But I noticed that just as in his opposition to the liberation of the serfs he had forgotten that in ordinary circumstances he himself would not be a master but a serf, so now he did not detect the contradiction when, a moment later, he remarked:

'Over sixty per cent of the population is illiterate. Russia is not ripe for a Constituent Assembly. The only salvation is a Tsar.'

Dr. Murgatroyd looked as though he were going to dissent. But Aunt Teresa at once remarked that she had every reason to believe that the peasants would welcome the return of a Tsar. ' "Give us back the Tsar," they say,' said Aunt Teresa, as it were on behalf of the peasants, although not having come in contact with any peasants ever since she left Russia proper twenty years ago, she could not speak from personal experience.

But Dr. Murgatroyd intimated that he did not favour emperors, though he did not mind imperialism, so long as it was 'democratic'. And the General, with startling logic, said that, in his view, the Bolsheviks (which name he prefaced by a string of lurid adjectives) should be opposed by all true democrats, because they were essentially anti-democratic, and that he, General Pshemòvich-Pshevìtski and his kind, would oppose them because they were what he described them to be in his string of lurid adjectives; and so in their opposition to the Bolsheviks he and his kind would have a common platform with the democrats, whose democracy they hated only second to the Bolshevik autocracy.

Yet the incorrigible General who had learnt nothing from the Revolution sought, as men of his type will, to apply to the future of his country principles that had ruined it in the past. The Imperial Russian Government had denied the people self-government on the plea that they were not educated; and it had denied them education on the plea that they possessed no self-government. And it had denied them both on the ground that 'they were happy as they were'.

'You do not understand Russia,' argued General Pshemòvich-Pshevìtski. 'The people are incapable of governing themselves. They are not ripe for it. Can you imagine the terrible oppression, the unspeakable chaos and misery of a country governed by uneducated workmen, by illiterate peasants? You know the result. It's Bolshevism.'

Having uttered that terrible word, he stopped to examine the effect on the faces of his listeners. All were non-plussed. But I ventured:

'If such be the terrible effect of ignorance and illiteracy, why, may I ask, had the Government denied them the necessary education and enlightenment?'

The General looked at me with infinite pity. 'My dear Captain,' he cried, 'our Government had enough sense to recognize the danger of superfluous education for a people who profess an autocratic form of government. They realized that to educate the masses was to make them discontented. They were right. Results have proved it.'

Aunt Teresa nodded emphatically, because this was just the sort of stuff which went down with her. 'What you want,' she said with conviction, 'is an honest man. The Russian people are an apathetic people. They don't care what government they live under so long as they get food and clothes and—are happy.'

Of this the General was—he confessed it with a smile—not so very sure, and he did not want us to go home with the idea that he was an out-and-out reactionary. Not a bit of it. We must move with the times. He was all for moderation. He stood (if his politics must be defined) in the *middle*, between anarchy from the left and anarchy from the right—a centre party, he explained, adhering to the good old sensible ideals of nationalism and honour. Yes. The General thought that the people might still be educated carefully and in moderation, and—who knows?—some day perhaps they may even have a Constituent Assembly and all that this meant. 'But at present,' he said in a cheery manner (putting off the evil hour which, if it had to come, well, it simply had to come, but, please God, would come tomorrow), 'at present'—he held out a paper-knife—'it is unthinkable—a complete surrender to Bolshevism!' He brought the paper-knife down with a bang.

And here at last Dr. Murgatroyd stepped in. The value of education weighed in the balance and found wanting, the utility of self-government reduced to a becoming level, and the worth of either played off against the other till one effectively disposed of both, the field was clear for his pet theory, the exposition of which he felt was now peculiarly appropriate.

His pet theory was the union of the Orthodox and the Anglican Churches. It was a fixed idea with him, the essence and the purpose of his life. For thirty years or more he had accosted archbishops, bishops, patriarchs, archimandrites, metropolitans, and such-like holy fathers in both countries with this obsolete idea. Dr. Murgatroyd was a singularly untidy, unkempt, dishevelled individual, and, no doubt, to advertise his liaison with that country he wore a costume after the style of the Russian *moujik*. He had been described by his enemies as 'the only Englishman who never washed', and he was persistent to a degree scarcely credible even in a correspondent. He had no conscience, no shame. He confronted kings and emperors, prime ministers and ambassadors and commanders-in-chief and every kind of religious enthusiast, and preached to them the union of the Orthodox and the Anglican Churches. Many seemed quite hopeful, and others were polite about it, but he thought it the crowning factor in world politics, the keystone of the Russian situation, the crux of the whole thing. If anything was to bring the two countries together, or avert wars, or promote trade, or kill Bolshevism, or save the world from every kind of evil, it was, he said, with certainty, the union of the Orthodox and the Anglican Churches. In his absent-mindedness it had somehow not occurred to him that the big idea of political domination through the medium of religion had died for ever with the temporal power of the Pope, and that whatever his concern for the Anglican Church at home the ordinary modern Englishman cared no more about the Orthodox faith than the ordinary Russian bothered his mind about the Church of England, should he have ever heard of its existence. But Dr. Murgatroyd was absent-minded to a degree only pardonable in professors. If you had told him at any hour of the day that he had already had his dinner, he would knit his brows and think hard for a moment and then say: 'Yes, perhaps you are right. Yes, you *are* right. Yes, I must have had my dinner.

Yes, I *have* had my dinner. Yes, yes, yes, yes.' But he never kept regular hours for meals. He scarcely ever had any regular meals, or, in fact, any meals at all. He simply felt no need for food. He said: 'All I want is a little tobacco.' He was one of that class of people who never have any money; for even if he had had any money, he would not know where he had put it. Similarly all his teeth had gone from wear and tear and lack of all care. But there he lived on without teeth, not that their absence did not cause him to suffer pain and discomfort (for his digestion, as in fact everything else in his constitution, had gone to pieces), but it had simply never occurred to him that something had to be done in the matter. His mind was continually occupied with other things.

'The most formidable weapon against Bolshevism,' said Dr. Murgatroyd, 'is religion. Here it is that we can truly help. Russia's salvation lies in the union of the Orthodox and the Anglican Churches. When I was in Moscow and Kiev many years ago I saw Archimandrite Theodosy, Metropolitans Theophanes and Hermogenes and Father Nikon, and they asked me to convey their warmest sentiments to our archbishops.'

'M'yes,' said the General. 'M'yes—of course—the Union of the Churches. But why is it that this Captain Negodyaev is so long in coming?'

He pressed the button in a prolonged, determined manner.

The aide-de-camp stood in the doorway.

'Well?'

'We've sent for the mechanic, your Excellency.'

'What a long time,' said the General apologetically to Aunt Teresa. 'Yes—of course—the Union of the Churches. But we must have propaganda for that.'

'Ah, yes, propaganda,' said Dr. Murgatroyd, and before we could stop him he had launched out on propaganda. This was his other craze.

He spoke with increasing speed.

'Propaganda is everything; it is almost as important as religion, but the most effective propaganda is propaganda conducted through the medium of the Churches—the union of the two Churches. We must develop a huge organization to counteract the insidious, lying propaganda of the Bolsheviks. The religious note must be struck. This is all-important. The people must be urged to stand fast and not let the Bolshevik forces of Antichrist prevail. In the defence of Christianity, we will argue, the Churches of Russia and England must combine their forces: this will lead us to the union of the Orthodox and the Anglican Churches. But we will not stop at that. This organization—this colossal organization—with headquarters at Vladivostok and London respectively, will be split into two groups: the first for the enlightenment of the Russians concerning their British Ally, the other for the enlightenment of the British concerning things Russian. It is imperative that an exceptionally capable man with an excellent knowledge of the language and conditions be given charge of the entire Association in order to co-ordinate and generally direct the work of this organization. Well, with your approval I am prepared to undertake the task. I have innumerable friends in both countries. I will get the bishops and the archimandrites to work together. Each group will be in uninterrupted communication with the other, acquire all available information on the spot, and pass it on to the people on the other side—and keep the pot boiling. We will buy up all newspapers, periodicals, printing presses in both countries, and so guide public opinion by issuing dailies, weeklies, hourly bulletins, leaflets, pamphlets, magazines, articles, books of every description, printed in large quantities, translated into all languages; some light books, some of them more serious works, some full of pictures, others of maps and diagrams and charts—but one and all directed against Bolshevism. We will mobilize all the best authors, artists, scientists, priests, and other people who know their subjects—sound and vigorous writers—and get them to condemn Bolshevism from the point of view of the peasant, the workman, the co-operator, the Church, the merchant, the schoolmaster, the professor. In a short while I hope a new literature will spring into being. We will then set up numerous libraries comprising all sorts of books on every kind of topic: philosophy, science, psychology, botany, gardening, poultry, mathematics, farming, sport, economics—all and sundry directed against Bolshevism: Bolshevism as a brutal and inhuman science; Bolshevism as a criminal psychology; Bolshevism as a ruinous economic system. Ugly gardening, hopeless botany, impracticable farming, immoral sport, misleading mathematics, impossible poultry—all as the result of the Bolshevik communist system. There is really no limit to which we cannot go! In addition special picture-books can be printed to preserve the coming generation from the insidious penetration of Bolshevik ideas. We will scatter throughout the country a host of photographers to collect scenes of Bolshevik atrocities. We will engage famous artists to paint pictures of rape, murder, pillage and outrage committed by communists. On the other hand, we will praise the courage and loyalty and discipline and devotion of the forces of law and order, and send them constant urgings to be of good cheer and courage.'

'M'yes,' said the General stroking his chin. 'M'yes. But why is this Captain Negodyaev not coming?'

He pressed the electric bell-button.

The aide-de-camp offspring stood in the doorway.

'Well? Have you telephoned at last?'

'The mechanic's drunk, your Excellency.'

'Send at once for the other mechanic!' snapped the General ferociously.

'Very well, your Excellency!' The aide-de-camp bolted.

'M'yes,' said the General, once more resuming the subject and turning to Dr. Murgatroyd in particular. 'Tell the Mr. Churchill, and tell the Mr. Lloyd George, and tell the President Wilson, and tell the whole world that the General Pshemòvich-Pshevìtski is firm, as firm as a rock, and he will fight the Jewish Bolsheviks to the last man,' he ended—pressing the button with violence.

The aide-de-camp stood on the threshold.

'Well, what about the telephone?' the General asked grimly.

'The other mechanic is on leave, your Excellency.'

'In that case,' said the General, pulling out his watch and looking at Aunt Teresa, 'dispatch a car for Captain Negodyaev, do you hear? A car *immediately*!'

'Quite so, your Excellency!'

The aide-de-camp dashed out of the room.

'M'yes,' said the General. 'M'yes—of course…'

Some ten minutes later Captain Negodyaev appeared in the doorway.

'Aha!' said the General grandly and graciously. 'I understand you have a wife and daughter in Novorossiisk.'

'That's perfectly correct, your Excellency. I have, your Excellency, two daughters,' Captain Negodyaev was explaining, turning pale as a sheet as he stood to attention:

'Màsha and Natàsha, your Excellency.'

'Quite, quite, quite,' the General chimed in impatiently.

'Màsha, your Excellency, is married, and lives with her husband, Ippolit Sergèiech Blagovèschenski, away in Novorossiisk, your Excellency. And Natàsha, your Excellency, is only seven, your Excellency.'

'Quite, quite, quite,' said the General impatiently, and turning fiercely to his aide-de-camp son:

'A telegram to Novorossiisk,' he snapped, 'to be dispatched *immediately*!'

The aide-de-camp tore off the ground.

The General pressed the button.

The aide-de-camp, like a jack-in-the-box, bobbed in again and stood to attention, trembling like a jerboa.

'Priority. *Clear the line*,' the General snapped savagely.

'Quite so, your Excellency!' The aide-de-camp, like a jack-in-the-box, bobbed out again.

It was as if the General had tarried long enough, and now having bestirred himself would show them that he meant business. He looked at Aunt Teresa to see if all this was pleasing her. She looked tender and vague.

As Aunt Teresa rose, assured by the General that no stone would be left unturned to comply with her wishes, she turned to Dr. Murgatroyd and thanked him for his most interesting and brilliant discourse. 'Perhaps you would pay us a visit,' she said over her shoulder.

Escorted by the General's retinue we stepped into the carriage and drove home.

26

A telegram awaited me as we arrived. With nervous hands I tore it open. It ran: 'Your scheme approved. Appointed liaison officer and military censor. Instructions follow.'

'And the letter! Where's the letter?' Aunt Teresa asked the moment she saw Beastly.

But the letter was for me. Uncle Lucy wrote to ask me if I

thought it would be feasible for them to go and live in England. It was impossible for them to stay in Krasnoyarsk, as well-nigh everything had been taken from them, and he asked me, if I so thought fit, to arrange for an early passage for them from Shanghai to England.

I was annoyed. In my irritable mood, I thought: others had perished in the grand commotion of the great world war and revolution. Why not my uncle and family too? This morbid instinct of self-preservation! Why doesn't he remain and perish? Apparently he thought that going to England was an easy matter. But was it? What annoyed me was the optimism with which some people deem it possible to get out of trouble. I suspected him, with all his surface pessimism, of being a facile optimist of a most distressing kind. When I was joining up to fight in the world war, he wrote to me as follows:

> I advise you to pay a visit to the War Office and see Lord Kitchener personally, and tell him that your constitution is not exactly suitable for the rigour and discomfort of the trenches, but that you are willing to 'do your bit' and do your duty by your king and country and are good at foreign languages and could thus be best employed in a sedentary capacity at the War Office itself, to the benefit of all concerned.

I thought of the nuisance of having them in our crowded flat, and advised against it.

At dinner Aunt Teresa questioned Beastly as to Uncle Lucy.

'Well, I've seen him,' he said.

'You've seen my brother, Lucy?' she asked excitedly.

'I've seen him.'

'Well?'

'He's a queer fish,' he said, 'and no mistake, your brother Lucy!'

Major Beastly had had a heart-to-heart talk with Aunt Molly, from which indeed it seemed that Uncle Lucy was a 'queer fish'. His father—so Aunt Molly said—had charged him on his death-bed to look after the remaining family. That death-bed scene seemed to have so impressed itself on Uncle Lucy's mind that ever since—according to Aunt Molly—he had neglected his own family. All the money he had made he would be sending to his sisters, and when his children were born and Aunt Molly wanted nurses, Uncle Lucy said he didn't believe in nurses. And when the children grew up and she wanted money for their schooling, Uncle Lucy, in withholding the necessary funds, declared that, with Tolstoy, he didn't believe in schooling. And when the time arrived for deciding on their future callings and professions, Uncle Lucy said he didn't believe in callings and professions. Till one day, with the eighth or ninth offspring, Aunt Molly kicked over the fence and managed the estate herself as best she could. Meanwhile, their number had been swelling, and when after having the family group taken at the photographer's they all marched home through the town garden, Uncle Lucy looked as though he were a guide conducting a crowd of sight-seeing tourists through the city grounds, and the family, except the very young ones, felt constrained. But Uncle Lucy's interest in them was not especially marked, and he would ask the same young daughter as each day he walked a portion of the way to school with her what class she was in.

'But what about our money?' interrupted Aunt Teresa.

'Oh yes. He said that, with Tolstoy, he didn't believe in money.'

'That's nice!'

'I tried to tackle him. But he said that in his house the subject was taboo.'

Next morning, being the fourth day since he last performed the operation, Major Beastly made a *stink*. Uncle Emmanuel at once lit a cigar, but said nothing. In the dining-room Vladislav shook his head. 'Enough to make you carry out the saints. In France,' he added, 'such a thing would not be allowed in a decent home.'

Berthe did not mind Beastly's *stinks* now. 'He has a tender skin—*il a la peau sensible*,' she would say, 'which can't stand the touch of the blade.' She confessed to me that she even rather liked his nostrils: there was something very frank, almost touching—*n'est-ce pas*?— about their vertical position, something that oddly reminded you of a dog who, at the command 'Beg!', displays himself before you in an unfamiliar pose.

Nevertheless, I thought the time had come to remonstrate with Beastly.

'I have a perfect right to shave as I like,' he rejoined.

'A man's rights are limited,' I observed. 'He has no right to make a *stink*, for instance, unless he be in a desert, alone with God.'

But nothing would shatter his faith in the soundness of his apparatus, and the same day, at tea, he turned to Captain Negodyaev with the offer to make use of his 'preparat'.

'Get some of that yellow moss off your face,' he advised.

'Thank you, I rarely shave,' said Captain Negodyaev. 'I just powder my chin, it's quite sufficient.'

Beastly suggested Aunt Teresa trying his 'preparat' on her own tender lip with a view to removing, as he put it, 'that moustachio of yours'. But Aunt Teresa's verdict was that Berthe should try it first. If Berthe came out of it without undue disfigurement, Aunt Teresa would feel justified in applying the method on her own lip and chin.

Towards evening Captain Negodyaev would be looking like a frightened rat. Having served under conflicting governments, he was afraid of persecution, and late at night he used to come into my bedroom and talk mysteriously of Red reprisals on White officers and of White reprisals on officers who, like himself, at one time or another had been forced to serve under a Pink régime. He would sit with me and talk for hours into the night, till the pale dawn mocked our yellow light.

27

The period of engagement, as all who've been engaged will know, is a period of transition, not wholly satisfactory. To please my august aunt, each day, for hours at a stretch, we sat in the drawing-room, where Aunt Teresa did her crochet work, I holding Sylvia by the hand; at long intervals exchanging silent looks of tenderness and passion—just as Anatole had done before his end, and Uncle Emmanuel himself in the sentimental days of his engagement to my aunt: when she let drop her head upon his martial shoulder. But my efforts did not meet with the approval they deserved: to Aunt Teresa, in the after light of her own romantic days, I did not seem affectionate enough, nor did she think her daughter adequately tender and responsive, and criticized my fiancée's dislike of these prolonged and silent attitudes, while Sylvia entreated: 'Darling, don't be soppy!' Aunt Teresa now went out with us (her health permitting, and when it did not so permit, objected to our going out at all). She did not like to leave us by ourselves, though we were cousins, and had been alone no end of times before we were engaged. And we were bored with her, bored with each other, and bored with ourselves. When left alone, after she had gone to bed, for want of something better, we kissed. It was as if, all of a sudden, we had lost our former faculty for making conversation. I sighed. Sylvia sighed. 'I wish,' I said, 'your mother would hurry up with our wedding.'

She thought a little, wondering what she could say.

'You are very naughty, darling,' she rejoined.

Sylvia liked to be kissed in short kisses.

'But don't you like long kisses, darling?'

'I can't breathe, darling, when they're too long; but I can breathe between each short kiss, if you know what I mean, and you can go on and on and on.'

I gave her a ring on which I had had engraved the message: *Set me as a seal upon thine heart.*

28

More Polyglots

It was the end of summer, and the rains had set in. A dark gloomy morning, the electric light burning as though it were evening. At last came the ring at the bell.

Mme Negodyaev, a crumpled lady with a face as though someone had once inadvertently stepped on it, held by the hand a smaller form with a pallid face framed in fair locks, and thin, thin legs. And to all questions Natàsha shrugged her shoulders. When I watched her drinking tea I noticed her faint finely drawn brow. And sitting at table among the grown-ups, sunk low in the chair and her chin not very far removed from the edge of the table, with a look of gravity on her face, she looked like a miniature reproduction of a human being. On board the boat that brought them she had played with English children, and Mme Negodyaev recounted, with pride in her face, that Natàsha could now already speak English. When she did so she spoke of 'my friends', 'my uncle', 'my grandmama'. I asked her about the Bolsheviks in Novorossiisk. 'Bolsheviks? What's it means Bolsheviks?' She shrugged her shoulders. 'Only lot of dirty mens in the street.'

I laughed at that. She laughed back—into the cup of tea, creating a little storm in the tea-cup. 'But I have lots and lots of my friends there. And my sister and my uncle and my grandmama. Ah! and I have left in Rush-ya my little kitchen—such a beauty thing—and plates my grandmama given me, lots and lots of plates and cups—such a lovely! Ah! such-such pity! Such, such *such*-such pity!'

Tired after the journey, supper over, she was at once put to bed. In her striped flannel nightgown, a slim little figure, she knelt up in bed and, looking towards the ikon of Nicholas the Miracle-worker which her mother had already unpacked and hung up in the corner, she closed her eyes, her thin palms together, and prayed: 'Dear Little God, pity our poor Russia.'

This over, her father and mother rejoined us in the drawing-room. I watched Mme Negodyaev's face as she talked. It was a face by courtesy only. 'My heart aches for poor Màsha,' she was saying. 'Hers is a hard life, for Ippolit is so strange. I have felt sorry for Màsha ever since the wedding day, when Ippolit began worrying me over the dowry, which he thought insufficient. I said to myself: "If that's what he is like now, what will he be like after?" And the very night after they had been married, Ippolit went out to the café by himself and sat there till early morning, drinking and playing cards. He soon took up another woman, and would go away with her for weeks on end. This Màsha tried to forgive him, because she loved him. He bought expensive presents for that woman with Màsha's own money, but she never said a word, because she loved him. Finally, he began bringing her to our house and, in fact, to Màsha's bedroom. All this, too, Màsha tried to endure, for she loved him very, *very* much. But when they left—Ippolit and the woman—they broke into the cabinet and took away the portfolio with all our ready money. Both Màsha and I don't think it was very nice of them to do that after all we've done for them; do you?'

I agreed. In fact, I was more emphatic; I said that indeed it wasn't *at all* nice.

In the morning Natàsha talked a great deal of what she had done in 'Rush-ya', as she pronounced that word. She spoke of Màsha with a sigh.

'And Ippolit?' I asked.

'Nasty mans,' she replied.

At once Natàsha became a great favourite with everybody. Even with the shopmen round about—even Vladislav, who rarely approved of anything that did not emanate from Paris. All day long she sang a sad, sad song of a strong Slavonic flavour that, however, seemed an improvisation, for it had no recognizable melody, though lots and lots of feeling. And as she was a little dull without toys she would come up to me and plead: '*Play* with me; oh, *play* with me!' Or she would steal up from behind, cover your eyes with her cool slender hands and ask: 'Guess! Guess! Who is it?' And she would wrinkle her nose as she laughed straight from the heart, upon recognition, a gurgling, bubbling laugh. Or she would come in sucking a caramel, her bright sea-green eyes sparkling, and command: 'Shut your eyes and open your mouth!' She scrambled up to my attic, where I was in the habit of doing my literary work, and overtook me kissing Sylvia's photograph. 'Oh, my darling! Oh, my sweet-heart!' I whispered. Natàsha looked on, issuing a long gurgling sound of delight— 'gug-g-g-g-g'—like a pigeon.

'Do you recognize the portrait?'

'Oh! how beauty! Oh! what a lovely!' she exclaimed. '

And your own photo?' I asked. 'Is that beautiful too?'

Natàsha shrugged her shoulders.

'Mr. Georg*es*!' she said whimsically. 'Mr. Georg*es*!'

'Yes?'

'Play with me; oh, *play* with me.'

'I am busy.'

'Oh, Uncle Georgie,' she said, pulling me by the hand, 'I love you. I love you, Uncle Georgie. Because you are so funny!'

Natàsha wrote little stories in Russian about a little boy Vanya who went to school and another little boy Petya who also went to school, but nothing beyond going to school seemed to happen to them, and the stories were all inconclusive. She also wrote a sad little poem about a child looking at the stars and thinking of God; and another of her mother (the woman who looked as though someone had inadvertently stepped on her face) whose great beauty she extolled and compared with a swan's. Natàsha had two baby goats given her for her birthday by a neighbouring farmer—one of which she called 'Bobby' and the other 'Beauty'.

Now and then Captain Negodyaev suffered from an acute attack of persecution mania, when, often in the middle of the night, he would bid his wife and child get up and dress in readiness for flight at a moment's notice. And they would sit there, all dressed up, in their furs and overcoats and hats and muffs and warm goloshes, in the heated drawing-room, Mme Negodyaev looking as if somebody had hit her suddenly between the ears with an umbrella, and she could not quite reconcile the fact with what had taken place immediately before. But Natàsha seemed to take it all for granted. With her parasol in her gloved hands, she would sit there, grave and quiet, one hour, two—until at last he would declare the danger over and send them back to bed.

These incidents, which were recurrent, would always cause my aunt *une crise de nerfs*.

29

And Still More Polyglots

The preparations for our wedding were complete, and cards had been sent out, when one November morning I was wakened ruthlessly by Vladislav at six o'clock (for usually they waken me with deference by first enquiring: 'Did you go to bed early last night?') and told by him, 'Your uncle has arrived and is waiting for you.

'Which uncle? Where? What? Why?'

In the adjoining dining-room, Uncle Lucy was pacing the floor up and down excitedly.

I began to dress hurriedly as Vladislav withdrew, but as luck would have it I couldn't find a vest; while there were drawers innumerable in the drawer. From the dining-room came Uncle Lucy's low voice to Vladislav:

'Quick. Quick. Quick. No time to waste.'

I pulled open all the drawers. The third drawer—all drawers, no vest. Why is it that when you look for a pair of drawers you always find another couple of vests instead? and when you look for a vest you can find only drawers? I do not know why it is so: I only know that it is so. It is a minor mystery of which the solution apparently (as of the major mystery of the hereafter) is not yet. But it damps my spirit, and I acquire a foreboding—which is ascribed sometimes to Thomas Hardy—of a relentless, wicked, mocking and malicious Providence.

Uncle Lucy's voice came through the closed door: 'Quick. Quick. Quick,' and I could fancy him pacing to and fro like a pendulum, with his hands behind his back.

'Your uncle, your uncle is waiting for you,' Vladislav came in again.

'Send at once for Mlle Berthe.'

'Yes, sir,' he said, and retired.

The reader may think I am unreasonable. But I can assure him (this book is not intended for women) that only last night the chest of drawers was full of vests—and not a pair of drawers in the neighbourhood.

'Berthe!' I exclaimed with the utmost demonstrativeness as she came in. 'How ridiculous! A drawer full of drawers—and not a vest.' The extent of my anger can be gauged when I say I felt that if I murdered Berthe the jury would acquit me and that I'd murder the jury if they did not. She looked at me blankly.

'Don't stand there like that, looking like Buddha.' This may have been a little rough. But I felt it.

She looked at me askance, and could not decide whether to be offended or not. The fact of the matter was she did not know what Buddha looked like. And I had forgotten.

'I may not be as handsome as some women,' she retorted, evidently offended, 'but, then, neither are you a beauty.'

Strange. What am I to make of it? Even while Berthe was in the room I glanced at the looking-glass: the effect was quite pleasing.

'Getting me up at this time of the morning,' she said. There was a slight note of peevishness in her voice which annoyed me.

'My uncle's waiting for me,' I said.

'And I'll tell your uncle!'

'Where's my vest?' I cried out in despair.

But Berthe is not a Latin for nothing. Before I could get a word in, she tore away—trr-trr-trr—unloosing torrents of recrimination, the brunt of which was: 'What have I to do with your *caleçons*?'

'Vests!' I cried madly, 'not *caleçons*. Vests! *vests*! I've a cupboardful of *caleçons*.'

'You have your man Pickup! You've Vladislav! While I'm only a woman!' she cried.

Perfectly so. I have Pickup. Vladislav is Captain Negodyaev's servant, but partly under my orders. Yet by some mysterious unwritten law Berthe rules over the laundry of the household. Besides, I do not like finding fault with my man, who is a soldier more than a servant. How like a woman to ignore the very circumstance by which she profits. 'Trr-trr-trr-trr——' She tore away, on and on and on, in floods of angry verbosity against which my French, I realized, was helpless. My French is rather like my piano playing—grandiose in conception but just a little blurred in execution. I slide over technicalities of grammar, I mix up cases and tenses, but on top of it all I put on a sort of dare-devil *Parisian* twist and make up for occasional inaccuracies by a really blinding speed. I make French people sit up. But my tactics proved of small avail in my dialectic duel with Berthe. When I was a child, a governess, Mlle Jardelle, would teach us French by insisting on our saying '*Passez-moi le sel, s'il vous plaît*' at table, or doing without it. I like to think that at that time my French was fluent; but I doubt it. In a crisis it deserts me, and I can only cry '*Enfin! enfin!*' And hard up for an effective repartee, I utter: '*Sacrebleu*!'

'*Enfin*!' she cried. 'I'm alone for the whole house. None of you do anything. Your servants do nothing.'

'I favour,' I said, 'a mild state of Bolshevism in the household.'

'Nobody does anything. Your aunt is a *malade imaginaire;* whines all day long. *Cet idiot de capitaine russe* only dresses and undresses, and gets his family into a funk. You are only thinking of your *caleçons*——'

'Oh, damn *les caleçons*.'

'Only me for the whole house,' she wailed, and off she tore—trr-trr-trr—on and on and on and on.

'I see now I ought to have done you in when I felt like it,' I said quietly.

'*À quoi bon*? You would be guillotined.'

'The jury would acquit me.'

'I'd like to see it!' she said, with savage glee.

'Look here, Berthe,' I said, making an effort to be serious and reasonable, 'I am an intellectual, an idealist. I am pained by conduct which falls short of my ideal.'

'Yes, you have such ideas, Georges.'

I shrugged my shoulders. 'I am afraid, Berthe, your philology has been neglected. *Ideal* is not quite the same as *idea*, you know.'

'*À quoi bon? Enfin*,' she said, 'I am alone for the whole house. You all sit all day long, no one does anything.'

'Berthe, my uncle is waiting.'

Dressed at last—without a vest, without even pencilling my brows that morning—I dashed out of the room.

30

In the dining-room, standing still for a while, was Uncle Lucy, a spectacled individual with a modest sandy moustache and a small pointed beard. He was pale; the only colour in his face was in his nose. 'Quick. Quick. Quick,' he said, 'no time to waste.' He explained that his family who had arrived late in the night were now at the hotel—all the lot of them quartered in three bedrooms, that the hotel was full to overflowing, and ruinous, and asked if he could bring them all over to our flat.

'But, uncle, we have scarcely any beds,' I said, with dismay.

He waved his hand—a gesture which reminded me of his sister Teresa. 'Anything will do,' he said. 'We can all sleep on the floor. Plenty of room'—he pointed round at the skirting. 'Times are different. Come on.'

'But wait, have some coffee first, Uncle.'

'No time to waste. Quick. Quick. Quick,' he said.

The clock on the shelf had just struck half-past six. We helped each other on with our coats, and went out into the street.

At the corner of the street we hailed a cab and drove on to

the hotel in the cold early morning air which bit at my ears. My uncle, I noticed, had large hairy ears, and did not turn up his collar. Uncle Lucy was very deaf, and hating to ask me to repeat my questions, replied on the off-chance, or not hearing my answers, nodded and meditated upon them. Before we alighted at the porch of the hotel, Uncle Lucy remarked that the whole back of my British warm had been besmeared with tar by my leaning against the back of the seat, and my uncle became very worried and apologetic as though it had been his fault. 'A little soap and benzine,' he said. 'I'll get it out for you with soap and benzine when we get back.' Uncle Lucy kept looking worried and taking another look at my soiled British warm and saying 'Soap and benzine,' but I only thought that sitting there without a vest I might catch cold, develop pneumonia, and finally die altogether. He insisted on paying for the cab when we alighted; and took me straight up to his bedroom.

Here I saw Aunt Molly, a tall, stout, milk-and-blood complexioned woman with small, kindly, brown eyes. She kissed me on the cheek, and her own glossy cheeks smelt of scented soap. There were two little girls tucked away in a big bed: one dark, the other fair; for both of whom Uncle Lucy was responsible. Whether Aunt Molly was equally responsible—for both or merely for one, and if so, for which of the two—was altogether less certain. For Uncle Lucy, I believe, was an infidel in these matters. But never mind.

'Your lost cousins,' said Aunt Molly.

'Which is which?' I asked, bending over them and kissing their wet mouths.

'This is Bubby—the darkie. And this fair one is Nora, our last.'

'And how old is Nora?'

'Two and a half,' Nora replied for herself.

'How many children have you got altogether, Uncle Lucy?' I asked.

He began counting them on his fingers—but got muddled in his score. He had been married more than once. And he had acquired so awfully many.

'Just wait a moment,' said Aunt Molly. 'I will bring Harry to you.'

I waited, and presently I heard muffled exhortations and a stubborn shuffling of feet behind the door. 'Harry!' urged my aunt.

'No!' said Harry, backing stubbornly and fighting his way out. But she dragged him in by the hand and brought him to me, confused and reluctant—a small boy of four with forget-me-not eyes.

'This is Harry,' she said.

He was dreadfully shy; he had seen a photograph of myself in military uniform, and was frightened of the sword. But left alone with me, he soon brightened up and began telling me about a dog he had seen run over in the street. 'Poor, poor thing!' he said. 'It was bleeding all over.'

'But why didn't you want to come and see me?'

'Because I didn't know what you were like.'

'Well, am I better than you thought, or worse?'

'No, I thought you were more worse.

'Will you play in my room?' he asked in a while.

'No. I am—frightened of you.'

He looked at me with encouragement. 'Why are you frightened of me? I'm very nice. That's all I can say. Are you frightened of cows?'

We passed into the other rooms. And only now did I understand what it meant to have Uncle Lucy launching on our accommodation. He was accompanied by married daughters, husbands, nurses, fiancées, and relatives-in-law of every sort. I was confronted by strikingly good-looking flappers who turned out to be my own hitherto unseen cousins, by boys of sundry ages, by babes and sucklings, by grown-up men and women, all, I perceived, related to me very closely, and bearing my own disconcerting name. Besides, there was my uncle's eldest son, a landscape painter, a promising young lad of about thirty-nine, who spoke a lot and drank a lot and painted little. Their knowledge of the English language was unequal. The little ones, who had an English nurse, conversed like natives. Their elders spoke with difficulty. For this their father was to blame. Uncle Lucy did not share Grandpapa Diabologh's passion for travel; he had been nowhere. Since his birth in Manchester he had not been out of Russia. The only sort of English people Uncle Lucy knew in

Russia were Lancashire mill hands and mechanics who called themselves 'engineers'—a term which, in Russia, implies a College degree. But as the Russian technical graduates possessed less natural aptitude for machinery than the English mechanics, there was some justification in the Englishmen's claim to the coveted term 'engineer'. These English mechanics, however, not having impressed Uncle Lucy by their refinement or education, he decided to send his sons to Switzerland and to Germany—countries of which he had had the highest account—and they returned with cheeks disfigured by sword cuts, and talking of a *Wechsel* in English when what they meant was a bill of exchange. And as Aunt Teresa now greeted them: 'How are you?' one of them said: 'Very nice,' while the other replied 'Very good.'

By various means these people and their luggage had been transported to our quarters. In the hall as I arrived was Nora. She stood there—a little mushroom under a mushroom hat. A little walking mushroom grown up in the night, it seemed—while Uncle Lucy wasn't looking. The children's overcoats and warm overshoes were removed in the hall, and at once there was heard a loud hoof-clatter—their strutting all over the rooms. Besides, there was a boy of one and a half, Aunt Molly's half-grandson called Theo, with long flaxen locks, who, having seen Don, at once toddled after him and pulled him by the tail.

I went to the office and returned a little before lunch. But in this short space our flat had already been turned into a squealing nursery and a bear-garden.

There were more human things about than there were beds and chairs and sofas, and when you rose you had to take care lest you stepped on some sprawling little Diabologh. The drawing-room, flooded by a host of relatives, was a babel of voices. Captain Negodyaev was standing talking eagerly to Uncle Lucy, who listened to him, with head slightly bent, through an ear-trumpet. Uncle Lucy had been a bit of a democrat in his day, and when the revolution came he hailed the revolution. But when the revolution, in its evolution, dispossessed him of his property, he thought the revolution was a mistake. Captain Negodyaev also thought the revolution a mistake, and it follows that Uncle Lucy and Captain Negodyaev had that in common that both thought the revolution a mistake. 'Bolshevism is a state of mind,' said Captain Negodyaev, with the air of enunciating a profound philosophical truth.

'An acquisitive state of mind,' retorted Uncle Lucy, laughing bitterly.

'Very truly said,' rejoined the Russian officer, nodding his head. 'We family men in particular feel the truth of this assertion. I have, Lucy Christophorovich, two daughters: Màsha and Natàsha. Màsha is away with her husband, Ippolit Sergèiech Blagovèschenski, in Novorossiisk. She's married, as I said, but is not happy. Poor Màsha! But Natàsha's here. Natàsha!' he called. 'This is Natàsha.'

Uncle Lucy beamed at her through his gold-rimmed spectacles, and touched her approvingly with his thumb and forefinger on the delicate chin. He then searched a long time in his pocket-book, and gave her a 200,000 rouble note—then worth about one and a penny. Natàsha curtsied and went away, beaming.

'Look! Look!' came her voice from the corridor. 'Harry, look!'

'That's nuffink,' said Harry. 'Daddy gives me—oh much more.'

'Oh, what a nice little girl!' Aunt Molly patted her cheek.

'Unfortunately, things being what they are, Marya Nikolaevna, her education is being neglected. Still, she is learning English without knowing it, which pleases me a great deal.'

'Oh, she can already speak English? What is your name?' Aunt Molly asked Natàsha in English.

'I don't know myself,' she said. 'I have two kinds of name, and I don't know what kinds it is.'

'She came out under her mother's maiden name so as to conceal her father's,' I explained.

Aunt Molly patted her again on the cheek; then went into her room, and returning gave Natàsha a banana. Natàsha curtsied, and went away beaming.

'*Ach*! Marya Nikolaevna, my heart aches for poor Màsha,' Mme Negodyaev was saying. 'Ippolit is a terrible man. You won't believe me if I tell you——'

Captain Negodyaev called Harry and gave him a caramel.

'What do you say?' said Uncle Lucy.

'Thank you,' said Harry.

'But when they broke into the cabinet and took away the

portfolio with all our ready money, well, both Màsha and I don't think it was a very nice thing to do, anyhow.'

Uncle Lucy, who, after a life of toil and authority, found his enforced idleness very irksome, offered to help Vladislav chop wood. 'There are so many of us now. All must help.'

'No, Lucy, don't be a fool,' Aunt Molly gently dissuaded him.

And Vladislav himself was not anxious. 'This is no proper work for a gentleman,' he was telling Uncle Lucy, who was getting in the way with the axe and retarding the man's work. 'You, sir, leave this to us who are used to it. In France——'

But Uncle Lucy, brushing the dust off his palms, had returned to the drawing-room, and, for want of anything better, was examining the pictures on the walls: all as dull as life. The children, strutting with a loud hoof-clatter all over the rooms, were saying:

'I like *this*.'

'And I like *this*.'

'And I like *this*.'

'And I like *this*.'

Till Aunt Teresa issued orders to stop that noise. Nora hopped about on one leg, with her tongue between her teeth in the effort, and her brother Harry, hardly taller, lounged about with an independent mien, his hands in his pockets. 'I have a dressing-table,' he said proudly.

'And I have a dr*a*ssing-table!' she echoed—and showed me the mantelshelf.

'Is this your dressing-table?'

Yesh.'

Harry came up and whispered in my ear: 'We tell her so s'e shouldn't cry. S'e's only a baby.'

'And this is my b*a*d,' she said.

'Silly! This is not a bed. It's a sofa,' he said.

'This is my shofa,' she said.

'I see this is where you sleep?'

Yesh.'

'Isn't she a lovely little thing? Come, lovie,' he said, embracing her.

'Why do you call her lovie? Is that her name?'

'No, her name is Nora Rose Di-abologh. Her name is Miss

Di-abologh. But I call her lovie. S'e's only a baby,' he said.

'And does Nora love you?'

'Yes. I love her and s'e loves me.'

'How do you know?'

'Because when I tell her: "Nora, put your arm round me", s'e puts her arm round me—and kisses me.'

'Your little sister is not a fool, Harry, you know.'

'No, she isn't.'

'And you're not a fool either, are you, Harry?'

'No, but daddy is.'

'Why?'

'Because mammy says so.'

Uncle Lucy stood in the middle of the drawing-room, his hand on his ear-trumpet and close to his ear (but talking himself all the while), and spoke of the heavy losses he had sustained, and expressed a fear lest soon he would lose all his possessions. 'Ruin,' he said. 'Irretrievable ruin.'

'*Courage, mon ami! Courage!*' said Uncle Emmanuel, smoking calmly a long, thick cigar, and he gave a smack on Uncle Lucy's shoulder—not too hearty, however, because he was still a little uncertain of his *beaufrère*. Although he had suffered material damage at the hands of the Bolsheviks, Uncle Lucy, I noticed, was not unsympathetic to certain aspects of their programme, and hoped that by their publication of secret diplomatic documents they would put an end to the immoral diplomacies of the past. Among other things, he expressed faith in the League of Nations. Uncle Emmanuel, on the other hand, professed a cynical naïveté in regard to human affairs. He did not believe in the League of Nations, laid stress on the inherent wickedness of human nature which he scornfully considered incapable of improvement and, moreover, had no wish to improve. Uncle Emmanuel had never profited materially by his cynical attitude, and had never had a penny of his own, and had all his life been fated to play a cringing role both before his superiors and his own wife. To Uncle Lucy, who had been a bit of a Socialist and withal a very rich man in his days, Uncle Emmanuel said: 'I respect your ideals, your impractical aspirations; but I am a man of facts, and have no faith in highfalutin theories: my purse is my politics. Yes.' And he looked round for applause. But as most of us knew that there was nothing in Uncle Emmanuel's purse, this statement was received without enthusiasm.

The dining-room was reorganized on the principle of treble shifts, and Aunt Molly, a big, full-blooded woman, presided over the long table surrounded by a multitude of her kin. Aunt Teresa, heavily powdered, bejewelled and wrapped in old lace, sat in a great arm-chair, propped up by pillows, a little to the side, to emphasize as it were that, unlike the others, she was an invalid. When she spoke across to Uncle Lucy she raised her voice with an air of self-sacrifice as though it were a cruel strain on her nerves. '*Ach!*' she sighed, when he did not catch what she said. And when she repeated louder the words she looked at the others to imply that she did so at the cost of her delicate health. When he spoke to her she closed her eyes, as though it were trying to her to make herself listen to his loud unaccustomed voice, as yet not modulated to her sensitive ear. Uncle Lucy continually asked questions about the progress of the Russo-Polish war, in which he was much interested, but could not hear my answers, and so turned to his wife. But Aunt Molly's intellectual powers had been sapped by a dozen children to whom she had given birth, and in her rendering of my account she mixed up events and issues in such a way that my uncle, withal a clever man, perceived at once that there was something very wrong about it. In desperation he turned to his son, a lout of eighteen, sitting at his side. 'What did George say?' he asked, and listened through the ear-trumpet.

'The Russkis have defeated the Polyakis,' the lout said right into the ear-trumpet.

'Speak up. Can't hear you.'

'George says,' shouted the lout, 'the Russkis have defeated the Polyakis.'

'Shame!' cried my uncle. 'Shame!' And I wondered what was a shame and why my uncle's Russophile sympathies should have turned Pole. 'Shame!' said my uncle, 'that you, an Englishman, can't talk English better than that.'

The lout shrugged his shoulders. Seeing that he had never been out of Russia and never spoke English at home, it was a wonder he spoke it as well as he did. Towards the end of lunch Vladislav brought my coffee machine. In forty-five minutes the coffee machine yielded enough for one small cup. Nevertheless, being polite, I asked Uncle Lucy if he wanted coffee, and devoutly hoped that he did not. But, as usual, he did not hear what I said. He had not as yet got used to my voice.

'Do you want coffee?' I asked.

'What?'

'Do you want coffee?' I cried.

'What?'

'Do you want coffee?' I yelled across the table, so that my own voice reverberated in my ears.

'Speak up. Can't hear you,' he said.

'George asks,' shouted Aunt Molly, to whose voice Uncle Lucy happened to be peculiarly susceptible, 'if you want coffee.'

'Coffee?... Yes.'

'Curse you!' I thought.

Luncheon over, Aunt Molly rose, followed by her offspring, like a hen by her innumerable chicks—'Chuck-chuck-chuck-chuck-chuck...' They ran in front, behind, and to both sides of her, as she moved into the drawing-room where she sat down on a soft chair, an ample, milk-and-blood-complexioned woman with small, kindly, brown eyes, her chicks surrounding her. She had been married a long time, but they kept arriving each year like a birthday present, or sometimes for Christmas or Easter. And when you saw her surrounded by cherubim with the same brown eyes (or blue like Uncle Lucy's) you felt moved, you spoke and treaded softly, reverently, feeling you had stepped into a sanctum, the holihood of motherhood, as if into the presence of that picture of Raphael. Some were by other mothers, and some, no doubt, fruits of Uncle Lucy's infidelities. Even so, you could never tell by her demeanour. To her all were alike. She had protested against Uncle Lucy's love affairs by ignoring him. But she ignored him so gently and meekly that he never noticed it.

And here I overheard a fragment of a conversation between Uncle Emmanuel and Uncle Lucy which I judged had some small connection with the financial nature of their recent correspondence. Uncle Emmanuel, the officer—which suggests swords, courage, honour (of sorts)—said to Uncle Lucy, the landowner—skins, mills, commerce, bills of lading—'I respect you more than I like you.' And Uncle Lucy surprised me by his ready wit in replying, 'And I like you more than I respect you.' Uncle Lucy, though he held forth a good deal on his poverty, had a pocket-book bulging with bank-notes of a high denomination—foreign as well as Russian. He had small deposits abroad, that was all. The Bolsheviks had taken the bulk of his money.

Aunt Teresa came up to her brother, put her head on his shoulder and said, 'Oh, Lucy, pity me! I am so faint, so ill, so weak, so miserable! I won't live long!'

'Speak up! Can't hear you,' he said.

'Oh, my God,' sighed my aunt, and looked up to heaven. 'If father were alive and saw the plight we were in!'

He looked at her with compassion. 'That's all right,' he said. 'You will receive your dividends as before.'

There was a pause, our hearts beat as if in a hollow.

'We are in debt,' she said in a whisper.

'That's all right, you will get your arrears.'

There were tears in her eyes. 'I must sit down,' she said. Uncle Emmanuel lit a cigar.

'What a pretty and well-mannered girl—Natàsha,' Aunt Molly observed.

'Yes, I am very fond of her,' said Aunt Teresa, with a brightness and gaiety unusual in her, 'and I rather like her mother. Her father is a queer fellow, quite harmless, though I must confess I'm not enamoured of his face, and I wonder what he does with himself all day. He's very meek and mild and servile with everybody, but at home he bullies his wife. He suffers from a kind of mania of persecution, and every now and then he sounds the alarm, wakes up his wife and child in the middle of the night and bids them dress—ready for flight at a moment's notice. And there they sit, all packed and ready, in their fur coats and muffs and hats and warm goloshes. Then he declares "All Clear!" and sends them back to bed. This happens about once a month or so.'

Aunt Molly sighed. 'I'm sorry for him. He looks so pathetic hopping on his wooden leg.'

The children's manner of acquaintance making, in its directness, reminded one of that of dogs. Seeing a photo of Uncle Lucy on Harry's 'dressing-table', Natàsha said, 'Oh, is that your daddy? He is very nice.'

'Ah, but he's not nice to mummy,' Harry said.

'I have a daddy too,' Natàsha said.

'No, you haven't.'

'I *have*! That Rush-yan gentleman—he my daddy.'

'I know, but we don't like his face, and we wonder what he does.'

'*Ooh*——! Nasty, nasty, nasty!'

'He's not your daddy at all,' said Harry. 'He's the stork that brought you.'

Open-mouthed, she asked, 'What's it means stork?'

'Because he hops about on one leg.'

'Sylvia, don't wink!' said Aunt Teresa. 'The wedding'—she turned to Aunt Molly—'will have to be put off till after Christmas.'

Sylvia, grave and timid in the presence of elderly ladies, was all 'Ha, ha, ha!' at the approach of her many boy cousins.

'Do you mind putting off the wedding till after Christmas?' I asked.

She stopped laughing. 'Just as you like, darling. Ha, ha, ha!' She at once became lively again.

Entering the dining-room on my return from the office, I saw a roomful of baby cousins at their evening meal. Napkined at the neck, they sat close at table on chairs that were too low for them, their chins touching the edge of the table, gaping around and swinging their legs. Behind stood their mothers and nurses, who urged them on with fine exhortations. Nora ate an egg beaten up in a cup; she held a teaspoon in her mouth upside down and sucked off the egg that clung to its convex surface, while her eyes wandered all over the ceiling. 'Some more br*a*d, mummy.

'Say *please*.'

'Please.'

'Isn't she a mess!' said Beastly loudly, and nodded heavily and guffawed several times in the doing.

Harry's forget-me-not eyes matched the blue-lilac rim of the cup and saucer out of which he was drinking, holding it in his two little fists and looking out from above, his eyeballs rolling all over the room.

As she finished eating Nora crawled off the chair, and at once there was the sound of her hoof-clatter. Natàsha ran after her: 'Ah! little Norkin!' Nora's legs were something in the way of a ship's screw: they worked evenly enough, but somehow did not modulate their pace to the peculiarities of the surface, thus often, for sudden lack of resistance, performing in the air with unexpected precipitation, like a ship's screw when it is jerked out of the water. In the same inconsequential way, she ran into Aunt Teresa's bedside medicine table, which was more than Aunt Teresa's nerves could stand. And Aunt Teresa took the opportunity to tell Nora what a sweet, obedient little girl she, Aunt Teresa, had been herself when of Nora's age. Nora didn't seem to care a bit, and while Aunt Teresa talked to her, was making very deliberate movements with her arms, as though affecting to fly. Aunt Molly, who was tired out, and had seemed angry with the noisy children, now that she had a moment to sit down, related tenderly their intimate histories from the earliest years. Aunt Teresa and Berthe professed a polite but unconvincing amazement at these confidences. A certain lady in Krasnoyarsk, Aunt Molly related, had organized a drawing competition, and Harry won a prize.

'Fancy that!' drawled Aunt Teresa, lifting for a second her eyes from the fancy needlework at which she was an adept and letting them fall at once.

'How clever of him!' said Berthe.

'And when Bubby was barely one, and we used to ask her, "What has Bubby got good ?"—"Good appetite," she said.'

'Fancy that—remarkable,' said Aunt Teresa, and at once began counting the stitches.

'*Charmant*,' echoed Berthe.

'When Nora was barely two, one day I asked her, "Do you love me?" And she said, "Would you care me to love you?" "Yes, I would." "Then I love you *dearly*," she said.'

Berthe beamed and purred like a cat, and Aunt Teresa first counted the stitches. 'Fancy that,' she said, and smiled rather belatedly.

'Well, Bubby,' drawled Aunt Teresa, 'are you a good little girl? And do you love your mummy?'

'Yes, I love her very much. I have a little pram,' she said, 'and now all my doggies can have rides in it, because if they are always running about and walking they will get so thin, you know.'

Uncle Lucy, ashamed of his enforced idleness, walked about

with a hammer, a chisel, and a sore conscience, strenuously trying to be useful. He came up to my attic and, watching my typewriter, said that he could construct a machine which would work by electricity in such a way that if I pressed the keys in my attic the typewriter would actually perform the work in the basement. It seemed a wonderful invention, almost worth while patenting. But when questioned by me as to the actual advantage of the typing being done in the basement while I pressed the keys in the attic, Uncle Lucy agreed that there appeared to be no visible advantage in such an arrangement. He went away swinging the hammer, and wondering if there was anything by way of a nail anywhere that wanted driving in.

The flapper cousins slept in the dining-room adjoining my bedroom, behind screens. And I spent hours in kissing them good night. At the dead of night, again and again I would creep out of bed and, with the air of one who has forgotten something, slip into the dining-room behind the screen to kiss my red-haired cousin good night—long, lingering kisses…

I dreamt: a host of polyglots marching, an army of polyglots marching relentlessly, marching on, on, on, on—a stampede of feet.

31

A Nest of Polyglots

And in the morning Aunt Molly asked me not to blow my nose quite so loudly as it wakened up the children in the night. While I was shaving, Harry came into my room, followed presently by Nora.

'Do you know what Nora said to me today?' he began. 'S'e said, "Good morning to you." ' And noticing the soap on my face, he pleaded: 'S'ave me! S'ave me!'

'And how's Natàsha?' I enquired.

His face at that showed no enthusiasm. 'S'e won't let us do anything,' he complained.

'Oh?'

'S'ave me!' he said. And while I lathered his face, he stood quite quiet, with a look of beatitude in his forget-me-not eyes.

'Now s'ave Nora,' he said.

'Nora, do you want to?'

'Yesh.'

And I lathered Nora's face.

They watched me dress with interest. 'What is this for?' Harry would ask, fingering a suspender.

'What is this for?' Nora asked. What Harry said Nora said; what Harry did Nora did.

'Daddy has one like these,' Harry said, fingering my braces.

'Daddy has one like these,' Nora said.

'Only better ones,' said Harry.

'Only b*a*tter ones,' said Nora.

'Who's better, Nora or Natàsha?' I asked.

'Myself,' he answered.

The act of dressing, I noticed, conduces to a peculiarly primitive mood of jocoseness, and I continued asking silly questions. 'Whom shall I drown?' I presently asked. 'You or Nora?'

'Drown yourself,' he said.

'Drown yourself,' said Nora.

'Come on,' I cried, suddenly assuming a forbidding look on my face as I walked up to him and took him by the sleeve. He side-stepped and considered a moment, and— 'Go to hell!' he said.

'Harry!'

'Go to h*al*,' said Nora.

'Who has taught you such dreadful language?'

'Daddy,' he said.

'Oh, pour some on me, pour some on me—some of that hair stuff,' he pleaded, watching me. I poured some on his head, rather lavishly. He stood very still, with the same beatific look in his forget-me-not eyes. But when it ran down his cheeks he closed his eyes with a grimace.

'What's the matter?'

'It bited,' he said.

'Now pour some on Nora.'

These interruptions of my morning toilet considerably retarded my routine. Life, I observed, was not worth living: by the time I had risen, shaved, washed, bathed, dressed myself, and so on, the day was gone, and it was time to go to bed. This was our life. A large family in a small flat—all doing this all day long. The activity was all directed towards getting clean—during which process they all got dirty again. The atmosphere of the place was sleepy and conducive to day-dreaming. Dusk fell soon in the winter. The heavy curtains were drawn, shutting out the icy-cold dusty snowless streets of Harbin, with the brilliantly illuminated windows of the shops closing down one by one as the town sank deeper into twilight, and we dwelt in the warm nicely heated rooms with the sumptuous leather sofas and chairs and the shaded lights behind silk Chinese screens embroidered with flowers and birds. The Chinese boys moved like ghosts, noiseless, in soft satin slippers on carpeted floors, listless shapes in long spotless white gowns. There was repose, soft, sumptuous repose writ large over the quiet interior; but when you entered Aunt Teresa's rose-coloured bedroom, and saw her in bed, about half-past five in the evening, among medicine bottles, family photos, especially those of her son, books, cushions, cosmetics, a writing-pad, a red leather *buvard*, screens on all sides, the rose-shaded light burning behind her, the scent of *Mon Boudoir* perfume lying in wait for you and stealing insidiously over your senses, you trod more softly than ever, you spoke in a whisper, you yawned, stretched, and yearned to wrap the quilt around yourself and yield to happy dreams.

Only the children were somewhat at variance with the atmosphere of rest. Nora would fall down suddenly from the most unlikely places. Once she fell from the top of the stairs, landing forthwith, without touching any intermediate steps, seated upright, on to the bottom step—palpably against all the essential propositions of the law of gravity. 'I did get a fright,' she said. The small children now had their meals before ours, and having finished theirs, would come into the dining-room and watch us eat—whereat Nora always begged for 'br*a*d'. But Harry, more reserved, only looked on from afar as we were eating (when there was something to be got he always went off and looked on from a distance), and when asked what he wanted would say, with some feeling: 'I'm not *asking* for anything.'

Nora was always eating, and when she wasn't eating she was drinking, and Harry was delegated by his mother to unbutton and button up his little sister's knickers—a duty which, in view of her phenomenal appetite and thirst, made a heavy demand on his time throughout the day. When there was any commotion or any unusual activity anywhere, there invariably came Nora's voice from afar, 'S'all right: *I*'m coming!' and there would come the uncertain hoof-clatter of her small feet, and the mushroom would toddle up on the scene of activity. Her name was Nora; nevertheless, she had light flaven hair combed and cut evenly over the forehead.

Natàsha and Harry liked playing at mummy and daddy together, Nora being the baby. But Nora did not care for the game, because they put her to bed, and she had to lie very still all the time; her part, in fact, differing so little from what she was in real life—'only a baby'. Whereas she wanted to run round the rooms stamping her feet, or to stand on one leg and make very deliberate movements with her arms as though trying to fly. But the three of them played together and developed a sort of tongue of their own, half-way between English and Russian, and there was, at first, a lot of 'vish!—bish!' about Natàsha's torrential English in which accuracy and everything else was sacrificed to speed. And it seemed as though this new language appealed to Harry and Nora, for when they spoke English they now purposely twisted the words as if for Natàsha's peculiar requirements. 'Give back, or no give back?' they would ask when accepting a gift. And when Natàsha spoke Russian to them she twisted her Russian as if to oblige them. They collected rubbish—all of them did. Harry took everything that Natàsha discarded, and Bubby took what Harry discarded. And what was no good at all for Bubby, Nora took. For a child coming from a Communist country, Natàsha displayed an astounding sense of property—even in rubbish, her rights over which she asserted with a vehement 'S'mine!' A claim to property sometimes disputed by the others with an equally determined 'S'mine!' And Harry would make off with some piece of rubbish of questionable ownership, when you would hear Natàsha's cries: 'What for you doing! What for you doing, Harry!' And rushing after him and being the stronger of the two by reason of age, she would snatch the thing from him—whereon Harry would give vent to his despair in Russian as he cried: '*Ne nado! Ne nado!*—This is *ours*!'—he had turned to me. 'Tell 'er it is *ours*. Tell 'er.'

Whereat Aunt Molly and Captain Negodyaev, having been attracted by the noise, smacked their respective offspring without investigation—mainly to oblige each other.

32

The Virgin

Our wedding was accordingly put off till after Christmas, Sylvia the while looking after Don or playing the *Four Seasons of the Year*. One of them—*Winter*, I believe—was so sad that as I listened tears came to my eyes, and I thought: how long? how much more? and, if one thinks into it deeply, really what for? The evening was in its full glory, perhaps a tarnished glory, a dying beauty cavernous with melancholy, as we went out. Uncle Emmanuel, who held a modest post in the Yugo-Slavian or some such Allied consulate, had made up a sort of uniform—it looked like nothing on earth, but it passed off as 'Allied'—and strode about in it seeking whom he might devour. Occasionally he would wear a monocle, but he complained that as he was short-sighted with both eyes the monocle was but a partial remedy. 'Wear two monocles then, one in each eye,' I advised. But he would have none of it. Uncle Emmanuel was anything but handsome and, to be exact, one-third my size, but imagined that he was irresistible to women, and now wore this home-made uniform in order, as he thought, to attract them the more. It is not easy to write of him. I can even think of a few people among my own acquaintances who would consider the revelation of these indiscretions as something, something—to use a strong term—not quite nice. I have a maiden aunt who would look upon all this as painful reading. But what do you and I care about such superstitions? It would be ungracious to condemn Uncle Emmanuel without trying to understand his nature. He had a passion for life, which to him was identified with the intimate charm of the feminine form in its greatest variety; and so he spent his days in quest of the red light. He was untrue to Aunt Teresa within the first week of their honeymoon, because he was a man who loved a lot. Uncle Emmanuel's good nature implied a belief in other people's good nature that sometimes was a little naïve. That night he booked a double bedroom at the hotel, for himself and his new friend—a charming brunette. But on the following morning when he intimated the desire to prolong his stay over the week-end he was informed that as the hotel was undergoing repair he must vacate his room by 1 p.m. that day. My uncle caused at once enquiries to be pushed, and was informed that if he travelled up three versts or so by rail he would be certain to obtain a room at a family *pension*—whither he and the brunette immediately repaired. The *pension* by its originality and charm exceeded all his expectations. Uncle Emmanuel explained that he was an Allied officer who had come out to help the Russian national cause. The nice old landlady—a Lutheran from the Baltic Provinces, a kind, God-fearing soul—was all wreathes and smiles. She understood the situation: an elderly military, a loyal Ally, just wedded to a young Russian wife—and naturally impatient. She would see that his honeymoon was as pleasant as can be. She understood. She had once herself been young and had married a much younger man than herself of whom she had retained the tenderest memories. She would go all out to make my uncle's honeymoon (as she imagined) a success. She took him to her heart: yes, she had had a husband once: a little man—she showed from the ground—just like my uncle.

'*Ah, oui! Charmé*,' Uncle Emmanuel said curtly.

An ardent lover nevertheless, it seemed. She cherished his memory. I translated this too to my uncle, who stood, a little impatient, with the tall brunette on his arm.

'*Ah, oui! C'est ça*,' he said, somewhat indifferently.

But he was dead, she confided.

He shrugged his shoulders.

'*Je regrette*,' he said.

Her watery old eyes looked at him tenderly. 'The gentleman bears his age lightly,' she said, by way of a compliment.

I translated this too.

It did not please him. It did not please him at all. *Age*! '*Enfin*,' he said, 'we cannot spend all our life standing here. Can madame give us a room?'

Yes, she would give him a room, one of the best rooms, to be sure. But her daughter had frank laughing brown eyes that pierced Uncle Emmanuel's soul, as he was signing the register. We at once ascended to the second floor where a tall, lofty, blue-papered room was assigned to my uncle, on the walls of which hung framed mottoes in German: 'Cleave unto the Lord'; 'God is our Refuge'; and 'Kept by the power of God'. She assigned for their exclusive use her private sitting-room, in which she sought to leave the newly-married couple, shielded from the glances of the curious, to their hearts' desire, and she undercharged them quite ridiculously for the food they consumed.

But just because she was good-natured, my uncle, a poor enough psychologist at the best of times, concluded that her good nature knew no bounds; and two weeks had not elapsed when he appeared again before the same (now somewhat grave) God-fearing dame, a little blonde, this time, upon his gallant arm, a rakish, cheery air about his face, as if to say:

'And here we are again!'

A veil over my uncle's doings.

On Saturday night there was a 'Gala Social-Democratic Ball' at the late Officers' Assembly building, and as Sylvia did not feel very well I had arranged to take my red-haired cousin. I was engaged to Sylvia—and this was as far as it went. The incredible tedium of our relation at this stationary point in our romance became intolerable. After a day spent side by side in Aunt Teresa's drawing-room one longed to shoot oneself. To account for my impending absence in the evening, I told Sylvia that I was dining with a General. She said nothing—looked sad.

In the afternoon on our way home to tea I bought a box of chocolates for my red-haired cousin, and another box for Sylvia who had come into the shop with me. 'This is for you.'

'And who's this other box for?'

'This other? For the General,' I said.

She said nothing, only looked wretchedly sad.

'What's the matter?'

'Oh, nothing,' she sighed.

(She already knew all about the red-haired cousin.) But she took the chocolates—and sadly, sorrowfully, went her way.

And as my red-haired cousin and I ensconced ourselves in the cab that evening, Sylvia, who had a sneezing cold, came out on to the balcony in her great coat—with the dark-brown curls dropping on her shoulder and the swollen upper lip she looked unkissable and unkempt—and watched us drive away.

The 'Social-Democratic Soirée' turned out a little 'too democratic' for the liking of my red-haired cousin. As we walked together in the ball-room, sunflower seed shells and orange peels were being dropped on us from the gallery, as a matter of course, and soldiers and sailors elbowed their way through the thronged space of the vast assembly-rooms.

'Who's that tall man with the long beard, who looks like Tirpitz, talking to the British Consul?' asked my red-haired cousin.

'That's the famous General Horvat.'

'What a beard!' she exclaimed.

'Yes. There is an anecdote attached to it. Some Allied diplomat had asked his wife: "How does your husband sleep: with his beard over or under the blanket?" "That depends upon the season," she is said to have replied. "In the summer, when it's warm, he likes to air his beard by keeping it above the blanket. But in winter, to keep himself warm, he tucks his beard under the blanket." '

She laughed at that, a little insincerely, as if mainly for my sake.

As the 'soirée' wore on, incidents occurred. Somebody had hit somebody else over the head with a beer bottle. Somebody had shot himself. Some officer had challenged some other to a duel —over nothing. To our surprise, we fell across Uncle Emmanuel—in somewhat doubtful company, I fear, comprising a notorious card-sharper, a secret service spy, and a young woman of the *demi-monde*.

'May I introduce you to the mistress of my brother?' said the card-sharper, as I approached. 'But I must warn you—and our friend here (he pointed to the spy) will confirm it—General Pshemòvich-Pshevìtski is her lover.'

'Nonsense!' said the lady. 'He only says this to ward you off. You don't know him. He is madly jealous of me.' She turned to Uncle Emmanuel and whacked him with her fan across the arm. 'Why are you so serious? Look at me, I am so gay, I'm always laughing. Ha, ha, ha!' Which sent a chill of gloom through our souls—and no one spoke.

'I hope you don't believe a word of it,' she turned again to Uncle Emmanuel. 'He's always telling awful things about me because he wants to ward you off and keep me to himself. That's why I do not love him. I can only love one who himself is pure. How I wish, Serge,' she turned to the card-sharper, 'that you were pure.'

'You ought not to wish that, my dear.'

'Why not?'

'You ought to love your equals.'

'What's this?' asked Uncle Emmanuel, and smiled sardonically when it was translated to him.

'What!' she turned on him. 'How dare you! Oh! Oh! *Oh*!'

She raised a desperate, terrific hue and cry.

'Madame, I assure you. I assure you, madame,' blubbered my uncle. But she continued screaming; and people rushed towards us and surrounded us, while she shouted something incoherent about a medical certificate—and then fainted.

'Come away,' I whispered to my uncle. 'For God's sake come away!' And having reclaimed my red-haired cousin from her dancing partner, we all left by a side entrance.

My red-haired cousin once escorted to the door-step, my uncle turned to me and timidly suggested going to the baths. I knew what these baths were like, and hesitated.

'You're married,' I reproached him.

'Well, and what of it? Can't I dine once in a while at a restaurant just because I have a kitchen at home?'

The contention seemed too reasonable to be disputed.

Dawn was just breaking as we set out for the baths. My uncle looked elated and pleased with himself, and sang (as if by way of adding zest to our adventure): *'Nach Frankreich zogen zwei Grenadier...'* He had been a German scholar in his day, which language he had studied with an eye on future military requirements, and he was fond of trotting out his knowledge on occasion. When I walked side by side with Uncle Emmanuel I took longer strides than I am accustomed to—in order as it were to humiliate my uncle. He was a little man—one-third my size—and ran beside me like a small fox-terrier, while I barged forward steadily like a big ship at the side of a tug endeavouring to puff up steam.

At the baths we were escorted into separate but adjacent

'numbers', each consisting of a dressing-room and bathroom, from where steam rose as if from the funnels of a railway engine.

Presently the Chink attendant came into the room.

'Soap?' be asked. And I translated for my uncle.

'Yes.'

'Loofa?'

'Yes.'

'Towels?'

'Yes.'

'Birch-twigs?'

My uncle considered.

'Yes,' he said.

'Nothing else?'

My uncle nodded.

'Japanese?'

My uncle shook his head.

'Russian?'

My uncle nodded.

The Chink went out, slamming the door, and his steps on the stone floor resounded loud and sharp in the hollow corridor. We sat silent, our hearts thumping. Uncle Emmanuel, a little shamefacedly, played with his watch-chain. It was stifling hot. Then he heaved a half sigh of relief, and said timidly: '*Que voulez-vous*?'

It was equally hot in my 'number'. Beads of perspiration ran down my face, and lingered on the tip of my nose as, crouching, I peeped through the keyhole into my uncle's domain.

Presently the door opened. Some lithe thing in a black hat and black silk stockings flitted past the keyhole and obscured my view. The black hat came off.... There was a rustle of crisp garments...

I do not know how all this strikes you. I am a serious young man, an intellectual, a purist, and disapprove of Uncle Emmanuel's sedate irregularities. A veil over my uncle's doings!

And now the Chink came into my room.

'Soap?'

'Yes.'

'Loofa?'

'Yes.'

'Towels?'

'Yes.'

'Birch-twigs?'

'Yes.'

'Nothing else?'

But I fear I am diverting from the purpose of my story. I came out feeling clean, pure, sanctified, as I rejoined my uncle. Such an uncle! He put his finger to his lips as we paced home through the slippery, frosty streets:

'*Silence, mon ami*!'

I was silent enough; and he held forth, as if in self-excuse:

'What I always say is this: outside, do as you like, it harms no one. But *chez soi, dans la famille*, which is the pillar of society, the sacred hearth, *le* 'ome…ah! that's another matter. On *that* point I am adamant. *Évidemment*, some husbands are not very *sérieux* nowadays and allow themselves *des bêtises* with the chamber-maids or—*enfin* with the cook. I *never*! *Jamais de la vie*!'

I was a little angry with my uncle—and said nothing.

'This,' he said, 'seems to me a very interesting building.'

'It only seems so.'

'Still, I think——'

'There's nothing to think.'

'What's the matter with you?' he asked.

'Leave me alone.'

'*Enfin*! you are not even polite today.'

I looked at him with hatred. 'Uncle though you be to me, I curse you!'

For a moment Uncle Emmanuel appeared to be a little staggered—but recovering, retorted: 'And I curse you, too!'

33

A Nice Lesson For a Purist

Next day—a Sunday—being Aunt Teresa's birthday, Uncle Emmanuel, following a long-established custom with him, recited two stanzas of verse of his own composition (but with a strong flavour of Musset) which he had prepared upon returning from the baths, comparing his old bride with birds and flowers, stellar brightness, and the pale beauty of the moon—while Aunt

Teresa complained a little more than usual of her nerves that day. The General, his aide-de-camp son, Dr. Murgatroyd, and a few others—of the local 'diplomatic corps'—had called on her that morning to tender their devoted homage. My aunt believed that it was only natural (since I was her nephew) that I should hold a high, exalted post, and to please her, I styled myself the 'British Military Ambassador'. And she considered that as I was the 'British Military Ambassador' our flat enjoyed extra-territorial rights and was in fact British soil (though being up on the fourth floor of a house owned by a private Russian citizen it didn't of necessity touch any soil at all). That claim was further strengthened in her view by the fact that she herself was born in Manchester. This impression grew so firm in the minds of all who dwelt in our flat that one day when the postwoman barged in rather clumsily and was abused by Vladislav, and, provoked, began to shout at him: '*Ach*, you yellow-haired devil, you!' etc., Vladislav silenced her with a terrific 'S-s-s-s! You ugly, cross-eyed old hag: this is not your Russia here to shout in; this is *England*, understand!'

For lunch there was a special menu, and as asparagus au sauce mousseline was just being served, there was a ring at the bell and Vladislav came in to say that a lady wished to see Uncle Emmanuel. He rose, and some little time afterwards he sent for me. The lady was the lady of the social-democratic ball. Being interviewed by me, she explained that she considered Uncle Emmanuel implicated in the question of her personal honour, he having laughed improperly at the insinuation questioning her purity, which she now wished to vindicate. It was a delicate situation. The lady pointed out that she had already gone to the expense of obtaining a Russian medical certificate, and now demanded a Belgian document to the same effect.

I hate sordid details (I am by temperament a romantic), but I translated to my uncle, who stood there, the colour flushing to his cheeks, his hands in his trouser pockets, an indignant man, a family man whose sanctum has been rudely invaded. '*Ah mais! Ce n'est pas un hôpital, par exemple!*'

I translated: 'My uncle says this is not a hospital.'

'Quite. I want,' she said, 'a medical certificate.'

'Madam, I am not a doctor,' I protested.

'*Madame, nous sommes des militaires et point des docteurs.*'

'Quite,' she said, 'but you must have a Belgian doctor.'

'*Ah, mais c'est une...une légation, quoi*!'

'This is a military mission—an embassy,' I translated.

'Strange—an embassy and no doctor!' she exclaimed.

'*Enfin, madame, ce n'est pas très délicat.*'

'This is not very delicate of you, madam, my uncle says,' I translated.

'But I want to see your doctor,' she looked at me.

'Madam, I'm not a doctor, I am... a censor.'

'But you must have a doctor.'

'*Je vous demande pardon, madame*, we haven't got one,' said Uncle Emmanuel.

'But it is nonsense, you must have one!'

'*Ah, je vous demande pardon, madame*, it is not nonsense.'

Vladislav expressed the wish to chuck the lady out. But Uncle Emmanuel, whose motto was 'Live and let live', protested: 'Oh, no, why? Why have a row? This is not a public bar, this is *un* 'ome, no *scandale* here, no, no!' In fact, he was not against meeting her outside—but never in the home! For in her own way, let me confess, the lady was not ill-looking. But he was diffident about making an appointment with her in my presence. I was courteous and patient, remembering that I was, after all, the 'Military Ambassador'. She too calmed down, but seemed to gain in muddleheadedness.

'You understand,' I said, 'that this is the British Mission, not a hospital.'

'Aha! I understand...I understand. In that case I'll come again tomorrow.'

'No, madam, you've come to the wrong place!'

She considered.

'Aha. In that case,' she said, 'I can bring my passport and my birth certificate.'

We sighed and then stood speechless, gathering breath.

'This, madam, is no doctor for you; this is the *Military* Ambassador, the *military* embassy,' said Vladislav, with an impatient air, as if he thought we were incapable of driving this piece of information into her.

'Where then is the other embassy?' she asked.

'The Consulate,' I said—by way of getting rid of her.

'Aha,' she said, 'in that case give me an introduction to the Consulate.'

'Get out!' said Vladislav impatiently.

'In that case,' said she, 'I'll come again tomorrow.'

He closed the door on her, and sighed.

'In France,' said he, 'they wouldn't have listened to her.'

No sooner had the lady gone than Vladislav handed me a card from an unknown lady with the words 'Daughter of an Actual-State's-Councillor' engraved beneath her name. Asked what I could do for her, the lady said she wished to thank me—generally.

'Generally? For nothing in particular?'

'Yes, yes, yes,' she said eagerly, smiling beatifically. Yes—and to present me with a pamphlet written by herself on the subject of phonetic spelling. I promised to peruse the document with care, but she continued calling on me several times a week to impress upon me that the problem of the abolition of the letter *yat* as well as the *hard sign* was of a magnitude and urgency such as the Allies in their task of reconstruction could not conveniently ignore. Till, thoroughly exhausted by the lady's pertinacity, I recommended her to the attention of my American colleague—and wished him joy of her. But he retaliated on me with a lunatic who claimed to be none other than the Emperor Francis Joseph desirous of being restored to his original position, and who henceforth petitioned me to that effect. One day, worn out by visits from the Austrian monarch and the daughter of the actual-state's-councillor, I dispatched them both together to my U.S. colleague, in a car, and wished him joy of both.

'This is terrible,' said Aunt Teresa, as I came into the dining-room.

'What is terrible?'

'Stepàn has come back again.'

'H'm.'

Stepàn was our coachman. Aunt Teresa with her delicate health could not walk much but had to take the fresh air, and so a carriage with two meagre mares and the bearded, disreputable-looking Stepàn was kept for her use, at the side of whom on the soft, sumptuous box Vladislav sat dressed up in a second-hand livery. Stepàn was a fatalist, and to all questions, including those of apprehension at his driving, would say: 'All is possible.' His attitude to life, if indeed he had one, was one of abject resignation. And of late Stepàn had taken to drink and had spilt Aunt Teresa. When she warned him not to upset her again, he said: 'All is possible'—and indeed spilt her again. After which she dismissed him. Two months ago she had dismissed him, but he remained in his bunk, taciturn and resigned, and nothing, it seemed, would dislodge him. For half an hour, perhaps, he would go out in the night and then come back to his bunk.

'Why not lock the door of his bunk while he is out?'

'There is no lock,' she replied.

'H'm.'

I spoke to him. Vladislav spoke to him. Uncle Lucy, too, spoke to him. We all spoke to him, and I got Captain Negodyaev to speak to him. But Stepàn would not budge from his bunk.

One day it seemed as if Stepàn had gone, and Vladislav, reporting the news, crossed himself with relief. But in the morning he informed us that Stepàn had come back in the night.

'Send for the General,' at last said Aunt Teresa.

The General arrived soon after three o'clock. '*I*'ll talk to him. *I*'ll manage him, rest assured,' he said when he had had his overcoat removed, and rubbing his hands, proceeded to the drawing-room, '*I*'ll tackle the skunk. Bring him in here.'

'He won't come here,' said Aunt Teresa. 'The trouble is that he won't go anywhere. He won't go away.'

'*I*'ll go to him. *I*'ll talk to him. *I*'ll manage the skunk, never you fear.'

We followed the General into the stable, above which the coachman Stepàn had his abode. The General kicked open the door of Stepàn's den without undue ceremony. An incredibly odious smell let loose on us, like a wild beast, so that for a moment we were, despite ourselves, forced back into the passage and the General pulled out his scented handkerchief and applied it to his nostrils. But Stepàn sat listless in his bunk, with a queer, peculiarly enervating look of complacent sullenness in his face, and never uttered a word. 'The skunk!' said the General, and at once began threatening the man. But Stepàn never uttered a word.

'I give you three minutes in which to clear out, do you hear, you skunk?' shouted the General. 'I'll this—I'll that—and I'll the other thing——'

But Stepàn never moved or uttered a word.

'You skunk!' shouted the General. '*Ach*, you bad subject! Why, I'll take and hang you by the nose on the nearest fence, you *bestia*! You grovelling reptile! You crocodile!'

But Stepàn never moved or uttered a word.

The General spared no pains. 'Am I talking to *you* or am I talking to this wall, you incredible blackguard?' he shouted again. And he cursed him, *and* he cursed him, *and* he cursed him, up and down, this way and that way, lengthwise and sidewise and crosswise and roundabout: '*Ach*, you son of this, and you son of that, and you son of the other thing.'

No good: Stepàn did not stir.

The General resumed with added zest, with renewed vigour, with incredible gusto. After a time he stopped, to take breath and to examine the effect which his threat had had on the man. It seemed as though it had had none.

'Tough stuff, these people,' the General said, and wiped his moist brow. 'Ugh! I've even perspired. I once had a batman—Private Solovyov. I was talking to him, do you know, as though he were a human being like myself—*talking*, you understand. His look was a blank—less intelligent than a cow's. Only when I began using strong adjectives, dragged in a few choice epithets bearing directly on his family tree, made mention of his mother, and so on, all in the recognized old way—"*Ach*, you son of a——" and that sort of thing, don't you know, well, then, and then only, his face began to light up as though after all there *was* a glimmering spark of reason lingering somewhere in that skull, and then, by shades, by grades, as I persisted with my adjectives, would you believe it, he almost became human; and actually said: "Quite so, your Excellency." This is the material we've got to deal with. Yes... Here nothing is possible. Nothing can be done with this *canaille*. And how are you?' he turned to Aunt Teresa. He looked at her tenderly. The sun played on his wrinkled brown eyes.

'I'm—as always. But this coachman, really——'

'Where does he come from?' he asked.

'Little Russia, I think.'

'Nothing to be done. Nothing to be done with that race! And what have you been doing with yourself all this time?'

'I suppose we'll have to keep him?' she sighed with dismay, her look betraying the suspicion that she no longer hoped great things from the General and thought that his bark was rather worse than his bite.

The General sighed and looked pensive. 'He may take to heart what I told him and go. I'll come again tomorrow, anyhow, and see.'

It was all of no avail. The coachman came back the same night. The General called the next day as he had promised. 'Tough stuff, these people,' he sighed when he heard the news from Aunt Teresa. 'As I told you, I had a batman once, Private Solovyov—a hard case, but in the end I managed to knock a spark of reason out of that skull. But this——' He sighed. '*Here*...nothing is possible.'

34

Green grow the leaves on the old oak tree...

As Christmas approached the children began to think of presents. The Russian Christmas was thirteen days later than ours, the reason being, according to Natàsha, that Father Christmas could not possibly be in two places at the same time. The children liked going to the big shop in the Kitaiskaya where, besides the splendid Christmas display, there was a man dressed up as old Father Christmas, who had to shake hands all day long with all the children who came to the shop in a long stream; and he seemed very angry and irritable, being more than fed up with his job. But the children revelled in him, such as he was. Berthe had bought a pair of scarlet felt slippers for Nora with scarlet *pompons*, and was knitting a little striped jumper to button her in, while Uncle Lucy was making three little chairs for the three little bears to sit on. Harry and Nora had no doubt in their mind as to what they wanted, and at night, before going to bed, spoke up the chimney: 'A peddling-motor, please.'—'A perambulator and a doll, please.'

'What would you rather have: a little horse or a little doll?' I asked Bubby.

'A little horse and a little doll.'

'And you, Nora?'

'Sometime when you have a *specially* lot of money——'

Well?'

'A *r*ittle house.'

'A doll's house?'

'Yesh.'

'And what is Father Christmas bringing you?'

'A perambulator and a doll.'

'Both at once?'

'I 'hink so,' she said.

On the afternoon of the 24th a parcel arrived, with a card from General Pshemòvich-Pshevìtski, addressed to Aunt Teresa and Sylvia, which, being opened, turned out to contain two sets of crêpe-de-Chine camisoles and knickers of Japanese make; Sylvia's being pink with little Chinamen stitched out by hand all along the border.

'Oh! how beauty! Oh! what a lovely!' Natàsha exclaimed as Sylvia held them up for inspection. Aunt Teresa's were green but without Chinamen. She was both confused and yet, I think, secretly flattered by the gift. It seemed too impudent for words—if the General had had any kind of...suggestion in mind. That he had coupled her with her daughter seemed reassuring. And yet, could he have had any thought of Sylvia's wearing them?—that alone was too impudent—and she even felt jealous. How tactless the man was, to be sure—the tall man with the stiff black moustache and the closely-cropped hair turning grey. Much, of course, must be forgiven him, since he had risen from a plain policeman! And, after all, he had just been over to Japan, and anything in silk was a natural gift in the circumstances. That was the trend of the innuendoes that she had exchanged with Berthe. But the knickers were nice and reminded her of her youth—though in her youth they didn't wear such knickers.

The whole week before Christmas had seemed unusually dull. Melancholy life. When I was a child home for the holidays, I sat on the hat rack and imagined I was a bird. The passing of the day, twilight—just like now in the Far East. And 'Far East' suggested that we were far away. But far from what?—the world after all was round.—A dreary day. You stand still, your nose pressed against the cold pane, and watch the movement in the street: life is passing swiftly. You are bored by life, but it is passing much too quickly: worse, you stand here at the window in Harbin and you think you ought to be somewhere in Adrianople. And it would seem that whatever you did—if you were to run out into the street, shout, dance, work, forget, go on a voyage, engage in politics, drink, marry, love—it would slip away even more quickly while you did not reflect; and the moment you tried to envisage it you would be leading again a still life.

Christmas Day was a cold but snowless and sunny day, and I was wakened early by Harry, who had come in for his present.

'What is it?' I asked.

He smiled his old man's smile, a little confused. 'I'm not *asking* for anything,' he said.

There was another shuffle at the door.

'Ah, Nora in her pom-poms!' said he.

She came up, a little mushroom, smiling all over, in her red shoes and striped jumper.

'Have you *bought* me something?' she said.

'You mustn't *ask*,' he whispered in her ear, stooping to do so. And both stood waiting. When they had got their presents they at once ran away with them.

In the dining-room was Natàsha—so pretty, so fragile, so happy in her new white and pink frock. 'Look me! Look me!' she said, turning round. 'Shut your eyes and open your mouth.' And I ate a chocolate. 'There will be trifle cakes, *vinaigrette*, meat, tea, pastry, cocoa!' she said roguishly.

'What nice shoes you have.'

'4.25,' she said.

'Shanghai dollars?'

She shrugged her shoulders, sucking a sweet the while. 'I don't know what's it means. Daddy bought them.'

She stood on, wondering why I was not admiring her new frock. She had curled her hair with paper overnight so as to enhance the effect upon Harry. 'Oh, I wonder what will Harry say when he sees me in my new dress! He will say, "Oh, Natàsha, isn't it beauty!" '

Harry came in, and Natàsha waited for him, a little confused, to notice her frock. But taking no notice, he said, 'Where's that peddling-motor?'

There wasn't one. Father Christmas up the chimney flue had played him false.

'Oh, damn!' he said—and smiled.

When Sylvia came up, like a China rose, in her champagne georgette, Natàsha relapsed into ecstatic delight: 'Look, look! What a beauty thing! Oh! Oh! Look!' And, indeed, Berthe's present could not have been more welcome.

'Ah! little Nortchik!' Natàsha cried as soon as she saw her, and at once began hopping about—and then lifted her by the waist, which you could see was no great satisfaction to Nora, to judge by her face. 'Leave me alone! Leave me alone! Stop it!' she said.

There she stood—like a little mushroom, red-cheeked, awfully appetizing.

'Isn't she just a little apple dumpling?' said Aunt Teresa. 'Come on your old auntie's knees, you little applie-dumplie.'

Nora climbed up Aunt Teresa's knees and putting her small arms round her neck tenderly—'Auntie Terry,' she said, 'have you *bought* me something?'

'Have you seen my dress, Harry?' Natàsha ventured.

'H'm...yes!' he said, looking at her, while she beamed all over. 'Have you seen Nora's pom-poms?'

'Shut your eyes and open your mouth,' she said.

Which he did at once.

'That's not a sweet!' he cried, spitting out the silver paper, while Natàsha laughed aloud her gurgling, bubbling laugh, hopping and clapping her palms together in ecstatic mirth.

While we were at our Christmas dinner, the virgin called, and Uncle Emmanuel went out to speak to her, and she pestered him for a Belgian certificate. His Christmas pudding was quite cold when he returned.

At four o'clock the tree was lighted. Uncle Emmanuel, who had donned his made-up Belgian uniform and waxed his moustache with especial care, gave Harry a toy motor which, being wound up, ran across the room and up against the wall. But Harry was very peevish and could not be prevailed upon by Uncle Lucy to take the slightest interest in the toy motor. 'Look here, Harry, look here,' Uncle Lucy urged—to save his own face and possibly to spare Uncle Emmanuel the sense of humiliation. But Harry would not look and turned his back to it. 'It's no good! I can't get *inside* it,' he said—when *Slap*! his father landed him one over the ear. Not at once, but as if on mustering enough self-pity, Harry began to cry softly. 'Come, come,' said the people surrounding him. 'I want a peddling-motor,' he sobbed, drying his tears with his fist. And thinking of it, he cried louder and louder and louder, until he had to be given the little cupboard Aunt Teresa had given Natàsha, my aunt promising to get Natàsha another one *exactly* like it immediately the holidays were over. Natàsha was reluctant. 'No, s'mine! s'mine!' she said. But Captain Negodyaev, out of deference to his hosts, at once ordered her to give it up.

'To keep?' asked Harry, incredulous, accepting the gift, with the old man's smile coming over his tear-stained face.

Natàsha cried softly.

'I will get you another one, Natàsha, a better one,' drawled Aunt Teresa. And Aunt Molly gave Natàsha a copy of *Uncle Tom's Cabin*, intended for Harry, to placate her for the temporary parting with the cupboard. Natàsha smiled through her tears at the book. 'No give back?' she asked.

'No.'

And she smiled away the rest of her tears.

Meanwhile the candles were flickering, rapidly burning down...Melancholy life. How it passes! even while it seems to hang so heavily on your hands. A little more, and we shall join the throngs who went before us. Then why don't we make haste and live? But how? How make the most of life? If you grip it, it runs through your fingers. While music played hilariously, life seemed to have stopped. Ah, if it were never to move on again I'd bear it: but it's stopped—and then, next moment, it will slip away—into the dustbin...What the deuce was the matter with life? I liked, for instance, spending Christmas in other people's homes because then I liked to think of my own home; but I never liked being at home. The children, who were between the ages of ten and fifteen, were all shy and reluctant, and I think looked on this Christmas tree as a nuisance. 'What extraordinary, unnatural children!' demurred Aunt Teresa. 'You *should* enjoy yourselves like everybody else!' Alas! You either do—or else you don't—enjoy yourself. There is no 'should' about enjoyment. Uncle Lucy was shy, too. Aunt Molly alone was sending forth sounds of 'Green grow the leaves' at the top of her not very agreeable voice, to her own not very efficient accompaniment on the piano, and urging us to join in. But no one did—at least not for some time. We stood around the wall sulkily and shifted awkwardly from one foot to the other, and perhaps regretted that Jesus Christ was born at all. Besides ourselves there were Stepàn's little nephews and nieces—evil smelling things with hair greased with butter—who also stood at the wall and shuffled their feet. At last, with some difficulty, and thanks to Berthe's initiative, the mechanism was set in motion: we began to go round, gingerly at first and feeling somewhat foolish, but gradually gaining confidence. Tall Uncle Lucy, small Uncle Emmanuel, Captain Negodyaev with the wooden leg—all but Aunt Teresa—went round the tree merrily. I thought: a few more æons, and we shall have joined the vast battalions which lie in wait for us and possibly begrudge us our temporary advantage. Why then is life so peculiarly unsatisfying? Why is there a streak of sadness, a deep strata of melancholy beneath all joy? 'Green grow the leaves of the old oak tree. Green grow the leaves on the old oak tree. They waggled and they jaggled and they never could agree: till the tenor of the song goes merrily.

'Merrily-y—merrily-y—till the tenor of the song goes merrily.'

'Gleen glow the leaves on the ole, ole tree,' sang the small children, while Nora lagged behind—

'navver could aglee——'

'They razzled and they jazzled,' came from Bubby, Harry, and Natàsha, and Nora sang—

'and the t*a*nner of the song——'

'Mère Lee——! Mère Lee——!' came Berthe's piercing soprano, a rendering which was an outrage on the national atmosphere of the song. 'They razzled and they jazzled,' Nora sang in her own time and tune, while—

'Gleen glow the leaves' came from the other three, when Nora, making up by a bounce, would cry—

'could *aglee*——!'

And Berthe shrieked like an engine whistle—

'Mère Lee*eee*——!'

From the many lighted candles the room had become very hot. Beyond the drawn curtains, Harbin was eclipsing into twilight, amid cries of Mongol drivers and the sound of cracking whips, the sense of two rival civilizations bordering on each other, the piercing wind sweeping the barren, naked streets, raising clouds of cold dust, and the town mercilessly cold but snowless, miserable, like a sleepless sufferer or a tearless heart. The wax candles burnt down sadly. The smell of burning pine. Music, laughter—and I wanted to weep for all living things. Oh, why must we live? Half realized revelry! Whom were we pleasing? A mere interlude—and then back. Back at the heart of the universe, listening to the beat and the waves universal rising and falling and breaking in and about us, dreaming of all things and none, sleeping—what deep, wholesome sleep—for ever and ever and ever.

The three little chairs of the three little bears were put in a row. Berthe, who had a 'working knowledge' of music, sat down to the piano, and Aunt Teresa, as a special dispensation on account of the high festival, joined her, brushing aside her long, black silk skirt as she sat down on the plush stool beside Berthe (who had moved on to a plain chair), and the two women struck together the opening bars of Liszt's Rhapsody No. 2, the children the while playing musical chairs. Harry moved very close to the chairs, ready to drop into each and even sitting down for a space and refusing to move on, and having fallen out of the game, joined again imperceptibly and strove irregularly to compete for a chair as before. Aunt Teresa and Berthe were belabouring the rhapsody, my aunt swinging her body a little to the always accelerating galloping rhythm, as though she were an expert musician, or else an expert horsewoman—or both. And possibly because the passage they were interpreting was one of chaos, they never noticed a discrepancy till Berthe turned the page. '*Voyons donc, Berthe*! I'm not yet half through the page!'—'*Enfin, Thérèse*!' Nor had *we* noticed anything, for chaos it should have been: and chaos it certainly was. The music having abruptly ceased, the children made for the chairs, and Nora fell out.

After supper Dr. Murgatroyd was talking of the psychology of the Koreans in the light of the teaching of Confucius, when he suddenly discovered that, leaning back against a table with a lighted candle on it, he had burnt a hole in the seat of his trousers. From the adjoining room came Beastly's resonant voice: 'No, my dear sir, you can't get out of that—ha, ha! Sit down, here you are, here's the pen and here's the ink, and get about it—ha, ha, ha!' he guffawed loudly.

'See here, man, you sit down right here, and write to your Marshal,' spoke Philip Brown's stern voice.

'But ze *maréchal* he be astonished,' protested Uncle Emmanuel excitedly.

'Never you mind, old chap. You write him a letter and ask him for the autograph, quick.'

'*Allons donc! le maréchal* he askèd for ze French Red Cross, and ze French Red Cross zey getted nothing. You send it all to American Red Cross.' Flushed in the face, Uncle Emmanuel expostulated: 'Excuse to me, 'ow can I ask? He askèd where is ze money. I say, Zey send it all to *Amérique! Nom de Dieu, enfin!*' protested Uncle Emmanuel, all his muscles agog with excitement.

'They're Allies—ain't they?' Beastly interjected.

'Sure we are!' said Philip Brown.

'Why, my dear sir—ha, ha, ha, ha!—you don't know your own silly business!'

'*Comment*?'

'Come on yourself! Get down to it and write to the Marshal for the autograph, here, now.' The two men standing over him, Uncle Emmanuel sat down to his desk and, with tears in his eyes, began to write to the Marshal.

The three little bears played nicely together, having moved their three little chairs round the table, though now and then Harry upset their shop, and then you heard Natàsha's voice: 'Harry! Harry! What for you doing !' and also you heard Nora's voice: 'Leave me alone! Shu*p* up! Harry! *Leave me alone*! Stop it! *Stop it*!'

'Whatever is the matter?' Aunt Molly asked.

'Nora's eaten my chocolate-cream,' Harry wailed.

'Because he's eaten my Easter egg last year!' Nora cried eagerly.

Slap! Slap! Slap! came from Aunt Molly—and tears galore from the children's eyes.

Then they played as before. They exchanged with each other some of their presents. 'Give back?' 'No give back?' or 'To keep?' Harry changed his chocolate stick with a little boy for a watch. 'I gave him this,' Harry said, looking the while at the watch. 'Is it worth it?' The little boy ate the chocolate stick and then cried and wanted his watch back. Harry pricked Nora's balloon, and, watching it, I thought: I'd like to die like that—fizzle out.

'Harry's been kicking Natàsha!' Nora complained to her mummy. But Harry, who heard this, only called out 'Nora!' put his arm round her, and off they ran together happily, neither of them caring a straw. Only Bubby played demurely alone.

At half-past ten, just before retiring to bed, Captain Negodyaev had a relapse of persecution mania, and he bid his wife and daughter dress—ready for flight at a moment's notice. They sat in the hot drawing-room, all dressed and ready, in their fur coats and muffs and hats and warm goloshes, till he declared 'All Clear!' and sent them off to bed.

Towards bed-time the children were overwhelmed with presents. They were dazed, almost unhappy: Nora dying from fatigue. Washed and put to bed, she knelt up and prayed: 'Gentle Jesus meek and mile look upon a little chile pity my s-s-s-simplicity. God bless mummy and daddy and granpas and granmas and uncles and aunties and cousins—and Cousin Georgie.'

Then Harry, too, rose on his knees. 'Green grow——'

He stopped. An impatient wave of the hand—'Not that!'—and fell dead asleep.

35

After Christmas our wedding was postponed till after the New Year. 'Do you mind, darling?'

'No, just as you like, darling.'

I looked at her tenderly. 'Lovie-dovie-cats'-eyes.'

'This is too soppy, darling,' she said.

Since early morning on New Year's day visitors had been calling on us. Franz Joseph came. The spelling lady came. The virgin came. After the virgin and the daughter of the actual-state's-councillor, there came a morose-looking Russian major general with pale mad eyes, whose conversation was largely incoherent. I was besieged by them, yet I liked them. They were good, well-behaved lunatics, trim and neat in their diminutive, harmless lunacy, compared with our war lords in their raving, disorderly madness. They were floating in a sea of bewilderment and confusion, but we who were waging this colossal war with seriousness and with method were more destructively futile in our pretensions, more grievously self-deluded. The world had got unhinged and was whirling round in a pool of madness, and those few lunatics were whirling independently within ours: wheels within wheels! And I received them with courtesy, to the pained astonishment of Vladislav, who, pointing at Franz Joseph, said: 'In France they wouldn't have spoken to that man.' So sensible and nice and relevant they were in their own little world of delusion that we, big lunatics, who were engaged in making war and revolution, allowed the little lunatics to roam in peace at large: out of a latent instinct of proportion that it would have been absurd to lock them up in the face of what was being done by admittedly sane people in our midst. Asylums and prisons were open: indeed, not in Russia alone. To give Europe her due, 'retail' murderers had been invited to vacate their prison cells to participate in the wholesale murder going on galore upon the battlefields.

There also came a Metropolitan. The *vladika* apologized for calling on a holiday—but the affair was urgent, for he had the welfare of the Orthodox people at heart. It was vodka—the undoing of many a weak soul in the past. For years and years the Government had seen fit to poison the Russian *pravoslavnie* people. The time had come, he thought, for the Church to take a stand. What should be done? Well, yes, he knew what should be done and would be glad if I could see my way to urge his scheme before the General. The vodka monopoly should be transferred forthwith to private interests. There was a powerful financial syndicate prepared to purchase the monopoly and he was in favour of their doing so, on conscientious grounds, for verily the Government could not continue this systematic intoxication of the *pravoslavnie* people. He was in touch with them. Yes, the syndicate were willing. He—well, ye-es, he had been approached by them.

'But,' I faltered, 'the systematic intoxication of the *pravoslavnie* population is to go on at that rate?'

The holy father leaned back and flung open his hands, just as Uncle Emmanuel was wont to do when he said, '*Que voulez-vous*?' He paused.

'Well, that would be a matter for their own conscience,' he said at last. 'We cannot control everything.'

'I see. The syndicate would then be personally responsible to God for the intoxication of the *pravoslavnie* population?'

'It is immoral for the State to poison the people it is called upon to govern,' said the Metropolitan, with a glint of righteous anger in his eyes. 'Private enterprise is another matter.'

He left me with the distinct impression that private enterprise was indeed another matter. And I equipped him with a card to Dr. Murgatroyd.

General 'Pshe-Pshe' (as we now called him for short) brought with him Count Valentine—a thin, ungainly individual with a high-pitched voice, whose one redeeming feature was his title. All afternoon I sat in my room in the attic and faked New Year's messages for Aunt Teresa, purporting as it were to come from local Jap and Chink officials and their wives, and as I showered them upon my aunt, she would exclaim: '*Tiens! Encore! Ah!*'—delighted at her popularity—while I went up and typed again. Natàsha stole up the stairs like a kitten, and entreated: 'Play with me, oh, *play* with me!' while I typed on, 'General and Madame Pan-La-Toon send greetings of the season to Monsieur le Commandant and Madame Vanderflint and wish them happiness in the New Year.'

'*Tiens! Encore une! Mais voilà un déluge!*' Aunt Teresa cried, opening the missives and smiling happily at Berthe. It quite reminded her of the old days.

36

Aunt Teresa Gives a Ball

It was already the middle of March, but the winter was still on, white, crisp, impenetrable. Aunt Teresa had become a social centre of the town; and perhaps what added zest to the adventure was the knowledge that our polyglottic presence in Harbin was only temporary—as temporary as life on earth. We specialized in being nice to everybody. Only the children were rather naughty. They would come up to any guest, however stolid, and say: 'You are awfully ugly', or Bubby would comment on her mother's looks as Aunt Molly came down the stairs in a new dress: 'Oh, mummy, you do look a fright!' We were an unusual set of people caught in an unusual set of circumstances and conditions. I like to think that we had, by the play of accident, escaped from much that has become threadbare and stereotyped in life. In the world war, the Russian revolution, things had taken place, strange shiftings of families and populations of which little has been heard as yet but the effect of which will tell one day

In the day-time I was censoring all manner of telegrams and letters—an indictment of the war: that anyone should waste his time and talents on being a military censor. Personally, of course, I didn't care a hang about the letters. It seemed to me that in a chaotic sea of gloom where age-long grievances sprang up like fountains to the surface, to censor private letters which someone wrote to someone else in the Far East of Russia was a farce to be enjoyed as such and nothing more. At this period I worked upon a thesis (for, as I have said, I am an intellectual and do not take wars very seriously)—a thesis named: *A Record of the Stages in the Evolution of an Attitude*. I would work in my attic on the Evolution of an Attitude and then run down to the drawing-room to kiss my red-haired cousin—and having thus refreshed myself, return to work. Life, in the meanwhile, was going on. One had a sensation—living like this far away in the East—that one was out of it all, out of touch with all the seething mental activities of the West. But the chances were, if one tried to ascertain the truth, that at the headquarters of Western thought the thinkers, wearied of the hollow mechanism of the West, were putting out their feelers towards the hollow mystery of the East. But one thought not of that: and so one felt 'out of it all'. When one scanned the glazed pages of Anglo-Saxon magazines and read the advertisements of new razors and fountain pens, how to cure oneself of gout, train one's mind, get an appointment, combining business with pleasure, grow hair, preserve one's complexion and teeth, furnish a house with all the latest conveniences, control one's digestion and liver and purchase new shirts, one felt that far, far away there *was* a 'progressive', sensible life, that one was wantonly missing the benefits of one's age. And one felt particularly 'out of it all'.

Do you follow my story? Are you interested? Is it all perfectly clear to you? Very well, then, let us go on. On Thursday, the 22nd, Aunt Teresa gave a ball to celebrate my betrothal to Sylvia. Aunt Teresa sent out gilt-edged cards to His Excellency General Pshemòvich-Pshevìtski *et fils*, Count Valentine, Major Beastly, Lieut. Philip Brown, U.S.N., Colonel Ishibaiashi, of the Japanese Imperial General Staff, Dr. Murgatroyd, and, although they shared our flat with us, Captain and Mme Negodyaev. And the orchestra from the American Flagship, which Brown had promised us, not having arrived, General Pshemòvich-Pshevìtski helped us out with a military brass band.

Count Valentine called the same afternoon and left a card of the size of a postcard which read:

COUNT VLADIMIR VSÈVOLODOVICH VALENTINE;

Assistant-Director of Posts and Telegraphs; Assistant-Inspector of Communications with the title of Acting-President (with plenipotentiary powers) of the Special and Extraordinary Conference convened for the discussion of questions arising in connexion with the requisition of quarters allotted to members of the Allied contingents in the Far East, and the unification of measures for the defence of the State against the enemy; and Supreme Inspector of the Provisional Commission for Inland Revenue.

And across the print he had written in pencil:

Called to tender congratulations on the occasion of the birthday of his Majesty the King of England.

But as I met him on the stairs it gradually transpired that the driving motive of his call had been to ask for British underclothing and possibly a pair of Army Ordnance boots. Count Valentine explained that his noble name derived from England and that for that reason he favoured English clothes. He bent down and felt my cavalry boots and said, 'Pretty.—I wonder where I could get a pair like these.' He fiddled with a button on my tunic. '*Très chic*! I should rather like a jacket made after your model if you will allow me to take it home with me for a few days. Unfortunately all my wardrobes have remained in Petrograd and I feel so dreadfully uncomfortable in these unbecoming clothes.'

I looked at him and thought: 'Your one redeeming point is that you are a Count.' He bowed again and again, and then vanished, still bowing.

The cold wind cut me in the face and wet snow fell in flecks from the dismal sky and vanished as it reached the ground. I drove home, elated and content. The house was being got ready under the competent direction of Vladislav. Sylvia, radiant, splendid, was dressing for the ball. Her shoes pinched a little at the toe and she was easily tired. I came up from the back. 'Lovie-dovie-cats'-eyes.'

'This is too soppy,' she wrinkled her nose.

But at the ball one somehow felt (if not behaved accordingly) as though one did the ball a favour by being there at all. 'Pshe-Pshe *fils*', the General's aide-de-camp, a short and freckled youth wearing the Don Cossacks' uniform, danced the mazurka with Sylvia, stamping his feet and jingling his spurs and falling down on one knee with superlative skill. There were many young ladies and as many young men, among them a French naval Lieutenant with a touch of grey on one brow, and Gustave Boulanger, a local Belgian bank official of about thirty-five, with a small yellow moustache, a large broad chin and small teeth. And each time he smiled he revealed a black tooth at each corner of his mouth. 'Ha, ha, ha, ha, ha!' Sylvia laughed. Surrounded by young men, she would at once begin laughing and be all 'Ha, ha, ha!' But Gustave Boulanger never said anything. He only stroked his broad chin with his two fingers and smiled.

By the side of my aunt was Dr. Abelberg, her latest physician. Aunt Teresa was always changing them, because as a general rule they found that there was nothing much the matter with her, and this she could not endure. It was as though they robbed her of her natural prestige. Aunt Teresa had long grown to look on death and sickness as her own peculiar monopoly and told us frequently that we would not have her with us very much longer. When Berthe fell ill with influenza my aunt resented it as an effrontery and gave it out as her opinion that there was nothing much the matter with Berthe. The last doctor but one had told my aunt that she must use her legs, go out and take a lot of exercise, play golf if possible; and she at once dismissed him as a bear. 'An unfeeling fool,' was her comment, 'who doesn't know his own business!' Until in Dr. Abelberg it really seemed that she had found her man. And naturally she had asked him to the ball. He stood beside her, a tall man of forty with a head as bald as a billiard ball and black hair on the temples; an affable man with a manner which is acquired from constant attendance on very nervous and difficult patients; a doctor whose sole force of argument in prescribing a medicine was that the medicine he prescribed could not do any harm. I sometimes wonder whether doctors die like flies because they have no layman's health-imparting illusion in the curative properties of medicine, and by involuntary auto-suggestion hasten their own doom.

'Must I go to Japan in the spring, Doctor?' she asked.

'To Japan... Well...'

'I know I ought. I ought, I ought!'

'Well, yes, you ought.'

'But you know I can't. How can I?'

'Well, I don't think there is any need—yet. It wouldn't do you any good. In fact, it might cause harm. Stay where you are and listen to my advice.'

'The Doctor keeps telling me that health is the first thing in life, don't you, Doctor?' she said, with a sly smile.

'Why, you can't pay too high a price for health.'

'I guess she pays you quite enough—ha, ha, ha!' guffawed Beastly.

'If I had better health,' she sighed, 'I would enjoy life. I would go to the Opera. As it is, we've only been twice—to *Faust* and to *Aida*.'

'I heard all about it,' the Doctor observed with a bow.

'Who from?'

'Friends. They said you were greatly discussed and looked charming.'

'When was that?' asked my aunt.

He looked puzzled and taken aback. 'Oh... Wednesday night.'

'Why, that was long ago—in the summer,' she said. 'I haven't been out anywhere since then. I was laid up all Wednesday. I had a most terrible *migraine* in the night. Indeed, at one time I felt so bad I thought I would not hold out.'

'I know, I was very anxious about you—very anxious indeed. Hope you feel better now.'

'Doctor,' she said, 'I think I must start taking *Ferros ferratinum*.'

Raising and dropping his forefinger, 'Best thing for you,' he said.

Indeed it seemed that she had found her man.

In the long interval Gustave Boulanger, who had a high but very weak tenor, was enjoined to give us a song. He coughed a little, stroked his throat in a nervous gesture as though adjusting his Adam's apple. Tuning his wind instrument. One had the feeling that unless he set it to the proper pitch, his voice might break out in quite another clef. His throat adjusted, he sang *Ich grolle nicht*, to Count Valentine's able accompaniment on the piano, but out of deference to Aunt Teresa and her deceased son he pretended that the words of the song were not German but Dutch. But my aunt did not care; besides, she knew German, and it was the Belgians themselves who had killed her son in the war.

When he finished, we applauded vociferously. But Gustave never said anything. He only stroked his broad chin with his two fingers and smiled. While Count Valentine was still at the piano the Chinese boys brought trays with little glass plates of ice-cream, and General 'Pshe-Pshe' approached to where Aunt Teresa was sitting, with a plate of strawberry-ice in his hand.

'No, thank you, General. The Doctor has forbidden me to have ice-cream.'

The Doctor looked pensive. Then:

'It's all right in my presence,' he said. 'Only don't have the strawberry-ice.'

'But I hate vanilla!'

'Well, it is really of no consequence. Only eat it very slowly,' he said.

While the dance was in full swing and Vladislav had strayed away from the front door, the virgin came in and while nobody was looking fainted in the waiting-room.

'Impossible! Impossible!' cried Aunt Teresa when Vladislav reported that a young woman was lying dead on the floor in the waiting-room.

'Impossible!' the Doctor echoed.

'But who is she? I say this is impossible!'

'Impossible!'

'But, Doctor, she's alive!' cried Aunt Teresa as she beheld the virgin twitching on the floor.

'Oh, yes, as a doctor I can confirm that fact.'

'I didn't believe it.'

'Nor did I.'

'Is that because of the heat in the room, Doctor?'

'Distinctly the heat,' he bowed.

She sighed. 'Well—it's hot in here.'

He sighed too.

'*Chaleur de diable*!' muttered Uncle Emmanuel.

'Telephone at once to the hospital,' commanded Dr. Abelberg.

'Telephone!—' repeated Vladislav in abject tones. 'Why, you can telephone, of course, or else not telephone. It's all one. In France there are properly equipped hospitals and things. But here'—an abject gesture—'you are safer at home than in the hospital. The other day they took my cousin to hospital, which was full up; they put the poor fellow on the floor in the corridor; he was still where they'd put him two days later, and on the third gave up his soul to God. "We've no time to bother. Told you we're full up," they said. And by the time they looked at him again his skull had split in two against the skirting.'

We tried all the hospitals, but all were full to overflowing; and it fell to Berthe to nurse the virgin back to life.

Aunt Teresa the while had returned to the drawing-room where General 'Pshe-Pshe', in a melancholy mood, was saying:

'I am not understood! Not understood by my wife, not understood by my daughter, not understood by my son; never! You alone (he brushed her pale hand with his prickly black moustache), you alone! Here I'm content. This is my spiritual home.'

Dr. Abelberg was the last to go.

'And what then, Doctor?' solicited my aunt, as she took leave of him in the drawing-room.

Folding his fingers as he spoke, Dr. Abelberg said: 'Salt baths morning and evening. Cold and hot compresses. Gargling before and after every meal. Tranquillity, tranquillity, and once more tranquillity.'

'And what about *Ferros ferratinum*? Leave it?'

'Leave it!'

I followed him out into the hall.

'Doctor,' I said, 'tell me about Aunt Teresa. Is there any real cause for anxiety?'

'Ah!' He waved his hand in an airy gesture and bent down to my ear. 'I wish I had her health,' he whispered. 'Why, she's as strong as a horse.' And he bid me good night.

37

Exodus of the Polyglots

After the ball Count Valentine called to tender his congratulations on the occasion of the birthday of his Majesty the King of the Belgians, and incidentally enquired if he could not have a Sam Browne belt like mine. General 'Pshe-Pshe' also called.

Closeted with Aunt Teresa, 'I am not understood,' he said, 'not understood by my family. But here in your midst I can rest, here I'm at home.' He brushed his prickly moustache against her slender hand. Tears came into his eyes. 'Yes,' he said. 'Yes.'

The wedding was to take place immediately a portion of my uncle's brood had left for England. The first batch of Diabologhs—comprising mostly sons-in-law and married daughters, nurses, sucklings, Theo among them—sailed on Thursday. At the station while we waited for the train, another babe came up to Theo, and in the simple way that babies have, bit him on the brow. The second batch of Diabologhs sailed on Saturday. My red-haired cousin sailed. The first clean-up, the first big sweep had been made, and one began to see one's way in the remaining mass, discern familiar faces. It looked as if at last Sylvia and I could marry in God's name and live in our own flat without encumbrance. Uncle Lucy remained with Aunt Molly and the small children. He walked about with a long face, swinging a hammer and trying to be useful, but looking thoroughly out of his element. Poor man! It was not the fault of his face: he had a soul that didn't smile. Also he had purchased roubles—and his pessimism on that count alone would seem rational enough. And already news had dribbled through that the first batch of Diabologhs had arrived in England and that my elder cousin, the artist of a modern school, for lack of other suitable subsistence, was now engaged in painting bicycles in Sussex; but still we two were not married. The War Office had obviously been losing interest in our adventure. Pickup was recalled. This was the first sign. And then, one day, there came a missive foreshadowing our complete withdrawal before long from the Far East. As I passed on the news at dinner Aunt Teresa's breath seemed to catch in her throat, and she looked a little pale. 'But what will you do? You cannot leave us all alone? And we cannot go to Europe with you as we have no means! Can't you write and tell them this at the War Office?'

'Can I be——' The last word was not spoken.

'Can't he, Emmanuel?'

'*Ah, mais non, alors*!' exclaimed Uncle Emmanuel, in tones of outraged military propriety.

'Strange! These people at the War Office understand nothing!'

The wedding had been fixed provisionally for April the 13th, but Aunt Teresa seemed sad, reluctant, and avoided all discussion tending towards any definite decision on this point. 'You never think of me, you never think of your poor ailing Aunt Teresa,' she complained, insinuating that my impending theft of her one remaining child was hard on her.

'I do. I always think of you, *ma tante*. I think: "Lord, how lucky for her to have such a splendid nephew!" '

My aunt did not behave as though she thought this was a superlatively brilliant joke; and, on second thoughts, I was inclined to agree with her that it wasn't.

'Naughty! Naughty!' Natàsha said, after a pause, shaking her finger at me. 'Naughty!'

'Georgie-Porgie, pudding and pie,' said my aunt.

'Georgie-Porgie,' she laughed her bubbling laughter: 'Georgie-Porgie-g-g-g-g-g.'

I looked at my aunt with compassion. Poor woman, she seemed to me a mental, moral, physical, and above all financial, wreck! 'You see,' I said, conceiving suddenly the thought of curing her by auto-suggestion, 'there's really nothing much the matter with you except what you yourself imagine. What you have to say is: "Every day, in every way, I am feeling better and better." '

'But I don't. *Enfin, c'est idiot*! How can I say I feel better if I feel worse?'

'Take care: you *will* feel worse if you say so.'

'But I do.'

'And I wish you joy of it,' said I, exasperated.

'But what *can* I say if I feel worse and worse? Do you want me to lie to myself?'

'Then say: "I feel the reverse of better and better." '

'Is that all right?'

'Well, at any rate it's better.'

But nothing came of it. Aunt Teresa told me that she had *une crise de nerfs* from my auto-suggestion. She assured me she felt worse. My aunt was not a good disciple of Monsieur Coué. The crux of it, of course, was that she did not want to feel better, or in fact to make us think she did so. But the small children took to Coué like duck to water. While my aunt felt worse and worse, Nora told us she felt 'b*a*tter and b*a*tter'. What it came to, anyhow, was that those of us who had felt bad didn't feel so well, and those who had felt well, felt well and better. The Doctor said that Aunt Teresa was not really ill. But Aunt Teresa thought that she was ill, and to all intents and purposes she felt the same as if she had been ill. Clearly then she had a 'complex'. I began to think of using for her benefit the discoveries of Freud and Jung with a view to liberating Aunt Teresa's 'complex'. I had only read a few pages of Freud's Introductory Lecture to Psycho-Analysis, while waiting at the Oxford Union for a friend. I knew, however, that the pith of the whole thing was that the 'complex' had to be dissolved to free the patient of his particular delusion or affliction. Clearly Aunt Teresa was in love with her own person. This, at any rate, was my diagnosis of her case. To 'side-track' my aunt's affections from Narcissus into normal channels had now become my earnest purpose. But I was not a little nervous lest, according to Freud, my aunt's Narcissus were 'side-tracked' on to me and she began to love me with a passion not entirely becoming to an aunt. I began by delivering a lecture on psychology. I spoke of motor-centres and bus centres and railway centres and the reflections of the conscious and subconscious mind—and that sort of drivel—for an hour and a half. My aunt listened strenuously and tried to look as if she understood. 'There is something in you that wants an outlet and cannot find it, and because of that is worrying you.' I took her hands into mine. 'Aunt Teresa dear, tell me.'

She was very still, but said nothing. And again I had the fear lest my aunt's Narcissus should begin loving me 'by transference'. My mood at that time was, in proportion to the preparations being made, steadily declining against marriage. I am not a cynic; but from what I've seen of married life in our own home, it has definitely put me off it for the remainder of my life. Only yesterday I heard a married man compare marriage to a rotten egg. 'Because,' he said, 'it looks all right from the outside, and before you taste it you do not know that it is rotten.' You may reproach me for fickleness in love. But what writer is sure of his livelihood with so fickle a public as ours? You may, for example, be reading this book—but it does not follow that you have bought it. Latterly my tongue would loiter with persistence round about my canine tooth. I came up to my shaving-glass, opened my mouth and looked in. What a cavity! Yes, wars were not to be fought with impunity. It was some time since I had been to the dentist. And it occurred to me that if I married Sylvia (who already had a gold crown at the end of her mouth) I would have to pay her dentists' bills in addition to my own, for all the fillings, crowns, fantastic bridges, and so forth, with which she would palliate the encroaching ruin of the years, ward off the desolation, till, one day, the disaster could be forestalled no longer, and she would order a complete set of artificial teeth—an upper and a nether plate—for which I, too, should have to foot the bill. Out of what? Out of literature, forsooth!...My grandfather rose in his grave.

Poverty—and the children catch measles. Winter—and a shortage of coal. From bad to worse, until you sit in your shirt-sleeves, maybe, in a one-roomed lodging, and having pushed aside the pans and saucers begin to write your book, *A Psychological Analysis of the Succeeding Stages in the Evolution of an Attitude*, the children howling 'I doan want to!' Sylvia, thin and angry and exhausted, perhaps turned into a shrew. To keep them from starvation you set your teeth and write a novel. At last it's finished. You send it to Pluckworth on the 7th of November and it comes back on the 15th of December, on which date you send it to Jane Sons, and Jane Sons return it to you on the 3rd of January, on which date you send it to Norman Elder, who sends it back on the 15th of March.

Suddenly I fell asleep. I dreamt that we were dining in a restaurant and Sylvia protested: 'I want French wine!' The waiter came, I had no money, and began to cry. I woke up in a sweat.

No, I did not want to get married.

After tea I went up to my attic, intent on settling down to a prolonged spell of solid work. But my tangled thoughts, revolting stubbornly, chased after those running streams of life which found their spring in Sylvia. Then, finally, I laid aside my papers and went to her. As I saw her, again I visualized our future life when I might be unkind to her; and because I wanted to be kind to her I craved to have this union broken before it was too late; and yet I knew that she, unconscious of future painful hours thus evaded, would suffer from the knowledge of a happiness missed; and it distressed me that I could not, without wounding her, explain these manifold considerations.

'Darling, frankly: do you want to marry me?'

'Yes.'

'Why?'

'It's so nice to be married, darling. To be always together. To live in the same house. To feel the same things. To have the same thoughts.'

Sylvia playing the *Four Seasons of the Year*. I take her for a walk, but think my own thoughts: though we couldn't be nearer, we couldn't be farther apart.

'This we can have without marrying.'

'But I want to have children...by you.'

'We'll send our son to New College.'

'Yes, yes.'

I used to say to Aunt Teresa in the course of our psycho-analytical experiments: 'If there is something that worries you try to isolate it and to tell me what it is—and we shall endeavour to side-track it.' I swear I never brought this on with an ulterior motive. And for some little time to come my experiments proved unsuccessful. Only as the time was nearing for our wedding and subsequent departure for Europe did Aunt Teresa tell me: 'I begin to believe in psycho-analysis. Something is worrying me, and that is why I feel so very ill.'

She sent for Dr. Abelberg and asked him whether there was anything in psycho-analysis.

The Doctor agreed.

After he had left she confessed to me:

'Dr. Abelberg asked me what it was that worried me. And when I told him that it was the dread of separation from my only daughter after the death of my only son, he said it was fatal for me to have anything like that to worry me.'

Poor Aunt Teresa! We did not show any sense of what we were doing to her. It did not occur to us that this was at all hard on her: to bring up her child, and then, suddenly, to see her go. She foresaw no prospect of following us to Europe. Most likely Uncle Emmanuel would enter Gustave Boulanger's bank, and then the last hope of seeing her daughter again would have gone. But we thought not of that. I boiled at the mere thought of a 'selfish' intervention on her part. Yet I knew that if I went away with Sylvia I would feel profoundly sorry for my aunt. That I did not feel so argued that I did not seriously believe I'd go away with her. If we had mingled our tears with hers and asked her to forgive us, she might have done so and resigned herself to her sad fate. But we did not do so; and once she had, with my aid, isolated her 'complex', there was no forgetting it.

The next I learnt was from Sylvia herself—when she told me 'It's all off'—crying, trying to restrain herself, and I, no longer knowing whether to be glad or to be sorry, or rather sorry against my very gladness, did my best to make her marry me, half satisfied, half mortified at my apparent failure to persuade her. We would get married first, I would leave and then return for her.

'No.'

At one time it seemed as though Sylvia resolved to take advantage of her whip hand—to avenge her suffering—and strike a blow for her own freedom, the feelings of her mother notwithstanding. But she collapsed in the doing.

Sylvia and Aunt Teresa mingled tears. But they were different kinds of tears. The daughter was a real heroine. She cried, but made a brave show, and only listened, blinking; and she never showed her wound, and sacrificed her happiness completely and without reproach.

And it was accepted promptly, without much ado.

'Sylvia! again!' said Aunt Teresa.

Sylvia blinked.

The tragedy of our position was not that Aunt Teresa dominated us into surrender, but that taking every circumstance into account—Aunt Teresa included—we could not make up our minds one way or another. My motive split: one portion of it became allied with Aunt Teresa; the other remained loyal to my love. But it is little use explaining the multifarious motives of one's thoughts and actions. I think this is a general mistake that novelists fall into. Why should I whitewash my conscience with your boredom, or waste my time in making the haphazard course of life seem rational in print? Why should I try to vindicate myself? Why pretend that I was reasonable or even logical? My conduct was confused, irrational. Who cares?

I considered the question from separate points of view—from the point of view of my present happiness, my future happiness, Sylvia's happiness if I married her, Sylvia's happiness if I did not marry her—and arrived at independent conclusions. I considered the question while I was undressing to go to bed, and while thinking of it, found that I had dressed again, put on my boots, and was tying my tie. Undressing myself once again, I considered the question again from all points of view simultaneously, displayed a truly Balfourian multi-sidedness. But, like my royal namesake from Shakespeare, I finally arrived at no conclusion at all. I am cursed with a Hamletian inaction. Russia has bitten me much too deeply. Why was I named Hamlet? Why this heart-splitting dilemma? Like him, I had an uncle—I had two uncles—but there was no clear reason why I should have murdered either of them. No such crude necessity in my case. Though perhaps it was my duty rather to murder my aunt. If it was, the reader must try to forgive me: I didn't do it.

38

And already—as the sentence once proclaimed is proceeded with without respite—so Aunt Teresa, once I was definitely off the cards, showed us her hand. I had suspected all along that she had someone up her sleeve. But her choice astonished me. To her, however, Gustave Boulanger seemed a candidate pre-eminently suitable. He was a Belgian, and he lived in the Far East. But sooner or later, his home would be in Belgium, and she still hoped that sooner or later they would all return to Belgium. Aunt Teresa's method of inveigling Gustave into marriage with her daughter was both swift and efficient and, if you remember my own case, not without precedent. She waited till they were to be found alone together, chatting innocently enough, when she dropped upon them, like an eagle from the blue, with her heartiest congratulations and best wishes for their future happiness. 'I'm so glad, *so* glad indeed,' she said, kissing them both on the cheek and taking them completely by surprise. Gustave coughed a little and adjusted his Adam's apple; but said nothing, only stroked his broad chin with his two fingers and smiled. And Gustave had to see his way to buy Sylvia a ring which she wore next to my own—that very same one which I once exhorted her to set me as a seal upon her heart.

It was difficult to know what Sylvia thought of it. Unlike myself, Gustave was not handsome. He had small podgy hands covered with freckles, and an absurd canary moustache. His large head had a bald patch on the crown which he vainly tried to cover up with what little hair he had left, and his teeth were ridiculously small considering the width of his chin. Gustave was a confirmed bachelor, and probably he did not favour the impending marriage. But it was difficult to know what Gustave really thought of it. It was difficult to know what Gustave thought of anything. For Gustave never said anything. He only stroked his chin with his two fingers and smiled. And each time he smiled he revealed a black tooth at each corner of his mouth.

I thought: We have lived our days carefully, sparingly, grudgingly. We have been cowards, preferring our life as a drab, moderate compromise rather than coloured in vivid stripes of joys and griefs. And now, she, my aunt, who has lived fully and recklessly and has landed on the rocks, wants to thrive upon the little savings of our happiness.—No more of it! No!

'No more of it!' I said.

'No, darling.'

'No what?' I asked, knowing that Sylvia, who hated trouble, was unduly acquiescent.

'No—what you mean,' she replied, blinking.

She looked as though she had something up her sleeve. But this, I knew, was merely an endeavour on her part to conceal her attitude of having nothing up her sleeve, of which she was ashamed. She acted almost without motive, following the line of least resistance, but feeling that in civilized society it was expected of one to be able to produce a reasoned motive for each action, she invented motives—sometimes after the event.

'No parting?'

'No, darling.'

'What is it all about then?'

'*Maman*,' she said—and was silent.

'Wants to part us?'

'Yes, darling.'

'Sixteen thousand miles apart.'

'So cruel!' she said.

'But do you *want* to marry him?'

'Darling, I'm so easily persuaded.'

She looked at me doubtfully, expecting a lead.

'Then let us run away together to England,' I said—rather uncertainly. I thought of the cost of the passage: my grandfather stirred in his grave.

She looked at me dumbly, her head bent, blinking.

'Shall we?'

'We can't, darling. *Maman*.'

She looked as if she wanted me to overrule her meek objection by a stronger motive, but I accepted it as valid, and she looked pained.

'Then what had we better do? Shall we marry—marry and separate? Marry and, for the time being, you remain and I go?'

She looked at me shyly: 'Just as you like, darling.'

'But—but what's the good if your mother will *never* let you go? What's the good? Besides, she might marry you off in my absence. No, she can't do that, but still, what's the use? Darling, answer me.'

'I don't care. Oh, it's going to rain. I must shut the window. What a wind! I don't care, darling.'

'But I do. And I'm damned if I'll do anything of the sort.' I smarted under Aunt Teresa's selfishness. I felt we were the victims of a crying wrong. 'Either we are to be married at once and you sail with me, or—or it's good-bye for ever.'

She was mute, very sad, and then said:

'Darling, I can't. '

'You must!'

'No, darling, I can't.'

'Yes, that's settled now. We leave together.' And even as I spoke the words I felt a pang for Aunt Teresa who had already lost her only son—and now her only daughter.

'No, no; it will make *maman* so sad.'

'Damn your *maman*! Damn all *mamans*!'

'Oh, what's the use of cursing? We've got to make the best of things, that's all.'

'We can only make the best of things by cursing.'

'Don't be nasty to me, darling.'

'I'm not nasty.'

'Be nice to me.'

'I am nice. And your *maman* would be a very nice person—if it weren't for her deceitfulness, dishonesty, meanness, and utter selfishness.' But because I knew full well the indecisions that really held me back, and was angry at my indecisions, I now transferred, with glee, my anger to my aunt, and my soul quailed under the weight of wrong, so that I nearly cried aloud for grief.

'We've got to make the best of things,' she said. 'Yes, darling, it's the only thing to do.'

It was not the only thing to do; but I could not do—whatever it was that wanted doing—and my heart felt sick.

'We shall meet again, we can think of each other,' she said.

'We shall most likely never see each other again.'

'Oh, don't; you make me so sad, darling.' She paused, and then said: 'I shall be true to you. We shall meet again somehow, I feel we shall. And don't flirt with anyone meanwhile, will you?'

I sighed. 'Well, I suppose we must make the best of things, that's evident. But—oh——'

'Never mind, darling.'

'Of course—it may even be for the best—who knows?' I said cheerily.

'Yes, never mind, darling.'

'We might not have been happy together after all—so cheer up!——'

She listened, blinking.

'Quarrelled, perhaps divorced later on——But why are you crying then?'

'I cry,' she sobbed, 'because it hurts me.'

She was on my neck, her wet cheek against mine, and I spoke tender foolish words: 'Oh, my little mouse, my little kitten, my little birdie, my little chicken!'

She stifled a sob. 'Not chicken.'

'Lovie-dovie-cats'-eyes.'

'Now, darling, don't be soppy.'

'But I'm so—for you,' I replied.

'No, darling, I don't like this soppy stuff.'

'Oh, well——'

She laughed her dingling silvery laughter which was a lovely thing.

Our spacious pessimism, what is it? The squeal of a puppy. Life hurts, and then the night is starless, the world a desolating void where the wind groans and mutters and complains in our echo. But we go on, amazed, a little puzzled, inert, day-dreaming and unquestioning. In the twilight of the drawing-room General 'Pshe-Pshe' was sitting at the side of Aunt Teresa, saying: 'My wife and I do not get on together well. My children, too, are not what they should be. But here with you I feel at home.' He kissed her hand. 'Here my soul rests.' He kissed her hand once more. 'This…my spiritual home!' Again he kissed her hand. 'When I go home, half of my soul remains here in this flat. Oh, my beautiful woman!' He kissed her hand. Aunt Teresa looked to heaven, as if pleading that this was a strain on her, the ailing delicate woman that she was.

'I see things through you and your being. If I hear a song that I think you have never heard it hurts me to think that it should have been in vain. If I hear a tune or see a picture, or anything like that, that is familiar to you, it hurts me equally, it hurts me more, to think that it has captured your attention, if even for a moment, perhaps your affection, your love, and that I—I—I—I couldn't, couldn't…nothing but blind indifference.' He could not speak. He was rent by self-pity; his heart was weeping tears. She looked to heaven, invoking strength to bear this—but not altogether displeased.

Harry stood in the doorway.

'What is it?' she asked, feeling foolish at his seeing her side by side with 'Pshe-Pshe' on the sofa.

'Nuffink. I'm not *asking* for anything.'

39

And he repulsed (a short tale to make),
Fell into a sadness; then into a fast;
Thence to a watch; thence into a weakness;
Thence to a lightness; and by this declension,
Into the madness wherein now he raves.

HAMLET.

It was the 11th of April, Nora's birthday. Aunt Molly had been away in Japan a week and she had taken Bubby with her, leaving Harry and Nora in the charge of 'Aunt' Berthe—for their own father, she felt was altogether too incalculable a factor to be relied on in these matters. The children played nicely together, and were not a nuisance. In the morning, before lunch, Berthe would take them out into town for an airing and they would walk in front of her, buttoned up in their warm padded coats and warm gaiters, Harry holding Nora by the hand. They would come back to say they had seen a big dog in the street; or Harry would climb the steps to my attic, where I was in the habit of working—'There'—and give me a big nail. Three times a week Harry went to the newly-organized school for Anglo-American children, and sometimes Nora was sent with him for company. He would walk in, with that old man's smile on his face, holding her by the hand, and she would sit at a desk next to a little boy (who pinched her occasionally), her legs dangling down, and draw something with the stump of a pencil. And when she twitched, because the little boy at her side was pinching her, Harry, sitting behind, put up his hand—'Please, teacher'—so putting a stop to it. She had been taught what to say when she wanted to rise and go out, which she did now with an air of independence, putting up her hand and saying: 'Please, teacher, may I?' and the teacher graciously nodded her head. But when she returned to the room, Harry, appreciating the position of things, put up his hand—'Please, teacher'—and, strolling over to his little sister, gravely buttoned up her knickers in front of the class.

I was working on my thesis *A Record of the Stages in the Evolution of an Attitude*, when I heard his steps; the door opened and Harry swung in in large hefty strides, looking mighty serious.

'There you are,' said he, producing an old rusty screw out of his pocket, 'this is for you.'

'Why aren't you at school?'

'Don't you know?' he said, astonished. 'It's Nora's birthday. Why don't you come down to have chocolate?'

'I am busy.'

'Well, never mind,' said he, 'I can take the present down to her.' He went over to my typewriter and began fiddling with the keys. 'I want,' he said, 'to type a letter to Mummy.'

'Well.'

He typed:

My dear Mummy how ar you getting on don has bit a bit of anti Berts nos of uncl is goto sell don. Nora ceeps geting eer ache I can reed books naw. nora can say her abc and can kant up to a hundrid wee hav a grama fon I can draw a kite and an open and klosd umbrela I hav got a woch. do you no hoo hav mee it. well i will tell you anti Bert gav mee it and I can tell the time. I——

He got stuck with the keys, having pressed several at once. 'Come, tell me what to say and I'll type it.'

He strolled about, swinging, his hands in his breeches-pockets.

'Well?'

He smiled that old man's smile of his, and then began:

My dear Mummy I am very good and have you not forgotten to get that chocolate from the station—have got quite a lot of toys and a bucket and spade. I've made a motor with two chairs and a shawl and all my toys are inside. I play very nicely and I am good. Auntie Berthe sleeps where you put the head and I sleep where you put the feet. I see all kinds of pictures in Auntie Berthe's room on the wall and Auntie Berthe's got a lamp with a glass on and lamp glass in crackling. I've got a water-can and some scales with a little drawer. Ginger always comes up, I always see Don. Ginger bite me. I written this letter myself. There is a little girl called Laurie and behind the barn there is a place with some bricks like a frame and it was all bumpy before and there were no seats before for Laurie to sit on because she was the teacher and all that bumpy earth. This morning I got up early and made it very flat and have put seats there so Laurie can sit down. It looks so nice now it's flat. Every afternoon we go for long walks and when we get home very tired we have lots of cups of tea and plenty to eat. When I went to the Sunday school treat I got most of the sweets and the others only had two each. I got twenty. And I fished a Noah's Ark out of a brown tub. Auntie

Berthe was hiding behind some bricks the other day. While Auntie was hiding I took the big milk can of lemonade and drank it all up and nearly choked; was all sick back into the can. Auntie laughed so much and Nora stopped crying and laughed at me being sick all over the can. Auntie Berthe's given me a nice looking glass and some nails. I told Daddy when he's finished making furniture I told him to make my peddling motor, put a screen on it at the back and tyres on the wheels. Auntie Berthe has got a dark brown cupboard with a big looking glass on it. Auntie Terry's case that Daddy gave her that she does her nails with I play with. I break nothing. Give my love to Bubby. A thousand pounds of love to you, Mummy. I've got real marbles.

Your son Harry Charles.

There followed nine big crosses purporting to be kisses.

I leaned back, exhausted, and yawned, and then gazing at Sylvia's picture on my table, took it up and, automatically, from habit, kissed it.

He looked at me brightly.

'Silly!' he said.

He pondered a moment, looking round, and then suddenly asked:

'Why is everything?'

By George! he was taking after me.

'But why is it,' he said, '——everything?'

I pondered a moment, stuck for an answer, and then answered him:

'Because…why shouldn't it be?'

He was satisfied—completely so.

'Harry, your wi*me*!' Nora called from the steps.

'Silly!' he said, 'they tell 'er it's wine because she's only a baby. It's cod-liver oil. Come down,' he said, 'Nora has a lot of people for her birthday.'

'People?'

'Children, not people; not grown-ups people.'

'Oh!'

In the dining-room, as we got down, there were many children. As fresh ones arrived, each, very pleased with itself, handed Nora its little present, which she snatched from them without as much as a 'thank you'.

'And who is this little boy?' I asked Harry.

'This is Billy—who pinches her.'

Nora looked round and smiled, her open mouth full of chewed cake.

'And don't you fight the boys when they annoy your little sister?'

'No.'

'Why not?'

'Don't want to get into trouble,' he said, looking at Nora the while, who was eating a long chocolate bar all by herself, till Sylvia observed: 'Won't you let Harry have a taste?'

'Well, Harry, you know what it tastes like,' she said, turning away.

When we settled down to chocolate, Uncle Lucy was not amongst us. For hours on end he would sit now in his study, brooding, brooding without cease, and we, stirred by curiosity, would open the door and peep inside. This popping in and out of heads irritated him not a little. Once, while going out with him, and passing a Lutheran church on the door of which hung a notice of the hours of service, Uncle Lucy precipitated his steps, concluding that the building was a bank and the notice the current statement of the rates of the money exchange. There was nothing very peculiar about that, but standing on the steps close up to the notice, Uncle Lucy still thought the building a bank, and said he wanted to go in and change 300 yen. He confessed to me one night as he was locking the front door that he must test the door twelve times to know that it was locked; and in the middle of the night, sometimes, he would feel the need to go and test it once again: or—he felt—irrationally—his youngest child might die. Seeing a dachshund across the street, he said, 'It would be nice to creep down on all fours and to bark like a dog—or else stand on one leg and crow like a cock.' And when Nora now went in to him to say that chocolate was on the table, her daddy 'did stand,' she said, 'on one leg and said he was a stork,' and she laughed and thought he was joking. After this, one by one, we all began to peep into his room to see if he was all right. 'Don't pop in peeping at me every minute,' he cried. 'I might be some uncommon animal in a zoo—people peeping at me through the hole every minute!'

We stopped peeping but began whispering to each other; for, indeed, Uncle Lucy was getting very strange. He did not come in to chocolate, but went up into the dark-room instead to develop some snaps. Of late, Uncle Lucy was always taking photographs and developing them in the dark-room upstairs. After chocolate, the children began playing together, at first somewhat gingerly, as if sounding one another; then more freely and boisterously. There was a boy with a withered arm, nevertheless very sturdy and strong and twice the size of Harry. Harry, in a wicked mood, came up to him suddenly, and—for no conceivable reason, but merely from an abounding sense of well-being—slapped him in the face. The boy's impulse was to strike Harry back, but he must have remembered that he was a guest and restrained himself, with a mighty effort. For two minutes or so he brooded over the offence, as if considering whether he should be offended or no. He could not stomach the idea that a boy half his size should have dared to strike him in the face with impunity. At last, he came up to Harry and—mildly, because he was the guest, almost amicably, with a propitiatory, extenuating smile—slapped Harry in the face. Harry looked as if considering whether he should cry, but since the boy with the withered arm smiled, Harry decided to take no offence and smiled too—unconvincingly. Two little girls with a little boy came in—a curly-haired, black-eyed, clean-faced and thoroughly well-brought-up boy, who presently, quite by accident, got a black eye from the boy with the withered arm, and went off crying softly. At once his two little sisters put their arms round his neck, kissing and consoling him: 'Oh, it *was* a knock. Oh, it *was* one!'—A microcosm of the adult world.

They bandaged the little boy's head up, and they all went on playing again. In the end, hardly one of them escaped uninjured.

'And now Nora will recite to us,' said Aunt Teresa, 'Little fly on the wall.'

'No, "Wee Willie",' she said.

'All right, "Wee Willie", then.' And placed on a chair, Nora said:

Wee Willie had a rittle *flute*
Which really was so *sweet*
That when he went out for a walk
He played it in the street.

And when the folks heard Willie play
They all began to dance,

The rittle *dogs sat down and howled,*
The horses did a prance.

So Willie's mother took him home,
And tucked him up in bed.
'I'll have to take away your flute,
It upsets *folks,' s'e said.*

All clapped; and, for an encore, she told us about Bunny who was white and *such* a size, who had long silky floppy ears and funny *wee* pink eyes.

Long after chocolate, Uncle Lucy came down into the drawing-room, where already a number of guests—my friends: local intellectuals—were gathered, and sat facing us, looking on sarcastically, never saying a word. He was pale, but his nose was redder than ever. 'What is consciousness?' I was saying. 'At the point where *all* the rays meet, there is a spark: that spark is . But the same rays meet in infinity again and again an infinite number of times (all straight lines being crooked in the infinite), and so all these other sparks are all these other *I*'s. But since we are, each one of us, the sum of the same rays, all *I*'s have their immortal being in the source of the One, eternally replenished by the fount of the Many: the finest distillation of this comprehension being the spirit we call God.'

Uncle Lucy as he sat there, listening, looked so wise, so derisively contemptuous in his silence; had such a seer's look in his eyes (as if indeed he were seeing through our intellectual foibles far into the future) that it silenced even the intellectuals. They felt as if Uncle Lucy had a secret message for ever hidden from their minds. They looked respectfully expectant. Even Dr. Murgatroyd stopped talking. Uncle Lucy's true secret, however—they did not know—was that he had quietly gone off his chump, indeed was already as mad as a hatter. Yesterday he had taken Aunt Teresa out for a drive and kept calling at shops without number, purchasing things—mostly cumbersome, useless things—without end, so that Aunt Teresa, sitting there beside him in the vehicle, thought that her poor brother had definitely turned the corner, and that his old vein of prodigious generosity was returning to him. But the extraordinary thing about it all was that the things he bought were conspicuously useless and unwieldy things—electric stoves, two ladders, a canary cage—depositing his purchases, as they drove on, at the railway station in charge of porters, at the theatre cloak-room, and suchlike places, which even to Aunt Teresa's unsuspecting soul appeared a trifle singular. Next day he came into the drawing-room, with that sulky Charlie Chaplin look we grew to know so well, and manifesting the wish to tune up the piano, took it all to pieces, to the minutest particles, so that afterwards he was unable to put it together again. He went out, and Aunt Teresa, frightened of meeting him alone, locked the drawing-room door. He returned, and finding the door locked, smashed the window.

Now he pulled out his watch and, declaring that it was half-past twelve o'clock, said that he had some snaps to develop in the dark-room.

'But, Uncle Lucy, it isn't six! What is the matter with your watch?'

'I've got to go by my watch—such as it is,' he replied very gravely and earnestly, and went off to the dark-room.

I went back to my office, and Uncle Emmanuel, who had lit a cigar, said that in spite of the rain he would come out with me. The pavement was a glittering sheet, like a wet waterproof, but the evening was misty and dark and the rain that wetted my face was completely invisible, and only as you came up to a lamp-post could you see how, in the radius of yellow light, the silver rain fell steadily from the sky. We took refuge in the barred doorway of a hosiery shop, whose windows were shuttered. A young woman was standing there, and my uncle took the opportunity of ogling at her through his pince-nez. And when I returned, after having vainly looked for a cab, Uncle Emmanuel was already speaking to her in his own tongue, while she only giggled and simpered. Presently we all moved along, Uncle Emmanuel holding his new friend by the arm. I parted with them at the back stairs of a shabby building, which they slowly ascended, but the rain having now become a torrent, I returned and stood under the porch, waiting for it to subside. Then, as I stood there, I heard strange menacing sounds from the back of the stairs up which my uncle had vanished. After a while, fearing that he might be in danger, I followed the sound of the menacing voice and gingerly knocked at a door on the second landing. There was no answer, but the thick drunken voice still boomed out menacing words, punctuated, as I now distinctly discerned, by Uncle Emmanuel's, as it seemed to me, feeble exhortations which sounded rather like 'Allies! Allies!' With an inward thrill of trepidation, I pushed open the door and, entering, perceived a huge fierce drunken Cossack 'carrying on' in the face of my uncle's clearly unwarranted presence, while the woman was doing her best to restrain him.

'This is my husband,' she turned to me. 'Returned unexpectedly.'

But here, again, I am in difficulties. My uncle was, as you may guess, the hero of an unseemly situation. I warn the reader to put down the book, for I refuse to hold myself responsible for the doings of my uncle. I am a serious young man, an intellectual. I blush all over, my very paper blushes as I think of him standing there—I can't. You must not press me to go any further. For there, if you please, stood my uncle—No; the less said of it the better. A veil over my uncle's private life. A veil! A veil!

'Cut you to pieces! Mince you up!' shouted the Cossack, his hand on his sword-hilt, while Uncle Emmanuel meekly repeated: 'Allies! We're Allies! *Vive la Russie*! Allies!'

'Allies!' shouted the Cossack, coming close up to him with savage glee. 'Allies! I'll show you some allies!'

'He'll kill him,' whispered the lady. 'He'll kill him, sure. Better give him something—some money quick! He'll kill him!'

'Give him some money,' I cried in French. 'For God's sake give him some money, quick!'

Uncle Emmanuel fiddled with his pocket-book for a moment, and then producing a 500,000 rouble note (at that time worth about 80 centimes) gave it to the Cossack, who grabbed it with his huge sabre-scarred fist, his body swaying uncertainly as he did so. 'Allies!' he snorted. 'H'm!'

He calmed down. 'Call yourself Allies!' he said, in a grumbling tone, no longer dangerous, and turning to go. 'Allies! H'm! That's right. Allies—in name.' He paused. 'I'll go and have a drink,' he said. And he went out, slamming the door after him.

My uncle looked at me, with confusion. '*Que voulez-vous*!' he said. '*C'est la vie*.'

But a veil over my uncle's doings. I went out at last, leaving him there. A nice lesson for a purist and no mistake!

I was sitting in my office, working on my book, *A Record of the Stages in the Evolution of an Attitude*, when the telephone rang shrilly at my side. I took up the receiver. It was Berthe.

'Georges, come home at once.'

She did not say why, but I sensed a tone of calamity in her voice. Before I could make myself ask she had hung up the receiver.

The rain had stopped and the big orange moon hung in the sky. The funny old man in the moon, as I drove home, looked sly in the extreme, and the road was all orange and unreal, and our whole life that moment seemed a series of ludicrous antics which we took so seriously to heart because—because we could not see, because we did not know. And then I thought that if when I got home I found Berthe standing on her head or Uncle Lucy standing on one leg and crowing, 'Cock-cock-cock-cock-orikoo!' I would not turn a hair, finding it in strict accordance with this orange light, this orange night, this orange moon.

When I arrived, I saw Harry, very tiny, very serious, below, proudly watering the flowers in the kitchen-yard out of a crooked tin; and two street urchins hanging on to the fence and gazing down at him with envy. The sight of him reassured me, but the absence of his little sister Nora made me feel uneasy.

'Harry!' I shouted down to him as I paid the cabman. But deep in his preoccupation with the 'water-can' he barely deigned to look up at me.

'Harry!' I said again. 'Where is Nora?'

He mumbled something, looking at the boys the while.

'Harry!' I repeated. 'Can't you speak up? Where is Nora?'

'In the w,' he said in tones of provocation, gazing at the urchins in confusion.

Relieved, I made my way into the house. Berthe met me in the hall. She looked at me with that intimate sad smile I knew so well, but there was in it, this time, no trace of reminiscence, rather of a tragic resignation, and the red stripe on the tip of her nose—the result of the dog bite—gave her gravity a very funny expression. It was that look which in effect implies, 'We live in a mad world: what can you expect?' And I answered it with a series of quick becoming nods of gravity.

'Your uncle,' she said, 'is dead.'

'Which one?'

'Uncle Lucy.'

'Oh damn!'

I could find no more. Bang! that is fate flying in at your door. I was amazed more than really shocked. It was so unlike Uncle Lucy. He was not at all the kind of man to do a thing like that.—So his life was finished, wiped off the slate.

She led me silently ahead and up the stairs. Before the dark-room where Uncle Lucy used to develop his snaps, she paused and turned to me. 'It's a dreadful day today,' she said. 'He has hanged himself.'

I opened the door and went in.

Ever since I had been born, some five-and-twenty years ago, I have been more and more astonished at the spectacle of life as lived on our planet. Others had struggled with the hangman on the scaffold: what has induced this man to do the ghastly job himself? In the name of what logic, in the name of what God was he cutting this capering figure? It was a suicide, you might say, with extraordinary features. Uncle Lucy was clothed in Aunt Teresa's camisole, knickers, silk stockings, garters, and a silk boudoir cap.

'What I want to know,' she said, 'is *how* he got into her cupboard.' And I had a vision of Uncle Lucy stealing into Aunt Teresa's wardrobe—and stealing out again on tiptoe, with the camisole and knickers and the boudoir cap.

'What *I* want to know is *why* he did it.' I could not think why, unless, perhaps, to vindicate his girlish name.

His ordinary clothes were behind the door. The face was livid; only his nose, for once, was pale, and the body was still warm but lifeless. He was hanging on the rope when he was seen through the window by a neighbour, who at first, owing to the extraordinary attire, took him to be a dummy. He was now lying on the floor, a wretched sight to behold.

'My God what had we better do? Send for the doctor?' she asked.

I looked at my wrist-watch: two adjacent holes on the strap had joined and the strap was loose, the watch hung under my wrist. 'A doctor! The matter is past a doctor. Though perhaps Abelberg had better come and look at him. I'm not exactly familiar with such feats. Poor man.' But in my heart I could find nothing but annoyance.

'Somebody must wash him,' she said with grave concern, and shuddered at the prospect of doing it herself.

'Doesn't need washing now. Clean enough for the worms.'

'Georges!' she cried. 'It's—it's blasphemy.'

These people are absurd.

'Do you know what the good Jesus said about the dead?'

'No; what?'

'That the dead had better bury their dead.'

'George!' she said, still uncertain if my words were in accordance with propriety. '*Quelle tragédie*!'

I have no tears to waste over this sort of thing. 'It's not a tragedy, Berthe: it's tragedy-bouffe.'

To hang yourself in a pair of Aunt Teresa's knickers—it's not the kind of thing you might expect to happen every day: it wanted some little getting used to. Suddenly, Berthe began to laugh (she couldn't help it). Indeed, though dead, he looked very funny. Her laugh gave me the shudders. And as she began laughing, she laughed louder and louder; she laughed at the idea that she should be laughing; it struck her as being increasingly funny. She tried to suppress it. She could not. She ran out of the room.

To die, I thought, must be like violent stomach-ache, when you exclaim, 'Oh my!' and are released, contented, with a blissful smile, into another world. Into the reasons necessitating this strange attire, into the tragedy of it I am unable to follow. Of course, he had worried over the loss of his Siberian property a good deal. And let us be just: he had also purchased a large quantity of roubles, which would justify any man laying hands on himself on that score alone. But I am inclined to think that the ordinary normal spectacle of life as it is lived on our planet had unhinged his mind: had proved too much for him. I pondered on the logic of the insane: perhaps they have a logic of their own. Or perhaps madness is the very antithesis of logic.

I found Berthe in the children's bedroom. 'I believe you and I, Berthe, are the only two sane beings on this earth. In fact, I am not even so sure about you. Why don't you spring at me and bite me in the shoulder?'

The children were awake. I went in and saw Nora, her small rosy head on the enormous pillow, like a pale cherry. She was crying.

'What's the matter, Nora?'

'Earache.'

'You've been in a draught?'

'I 'hink so,' she said, and cried.

It transpired that during the day she had drunk water out of the drain-pipe in the yard, and suddenly in the night fear seized her, and she cried: 'Don't want to die.' In the rough-and-tumble she had scratched her leg, and the little boy with the withered arm had evidently preyed on her mind, and through her choking sobs 'Don't want to die,' she interjected, 'withered leg . . . oh, I don't want to die.'

'Nora, but what is the matter, dear?'

'My leg's withering,' she sobbed, 'but I don't want to die.'

At last she calmed down. Berthe got her to kneel in bed and say her prayers again, which she said: 'Mammy and daddy, granpas and granmas, uncles and aunties and cousins—and Cousin Georgie.' Then she was tucked in once more and at once went to sleep.

'S—sh!' whispered Berthe. But Harry made overt signs to me, and moving on tiptoe I strolled over to him and sat on the edge of his bed. He tucked in his feet: 'You can sit back now,' he said. 'It's all right.'

The moon looked blurred, as if behind a film, and more apart, more distant, and I wondered if one could be happy on the moon. Nora, who must have dreamt of the little boy Billy at school pinching her, cried out in her sleep: 'Leave me alone! *Leave me alone*! Stop it! *Stop it*! Shu*p* up!'

Then Sylvia, flushed and terror-stricken, flitted in: 'Aunt Berthe, *maman* is in hysterics, *une crise de nerfs*…'

It was a damnable night.

40

Next day Aunt Teresa did not rise from her bed, and Berthe attended to her with hot and cold compresses, valerian drops, pyramidon, aspirin, and a number of lotions. Aunt Teresa's nerves were so badly upset by the suicide that even Aunt Molly herself on arriving two days later from Japan had to take turns with Berthe and Sylvia at Aunt Teresa's bedside during the night. Uncle Emmanuel returned in the early morning, from the Cossack's, and was so dumbfounded on being told of what had happened that he found nothing to say. Aunt Molly came back, and to the end of her days she would never cease regretting that brief holiday in Japan. And although it was clearly a matter of death, '*C'est la vie*,' said my uncle, pressing her hand.

General 'Pshe-Pshe', hearing of the calamity, called on Sunday morning to tender his condolences. He bowed low over Aunt Teresa's hand and brushed his prickly moustache against it. Then, for a brief space, he sat still, in homage to the deceased. He cleared his throat to show that it was over. But Aunt Teresa was the first to speak. Her poor brother! Who would have thought it! It was such a shock to her nervous system that Dr. Abelberg, who had begun to cure her, had abandoned his treatment in despair. She had not a wink of sleep since the calamity! And indeed her face looked white and pasty and transparent against the morning light. The General said that he had come as an old friend with the one wish to be of help if they would let him. Would they like a band?

'A *band*?' exclaimed my aunt.

'*Pardon*,' said Uncle Emmanuel, addressing himself *viâ* me with his unfailing courtesy, to General 'Pshe-Pshe', 'what kind of band does his Excellency mean?'

'The military band which assisted at the ball,' the General replied, with a timid smile.

'For the funeral!' exclaimed Aunt Teresa. And we had visions of the carcass of Uncle Lucy being galloped off at full speed to the cemetery to the wafting strains of the mazurka.

'But they will play the funeral march—appropriate to the occasion,' explained the General, with the same tender timid smile on his face.

'Ah, that is perfectly all right, then,' said Uncle Emmanuel, completely satisfied. 'That's all right. The General is too amiable.' He bowed courteously. The General bowed back.

Another stiff little pause.

We anticipated difficulties in regard to the burial of a 'suicide'. But in the face of the general chaos, no real restriction was put in our way. Indeed, why should there have been? Had a man not the right to cast off his own shell? But a minor hitch had none the less occurred in the choosing of the grave site. Uncle Emmanuel cleared his throat. 'We expected,' he said, 'certain difficulties in regard to obtaining a licence for the burial. The death, of course, is not a—a—' he flung out explanatory gestures—'an ordinary kind of affair, and we expected——'

'Oh?' The General cast a quick enquiring look at Aunt Teresa. 'Has anyone said anything?'

'Well—yes,' Uncle Emmanuel admitted.

'Who?'

'The keeper of the graveyard. But no one else has.'

'Let him come to me,' said the General, all his native ferociousness coming into his manly face. '*I*'ll talk to him! *I*'ll settle him quickly enough!' He would, he declared, stand no nonsense from anyone in this city so long as he had his troops in it—he did not know how much longer that would be, and he was bound to say that if the Allies did not change their mind (some people's blindness must be a blessing in disguise, otherwise he could not account for their survival), yes, he was bound to say that if the Allies did not change their mind and send him reinforcements he would no longer be master of the situation, and then anything might happen and *any* keeper of *any* graveyard would do as he pleased; but so long as he, General Pshemòvich-Pshevìtski, was still in command he would see that they, his friends, were properly protected. Uncle Emmanuel bowed. The General bowed back. He respected Madame Vanderflint and Monsieur le Commandant ('Ah, his Excellency is too amiable,' Uncle Emmanuel punctuated the flow. Mutual bows), he respected them, and it was his wish to mark his esteem for the deceased without at all enquiring into the manner of his death. He also wished to mark his esteem for Mme Vanderflint, and though it was not in strict accordance with the regulations, which laid it down that such military honours were reserved for the military, still he supposed that the deceased had served his term of military service in his time——

'No,' interrupted Aunt Teresa. 'My poor brother was a British subject, and there was no compulsory military service in England—at least before the war.'

No matter! The General in his esteem for the lady would

waive that point also and fire a military salute at her brother's grave.

'What?' asked Aunt Teresa, not understanding perfectly.

'A firing squad,' he said. 'I'll order firing.'

'Oh, no!' she quailed. 'Please not, it reminds me of Anatole, my son, I couldn't stand it.' And suddenly, before anyone was prepared for it, she began to sob.

'Blank cartridge,' he said, looking round sheepishly.

'That's all right, my angel, that's all right, my dear,' Uncle Emmanuel consoled her. 'No one will do it if you don't want it. No one will do it.'

At this moment Aunt Molly entered the room. The General rose with military precision and clicked his spurs before her and bent over her podgy hand with the solitary wedding ring. 'Whatever is the matter?' she asked, seeing Berthe run out for the valerian drops and Aunt Teresa in hysterics.

'Ah, they want to shoot at the grave, as if hanging were not enough,' Berthe muttered angrily, as she swept past her.

'Hanging...shooting...' mumbled Aunt Molly. 'Why? Why?' And having unwittingly uttered the word and seeing Teresa in tears, she too began to sob into her handkerchief. The General shuffled his feet awkwardly, till, Berthe having arrived with the drops, Uncle Emmanuel took me by one arm and the General by the other, and spoke to him, *viâ* me, in these terms: '*Ah, mon général*, you must excuse my wife, her nerves have all gone to pieces, and my *belle-sœur* did not understand the nature of the honour you were going to accord her poor husband. *Qu'est-ce que vous voulez*? She has been brought up in civilian surroundings—in the country—far away from cities and towns; *évidemment*, her husband and relatives were all civilians, unacquainted with the code that we—*nous autres militaires*—share together as our precious heritage, and you must forget this little episode, *mon général*.'

I translated.

41

Von dem Dome,
Schwer und bang,
Tönt die Glocke
Grabgesang.

SCHILLER.

Aunt Teresa, already seated in the carriage, waited for Berthe and Uncle Emmanuel to join her; but Berthe, with that quick intuition for succour, divined where her help was most needed and said she must walk by the side of Aunt Molly, who insisted on walking behind the coffin.

'Emmanuel!' exclaimed Aunt Teresa, 'you will sit with me in the carriage.' But, strange as it may seem, my uncle this time took a firm stand, though, as always, his answer was tender. 'Ah,' said he, beholding my uniform, 'it behoves *nous autres militaires* to march behind the coffin. It would not look well if I sat with you in the carriage, my angel.'

'But, Emmanuel! I can't be sitting here all alone!' remonstrated Aunt Teresa in tones of acute anguish. 'I feel very faint and ill! I must have somebody at my side.'

And to comfort her, Natàsha was put into the carriage.

At last the procession moved on. Uncle Emmanuel had donned his uniform for the occasion and had a broad black band stitched round his sleeve. I had fished out '*le sabre de mon père*'—a long clumsy thing in a leather scabbard. I had bought it cheap in a second-hand shop in Charing Cross Road; it was an obsolete cavalry sword of pre-Waterloo pattern, being much too long even when you sat on the top of a horse, and therefore long since discarded. I carried it well forward, walking side by side with Uncle Emmanuel, on the heels of Aunt Molly and Berthe, at the slow funeral pace set by the General's brass band. And it seemed to me that Uncle Emmanuel was glad that now he could keep step with me, without effort, that his strides were as measured and dignified as my own. Alas, it was a funeral march. My spurs softly jingled; involuntarily I looked down at my feet, conscious of the superiority of my cavalry boots which Pickup had polished up to the last pitch, so that they shone like the veneer of a dark-brown piano. My uncle's ill-fitting boots and incongruously light leggings were detestable. Only an officer of the Latin race could put up with the indignity of such a uniform. As the hearse moved through the streets, peasants took off their caps and crossed themselves. An American captain saluted that sunshade salute, and seemed glad of the opportunity. He was smart, but his boots, though good, were much too low. I daresay he thought mine too high. Poor Uncle Lucy! he did not suspect the homage accorded him on all sides. What futile waste of gesture: if the dead can really see the living one may assume that they are above such vanities. Yet this was a farewell from a stray brother who lingered behind to a brother who had set out on a journey. A Chink whipped his horse up a steep hill. Two little girls, looking on, said: 'What a cruel man!' And Uncle Emmanuel upon my having translated, said: 'The little hearts are compassionate.' A very old man in charge of three cows and a bull found that the bull had galloped off at the cross-roads in the opposite direction to that of the cows, and he could not make up his mind which way to go. He was too old to run after the bull, and the cows meanwhile had also walked off, and so he stood still, reflecting in anguish, while the street urchins laughed at him, teasing him: 'Beaver! Beaver!' And Uncle Emmanuel said: 'They are cruel and heartless, the little ones!'—This was life. And how was death?

We went by a long winding road into the country, between two rows of trees. Aunt Molly looked hot in her long astrakhan coat and warm felt goloshes slopping in the mud. Soon, too, Pickup's labour was wasted: my boots were covered with dirt. The road before us seemed endless. I had a feeling that I'd like to mount a steed and ride away from these mourners, this dead, from their red weeping eyes and the deadly boredom of living, gallop on without looking back, on and on, on and on.

At length we had reached the lonely Lutheran cemetery in that far-away lonely suburb, and the hearse and the carriages halted. We followed the bier through the great silent gate that bore the message: *I know that my Redeemer liveth*. It was the 14th of April; two days ago it had been bitterly cold and snow had fallen in heaps and covered everything at a distance. But that morning turned out hot, even stifling, and now as we entered the lych gate, the awakening verdure exuded upon us so strong and pungent a scent that we felt as though we had entered a hothouse. The procession turned to the left, the wheels leaving deep furrows in the muddy snow. But the sun played on a thousand well-kept tombstones and sepulchres: evidently in this forgotten, far-away nook of the world people had been dying, people who are cared for, who are not forgotten. The trees were stripped of verdure, but green was just sprouting. Behind the open grave which swilled in water there were birches—dear, modest birches!—and at the side, as if guarding the grave, a young weeping willow with the leaves golden in the spring sun. They had been trying to pump out the water, but the pump—or the people—proved unable to cope with the floods of the melting snow, and when the coffin was lowered there was an unpleasant sound of its splashing, as if it had been dropped into a well. How strange, I thought: Uncle Lucy, who was born in Manchester, and spent his life in Krasnoyarsk, was put to bed with a shovel in a Lutheran graveyard on the soil of a Russian concession on the Chinese Eastern Railway. When the coffin was being lowered into the swilling grave, Uncle Emmanuel and I, who stood a little forward, stretched ourselves up to the salute. The Lutheran pastor—for want of an Anglican minister—read the service in sonorous German. We precipitated to the edge of the grave. Aunt Teresa and Natàsha dropped flowers on the floating coffin; then Aunt Molly dropped two China roses. We followed her with handfuls of sand which fell on the hollow-sounding lid. I stood to the salute, and Uncle Emmanuel quickly put on his cap and emulated my example; the pastor said a few last words. And the men vigorously handled their spades.

There was no other sound than the chirruping of birds; the sun beating upon us, on the sprouting young green beneath the thawing snow, spoke of the passing of winter, of the awakening of life into spring, then into summer. The eternal cycle. And suddenly—for no reason—the thought of the gold bridge in Uncle Lucy's mouth swam into my mind. It would outlast the ages! In these decades his teeth, his mouth, his body would be gradually decaying in the swilling grave, but the solid gold would be immune from change, and then, one day, there would be a moment when nothing whatsoever remained of his once active body, and the solid golden bridge would fall upon dry dust. The sky was kindly, the morning friendly and tranquil. I thought of this terrible death penalty that hangs over us all—when we shall fall asleep and not waken. No: waken, but far beyond this. In my soul I keep captive the soul of the world as hostage for my immortality. I have released it now: and we are one: and I am dead. To die could not be stranger than to come to life. He died—and was disillusioned in death. 'Where was death?' And there was no death. And perhaps he longed to explain, to tell us that there was no death, that death once dead, there was no dying then. Passion, in the nature of the satisfaction it seeks, is not a craving for acquisition, but rather for the release of the forces oppressing us. In the same way, death may be the release of those forces that had 'licked us into shape', and kept us in the mould of our particular individuality too long—a satisfaction akin to the physical, but lasting longer, perhaps very long, perhaps into eternity. Death, I thought, is the merging of a particular vision in the sea of bleak generalities, the ending of all limiting and exclusive perspectives, the grandest of all disillusionments.

And then, as one felt that all was over and it was time for us to go, Aunt Molly who had so far made heroic efforts to contain herself, suddenly trembled, her face changed, quivered, and she began to sob at first softly, quietly, then louder, in odd little jerks, nervous convulsions. For a moment we gazed helplessly, and I thought I could read what was in her mind. How she had worried the long years through over his diet and digestion, over his socks when they were damp, seen to it that his bed was aired for fear he might catch cold; and now she was to abandon him to this swilling grave. How strange! The ancients had a fitting sense of delicacy in these matters. They left food and clothes and all the necessaries with their dead before abandoning them to their long sleep. Aunt Molly, the tall, stout, milk-and-blood-complexioned woman, was now about to faint. And we, not failing in sympathy but shy of demonstrance, stood as in a trance, reluctant to give succour. All but Berthe, who, again, was first at her side. '*Pauvre amie*!' she said in wailing doleful tones as she slipped her own sinewy arm round Aunt Molly's big sobbing frame. 'Come with me, *ma chérie*, come along, come with me.'

We made our way back past innumerable monuments and stopped before a mosaic erection of the Island of Death still as doom in the shadow of cypresses. We halted a moment, and then continued our retreat. Our eyes caught the inscription on a tomb:

A faithful wife,
A loving mother,
Not dead
But gone before.

We walked on and presently stopped again and read: '*I have held faith.*' I walked in silence beside Uncle Emmanuel, Aunt Teresa and Count Valentine on the grassy edge of the path, the wet grass tingeing my boots, inhaling the scent of fresh verdure, and again I felt that soon spring would be far advanced, then there would be summer. Somehow, as slowly we made our way back through the cemetery, where thousands of mortals, gone before us, lay peacefully in the glittering wood that was awakening in spring revivification, I forgot the coffin floating in the swilling grave; I thought only that he lay here for ever, sleeping through the onset of ages in eternal forgetfulness.

We walked on, thinking, until we passed out of the Great Silent Gate. Then, once again, we were in the world of the living.

Oh, no, Aunt Teresa did not begrudge Aunt Molly the place of principal mourner. Whether her memory went back to days of early childhood when she had played together with her little brother in dreary Manchester, I know not. But Aunt Molly had been his wife, had rendered him innumerable intimate offices—which, strangely, women as a rule are not averse from doing for those they love. She had known him in all his moods, she knew in detail all his plans, his worries, his complaints, had suffered from his temper—and infidelities. As they ensconced themselves in the carriage, it was as if Aunt Teresa, red-eyed but not weeping, had been relegated to the posture of a dowager-queen, and conscious for once that our compassion was focused not on her, '*Ma pauvre Molly*!' she said: 'We both have become orphans!'

'Don't cry, dear,' said Berthe. 'It won't help. There...I'm crying myself.'

I banged the door from without, and Berthe, who was sitting on the small seat, turned the white bone handle from within, and the carriage moved and drove off. Sylvia, Gustave, Philip Brown, and Beastly got into the second carriage; Count Valentine, the General, his A.D.C., and Mme Negodyaev into the third; and Captain Negodyaev, Uncle Emmanuel, Natàsha and myself into the fourth, and followed. We drove in silence. Uncle Emmanuel's behaviour throughout had been that of a correct disinterested spectator. Only now and then, as we drove home, my uncle would say something essentially trivial—'There seem a lot of houses,' or 'That man seems to be talking to himself.' About half-way home we saw the virgin drive past with an officer. My uncle leaned out of the window and waved his hand to her, and was about to shout something, but '*Mon oncle*!' I restrained him, just in the nick of time. I was very hungry and enjoyed the quick drive. I sat and thought: they have put you into a dark wet hole and covered you with earth: while I am driving home to have my lunch! Yet on one of the seven days of the week I am bound to follow you, and there is no escape. If I do not die on a Monday, Tuesday, or Wednesday, the chances of my doing so on a Thursday, Friday or Saturday will be increasingly more probable. And should, by a miracle, my death not come off on any of these days, it will be imminent on a Sunday. The certainty of it is appalling. A friend of mine—a profound reader of character—characterized me, with astounding penetration, as the Strong Silent Man of the Kitchener type. He was quite right. At the funeral of Uncle Lucy I did not weep—nor did I want to. I thought of my own death, and thus side-tracked my emotion and spent it on myself. But now I thought: who is the next on the list? Aunt Teresa, by the looks of her, could have spared herself the journey back. But then it was not always the old and delicate who went first. She had taunted Uncle Lucy with her death, and he died before her, and she might go on living till she was a hundred, while some young slip of a thing, a newly-fledged spring chicken, departed without warning.

When we got home, the children were playing ball in the yard. They had been told that daddy had gone—gone away. And they did not worry overmuch, as they thought that when he had done his job he would in his own good time come back. Only Bubby was heard to say: 'I want my daddy.'

'S—s—sh!'

'But I *want* him.'

But her daddy, as the Russian saying is, 'had bid them a long life'. She had been his favourite.

In the house it was like a removal day. All doors were open and a draught promenaded the length and breadth of the flat; a strange dog was being chased out of the hall. Aunt Molly seemed as though in a trance and never opened her mouth. But when she returned to the great emptiness of the room that was once his abode, she collapsed in a chair and wept—wept fully, unstintingly, and the tears like a flood streamed from her stricken eyes. While in the drawing-room Aunt Teresa was receiving the condolences of the 'diplomatic corps'. Lunch was not ready. The table wasn't set. Nothing was ready. Uncle Lucy with his funeral had upset everybody. In the corridor somebody was looking for Uncle Emmanuel. He went out. It seemed the undertaker had come for payment; the cabs too had to be paid.

Returning, he took me amicably by the waist. '*Mon ami*,' he said tenderly, 'go and settle it with these people.'

42

Now that I look back on it from the vantage point of many months it is clear to me that Uncle Lucy's life was a crescendo towards madness, culminating, as you will have seen, in this extraordinary suicide in Aunt Teresa's knickers, camisole and boudoir cap. Why did he do it? Well may you ask. Yet the explanation is, perhaps, more simple than we think. It may have been because he knew that he was going mad that Uncle Lucy hanged himself, and hanged himself the way he did in order to do justice to his madness. What was the reason? I wondered whether it was monetary worry, or disillusionment in life; or whether, again, it was to indicate that it was the element of woman, '*das Ewig-Weibliche*', and more particularly woman's love of plumage, which had caused him to set out to meet his Maker in his sister's mauve silk stockings and the boudoir cap. I cannot say, I do not know, I can do nothing but record the sad and somewhat singular fact.

You will be wondering why I am writing of it at such length.

It is because I am a novelist—and a novel, as no doubt you are aware, is not the same as a short story. Aunt Teresa, when I went to her, was sitting up in bed, propped up by many pillows, and a soft transparent shawl on her slim shoulders. On the wall I saw an old photo of Anatole, and next to it another—Harry holding Nora by the hand. The mingled scent of medicine and *Mon Boudoir* aroma attacked my nostrils, till, staying with her for some little time, I got used to both. When Anatole was killed Aunt Teresa was so grief-rooted that the thought of wearing mourning for her son had never crossed her mind. But now with Lucy's death—who had frightened her with his moodiness and threats, and worried her with many an unpleasantness—she would not let the opportunity go by and sent at once for seven yards of crape, as well as black-edged writing-paper and envelopes to match in order that she might immediately attack a number of outstanding letters of condolence. 'Berthe!' she called out.

'Yes?'

'I must have black ink. I can't write in violet ink!'

'Why not?'

'How insensitive!'

There were a great number, but she was warming to her task. To answer letters was her mission, joy, and gift in life. If you wrote to Aunt Teresa on any subject whatsoever you always had a letter by return of post. '*Mon pauvre frère*!' she wrote, and stopped. She used a lot of exclamation marks. But even so, her task today was not easy. 'He had complained of sleeplessness!' she wrote. She stopped. The trouble was to say it all without making a farce of him and her. He had hanged himself, to Aunt Teresa's lasting shock, in her clothes. She could not forget this. And she did not mourn him as she felt she should have done, because she secretly resented the highly unconventional manner of his end. It did not follow the canons of good taste. It was not pre-eminently a respectable death. It was so irregular. It was awkward to tell people how he died. What made it worse was that the crêpe-de-Chine camisole and knickers—green, embroidered with flowers—were the General's souvenir brought back from Japan. The most astonishing thing about it, the most distressing, too, was that it was—well, funny. It required feats of self-restraint to bear down an involuntary impulse to giggle as she wrote about his death: '...I do so miss my poor brother Lucy!'; or, when she told about it to a sympathetic listener, to suppress a sudden chuckle as she thought of her poor brother in her knickers and the boudoir cap; so hard to keep your face straight. It seemed so wanton, so extraordinarily unnecessary. The absence of any trace of logic in his choice of conduct baffled her. She wanted to feel sorry, she did feel sorry for him, but it was so—deuced funny, and she reproached herself for that. She did not know that one could laugh and be serious at the same time. Aunt Teresa was never violent, always spoke calmly, quietly. She said: 'Other people get excited. Your Uncle Lucy, for example—he is dead, and I don't want to say anything against my poor brother—but I—(she cried softly)—I am different. I have to keep it all here (she pressed her palm to the heart), all to myself!' She had taunted him with her approaching death, and once he was affected and even cried—but he died before her. And I thought that Aunt Teresa could still be sighing and complaining when the youngest of us would be pushing up the daisies.

A decent (but not too long an) interval having elapsed after Uncle Lucy's death, Aunt Teresa sent out cards, the first half of which read: 'Commandant and Madame Vanderflint have the honour to inform you of the forthcoming marriage of Mademoiselle Sylvia Vanderflint, their daughter, with Monsieur Gustave Boulanger', while on the second half of the parchment Mademoiselle Boulanger stated, in identical terms, that she had the honour to announce the forthcoming marriage of Monsieur Gustave Boulanger, her brother, with Mademoiselle Sylvia Vanderflint. These cards were placed in large parchment envelopes and dispatched to Count Valentine, Dr. Murgatroyd, Colonel Ishibaiashi, Philip Brown, Percy Beastly, General 'Pshe-Pshe' *et fils*, Dr. Abelberg, and others, even to the legendary General and Madame Pan-Ta-Loon.

And already ties were being artificially cemented. Aunt Teresa had paid a visit to Mlle Caroline Boulanger, an elderly spinster, heavily powdered, and the children had been asked to tea.

'Uncle Gustave will take us to the Logical Gardens to see the lion this afternoon,' Harry said, strutting about in his long trousers.

'Are you afraid of the lion?'

'Yes,' he confessed.

'And where have you been all this morning?'

'To Sunday school,' he said.

'What have you been doing there?'

'Singing,' he answered.

'Hymns?'

'No.' He wrinkled his nose. 'Sumfink about Jesus.'

'And what was the sermon about?'

'Oh, all about hell.' He reflected a moment. 'Any ice-cream at hell? No? Only at heaven?'

'Yes.'

'We are going to Aunt Caroline,' said he.

'And who's Aunt Caroline?'

'S'e is a lady with a dog and two cats,' answered Harry.

'And what will the dog think of you, Harry?' said Aunt Teresa.

'I don't know what he'll think of me in my long trousers.'

In the afternoon, while the children were at Gustave's, General 'Pshe-Pshe' called on Aunt Teresa.

'I am not understood! not understood!' he said. 'Not understood by my wife, not understood by my daughter, not understood by my son; never! You alone——' He brushed her pale hand with his moustache. 'Not understood! But this is a harbour of rest, an asylum.'

The last allusion, in view of Uncle Lucy's sad end, was unpleasant, and Aunt Teresa winced just a little.

Moreover, the General confessed that the political horizon, till recently so serenely blue, was not too cheerful. He expressed incredulity at the levity of the Allies. 'I simply cannot understand their folly in ceasing to support me, for surely they must know that I can never hold out without their help, since the entire population of the country is against me. Such want of logic on their part! They must have lost their faculty of reasoning. What *were* they thinking? The Mr. Churchill is the only politician left who sees eye to eye with me. I have always had great faith in the acumen of this brilliant and courageous statesman. Like myself, he is prepared to take chances on behalf of his country, irrespective of all consequences. In our modern world this has become a quality rare among individuals, and therefore all the more to be treasured when it is found. But, I am sorry to say, his own countrymen do not always see eye to eye with him.'

Yes, he marvelled at the Allies. The more he thought of them, the more he marvelled. The General wanted to see law and order established in Russia. The population did not understand him, and—what more simple?—in order to administer the land, the General's idea (not to put too fine a point upon it) was to invade the land by first killing off the population.

'How will you do it, General? You have no men.'

The General thrust his hand into the front of his coat, after the manner of Napoleon Bonaparte, and said, in a stern, robust voice, looking ruthless:

'I will fight on with the pistol and the gibbet.'

'General,' I sighed, 'you can hang or shoot a criminal when public opinion is behind you, but you cannot shoot or hang the public, even though you may think it a criminal public, when its opinion is that *you're* the criminal.'

He looked at me with infinite reproach, as if to say: '*Et tu, Brute*!' He was silent, and then said: 'I am doing my duty before God and the fatherland.'

Aunt Teresa's blanched face with the enormous eyes turned to him. 'Dear me! How will you do it?' she asked, not without some concern. 'How will you fight? You have no men.'

'To the last man,' he said, and looked into her eyes, her deep St. Bernard eyes. He loved her, as it were, in retrospect; those years before he met her, when she was young, to him were years of separation, and now! and now! at last they met again, and in the present the whole past was reconstructed for him in this after-word, this evening glow of love. He bent over her slim white hand and brought his lips against it; this touch was to atone for all that he had missed. And she looked up to heaven with her beautiful, her lustrous, large eyes as if this woman who had never loved should pray: 'I wish I could. I want to do my earnest best—alas! it is not in my power!'

On Friday morning Beastly was to leave for England. He had been laid up with dysentery through the whole of March and first half of April, and was faithfully looked after by Berthe. Dusting his hat for him while he put on his coat, 'Write to me sometimes, won't you, Percee,' she said. 'You know how precious you are to me.'

He made his last *stink* on a Wednesday, and then left on the Friday. But owing to some misunderstanding regarding his passage, he returned at the end of the week and made *stinks* on the subsequent Tuesday, Friday, Monday, Thursday, and Saturday.

43

The Badge

Came the wedding-day, even as the dreaded day comes to the condemned, as comes the moment for the trembling rabbit when it must jump for dear life—inexorable, relentless day. Somehow we had hoped that such a day was impossible, but the day came on to prove that it was possible, a bleak day—April the 28th. The snow had not yet been cleared in the streets, but it was already warm and the pavements were dry as in summer.

Since I awoke that morning I was on tenterhooks. A dreary day. I stood at the window, my nose against the cold glass: a time when you would kill yourself for a song. A fly at the window—a mosquito in the damp—looked puzzled with life. We are half alive, half asleep, wondering why we are; could we but grope out of this slimy bog, where we had sunk, into the light from which we fell, perchance we'd find our wings.

On the floor lay my kit all spread out, and the Chink boy was packing. I looked down on to the street below—and suddenly I saw a visitor at our door: a bent old lady in a mushroom hat pulled down over a grinning skull. 'Madame Death.' And standing on the doorstep, looking at her, was Natàsha. A shiver ran down my back. But Madame Death bent double, and vanished in the backyard.

I resumed my packing. Natàsha knocked at the door, came in, proud and a little confused, put a new shaving-brush on my table—and ran away again. Her gift at my departure!

I called her back.

'Natàsha, who was that old lady outside?'

She shrugged her shoulders. 'What's it means a lady? No lady. Some mens outside—a lot of dirty mens, but no lady.'

I took up the shaving-brush and examined it. You drift along in life, I thought, and you drift into some Captain Negodyaev with a Natàsha. Attachments; partings; the keeping up of correspondence; the dropping of it, the drifting out of sight and call. How queer. And when I think of the sights, the people, the opportunities I miss at every turn, will go on missing, my heart stops dead, I gasp for breath, I clutch a chair…

Uncle Emmanuel had donned his uniform for the occasion, and his full medals, and I attached '*le sabre de mon père*', that silly sword of the 1800 pattern long since discarded for its prohibitive length. At one o'clock the service began. There was sun in the church, but bitterness in my heart. I wore my love, a rosary of pangs, on her behalf and on my own. My soul quailed as I met her eyes. If I had been weak, still, was that a reason why she should have tied herself for life to this grotesque individual with a canary moustache? I felt offended—but couldn't say who had offended me. As the organ soared forth, I felt my soul weep for her. I grieved for my Sylvia; the thought that I had in the past offended her racked my heart: I seemed to be in her soul, to feel myself an inmate of her dolorous being. And when it was all over, and they came up to Aunt Teresa to be blessed and kissed and congratulated and Gustave murmured softly from beneath his soft moustache, 'She has brought joy into my life', I could not contain myself, and muttered as I pressed her hand: 'I wish you joy of it!' I walked home along the windy icy streets, my two legs jerking forward: two wooden sticks propping up a heavy vase of grief—my heavy heart.

I strayed into the dining-room, where the table was being laid under Vladislav's direction and watched eagerly by Natàsha.

'There will be turtle soup, duck and mushrooms and pears with ice-cream!' Natàsha imparted, with glee in her sea-green eyes. I complimented Vladislav on the appearance of the festal dinner-table.

'Yes, not bad,' he agreed. 'But a long way off the French! Paris—that's a town, you might say. Streets, shops—in a word, a joy to behold! But here—*ach*!' He waved his hand with the air of a thwarted artist. 'What's the use?'

At dinner there was turtle- as well as ham-flavoured thick soup; sole with sauce made of champagne and cray-fish; saddle of baby lamb; braised duck stuffed with birds' liver and mushrooms with salad; celery with Parmesan cheese; Comice pears with cream ice and black currant jam; 'petits fours'; and baskets of fruit. The dinner was prefaced with sherry and bitter and monkey-gland cocktails, while throughout there was vodka, Château Lafitte 1900, and champagne of the brand 'Œil de Perdrix', the feast being wound up with 'Fine Champagne 1875', coffee, benedictine, curaçao and salted almonds. Aunt Teresa was anxious that it should be in the Russian custom, for fear of outraging local society. Dinner, accordingly, was at three o'clock in the afternoon. General 'Pshe-Pshe' supplied his batman, his own A.D.C. son, and a quantity of cutlery and china. A brass band (the one that had played at the funeral) had been installed by General 'Pshc-Pshe' in the dining-room and played flourishes on every suitable—and unsuitable—occasion during dinner, and the smell of the soldiers' highly polished boots was no less pronounced throughout the meal. There is in Russia what seemed to me that day an inane custom of bringing in at these nuptial feasts the word 'bitter'—at which the bride and bridegroom have to kiss.

'Strange,' said the General, 'this bread is bitter, and this wine is bitter.'

'Bitter! Bitter!' all the guests shouted exultantly.

Sylvia and Gustave kissed. He just touched her with that absurd canary moustache of his. Imagine my feelings. The General flicked out his thumb at the band, and the band played a flourish.

'Yes, that's the real Russian fashion,' laughed Aunt Teresa.

There were many toasts drunk, and at the end of each toast the band played a flourish. And even when there were no toasts, now and then, when the General flicked out his thumb, the band played a flourish. Afterwards they played flourishes of their own accord: at the stressing in conversation of a sentence, at the emphasis of a word. At the least ostensible noise of any kind, the band played a flourish.

'Ha-ha-ha-ha-ha!' Sylvia laughed.

The band played a flourish.

I sat there between Captain Negodyaev and Beastly, and listening to the inner voice in me reproaching me for the barter of my happiness, I reflected thus: the difficulty about happiness is that its technique is thoroughly unsatisfactory; that you cannot get it quickly when you want it, or easily enough to be worth having; the sacrifice demanded for its sake is apt to outweigh the motive, and, knowing that, you are loth to take it on. I was loth to take it on; and here I sit—and suffer. Still, I consoled myself that she was to me a white elephant, that on my journey in search of perfection she was a sort of luxurious trunk, a gorgeous globe-trotter for which I had no kit. She was a precious stone, a jewel I could not afford to buy. Yet beneath all these consoling reflections there lurked a truth, unheard but still disturbing, that I had missed my greatest chance of happiness in life as I might miss a train.

'Bitter! Bitter!' shouted the General exultantly. Sylvia and Gustave kissed. (Oh, where was my sword!) The band played a flourish.

I was not in pain; I only felt a heavy dullness—a spiritual headache. To-day was Saturday. What would I do now? Tomorrow was Sunday. A day of celebration and repose. A red-letter day—yes, red with anguish! And as for my sailing home—I could have only waved my hand!

As the first course was being removed the General rose and proposed the health of the bride and bridegroom, while the band played a flourish. After that, Captain Negodyaev got up and proposed the health of the bride's parents. Then speeches were made of a national character, and the General drank to the glory of the Belgian Army, the band playing, somewhat inaccurately, the Belgian national anthem. Whereupon Uncle Emmanuel rose and drank to the revival of Russia, the General, as senior Russian officer present, responding, and including England and the Allies generally in his toast (having in his festal mood forgotten their betrayal of him). 'Turning to our latest ally the Americans,' he said, 'I must observe that although they are a godless people they are nevertheless a deuced clever race. Gramophones, goloshes, footwear, vehicles, inventions, and all sorts of rubbish—they can do all that; or construct a railway, let us say, across the ocean—at that they are past-masters. The Americans! Hurrah!'

The band played a flourish. I and Beastly responded for England. Then Colonel Ishibaiashi rose to respond for Japan; everybody leaned forward and strained his attention.

'I have an honour very much,' he said, 'to speak for the honourable officers of the Allied Forces. A band of Bolsheviki that appeared Cikötoa from north-east who proud but weak retired hearing the arrival of our alliance. Perhaps they spied us and felt very much anxiety, they retired far and far at last. Therefore we can hold the peace of Cikotoa and the safety of the principal line of the railway, unused our swords. Now it has become unnecessary to stay a strong force here any more. Therefore my Commander ordered me let the alliances to return to Harbin. Soon after you will triumph taking a great honour. We accomplished our duty by your a great many assistance. I offer you my thousand thanks for your kind relief——'

Here Beastly, very red in the face, leaned over to Colonel Ishibaiashi. 'Stop talking shop, old bean,' he said, 'and tell us instead something—er—interesting—something about your damned old *geisha* girls, don't you know.'

Colonel Ishibaiashi showed his teeth. 'Ha!—Ha!—Iz zas so—zzz?' and turning to the bridal pair, 'I wisk,' he said 'your happy in this occasion. It is a little entertainment on the battlefield, but I hope you will take much *saké*, speak and sing cheerfully.' And he sat down—while the band played a flourish.

The General, who only a few moments before had urged Allied solidarity after the war, now, perhaps from excessive drink, all at once displayed a weary cynicism and disenchantment. '*Ach*!'—a weary gesture—'it's all talk, all talk. They talk of preferential treatment for the Allies, the best-favoured nation clause, and that kind of rot. But in practice what does it all amount to? We Russians, for example, have done no end of good in Armenia. But when one of our lot went to have a shave in Nahichivan, the barber spat on the soap before lathering his face. He, of course, jumped up, disgusted, and went for him. "Don't you get flurried, my beauty," the barber replied. "This is a favour we're showing you—preferential treatment. With any ordinary bloke we first spit in his snout and then rub on the soap afterwards!" Yes. That's what it amounts to—no more—he!—he!—he!' the General laughed feebly.

And looking at this mixed assorted crew, I thought: why the devil should nations fight? The shallow imbecility of 'alliances', of this or that national friendship: all nations were too uncommon and too alike to warrant any natural camping based as it were on personal preference. It was absurd. Yet they all behaved as though there were some real lasting advantage in such a stampede for safety. There were fools who advocated wars for economic reasons, and when, after the war, victors and vanquished alike rotted in the economic morass which the war had made, they forgot the economic argument (till they fomented a new war). It was incredible. No one wanted the war, no one with the exception of a score of imbeciles, and suddenly all those who did not want a war turned imbecile and obeyed the score of imbeciles who had made it, as if indeed there were no alternative to war—the simple common-sense alternative of, at any rate, not going to war about it, whatever happens: seeing that whatever happens cannot in the nature of the case be worse than war.

What a mixture we were, even within each nationality. The Russian batman Stanislav was more of a Pole than a Russian; Brown was more of a Canadian than an American; Gustave more of a Fleming than a Walloon, and I—well, you know who I am. And—to make the gathering more truly representative of the late World War—there was a youthful British officer, one of those young and simple and good chaps who, in wars waged for freedom, civilization, the avengement of national honour, the suppression of tyranny, the restoration of law and order, and such-like blood-exacting sacred causes, are freely sacrificed by the thousand, and their conception of the world is a vague sense that something is wrong somewhere and that somebody ought to be hanged.

So they set off to their doom, cheerfully, on the off-chance that their foe is that evil whose blood they are after, and having set out on their righteous (and adventurous) cause they now care but little about the origin of the wrong. And so they set out to kill and maim, and to be killed and maimed in turn, cheerfully, in the 'old bean' sort of fashion. Their mode of thinking, their manner of talking, is at one with the state of their soul. They go about asking everybody all day long: 'Do barmaids eat their young?' They strike on a happy phrase like 'You're all shot to pieces', and it becomes a sort of standing sentence applicable to any person at any given moment. Or they pick up some phrase like 'The odd slab of bread', and then go on referring to 'The odd slab of beer', 'The odd slab of sleep', 'The odd slab of wash', and the odd slab of everything. Their conversation deteriorates into relating to each other in the morning the number of whisky-and-sodas they have consumed the night before.

'Bitter! Bitter!' shouted the General.

The band played a flourish.

Sylvia and Gustave kissed.

I have often read in novels and I have heard it said 'How prettily she laughs', and it has always left me cold, because I could not conceal the thought of the underlying artificiality of such a pretty laugh. A laugh to be pretty, it seemed to me, must be natural and unconscious. But now, though I had seen her laugh no end of times before, I thought with eagerness, I thought in exultation: 'How prettily she laughs!'

What a beauty, what a treasure, for sure, I was giving away. And to whom, of all people! How stupid. To miss one's happiness by worse than an oversight, to surrender heedlessly the one thing that one should have kept. And the devils of hell, ten thousand strong, hissed into my ear from every hidden crevice of my brain: 'You have missed your chance, missed it! missed it! missed! missed! missed!'

'Bitter!' shouted the General.

Sylvia and Gustave kissed.

The band played a flourish.

Facing me sat Harry, and suddenly he asked:

'Where is God? Is He everywhere?'

'I suppose so.'

'Is He in this bottle?'

'I suppose so.'

'But how has He got in with the cork on?'

'He was there, I suppose, before the bottle was made.'

'But how is it He hasn't got drowned in the wine?'

'He can exist anywhere, I suppose.'

'But I can't see Him,' said he, peering through the Château Lafitte 1900.

'Nor can I,' I confessed, 'as yet.'

But having found an opening, Harry would not shut up any more, and for the rest of the meal kept pestering us with questions, such as: 'Is the halo fastened to God's head with an elastic?' Or 'What would God do if a big tiger suddenly rushed at Him?' Or, descending to a lower plane, 'Why can't you chew milk?'

Dr. Murgatroyd had just arrived, after a particularly trying journey, travelling six thousand versts from Omsk in an old cattle-truck without springs. In the present state of things it was indeed a rare occasion when the train did not stop every few versts in consequence of some congestion on the line. But as it happened, Dr. Murgatroyd's truck had been hooked on to the special train of a certain combative general who was grimly intent on making his way through to Harbin with as few stops as possible, and to make his determination more grimly felt by others he had an armoured train in front of him and another at the back of him. And Dr. Murgatroyd, seated for days on end on the floor of his cattle-truck, alone amid shells of sunflower seeds and peel of oranges—the sole food on which he lived—careless and indifferent as he was, he yet prayed to heaven that the train might stop if only for a moment. But the warlike general, in his grim determination, voted otherwise, and so seated and shaken to pieces, Dr. Murgatroyd finally arrived in Harbin. When the door of the cattle-truck was pulled open, the railway authorities beheld the curious spectacle of Dr. Murgatroyd, unshaven and unwashed, lying on an enormous heap of sunflower seed shells and orange peels, perusing a book. Dr. Murgatroyd had intended to give a lecture at the local Institute on the subject of the Union of the Orthodox and the Anglican Churches, but, cruelly shaken by the journey in the cattle-truck, he hesitated.

'And what was Omsk like just before the evacuation? I can well imagine!' asked Captain Negodyaev at the dinner-table.

Dr. Murgatroyd expressed a look of ominous significance. 'These days,' said he, 'we live on a volcano.'

'Very truly said. I have myself two daughters, Dr. Murgatroyd, and I feel anxious for their future. Màsha, poor thing, is married. But Natàsha is here. That is Natàsha over there.'

Dr. Murgatroyd looked across the table absently and pitched his fork into a sardine.

'I regret that in the present unsettled state of affairs her education is being neglected. But then she is still only eight, and already speaks English like a native.'

'That is very necessary,' said Dr. Murgatroyd. 'A closer knowledge of the two languages will inevitably draw the two countries together and facilitate the reunion of the Orthodox and the Anglican Churches. At Omsk I had a conversation with Metro-politan Nicholas and Archimandrite Timothy, and both ecclesiastics seemed struck with what I had to say.'

The Russian national cause had swayed to and fro with the territory held, the champions of that cause, irrespective of the fortunes of war, losing increasingly national colour through support by foreign troops, and the champions of the Revolution gaining it by their defence of the centre, the historic citadels of real Russia against foreign 'invaders'; in addition, they had the revolutionary cause undisputed. And one began to ask: Who are the *Russians*? The masses outnumbered their ancient leaders. They had their own leaders. The ancient leaders found that they had no one to lead. Their Russian national cause was now a void cause: its Russian nationalism having deserted to the enemy with the ground itself, leaving a labelled carcass. The ancient leaders became crusaders on the coast: their cause was a lost cause, in addition to which it became a personal cause and an international militarist cause. It was, I think one may safely say, a hopeless cause, with the bottom knocked out of it. The tug-of-war was a rout. The revolutionaries had won the national Russian cause in addition to their own revolutionary one.

It is like this that the Russian Revolution presents itself today. But at the time of happening it was a conglomeration of disorderly incidents, of vile crimes and arbitrary acts, of petty vanities and senseless cruelties, of good intentions frequently misplaced and more frequently misunderstood, and people meaning often the same thing mutually intent on murder. It was thus that the Revolution affected Dr. Murgatroyd and many others of his outlook; and for the disorderly clamour of long-suppressed urgencies and the growing chaos in the economic life they refused to recognize this tempestuous movement as at all inevitable, but ascribed it to the follies of this or that politician, to the work of German or Jewish 'agitators', or regarded it as a bad joke.

Dr. Murgatroyd had been a busy figure in those days at Omsk.

He had conducted, with considerable vehemence, an anti-Bolshevik propaganda, and in his zeal and fervour had overstrained his object. He had painted the Bolsheviks in colours at once so black and lurid, made their atrocities appear so extravagant and flamboyant in their ghastliness, that when the Siberian soldiers, whom it was his task to whip up into a fight against the Soviets, beheld the pamphlets which Dr. Murgatroyd turned out for their consumption, they were seized by a panic. 'No! if they're as bad as that,' said they, 'we're off'—and deserted in battalions. Dr. Murgatroyd had made the Kolchak cause his own. At that most critical time, when the fate of Omsk hung in the balance, he was invited to attend an extraordinary sitting of the Council of Ministers in order to take part in the debate as to the possible evacuation of the city, and Dr. Murgatroyd, not a military gentleman, had made a speech in Russian, drawing the attention of the ministers to the lamentable condition of the city gardens, and suggesting that the British representatives might be approached in order that a few experts in garden-planning might be dispatched without delay from England—a country which, as Dr. Murgatroyd explained, excelled in that particular art. His untimely solicitude on behalf of the city in process of evacuation was not fully appreciated by the members of the council, for it appeared they had some difficulty in understanding his Russian, so much so, that when at the close of this memorable sitting he walked up to a venerable grey-haired general to ask him what he thought of the speech which he, Dr. Murgatroyd, had made in Russian the venerable general, with a charming smile, expressed regret at having in his youth neglected the study of the English tongue, in consequence of which he was rather at a loss to catch the meaning of everything that Dr. Murgatroyd had, no doubt, so wisely and admirably expressed.

'I want to give up journalism,' said Dr. Murgatroyd, 'and go into politics seriously, on my return to England.'

I said nothing. I thought: in so large, clumsy, inaccurate, uncertain, fumbling, blundering, blustering a body as politics, one fool more or less does not matter.

'And what will you do after the war now that you are grown up, Alexander?' Sylvia asked.

'What would you like me to do?'

She thought for a while. 'You don't like militarism. Well, in that case I should like you to go into the Navy.'

'Of course there's the uniform—travels in foreign parts—dances—flagships—eguilettes. But to think of it, that a man should go to the trouble of being born, reared, educated, for one sole purpose in life: to drive a hole in another people's vessel and send it to the bottom of the sea. In anticipation of that task he reads and writes, plays and loves, but all this is merely an interlude, a diversion in which he indulges till comes the grand proud moment of his life: he drives a hole in some other people's vessel and sends it to the bottom of the sea.'

'You are angry,' she said.

I was angry: I visualized '*le sabre de mon père*', and then I looked at Gustave. Why did I let another have her? Terrestrial love is not for ever—perhaps once in all eternity. I suddenly began to think: she is disgusted with me because I did not ignore, did not overrule her problem of deciding between happiness and sacrifice by simply taking her away. If not for this dilemma, these subversive solaces, I could have sat now beside her who was my love. What hypocrisy my pretending I was debarred from acting thus by considerations of my aunt. Why was I not of the Stone Age when I could have clubbed my aunt and carried Sylvia away? I had given up my precious claim—I who could have moulded her to my will. She was like wax—and like wax she had been moulded by what?—by the sloppy selfishness of Aunt Teresa! Oh, it was not easily to be borne. It was not to be borne!

Love is kindled by the wind of the imagination, blazed into a consuming flame by these trivial, unreasoning, and utterly contemptible twin-brothers—regret and jealousy—who are yet stronger than the human will. Stronger because they have secured an unfair leverage upon it. As a child can lead a bull by the ring in his nostrils, so they, too, fasten to the nerve centres, as it were, of human happiness and pain—and conquer shamelessly. It isn't strength of will, nor the visible amount of damage wrought in you; it's the particular leverage by which pain digs up your soul that matters. And the leverage by which I was made to suffer out of all proportion to my loss was the thought that it had been entirely my fault that there was any loss at all. So far our relations had been as simple as those of a cock and his consort. All I did was to say: 'Cock-cock-cock-cockoricoo!' And Sylvia after me: 'Cock-cock-cock-cockoricoo!' The same trait I observed in Harry and Nora. What he said, she said. And even when I quoted something like:

The Spanish Fleet thou canst not see, because
It is not yet in sight.

Sylvia, though she neither knew nor cared whence this quotation came, would echo gladly:

The Spanish Fleet thou canst not see, because
Ha-ha-ha-ha...not yet in sight.

I hungered for her being. I was jealous of myself, of the days when I strutted about like a cock and she followed me like a pet hen and echoed all my sounds. And the thought occurred to me: that in eternal hell nothing but our memory will be left us to tease us over that which we had wilfully denied ourselves in life.

'Bitter!' shouted the General.

They kissed. The band played a flourish.

Beastly and Brown, who sat side by side, were boasting, it seemed, for all they were worth.

'Gently! Gently!' I prompted.

'That's all right,' he guffawed. 'I believe in talking to an American in his own language! Ha! Ha! Ha!'

As the dinner progressed, Beastly and Brown grew more and more tender and brotherly. Captain Negodyaev, on my left, soulful from drink, nudged my arm, and looking at Beastly said: 'I am a captain, he is a major. But we have no majors any more. A Russian staff-captain is equal to your captain, and a Russian captain to your major. So he is a major, and I am a captain, and we are brothers-in-arms, and I want to give him something. Wait, I want to give him something, because he is a major and I am a captain, and we are brothers-in-arms. I want to give him something. Tell him so.'

'What?'

He took off his badge. 'This is my regimental badge,' he said. 'I want to give him this because it's my dearest possession, and he is a major and I am a captain, and we are brothers-in-arms. Tell him so, will you.'

I nudged Beastly's arm, but he was busy talking to Brown and only said: 'Half a mo.'

'He is busy,' I said.

'Tell him that it's my dearest possession. I had it on my breast when the bullet struck it and so saved my life. I swore then I would never part with it, but would hand it on to my daughters and their children. But to-night I want to give it to him because, as I say, he is a major and I am a captain, and we are equal in rank and brothers-in-arms, and it's the most precious thing that I have. I want him to value it. Tell him so, tell him.'

'Half a mo,' Beastly said, as I nudged his arm, and went on saying to Brown, looking at him with dim, soft eyes:

'You're a jolly good fellow, old Philip, and I don't mind the United States joining the British Empire any day—any day.'

'Gee! You're a swell guy, Percy,' said Brown, 'and we'll join your empire the day you transfer the capital to Washington.'

'Look here, Beastly,' I said. 'Negodyaev——'

'One man at a time, one man at a time.'

'Tell him,' Captain Negodyaev urged, 'how dear it is to me.'

'Oh, God, wait a little, man!' snarled Beastly. 'I can't talk to two men at a time.'

Captain Negodyaev expostulated vociferously.

'Just you dry up, ole man! Don't you get too excited,' said Beastly, turning to him with dull eyes.

'But he wants to give you his badge,' I explained.

Captain Negodyaev gave me his badge, which I handed over to Beastly.

'That's all right, old bean,' he said to the Russian, pocketing the badge, 'but I can't talk to everyone at once, can I?' And he turned back to Brown.

'Did you tell him? Did you explain to him?' Captain Negodyaev accosted me. 'Will he value it?'

'Oh yes, he'll value it all right.'

'But he didn't say anything.'

'He was busy talking to Brown.'

'But this is my dearest possession.'

For the rest of the meal Captain Negodyaev was taciturn. He

was no longer soulful but speechless, as if mortally hurt. But I had my own worries, and I could not be bothered with his. People, objects, conversations were the 'atmosphere' charge with my love. There was only one thing—my jealous love, and all the other things claimed my attention and added to my suffering. I saw her sitting in the evening, the soft lamplight on her dark head. I heard her laugh, or play the *Four Seasons of the Year*: the tune which made you want to cry. To be running with her in a field, to tramp the down with her in the rain, to dream of her as she sat at dinner one night in her champagne georgette, looking the tenderest of fairies, her dark velvety eyes blinking bashfully, softly. And then one wakes—she is not there. I fancied writing to her from afar: 'It's now past midnight. I've just come back from a dinner where I'd heard someone say "Sylvia"—and the thought of you went through my heart like an arrow. I couldn't hear what my neighbour was saying; I listened politely, but my soul was with you, thousands of miles away. Where are you, Sylvia-Ninon?

Frisch weht der Wind
Der Heimat zu:
Mein irisch Kind,
Wo weilest du?

'And I think: perhaps she will get this letter as she is dining out with Gustave, and will read it to him in cold blood, like that letter from the man in the rubber trade which she once read out to me. I can see you so clearly before me. I can't forget those eyes, those luminous, lustrous eyes, that soft cooing voice: "Alexander, listen. You never listen when I speak to you, just like water on a duck's back" (oh, wouldn't I listen now!), and those soft kisses, and our love.'

I remembered suddenly that the only thing that I had ever said to her that was at all encouraging, the only thing which showed any other than a sexual interest, was: 'You shouldn't eat so many chocolates; it's bad for your teeth.' And this, after having reluctantly bought her a box of Gala Peter—at five shillings a pound.

Love is like a match lit in the dark: it illumines all the lurking sensibilities for pain—your own and hers. How senseless, how unstable! Gustave looked triumphant at the end of satisfied achievement. And swiftly I conceived a situation typical of the incongruity of life. A plot for a short story. While one man was down and out, another, who has succeeded, was holding forth on the glory of struggle!

I felt a surface unhappiness which dominated the depths of my real happiness; I fretted, but all the time I felt that I was fretting over things not worth the pain. We were so earnest, so unforgiving, exacting, intense; we were shouting ourselves hoarse till we were deaf to the real inner voice which even in moments of peace seemed scarcely resolute enough to make itself heard; and beneath it all was the sense that all this, as it were borrowed emotion, though consuming and painful enough, was trivial and unnecessary.

'Champagne! Champagne!' The sound of flying corks, the sparkling wine, voices, music…I felt sorry for myself, jealous of my former casual self whom she had loved, of the thought that she had loved me when I was not worthy of her love, and that now I could have kissed her feet she should care for me no more. And as I watched her tears came to my eyes.

Dinner over, I was invited to play, literally dragged to the piano. I played that voluptuous bit from *Tristan*, but it aroused no enthusiasm. I was dishonoured. Dr. Murgatroyd gave us a comic song, which must have been a modern comic song about the time of Joseph Chamberlain. Mr. Walton, the British diplomatic representative, who, according to *Who's Who*, was 'privately educated', had been instructed in the art of playing the piano, and urged by the military (who looked upon this distinguished civilian as withal a good fellow), took his position at the much tried upright piano, while we others, linking up in a brotherly trellis-work of interlocked hands, made a large circle: General 'Pshe-Pshe' standing by Uncle Emmanuel, Beastly by General 'Pshe-Pshe', Colonel Ishibaiashi by Beastly, I by Colonel Ishibaiashi, the French Colonel by me, and as the music began, shaking our crossed hands with more and more emphasis to the slow deliberate rhythm of the Auld Lang Syne, our shining faces as we sang out expressing beatitude and loyalty everlasting. Having completed the song, Mr. Walton repeated it with more precision and deliberation, Percy

Beastly stressing the handshake which, as it were, determined that the word of Britain was as good in peace as in war. The Italian did not lag behind in warmth. Little Uncle Emmanuel, by the gravity with which he kept up the rhythm, showed that he had given his all, and had nothing more to give. Captain Negodyaev, probably still thinking of Percy Beastly's boorishness, looked gloom itself, and, even as his country, stood aloof and only shared half-heartedly in the triumph of the Allied arms. Brown's attitude, in its frank bright smile, betrayed the thought that though, to a Yank, foreigners all of us, we were a decent bunch, and that 'better late than never' was, after all, worth something to us, conceal it as we may. And the Frenchman in his cool but amiable detachment showed that he did his level best to recollect that France had had some small assistance from outside in winning her victorious war. On and on, on and on, our eyes shining, the sweat running down our faces, our clasped hands came down with a deadening thud to the ever-slackening pace, but gathering emphasis, of the song. If this was not the high climax of victory, the last pitch of the paroxysm of rejoicing, the apotheosis of triumph, the Allied cause victorious *in excelsis*, then there was no Allied cause. Mr. Walton, as if feeling that it was the Allied cause *in excelsis*, interjected between each bar of quavers two semi-quavers with his left hand low down on the scales, the effect of which can be imagined. Beastly stressed more and more violently, till one felt that one's hands would drop off; the Jap sang louder and louder. Victory was ours. The enemy lay prostrate. Heaven had triumphed.

As the time of jollity came to an end and we were dancing in one another's caps in the corridor (General 'Pshe-Pshe' in Colonel Ishibaiashi's, I in the Italian Major's, the French Colonel in mine, Beastly in the Czech's, the Jap in the Yank's, and so forth) suddenly I noticed Captain Negodyaev's badge on a table in the hall. I picked it up quickly and went into the dining-room where he stood by the fire-place, brooding, and handed it back to him. 'There.'

He took it darkly. Then, suddenly, he flung the badge into the fire, which, however—it being spring—was laid but not lit. 'Well, that's his affair,' I thought, and went out into the hall to see the guests out.

When I returned to the dining-room I saw Vladislav crouching at the fire-place, and Captain Negodyaev standing over him, saying:

'You blithering idiot! What are you squatting and staring at me for? Look for the damned thing! Look for it!'

44

Let him kiss me with the kisses of his mouth:
For thy love is better than wine.

'Sadie.'

'Yes. Sadie. I am afraid I shall always have that name now.'

The evening sun pressed through the window, over the carpet, over the silk chair. The flies raced like mad round the globe. They seemed to make this their headquarters—a meeting-place. And a wasp, too, was not long in coming. For a moment, we were alone.

'What can I say? What is there to say?' My words choked in my throat.

'Little Prince, you cannot be as lonely as I am.'

The sun vanished, vanished from the carpet, from the silk chair. The flies dispersed to the windows and walls. It had become difficult to breathe. The clouds gathered more and more ominous. A sudden gust; the garden gate slammed. Then a few large and warm drops pelted the hard dusty road, and at once there was the sound of fine rain on the leaves and the hum, long and loud, in the air. And from afar rolled the dim basso of thunder. Already the lightning zigzagged once or twice, in front of your very brows, it seemed. The rain was one mass of grey vertical mist. We stood at the window, inhaling the fresh breezy boon. How long would it last?

'*He*?'

'He is there, with *maman*—talking.'

'Gustave——' I sighed.

'I don't like his name.'

'Why? Flaubert was called Gustave. It ought to be distinguished.

It's no worse than mine any day. Georges—there's only Georges Carpentier. Unsuitable association for an intellectual!'

'If it were just the name…' She looked at me. Suddenly, shyly: 'I dreamt last night you and I were flying in an aeroplane,' she said. 'I threw out two of your books, and you were so angry, so angry—you leapt after them straight out of the aeroplane, and we were so high up, so dreadfully high up. I cried my eyes out, but they could not find you. Afterwards somehow you returned—but how I forget.'

I looked at her. My soul, after much pain, had become strangely quiet. I just looked at her and could not speak.

'In the *Daily Mail*,' she said, 'there was an article the other day about love—*How to win and keep a woman's love*.'

'The *Daily Mail*…*The Daily Mail*…But why the *Daily Mail*? Why do you read the *Daily Mail*?'

'Because I like these articles they have about love and things. I follow them to know how we stand, how we love each other, you see? You should read them.'

'I have been so weak,' I wailed melodramatically—and really feeling the part. 'So miserably weak, so indecisive. I have imbibed this curse of a Hamletian vacillation with the name, I suppose.'

'Never mind, darling, we shall travel. We shall come over to Europe one day and see you; won't it be nice?'

'And Gustave!' I wailed, almost in tears. 'Gustave! Gustave! of all people! Casting pearls——So silly, so really idiotic when one comes to think—isn't it? Why was he dragged into this affair? Oh, when you consider, think ahead, weigh up, select—it's almost better, really better, if you never thought at all.'

'Never mind, darling.'

'I deserve what I got—and with interest—I deserve it, honestly. But you; why *you*? Why should *you* have been let down as you have been, by me and your mother—me and your mother!'

'Never mind, darling. He doesn't count. Nothing will count. We shall think of each other all the time, and nothing, nothing will count.'

I looked at her, I looked long and steadily, and her eyes blinked several times in the interval. I looked—and suddenly the tears welled up from my eyes. 'Queenie!'

'What?'

'My little queenie.'

'Yes…Prince.'

'What?'

'My little prince.'

'Yes. Oh, must we part?'

'How cruel!'

'Sixteen thousand miles.'

'Don't, or I shall cry.'

And the evening seemed to listen, to grieve, to sympathize with our losing each other.

'The fact of the matter,' she purled, looking into my face with her dark velvety eyes, 'is that I shall never see you again.'

'Gustave!' called my aunt. He went back to her.

'There, he's coming now'—Sylvia turned to me as if to go. She liked Gustave well enough against a background—the background of other people; the more the better. Being alone with him was another matter. Then he was like a thread pulled out of a pattern—a poor thing. When she was engaged to him she would never be alone with him, but insisted on going out with friends, myself included. And now she must be pointedly alone with him.

'Gustave! Good night,' said my aunt. 'Sylvia won't go home with you to-night. *Elle n'ira pas.*'

And, again, I was reminded of military orders: 'B Company will parade.' But she deigned to add:

'She is too tired to-night and will stay at home. *Elle restera à la maison. À demain, alors*!'

Gustave just raised his faint brow a little—as though it came to him that the practice was rather against precedent in most marriages. He gulped once or twice, coughed a little, and adjusted his Adam's apple. He pulled at his collar in a timid gesture, cleared his throat half-heartedly, and said, 'Well, then, good night, *maman*.'

'Good night, Gustave'—she touched his faint brow as he bent over her and licked her blanched hand— '*à demain*!'

For a moment he stood there as if wanting to say something, then gulped and went out.

He was gone.

If you doubt this, I simply say to you: you do not know my

aunt. We stood there, Sylvia and I, it seemed both of us breathless. The thing was too sudden. Even Aunt Teresa herself looked as though she had astonished herself. Suddenly I understood the secret power of that woman. I understood—what so far I had failed to understand—how she had managed to take her husband with her all the way to the Far East in the midst of 'the greatest war the world had ever seen'.

'Now all go to bed. Ugh! I feel so done up.'

'But it's barely eight o'clock!'

'Never mind. All go to bed. You are leaving early tomorrow.'

I strolled about the house, pondering on my departure. My trunks were packed. My cupboards bare. My hours void.

Sylvia was in the drawing-room. She rose to meet me. 'I'm so glad you've come.'

'Why, darling?'

'I felt so sad just now. I had a bath—and suddenly I felt so lonely—lonely—lonely—as if I were all alone in the world.' She blinked. 'I have only you to talk to.'

A kiss.

'O—o—o!'

'What?'

'A sore on my lip.'

'Never mind.'

'Sylvia!'

'Yes.'

'Sylvia!'

'Yes.'

'Sylvia! *Sylvia*! Sylvia! Sylvia! Sylvia!...' I murmured in varying accents, rapturous intonations, as she nestled closer to me. We were alone, and the world had shrunk into a corner of our soul, listened, and was silent.

I kissed her on the eyes—her hazel eyes—her warm and tender eyelids. 'There. And again. And again.'

Sylvia kissed impetuously, as though there were no noses on our faces which got in the way. I kissed more carefully, avoiding the noses. And, by this time, kisses for me had become as plentiful and unsought as chocolates at a birthday party. Through the open window there came the smell of spring—the fragrant moist and heavy odour.

'If you go on loving me, and I go on loving you—what else do we want?' she said.

'We want each other, of course, in the flesh.'

'We can still love each other, *think* of each other.'

'*Think*!' I echoed sardonically.

Outside was spring, as beautiful as the last, as beautiful as the next. The sun had come out, but the rain still fell slowly, perfunctorily.

How, after a run of ill-luck, of despair, life blossoms out unexpectedly.

We went into the garden, walked under the trees, felt the rain-drops on our faces—cool, clear, splashy silver drops. When life smiles on you, it compensates for all. The beeches, dark and delicate against the fading sky, like Sylvia's lace hat, stood passive and unquestioning, and there seemed wisdom in their unquestioning acceptance of all things, in their taking life for granted; wisdom—and a sadness.

'Put on that champagne georgette, put it on for me.'

'But it's a ball-dress, darling.'

'Never mind. I love you in it. I want to remember you in it—for ever.'

She looked serious, blinking. 'Will you, darling?'

'Yes.'

She went in, and I remained, and, waiting for her, paced the lawn and watched the trees listless in the melancholy of revivification. I remembered suddenly last spring, our love, my mood one evening. There was the memory of a promise unfulfilled—of former springs—in this early breaking rigour as I drew a full breath of the twilight dampness that engulfed me, a promise that I knew would never be fulfilled this side of the grave. And I felt sad. Not because we two were destined to be parted, and I was leaving on the morrow. I think that were we never to be parted I would have been just as sad. Had I been thieved of love—as Gustave was that evening—I know I would have felt, and felt acutely, the melancholy of reviving life. But I had been rewarded handsomely and unexpectedly, yet it was spring—and I was sad. This sadness we attribute to terrestrial reasons but that visits us in spring, like a haunting phrase of music, this sadness without reason—what is it? Is it regret because we, fragments of a single soul, grieve in separation, lament our being 'misunderstood'? But if we cannot understand ourselves! if at our best we are half empty, what answer can we give each other, we who have grown sceptical, and justly so, of answers, we broken melodies who can but ask and ask (because there *is* a question, and so there *is* a Something) when we are joined at last in the grand union of a universal soul: what message shall we send unto the skies but yet another question, 'orchestral' but unanswered as before? Till we lose heart and cry in anguish: How long, O Lord, how long?

Upstairs in the drawing-room Sylvia, in her fragile champagne georgette, looking the tenderest of fairies, came up whistling and hopping slightly on her toes.

'Oh, how I love you!'

'Oh! Really?' she said. 'Oh! Oh! I see.' She talked to herself, cooing like a dove. We sat on the sofa. I examined her rings, and a pang shot through my heart at the sight of the ring next to her wedding-ring. And, as if divining my thought, she took it off and showed it me silently. This: *Set me as a seal upon thine heart.* And our eyes clouded.—Then, in a newspaper, she came across a poem which she thought fitted the occasion, and read it out to me in a whisper:

Some day our eyes shall see
The face we love so well,
Some day our hands shall clasp
And never say 'Farewell.'

'I want a lock of your hair.'

'Yes, darling, you can have whatever lock of hair you like.'

I fetched the scissors.

She took two of my cards, on the one side of which was: 'Captain G. H. A. Diabologh, British Military Representative, Harbin', and on the other she copied the poem, reading out as she wrote:

Some day my eyes shall see
The face…no, the boy I love so well,
Some day my hands shall clasp——

'Not "my hands", surely. You don't want to clasp your own hands. You can do that all the time.'

'Well, "our hands", then.'

'Lips, not hands.'

'Yes, lips. Some day our lips shall clasp—but not "clasp" surely?'

'No, meet.'

'And never say "Farewell." '

And having completed both cards, she handed me one and kept the other, as keepsakes for eternal remembrance.

'And the petals of this yellow flower.' She gave me a petal, and kept one for herself.

'Yes.'

There was silence.

I looked at her. 'Why don't you say something?'

'There's a great lump in my throat,' she said, 'so talking is impossible.'

I went over to the piano, and striking up a few bars began to compose on the theme of farewell. But the result was abominable.

Sylvia opened a page with strings of demi-semi-quavers—thick as blackberries. I struck a few notes and then stopped. Crochets and quavers depress me. And when I cannot read difficult music I sound a few bars and then pretend it's no use going on.

'Go on!' she enjoined.

'I'm not in the mood.'

And I played *Tristan* instead. I played louder and louder and louder. The door opened suddenly and Berthe came in.

'Your Aunt Teresa asks you not to play so loud; she does not feel well.'

'Oh, bother!'

Berthe counted fifteen valerian drops into the glass which she held in her hand, and then departed.

To get away from them!—*to get away from them*!—to be undisturbed for the night—that is what we wanted and craved for above all else.

I looked into her eyes.

'Darling, I do, I *do*, I *will* miss you. But I shall come back,' she said.

I played softly—improvising again as I went along.

'What is this?'

'Set me as a seal upon thine heart.'

She smiled.

'It is, really.'

Sylvia, so light, so fragile, pale and delicate in her georgette, like a China rose, sat behind me on a high marble table (on which Dr. Murgatroyd once upon a time had burnt the seat of his trousers), gently swinging her legs. Suddenly, as I played, tears welled up from her large hazel eyes.

I looked at her. 'Did you see my crying, dear?'

'No.'

'As I played I did.'

'Don't cry. If you cry I shall cry too.'

'But you had tears,' I said, a little jealous. 'I saw.'

'A little.'

I improvised and improvised till, in the end, I came a cropper. I was sorry now for all we did not do: for the walk we never took; for the kiss I did not press nor linger over. 'For ever and ever and ever——'

'Never mind, dear; you shall come to me to-night,' she whispered.

'What?' I stifled a gasp of surprise, but could not help looking incredulous at this news too good to be true.

She said: 'Come to me, dear, to-night, after ten, when they are all asleep. Promise me!'

'You want me to?' I said complacently, checking my surprise instinctively for fear that my shock might shock her off her declared intention, as I would to anyone who offered me the sum of £100,000—to preclude its seeming unnaturally generous to the donor. 'You want me to?'

'Yes.'

And I daresay since, as I now perceived, she had deliberately imparted this unexpected piece of news in a complacent tone so as to startle me the more into a thrill, my own complacency (the policy of which she did not see) was somewhat of a disappointment to her. I ought to have thrilled with gratitude at the new lease of love that she was offering me; but the novelty of it by now had worn off a little. 'And Gustave?' I said uncertainly, anxious for confirmation.

'Well—it's the last time. So he shouldn't mind.—I mean—it being the first time. And besides,' she said, 'he won't know.'

'He might find out.'

'He'll find out nothing'—she shook her head. 'He's such a ninny!'

'You—you are sure you don't mind, darling?'

'All young people who love each other live with each other.'

'Of course they do! Of course!'

The reader knows that at the time of her renouncing me, without a murmur, at her selfish mother's bid, I was touched profoundly by Sylvia's self-sacrifice. Passion had become compassion. Oh, what a high, exalted form of love! But when suddenly the tables turned, I thought: 'Why not? After all, why should my silly aunt have it all her own silly way?'

You will have to square my aunt over it, whether you will or no. This whole business of our love had been so tampered with by Aunt Teresa that it was, for all practical purposes, out of our hands. And now, after a long series of reverses, the opportunities simply played into our hands. To have acted differently I could not have been George Hamlet Alexander Diabologh, nor she Sylvia Ninon Thérèse Anastathia Vanderflint. So if blame you must, blame Aunt Teresa. I have no words strong enough to condemn her reprehensible behaviour. It was wicked. It was unforgivable. It was—it was a damned shame!

At about twenty minutes before ten I sat in my attic and watched the town dissolve in the gathering gloom. Foolish associations press into one's brain—*Götterdämmerung*. I scanned the pages of a book devoted to a scholarly analysis of the difference between what is 'subjective' and 'objective', and meditating on this difference nearly fell asleep. I am, as you may know, an intellectual. I smoked one cigarette, then lit another, and when the clock on my table struck ten, I threw away the cigarette, and went to Sylvia.

I do not know how far you are prepared to follow me in my attempt to leave nothing out. I am an inexperienced writer, a new hand at this business of depicting life. However that may be, I knocked at Sylvia's door. There was no answer. I went in. And there was no one there.

I caught the scent of *Cœur de Jeanette*, and of powder. Here I sat in Sylvia's room, looked at her girlish books, her girlish things. And I grew sad, sad at my departure. For some reason this insistent passage from Maupassant, which I had run across in Arnold Bennett, clung to my brain and would not let go—'How I have wept, the long night through, over the poor women of the past, so beautiful, so tender, so sweet, whose arms have opened for the kiss, and who are dead!' And it seemed as though Sylvia were already dead, ruined, gone—the way of all damnation!

I stood up. I saw my face in the glass. I combed my black mop of hair back from the forehead with her comb: it gave me a secret thrill of pleasure to do so. The comb sparkled. How exquisite, how overwhelmingly happy was life! The big bird had stirred its wings in me, ready to fly. I looked round. I could wish I had flowers—to invade our room with flowers, as in *Le Lys Rouge*. But now there was no time. On the stained and tattered wall there was a copy of an English oleograph—heaven knows how it had found its way here, and why Sylvia had not had the impulse to remove it—of a young woman in wedding dress and a bouquet of roses in her white-gloved hand, bearing the inscription: 'An anxious moment—waiting for the bridegroom.' And I thought: '*Our* roles are reversed.' I looked out of the window, my brow pressed against the chilly glass, wondering, hoping, doubting, the town eclipsing into darkness, the growing string of lights winking steadily, demurely. The flowers on the wallpaper. How they complement each other in making figures! Tick-tick, tick-tick—this is æon beating upon æon, time receding into the past, life running down. On the table was a bronze bust of Sylvia done by a young sculptor of our acquaintance. What beckoned those shoulders, those breasts? What raptures did they cajole? Suddenly I felt that I was basking in the heat of the sun, bathing in empyrean anticipations: this beauty I had always looked for and somehow always missed was mine—to be mine almost any minute. It was as if the future and the past had merged into one vast vague dream; but the present has come to stay, has become momentary and eternal, and intolerable enough on that account. And I thought of how, when all this tribulation and excitement should be over, I would return once more to my peaceful, sober treatise in connexion with the evolution of an attitude.

Then she came. She did not speak; she only looked anxiously at the door. I went immediately and locked it, once, and then again, thus feeling that we were doubly secure. She put her finger to her lips: 'S—sh!—If—if anyone should knock you'll have to go into that cupboard, darling, because I'll have to open the door.'

'All right, I'll go into the cupboard, my sweet—I'll go into the cupboard,' I said in tender acquiescence. For more than ever before she was in my soul.

We live in an Anglo-Saxon world. Now, had I been writing these pages in the language of beautiful France, I would have written with a Maupassantian, an incredible, candour. But we live, as I said, in an Anglo-Saxon world—a world of assumed restraint. However that may be, I felt the sharp thrill of the first touch. A vaster power than ourselves threw us together: a combustion of elements outside our ken. We were awed, breathless. Standing behind her, her lovely weight against me, I kissed her in the warm hollow of the shoulder, and she threw back her head. Whimsically:

'I'm your wife?'

'Yes.'

Her eyes gleamed darkly as I leaned over her, like pools in the evening; and I could even see myself in them, my khaki collar and my tie pulled crooked in the eagerness of our embrace: and the pools reminded me of Oxford, though what I really pictured were not pools at all, but the dark canal that runs outside the wall of Worcester, where I had walked in days gone by. Why should the image of these things thrive to life even as we kiss? Why should our imagination roam so heedlessly? Shall we ever capture anything wholly and completely, and hold it, hold it fast?

I knelt and kissed her knees. 'And these lovely little Chinamen!' I felt as I might feel if I had been privileged to attend a private view of the Royal Academy. I felt elated. I forgave Gustave. I forgave the whole world. 'It must be all handwork, I imagine.'

'But of course.'

'Why of course?'

'You are so stupid, darling.'

'Why?'

'The General got them in Tokyo.'

'God bless the General!' I cried, embracing her. I felt full of an uncontrollable gratitude. I felt grateful to the world at large. Gustave had been relegated to his appointed place. All was well in this best of all possible worlds! There was a God in heaven after all.

'They have lasted a long time,' I remarked.

'They are durable.'

'God bless him—the General,' said I, with redundant heartiness.

'*Maman*'s are without Chinamen; but they have flowers also embroidered.'

'I know them,' I said; and, stupidly enough, I blushed—as though I had given myself away. So stupid, since no one in his right mind could suspect that my relations with my aunt could be anything else but cordial.

'Who would have thought—that other pair—*maman*'s—had seen different days?'

I bent my head in mute homage. The still angel flew by. 'Ah, well!——'

But when she came to me with her real ruby lips and in the unstained whiteness of her skin, I thought—I thought of strawberries and cream. And there rose in my breast an overwhelming feeling of gratitude, gratitude for her old trustfulness. She came to me as my long-awaited bride, without sham protests, taking as it were the implications of our love for granted. What struck me especially was that she yielded herself to me gaily, laughingly, as if indeed the nature of the pleasure was gaiety. She looked felicitous—she wore a holiday air. She smiled all the time. I expect she was having the time of her life: and not the least so because she thought she was the cause of my having it, too. And I loved her. Those magical mysteries: the convexities and concavities of the eternally alluring feminine form! A whirl, a dream, a trance. Her warm soft tresses fell round her neck on the white pillow; they were dark brown gold in the moonlight. I am a serious young man, an intellectual, but I confess I felt the savour of existence. She was beautiful, passionate. And I am not a Diabologh for nothing. My uncle married thrice, and could not count his children on the fingers of both hands. My father, Aunt Teresa tells me, had had innumerable love affairs. You know the record of Uncle Emmanuel. Uncle Nicholas was born in circumstances of romance. I admit I haven't all their blood. However that may be, I felt proud and glad beyond measure. To hold in one's arms the quivering young body, the warm soft ivory of a woman whom one knows beyond any shadow of a doubt to be a beauty is a pleasure, I can tell you, not to be despised even by an intellectual.

'Isn't it lovely?' she purled.

Well, it was. Very much so.

And now already there was something tragic in this our attainment of happiness, as though we had reached the end of a long and steep lane, behind which loomed a precipice. Now there was nowhere farther to go, and we halted, and wept. 'Darling!' I kissed her, and my kisses were not what they should have been—not at all what they should have been. And she felt it.

Then I laughed.

'What's the matter?'

'You are my bird in hand——'

'I wonder if *maman*'s asleep?'

'I hope so.'

'I wonder what Gustave is doing?' she said.

'I hope he's asleep too.'

'I'm his bird in the bush.'

How queer! We had at long last succeeded in escaping from the others, in being alone, we two by ourselves; and apparently we could find nothing better to do than to talk of the others. And we were still sad, sad in our meeting, as though we had not met at all. She had only me to talk to. I had only her to talk to. And we did not talk. Happiness is always somewhere else. It is one of the failings of our common nature that our pleasures are chiefly prospective or retrospective.

'Darling, go into the dining-room and bring me the playing-cards out of the drawer in the little table by the window.'

I went, but could not find them. I can never find anything. She slipped on her pink dressing-gown, and returning, brought the cards, and, spreading them on the quilt, began to play patience with herself, and afterwards telling her own and my fortunes, cooing the while like a pigeon. There was a fair lady who would come into my life; a long voyage; an early death—and the usual prophecies of this kind. I took no heed. Now, it would seem, was the time, the love climax, for which we had always waited, which palpably is the real note on which a novel should be ended: instead Sylvia looked preoccupied with her pack of cards which she had laid out over the quilt, and speculated on what happiness there lay in store for us in years to come.

I watched her comb her hair and wash her face and brush her teeth; then get into bed—so trustfully. She sat there, a dark-curled, large-eyed, long-limbed little girl. Quickly she raised herself on her knees, and bringing her fingers together and closing her eyes—like an angel child—hurriedly mumbled her prayers; then fell back on to the pillows and pulled the sheet to her chin. Because tomorrow morning we should have to part, we felt that night as though tomorrow morning one of us was going to be hanged. Sylvia lay there, listless, the sheet drawn to her chin, looking at me—so serious, so demure—and as I watched her and heard the clock ticking away the æons, visualized the liner which would relentlessly take me away from her, farther and farther away—until one evening, standing at the rail, I would see the lights of England in the distance as the rolling liner hooted shrilly in the gloom; and at these farthest points apart upon earth's girth we shall indeed have parted to all eternity!

'Darling,' she said, 'you have come to me.'

I was grateful. Somehow I could never make myself believe that another human being loves me. She looked at me whimsically:

'I'm your wife?'

'Yes.'

She was warm; she lay there all in a bundle, purring, 'Mrr-mrr-mrr…'

'I told you you could cuddle me, but you are pinching me.'

'It's all right—it's all right—it's all right,' I reassured her.

'Fairy!' she said.

'My darling, my angel, why did you torture me then? Why?' The wedding-dinner now appeared a happy, happy thing! 'Why did you torture me?'

But she purrs, having bundled tightly around me, 'Mrr-mrr-mrr…'

And we never gave a thought to Gustave!

I lay there, surrounded by a mysterious, inexplicable, utterly puzzling universe, and reflected on what it could all mean. What the deuce could it all mean? The moon had gone; and the street was discernible only by its string of lights. I thought of life and love and what they have to offer, and how shamelessly they emulate the methods of commercial advertising. The alluring posters and signboards. The promise of what-not revelations! And what does love reveal! That concavities are concave, and convexities convex. Son of man! Is that all there is for you? Will it ever be so? There is little to choose between hunger and satiety. And as I lay there, the trees now only visible in silhouette behind the glass bowed to me their respects, and the leaves, moving like fingers—'Tral-la-la!'—beckoned playfully as if to say: 'There you are on the summits!' Silly things.

'Love. Either it is a remnant of something degenerating, something which once has been immense, or it is a particle of what will in the future develop into something immense; but in the present it is unsatisfying, it gives much less than one expects——' Chekhov once noted down in his notebook. And I agree. I am a serious young man, an intellectual. I am so constituted that at these moments when it would seem most proper to expand, to drink life purple, to invoke brass trumpets, I suddenly lose heart. My thoughts went back to my *Record of the Stages in the Evolution of an Attitude*, which was the central thing round which the world revolved. All this other was—well, inevitable rather than overwhelming—and just a little silly. We two had been separated, had withheld from each other that which, when it had grown into a grievance, seemed nothing less than Paradise lost. And now that we had remedied our grievous deprivation, we found that when we had given all we had to offer, perhaps it was not so very much. The night was long, and sleep was a good thing. Perhaps the great point about these things is that they restore your sense of balance; that unless you have them you will store too high a value of them. And you will think you haven't lived.

She was with me—altogether mine; I was assuaged; and I could think of other things. I lay still, and my soul went out to the world. That surging passion in me of a while ago was torn out by the roots, and the memory of it was now no more than of an eaten sweet. Released at last, my soul went forward with another, finer, passion of the mind, and I could see things, near and distant, with a minute acumen teeming in a pool of quivering sunlight. I suddenly perceived the difference between the subjective and objective aspects at the succeeding stages in the evolution of an attitude. And thinking of this difference between two aspects, I just as suddenly fell asleep.

'Oh, my goodness,' she said, waking me.

'What?'

'You *are*—you *are*——'

'What?'

'Oh! But you are leaving, Alexander, tomorrow, and—oh!'

'The best of friends must part.' I rubbed my eyes.

'Perhaps we shall never see each other again.'

'As your father says, "*Que voulez-vous? C'est la vie!*" It can't be helped. But I am awfully sleepy, you know. And tomorrow morning I must be off.'

'Oh! You know you *are*—you *are*——'

'What?'

'Well, never mind,' she said, and turned her back to me.

'Well, if one can't sleep then one must do the next best thing—think.'

I was silent, thinking.

'What are you thinking of?' she asked, without turning round.

'Well, I was reading this evening—just before I came here—a book that, to my way of thinking, defines very clearly the difference between the subjective and objective attitudes in life and letters.'

But when I spoke to Sylvia of the confusion of the terms 'objective' and 'subjective', she looked as though she thought that it was a confusion which I succeeded in confusing further still in my painstaking efforts to elucidate the difference; and I think she felt sorry for me. The trouble was that Sylvia, with all her charm, was not an intellectual; but though I felt that my endeavour to raise the level of our conversation was doomed to failure in advance, I nevertheless went on: 'What is the meaning of "better", unless it be "better fitted to survive"? Obviously "better", on this interpretation of its meaning, is in no sense a "subjective" conception, but is as "objective" as any conception can be. But yet all those who object to a subjective view of "goodness", and insist upon its "objectivity", would object just as strongly to this interpretation of its meaning as to any "subjective" interpretation. Obviously, therefore,' I continued, looking at Sylvia, who only blinked repeatedly the while, 'Obviously, what they are really anxious to contend for is not merely that goodness is "objective", since they are here objecting to a theory which is "objective"; but something else. But something else,' I said, looking at Sylvia.

'Darling, talk of something else,' she said. 'This is difficult for me to understand.'

I am an intellectual, and I do not like to be interrupted in the midst of an elusive analysis, the less so when this analysis is none too clear even for an intellectual.

'I'm an intellectual,' I said. 'A purist. I can't be for ever kissing and cuddling.'

'You talk to me like a teacher,' she complained.

'All the more reason why you should listen attentively. And so where have we left off? Ah, yes: *but something else*. And it is this same fact—the fact that, on any "subjective" interpretation, the very same kind of thing which, under some circumstances, is better than another, would, under others, be worse—which constitutes, so far as I can see'—(I looked at her again, and she gave me a bright, anxious gaze, as though frightened that I might lose the thread)—'so far as I can see, the fundamental objection to all "subjective" interpretations. Is that quite clear?'

Sylvia only blinked. She looked at me sadly, as if wondering who were these subjective and objective animals that sapped my nervous force, and she had a suspicion, I daresay, that these activities of mine were in excess of life.

Then I craved for sleep. Sneaking thoughts kept creeping in, that it would be nice to have a bed to yourself and to go to sleep in it royally, as last night and all the nights before to-night. I wanted to sleep diagonally, crumpled up as I always sleep, and her presence across my path annoyed me a little. Then suddenly I began to laugh.

'What are you laughing at?' Sylvia looked up, surprised.

'Because this reminds me of my grandfather when, having just joined up in the war, I visited him at Colchester, just before his death. I wanted him to notice me in my uniform, but he would talk of nothing else but his dead father and how he had fought at Waterloo—and never took any notice of my uniform.'—At which I laughed again.

'Why are you laughing?'

'Well, you see, there were only two beds in the house: my grandfather's and my aunt's. As it was contrary to custom that I should share a bed with my maiden aunt, I had perforce to share it with my maternal grandfather.'

'But why are you telling me all that, darling?'

'Well, because, you see, he rolled himself round twice in all the available blankets—just like you now, in fact—monopolizing the whole of the bed, so that I had to lie on the iron side-bar—just like now, in fact—and "Keep warm, George," he said; "ah! there is nothing like keeping warm!" He died a week later. He was ninety-two, good old chap!'

Sylvia tickled me.

'Go to sleep,' I said tenderly.

'Kiss me good night.'

I kissed her tenderly on the left eye. Beautiful, beautiful eye!

'You are leaving tomorrow,' she said woefully.

I kissed her again, close on the mouth, with considerable passion, and then said:

'Go to sleep.'

And she purred as she curled up close to my side:

'Mrr-mrr-mrr…'

The light was out. My thoughts went out to some imaginary girl, stranger and less obvious than Sylvia—some other girl in some other stranger and remoted place, some other place where I could lose this thing, this cursed thing, my soul. The clock on the table at my side ticked away the æons. It was dark, and I could hear the measured rhythm of Sylvia's breathing. A black mosquito, like a black shark, swam up in the air and attacked me with a pertinacity astonishing in one so frail. But he had forgotten to silence his engine, and his buzzing announced his approach at my ear with the blare of a brass trumpet; which proved his undoing. In a flash I dispatched him back to his forefathers!

Then, unnoticed, I lapsed into sleep. I dreamt that my old teacher of mathematics, whom I had hated at school, was trying to sell me a number of *Corona* typewriters, and that though I already had one I was constrained into buying another—and suffered deeply. If we can suffer thus in sleep—meaninglessly and unnecessarily—perhaps in life we also suffer meaninglessly and unnecessarily. And as I was suffering thus in my sleep, bemoaning the expense of a superfluous *Corona*, suddenly I must have jumped clean out of bed.

'Oh, darling, I'm sorry I frightened you,' I heard Sylvia's voice as if coming from another world.

'What! Where! What!' Then, still in a trance, I got back into bed and at once fell into a sound dreamless sleep.

To wake in the morning and to see her profile; a head framed in dark locks, all locks to the shoulder, a delightful nose, ever so slightly *retroussé*, her eyes closed, clearly defined, thin, as if pencilled black brows; her dark head thrown into relief by the white pillow on which it rests sideways—these are the sweets of life. To hold a fragrant lovely warm body in your arms, to inhale the delicious scent of *Cœur de Jeanette*, to murmur sweet, tender, whispered things, and to know all the time that she is yours, your Sylvia-Ninon—oh, it was good to be born, good to be born, good to be born! Those pursed red lips, her face against your face, and when she winks you feel the impish movement of her lashes on your cheek, and without seeing it you feel her smile—oh, what a fund of secret gladnesses, of intimate delights! You roll over and kiss her closed eyes, and she, half reluctantly—for she is awfully sleepy, awfully hard to wake—smiles at you, purring the while like a kitten: 'Mrr-mrr-mrr…' This is meet, this is meet, I say, even for an intellectual. And her nose! That exquisitely shaped little nosy! The lovely outline of her nose as her head rests sideways on the pillow. How is it that I did not notice it before? If you cannot catch my exultation, if you needs must present a cold front of indifference, it is, I *know*, because not having seen it you do not know. I know: because I've seen it. (It is absolutely necessary that we should understand each other on this point before we can go any farther.) It was like a fairy-tale, and Sylvia, with her locks and childish face, was like a fairy child.

And I felt a pang of pity at the thought that I shouldn't have perceived its charm till that last morning when I was leaving her for ever: that the first time must needs also be the last.

But indeed Sylvia is hard to wake. Every time I touched her arm she drew it away with a drowsy frown. 'Darling,' I whispered, 'it's the last morning: I am leaving today—soon.' She only murmured into her pillow, 'I want to sleep.'

'But you will be able to sleep for the rest of your natural life: I am leaving in a few hours!' I wailed in tones of anguish. She only purred in answer: 'Mrr-mrr-mrr…' Sleeping apparently was more important. Sometimes I despair of life.

'I dreamt,' I said, 'I dreamt of a beautiful girl in ballet dress, who kissed me, and my heart was full of love. And now she's gone.'

'Oh!' she said, quickly awakening. 'Oh!'

'But, darling, she was fair. You're dark—and she was fair. I can love you both, can't I?'

'All the same,' she replied, not as perturbed as she might be. But she turned her back to me.

'Wake up! It was only a dream.'

'All the same, you shouldn't have dreamt it.'

'I couldn't help it!'

'I'm glad I frightened you now.'

'Frightened me?'

'Don't you remember?'

'No.'

'I heard an awful noise outside—*maman* calling out "Berthe!" Then Berthe's *pantoufles.* I leaned over to the little table at your side to strike a match, and you were so frightened you jumped straight out of bed.'

'I didn't!'

'You did!'

'Did I say anything?'

'You said "Hell!" '

'I didn't!'

'You *did*! You said it five times—like this! "Hell! Hell! Hell! Hell! Hell!" '

'How queer! I don't remember a thing. Only being a little frightened in my sleep, perhaps.'

And when afterwards I saw her take her little toothbrush, the sight of it, dilapidated and red-stained, and of her pathetic squeezed-out toothpaste tube, made me feel sad. Why? Since surely she would be able to afford to buy herself another. Nevertheless, with a heartfelt pang, I said:

'Oh, that little brush…'

'Why, darling?'

'And your teeth and all. Is *he* to take care of you?'

'All this should have been for you.'

'It should, it *should*.—But should it?'

I looked at the clock, at her sad look. The boat sails, your feet sail, your chest with your heart remains—you topple over. Unhappiness!

'This little brush…So pathetic…I see you use red toothpaste.'

'Yes.'

'Carbolic?'

'Yes. Why?' Sylvia is always suspicious of me.

'Just so. I use white—Pepsodent.'

'Yes,' she said. She always says 'Yes'—softly, whisperingly.

'Sylvia, darling!'

A kiss.

'Sylvia-Ninon!'

A kiss again.

'You little…prince.'

Twenty-four kisses, mostly in one.

'Ha-ha! I've been trying to screw your top on to my toothpaste!' she laughed.

'Dearest,' I whispered, 'I love you as ever, and more than ever—fervently, passionately. I love your frankness, your kindness of heart, your trustfulness. I love these eyes, these curls, your movements. I love you, oh! how I love you—with my soul—with my soul…'

'Darling,' she said, 'go and turn the tap on for me in the bathroom.'

45

It was the 29th of April, but already sunny and warm. Spring was beginning in real earnest. I broke my front collar-stud, and therefore was later than usual for breakfast. To my surprise, I found Aunt Teresa already dressed and heading the breakfast-table. Usually she took breakfast in bed. And I appreciated the compliment. It was because I could not bear to see Sylvia in the podgy freckled hands of Gustave that I was leaving this Sunday, though the boat on which I had booked my passage did not leave Shanghai till ten days hence, and my plan was to spend a week travelling through China.

'Today it's warm, hot,' said Aunt Teresa, 'you can sleep with the windows open.'

'Did you, *ma tante*?'

'I didn't sleep at all.'

'I heard an awful noise in the night, *maman*, and your crying "Berthe! Berthe!" ' said Sylvia.

'Well you might!' she groaned.

No! Emphatically she would not stand this any longer—for the love of *anyone*. (And at her words it was as if a hand of ice was laid on my heart. Could it be that Aunt Teresa knew about us?) She would put up with it no longer, unless we wished to see her go clean out of her mind! Suddenly in the middle of the night she woke. The door she had shut was half-open. It seemed as if somebody in a white gown had entered the room, holding a candle. She was too frightened to cry out. The light had vanished. But somebody stood at her bedside breathing on her. She stretched her hand for the matches, and as she did so a box was handed to her in the dark. Who did it? She lit the candle on the table at her side: and there was no one there. A picture postcard stood on edge. Who made it stand? Who kept it in that position?

It was clear enough. She was haunted by him. He lay beneath the sill, with the weight of a massive tombstone upon him. Yet apparently it was not enough. She had burnt her camisole, her knickers, her silk stockings, garters, and the boudoir cap, but it wasn't any use. He brought them back to her in her dreams. She developed an aversion to *all* knickers, camisoles and even combinations, whether new or old; she had a secret fear lest in some mysterious way they were *all* contaminated. She knew not what to do. Give up wearing them? Was it either just or fair? Always she would dream the same awful dream: Uncle Lucy returning to her again and again, showing his teeth (as he had done when listening, without comment, to the local intellectuals), with that last strange grin on his face, intimating by what he carried in his hands that no matter how many camisoles and knickers she might burn, whatever new and different ones she might purchase, they were still the same—the *original* ones. It was as if he brought them back to her each time out of the flames. Each morning, on waking, they were there across the back of the chair. She didn't like to touch them. True, she marked every fresh pair she bought in variegated thread. Yet he may have replaced them in the night *with the identical marking*. She never knew what he might not be up to. Besides, she really could not go on for ever purchasing new underlinen. The moral was: she must leave the haunted house.

It is well known that far-reaching, lasting decisions are nearly always taken in a whim or mood that will not last.

'Emmanuel!' she said. 'We are going back.'

'Going back where, my dear?'

'To Belgium.'

'But, *ma tante*——' I chided in.

'No, George, no!' She was determined to go, whatever the difficulties. She could not stop here another week. Uncle Lucy had breathed on her; she was certain of it.

I did not oppose.

'It won't take long to pack. We must all help. I shall write out the labels.'

I grew alarmed, however, when she turned to me and said: 'When is the next boat?'

'Which boat, *ma tante*?'

'The boat sailing for Europe—leaving Shanghai.'

'Oh—well—God only knows. My boat—the *Rhinoceros*—sails Wednesday week.'

She considered.

'Why not,' she asked, 'sail on the *Rhinoceros*?'

'So soon?' said Uncle Emmanuel.

'But he *breathed* on me! I can't stay here! *mon Dieu*!'

'Perhaps change the room?'

'He will come to the other room—I am sure of it.'

'But the fare, my dear?'

She considered.

'Gustave will have to get us a loan at the bank.'

The door opened and Gustave, with a red rose in his buttonhole and two bouquets in his hand—one for his mother-in-law and one for his bride—entered. And I surveyed him with a feeling of double curiosity.

'Gustave,' she said, accepting the flowers without comment, 'we are leaving.'

'Leaving where, *maman*?'

'For Europe—for Belgium.'

'When?'

'Soon. At once.'

He looked first at her, then at his bride.

'Poor child, she will feel the parting.'

Aunt Teresa looked at him vaguely. 'Sylvia, oh, she is coming with us, of course.'

'But—my wife——' he stammered. 'She must stay with me.'

'Gustave,' she said very quietly, 'stop it. I can stand a good deal. But there is one thing I simply cannot stand at all—anyone disagreeing with me. Stop it. Stop it! For *God's* sake.'

'But—she—she's my wife.'

My aunt gave him one furtive look.

'You want to *kill* me?' she asked.

Gustave said never another word.

'Today is Sunday. We leave on Wednesday,' ordered my aunt.

'But all the packing,' Berthe wailed. 'And all the thousand and one little things we leave unsettled.'

'Gustave can wind up our affairs.'

Gustave sat silent, as if a little dejected.

'Gustave!' said my aunt. 'You must try and obtain a transfer to Brussels as soon as you can—and, to start with, a long annual leave.'

Gustave only smiled, and showed a black tooth at either corner of his mouth, and there was perhaps an indication in his faintly sardonic nod that Gustave regarded such a contingency a remote one.

'*Courage*!' said Uncle Emmanuel.

'*Alors, en avant*!' commanded my aunt. 'I can't endure this exile any longer. I must have a complete change. And at Dixmude I shall at least have *Constance* to look after me.'

'Hasn't Berthe then looked after you?' I asked, looking across at Berthe with a twinkle.

'Berthe,' said my aunt, 'is not a trained nurse.'

'What about the flat?'

'Gustave will look after it.'

Then the packing began. It began in real fury. For we had only three days. We worked as if stripped to the waist. All the boxes and hold-alls and cases and trunks had been hauled down from the attic, and were being filled, filled to overflowing, to the point of bursting, tightly strapped up—and still the travail went on night and day: while Aunt Teresa, ensconced in her soft bed, was writing out the labels. Captain Negodyaev, hearing of our sudden flight, had a violent relapse of persecution mania and begged us piteously, for the love of all saints, to take him with us to Europe.

'Why, man, you're all shot to pieces,' Beastly observed, surveying the Russian's tremulous frame with compassion. 'I daresay you had better come along.'

'And my wife and Natàsha?'

'Yes—why not?'

Captain Negodyaev was wringing Beastly's hand with gratitude. But the question of their going with us in the last resort depended—though why it should so depend no one really knew—on Aunt Teresa. And finally my aunt said: 'Yes.' Gustave was to see his bank manager and director the same day (though it was Sunday and the bank was closed) to arrange for a substantial loan; and Gustave came back to say that he could do this only on the strict condition that on his return to Brussels *Père* Vanderflint took instant steps to sell his pension.

'Yes, sell the pension,' Sylvia agreed.

'Well—yes,' said Aunt Teresa.

'Yes, my angel,' Uncle Emmanuel rejoined, not without some concern. 'What shall we live on, however?'

She did not answer at once. 'There are ways and means,' she replied.

This too, it seemed, could be got round. Gustave had relations who had an interest in a number of cinematographs in Dixmude, and an uncle on the city council, and possibly—he could not say for certain—but possibly some sort of post as films censor or something could be promised his father-in-law on arrival in Dixmude, carrying with it a modest stipend, which would, however, compensate him for the loss of the pension.

'Yes, that will do very well,' Sylvia said gaily.

Between Sunday and Wednesday we lived in a whirl and a trance. Removing. Here they had settled, by all accounts for a long stay, and were gradually nearing the inevitable doom—flagging, sagging, fizzling out. And now—suddenly—removing, living again, beginning anew, planning, struggling, bracing. 'Oh, my God!' Berthe, wedged in between trunks, wailed aloud. And, with this, spring was beginning. Spring was beginning. Over half the globe it was beginning, a verdant hope renewed. I hardly saw Sylvia. The moral issues were happily out of our hands. If there is a seat of justice, a day of judgment, Aunt Teresa will, in her own good time, answer for this curious mismanagement of the *convenances*. Meanwhile I decline to discuss this delicate subject any further. I wash my hands of the whole business. Gustave was not an eagle. And if I were Sylvia *I* should not have gone back to him. But then, nor would I have married him in the first place. She married him, and she went back to him—till Wednesday morning. It was her affair. I have no comment to make. Indeed, I have nothing further to say.

On Tuesday afternoon Aunt Molly paid her last visit to Uncle Lucy's grave; and on Wednesday morning at quarter to ten we were ready to drive to the station.

'There are only two more questions,' said Aunt Teresa, as she was putting on her hat. 'One is Vladislav.'

'That's all right,' said Uncle Emmanuel. 'I've spoken to the General about Vladislav. And I have recommended him for the Cross of Saint Stanislav.'

'And the other is Stepàn.'

'I went to Stepàn,' I said. 'He is still in his bunk.'

'Gustave,' she said, 'you might keep an eye on Stepàn.'

'*Oui, maman*,' said Gustave, and touched his Adam's apple.

'And now we can be off.'

'Come on, Harry. Come on, Nora,' Aunt Molly called.

'Oh, where's my umbelera?' wailed Natàsha.

'There it is.'

'Come on.'

On the stairs as we went down we were stopped by the daughter of the actual-state's-councillor.

'No time'—I held out a warning hand. 'We're leaving.'

'I won't be long. The main feature of our proposition for the reform——'

'Quite so, but, you see, we are pressed for time; we have to catch a train.'

'Yes, yes, yes. I won't be long. We want, if the Allied Governments will assist us with our alphabet——'

'Quite, but we are afraid to miss our train.'

'Yes, yes, yes. I won't be many minutes. Primarily, we want to introduce phonetic——'

'But, really, we shall miss the train——'

'*Madame, nous sommes pressés*. We have no time; our train is leaving,' intervened my uncle.

'I will be brief and outline the scheme in a few concise——'

'Good-bye!'

We swept past her.

46

General 'Pshe-Pshe' was at the station in his grey coat with a scarlet lining, and I instructed our guards—two Hungarian prisoners-of-war awaiting repatriation and dressed up as Tommies and led by an old squinting British corporal—Corporal Cripple—now proceeding to his Tientsin station for discharge—to accord the General the requisite military honours. But they were a sleepy lot of fellows, and presented arms to an excise clerk instead, much to his delight. We made what military display we could, but the War Office had long since withdrawn our men, and our parade was not redeeming. Colonel Ishibaiashi had sent a guard of honour. The little Nippons in their red-banded caps looked smart enough, but the officer, every time that he shrieked the word of command, sounded just as though he were being skinned alive, so that the Russian peasants who gazed on from behind the fence laughed aloud in derision.

The General had ordered the meagre Russian military band to come and play us off, and we could see them coming: the movement of the drummer's arms, the puffing of the soldiers' cheeks, but not a sound of it could be heard before they were actually abreast of us. There are perhaps few things spectacularly more pitiable than the disintegration of a once resplendent army. Count Valentine also came and conversed fluently in florid French with Berthe, tapping the while his new leggings, procured from the British ordnance stores, with a light bamboo cane (likewise of English make). The Metropolitan also came. Dr. Abelberg came. Philip Brown, who was going to Shanghai by train to join his ship which had already sailed from Vladivostok, wanted to be photographed in the act of saying farewell to 'his girl'. He was being seen off by his cousin, who was only a sergeant in the American Expeditionary Force, but told his Russian sweetheart that it was more than being an officer. It was a lovely day in spring. We were going by a special train given us by General 'Pshe-Pshe', who presented Aunt Teresa with a whistle on a white silk lanyard which she was to blow as soon as she wished to set the train in motion. It was the most luxurious train at his disposal, and was manned by Czech personnel. The engines, ready to start, breathed: puff-puff-puff. The Czech drivers looked at us from above their perches with a dare-devil air: 'We'll drive you as you've never been driven before!' That was their look.

'It's a fine engine,' I said, looking back at Vladislav, who stood with a complacent gaze, surveying his well-polished high boots.

'An engine. It's only an engine in name. In France, ah!—there they have engines! Such engines that once you have got them going you won't stop them again! Yes.'

The spring sunny freshness; I breathed in the air; I paced up and down in my brown highly polished top-boots. O Life! Vladislav—he was all right. He would get through revolutions and counter-revolutions, through red and white and green terrors without coming to much harm. He would wander on from the coast to the Urals, from the Caspian Sea up the Volga and back again to the south, to the west, to the north, to the east, round and round. He was all right.

'Keep out of the Army, my son, and you'll be all right,' was my farewell advice to him.

And then we parted with the General. There was a worried look on his face: his troops had already been disarmed, and he had been nicknamed 'Commander-in-Chief of all Disarmed Military and Naval Forces of the Far East'. Before leaving—he was in a hurry—the General bowed low over Aunt Teresa's pale bejewelled hand, and brought his black moustache against it in a prolonged exquisite expression of farewell. She looked moved, charming—with sad, beautiful St. Bernard eyes. He went away rather briskly, with visible emotion, and did not notice the omission of the guards.

Gustave stood on the platform at the open window of our coupé. 'Write, Gustave,' said Aunt Teresa.

He gulped once or twice, his Adam's apple withdrawing and bobbing up again conveniently, pulled at his collar in a timid gesture, cleared his throat half-heartedly, and said:

'*Oui, maman.*'

'You must really make an effort to come home—to get a permanent transfer to Brussels or Dixmude,' she said.

'Yes,' Sylvia echoed.

Gustave coughed a little and adjusted his Adam's apple, but said nothing. He only stroked his broad chin with his two fingers and smiled, revealing a black tooth at either corner of his mouth.

'*Allons*!' said my uncle in a tone one might use to a small boy shirking a plunge into the water, urging him to be a man. '*Allons*! One must make a try. One must exert oneself.'

'Come. Never say die!' offered Beastly, who always took a leading share in any conversation, however intimate, once he was present.

'Come. You must *demand* a transfer,' urged Aunt Teresa, 'or immediate annual leave.'

Gustave did not look hopeful. To be perfectly candid, I]do not remember any man who, despite hearty urgings to the contrary, looked less hopeful. He seemed oppressed by the magnitude, the problem, the distance, and the vagueness of the whole proposition.

'*Courage! Courage, mon ami!*' urged Uncle Emmanuel.

'Good-bye, Gustave,' said Sylvia.

They kissed.

'Good-bye.' He looked as though he were going to cry. I remembered how he had said in church, 'She has brought joy into my life.' And it was as though the sun had gone as suddenly as it had come out.

'*Courage, mon ami*!'

'*Adieu, mon pauvre Gustave*!' That was all his mother-in-law had to say to him. But it may have compensated him all the same. I don't know. I don't care.

But when he advanced to the window, and with a self-conscious self-effacing smile moved towards the children, I felt that he was a member of the family, that he was attached to us, and had been cruelly wronged; and a pang ran through my heart and my conscience was ablaze.

'Good-bye, 'Arry,' he said.

Harry's face suddenly quivered and winced into a protracted, leisurely sneeze that ran its full course of development to a climax, discharging in thunder; he unfolded his handkerchief, blew his nose twice with a trumpeting sound, replaced the handkerchief, and then said:

'Good-bye.'

My aunt blew the whistle on the white lanyard presented to her by 'Pshe-Pshe', the old gallant. It was a beautiful morning, so fresh; the engines puffed on mightily, only awaiting this signal. Now they would set off.

'*Adieu, Gustave*!' And she lowered her bejewelled hand to his thin lips hidden under the soft canary moustache.

He smiled back timidly. '*Adieu, maman*!'

Now in England you sit in the corner seat of the compartment at the window, somewhere, let us say at Nuneaton, and quite imperceptibly, while you sit, with your hand in the sling, the train glides out of the station. Not so in Russia. At first there was a jerk, as if the two engines tried to do something that was obviously beyond their strength. The jerk was so violent that a portmanteau shook on the rack and hung in the balance. '*Allons donc*!' muttered Berthe, while Uncle Emmanuel made propitiatory gestures, as if to say '*Que voulez-vous*?' We were settling down again—when '*Whack*!' came another jerk, and this time all the coaches all along shook, moaned and screeched piteously. *'Ah mais! Ce sont des coquins ces machinistes tchèques!'* uttered Uncle Emmanuel as he hastened to restore two of Aunt Teresa's hat boxes to the rack from which they had fallen—when '*Whack*!' came yet another jerk, more moderate this time, as though, after all, the task the engines had set themselves was not entirely beyond their strength. Then came a fourth jerk, and it seemed that the engines, in spite of all, were succeeding—succeeding. Sylvia waved her gloved hand. But her mother blocked the window.

'Now mind you write, Gustave.'

The engines were already gathering strength, and slowly, but rapidly gathering speed, we were moving. And Vladislav waved his cap in the air and, timidly but none the less exultantly, as the train went faster he cried:

'*Vive la France*!'

The train drew out, and Vladislav and Gustave with the platform they stood on slid away out of sight, out of call. I stood at the window and looked at the vanishing outskirts: a few mills, a few factories, a cemetery; then there came fields and woods. The engine gave a shrill whistle. The train rattled on with increasing speed, swayed at the curve—and all these things had become of the past.

Puff-puff-puff—and the accompanying shatter and rattle was not at all disagreeable. We were moving. After all the waiting and running about we were sitting still and were moving. I sat there, my head propped up by my hand, and thought: '*Pauvre Gustave! Pauvre Gustave!*' I was the only one of the whole crew to shed a tear for him—and it was not a crocodile's but a real genuine tear. What could I do? Even had I handed Sylvia to him through the window, what would have happened? Picture Aunt Teresa pulling the alarm-cord. It was his luck and my luck, and fate alone knew who of us two was the lucky one. I would not have you put this down to Sylvia or myself. It was very simple—our love affair had been upset by one of Aunt Teresa's arbitrary acts: now it was reversed by another. On taking thought, we were content to leave our love to fate and Aunt Teresa. '*Pauvre Gustave! Pauvre Gustave!*' I could but repeat to the shattering rhythm of the train. To those who would cast the first stone at me for my betrayal of Gustave I would say this in my defence: Gustave was an enigma. He said 'Yes', or else he said 'No', and this he seemed to say according to whether you wished him to say one or the other. He was the type of man that you will find playing second fiddle in an orchestra: reliable but timid, and no good as a conductor. Gustave got the worst of the bargain. Or so it seemed on the face of it. But he was a patient man, and patience to the patient is as natural as impatience to the impatient. I was impatient. But my aunt was a fool, a blind, egotistical fool.

'A penny for your thoughts,' she said.

'Never mind my thoughts.'

I looked out of the window. The green fields were whirling round; a few trees glimpsed; a forest flew by.

'Look at the spring!'

Nora looked, and saw gee-gees and moo-cows and ba-lambs and nanny-goats. The train raced on as before. Sylvia sat facing me, in her big velvet black hat, her wide-awake eyes sparkling in the morning sun. And looking at the window, with an unending smile on her face, 'Are you frightened of bulls?' she asked.

'Very.'

I thought: she is mine, mine for ever. And my heart gave a pang for Gustave. I wanted to speak to her, urgently, privately. I made signs to her to come into the corridor. She turned her head away from the sun, and looked at me with her dark velvety eyes, shook her head, and looked back at the window, smiling away in the sun.

'*Yes*,' I insisted.

She did not respond.

I wrote on a slip:

Come out into the corridor *immediately*, or I shall never forgive you.

She wrote in answer:

You are so stupid, darling. The people are laughing at our soppy ways.

From under her broad-brimmed black hat she looked out with her enormous eyes at the sunny fields and smiled to herself without cease.

At one o'clock we took lunch in the restaurant-car. The train went on—puff-puff-puff. The field, drenched, seemed to sink in the river, and dark stems of trees showed out of the water in all indecent nakedness. Spring was beginning. Then over half the globe spring was beginning, as we rolled through an unsettled country that had been in a better way before we tackled it. Moods, reminiscences pressed into my heart. Once on just such a day, in just such a mood, at Oxford and in spring, I had gone to Magdalen citadel encompassed by a Chinese wall and steeped in tender foliage, and from an open window came a phrase of Chopin like a question addressed to the hollow blue. Oxford now would be a mass of green, white, tender pinks, tremulous like the sea. The green elms stretched out their arms to the sky. Why? Because, like us, they were thirsting for things outside themselves. Their own beauty was lost on them, wasted. But when the rain came the drenched birches drooped their glittering limbs and cried. Because, having quenched their thirst, there was nothing left them—nothing left outside the anguish of desire! And now, as we rattled past on our way, the tall pines roared and the slim young birches lashed together in the wind; prisoners rooted to the ground, they stood there and deplored their cruel fate. Later, in the tinge of evening, they shook their heads, looked older, wiser and resigned—but sad, sad.

There was more dignity in their vague dreams than in all our farcical preoccupations. For it is the vagueness of a dormant world that lies behind our subtle thoughts as, maturing, they shrink into precise expressions. And so, perhaps, these beeches, dreaming, do not seek to apprehend and, not seeking, apprehend in full.

'The logical conclusion of life,' said Captain Negodyaev, 'of all joy, sorrow, suffering, exaltation, consciousness; in a word, of being—is not being.'

'But dreaming?'

'No.'

'What is the meaning of life?'

'Life is meaningless. Perhaps it is there to give meaning to death. After life we are content with death.'

'I don't believe it. If the whole world be unreal, then where is the real world? (This, by the way, is not a question but a statement, an assertion that the only reality is *I*.) And when I want to die, to be extinct into nothing, I only mean I am tired and want a pillowed sleep with happy dreams. The thought of death—of the complete annihilation of my *I* is as unnatural and impossible as eating myself up and leaving no crumbs behind.'

'Darling, do talk of something more interesting—something which is easier to understand,' Sylvia demurred.

'You believe in immortality?' he asked.

'I have not sufficient data not to believe in it. It is no less a miracle that I should exist in a body than that I should exist without one.'

'I don't believe in things of which I have no tangible proof,' he said.

'Which means you disbelieve in everything except your limitations.

'How so?'

'Your limited knowledge stops short this side of death, and you give your verdict in favour of this knowledge. But for me to believe that death is the end is like giving a verdict in the absence of innumerable witnesses to the contrary who had been prevented from appearing by some flood or fire. The unexplored possibilities of what *might* happen after death are so incalculable in the face of our provisional assumption to the contrary that as well we may deny the future generations inventions and discoveries of which we have no knowledge.' I sighed.

'What is it, darling?'

'Oh, nothing,' I said—and thought: '*Pauvre Gustave*.'

An hour later we stopped at a country-side by the river. How quiet, how idyllic.

Then we went on. The blinds in the train turned pink from the sunset. The grinding and clanking subdued: we rushed into a tunnel. Again we rushed out, polluting the air of the hill-side.

By order of the General we had the special train, but no sooner did he leave us than they began unhooking one coach after another, till we were left with half. '*Le sabre de mon père*' was in Aunt Teresa's case with her umbrellas, and my eloquence proved helpless against the villainy of local station-masters. For lack of space I went in with Aunt Teresa, Aunt Molly, Berthe, Sylvia, Uncle Emmanuel, and Harry. In the adjoining coupé were ensconced the Negodyaev family, Bubby, Nora, and Nurse. In the third compartment, Beastly, Philip Brown, and several strangers.

'Give your *maman* the corner seat, *chérie*,' said Aunt Teresa. This roused my dormant sense of gallantry. I surrendered my cherished corner seat to Aunt Molly, perceiving in advance that I would be rewarded for my sacrifice; for I was now by Sylvia's side. Our women were chattering like birds. Presently they got Uncle Emmanuel and myself to haul down a heavy supper-basket of immense proportions and dug into it. Tea, coffee, fruit, cakes, biscuits, sandwiches, and such-like luggage made its appearance. At wayside stations I had to run out to buy bananas, soda-water, and so forth. The evening sun, showing through the cream-coloured blinds, cast a pink light over Sylvia at my side. The train rattled on. Berthe and my aunts were still chattering. Their talk was boisterous and easy. Berthe was relating how when, many years ago, she travelled with her father there was a young man in the compartment with them who, in the process of settling down for the night, was taking off innumerable articles of underclothing, of which, however, there really seemed to be no visible end. They laughed. But Aunt Molly was silent. Looking through the window, I saw our train overtake a peasant driving in a cart. For a moment I could see him clearly to the minutest detail of his podgy face and cap, and I endeavoured to imagine the real 'I' of that man as if it had been myself sitting in that jolting cart; then the road which had been running alongside our track began to drift, and swiftly our ways parted, parted beyond sight and recall and remembrance. So it is in life, I thought, and I could see myself, a little light, a bundle of experiences, boring my way through time-space, past other bundles, bleak faces, eyes like lighted windows, all hurrying through what trance, what world of appearance, to what purpose, what goal? On, on, and on. The lights were being lit, the train hurried southwards. As Berthe and my aunts began to settle down for the night, they did strange things with their hands beneath their blouses, and their waists expanded automatically, and the creatures became flabby and unattractive, like empty sacks of oats. Sylvia alone did nothing to prepare herself for sleep. When night came, the shades were drawn over the electric globe and the window-screens lowered. The train rushed and roared through the dark. I stood for a while in the swaying corridor and looked through the wide black panes at the string of lights. What a lot of houses they have built: how they plod and multiply, these human beings! As we had settled down to sleep, the train, on the contrary, seemed to have grown more lively, and gathered speed, caring apparently nothing for darkness or sleep, and raced on with light-hearted gaiety, while we could only stretch our aching limbs and sigh. Sylvia was asleep. Through all the grinding and clanking, what sweet dreams would she be dreaming . . . perhaps of me? She had lain in my arms as the night drew out and the morning hours crept in sulkily, one by one. And now, like an angel child, she was asleep. These lines from Maupassant came back into my mind:

> How I have wept, the long night through, over the poor women of the past, so beautiful, so tender, so sweet, whose arms have opened for the kiss, and who are dead! The kiss—it is immortal! It passes from lip to lip, from century to century, from age to age. Men gather it, give it back, and die.

It was interminable night. Carefully I moved my foot to hers and felt her ankle. She never stirred. Yes, she was asleep and leaning on my shoulder.

Presently she sighed, tried to readjust her head upon the pillow, then gave it up as a bad job, opening her eyes.

'Put your pillow on my knees.'

She did. 'Better now.' She closed her eyes. I looked at my watch. It was past 3 a.m. All were sleeping. Then Harry, who had been sleeping with his head on Berthe's lap, woke up. He muttered: 'Yesterday the train went; today it's stopped.'

'Sleep, my little one,' Berthe whispered, 'sleep, my darling. You've woken in the middle of the night. The train went yesterday and today too; it has only stopped for a few minutes and will go on directly. Sleep, my darling.' She kissed him on the forehead. 'Sleep, my little one. There.'

He shut his eyes, but opened them again after awhile with the remark, 'Where's Nora's monkey?'

Berthe tucked the cloth monkey in the front of his coat; he shut his eyes. But soon afterwards he woke again, announcing his intention to hang the monkey.

This roused the rest of us, and no one any longer tried to

sleep. I raised the window-screen. The grey dawn, showing feebly through the rain-stained window, mocked at the electric light. The air in the coupé was heavy. Uncle Emmanuel yawned into his hand and opened the door into the corridor. It was chilly. The ladies bucked up. Powder-puffs, hand-mirrors, and the like came into play; hands and eyes got busy; coiffure and complexion was remedied; scent poured out galore. And not a drop of water all the time. Water was not mentioned. Water was not thought of! Sylvia had a tiny orange-coloured crêpe-de-Chine 'hanky'—that was all she used by way of toilet. It seemed to me touching. But had she used a bath-towel or nothing at all, it would have appeared to me—for such is the nature of love—equally touching.

The train raced towards Changchu. Another train hove in sight, and the two trains raced side by side: now one was ahead, now the other; till their ways took them asunder and the other train raced away out of sight.

At ten o'clock in the morning the train, exhausted, pulled up at Changchu. I looked out. Silence. Dusty foliage. Chinks squatting on the ground and staring at the train. Lemonade and oranges on sale on the platform. Sunshine. What a country! Peace. Relaxation. It goes on in that benevolent, watching, smiling sunshine. We got out and repaired to the hotel for lunch.

Before lunch Aunt Teresa drank a cocktail with a cherry on a matchstick. It was a lovely day in spring. We sat on the open veranda and talked.

'Now do we live after death?' asked my aunt.

'The answer,' said I, 'is in the affirmative.'

'How can we know?' Captain Negodyaev interjected. 'We have so little to go upon.'

'A plain reason for not going upon it. Seeing that, when all is said, life is a miracle, it would be a miracle indeed if the miraculous never occurred.'

'But you seem certain.'

'There are umpteen ways of being alive, but there is only one way of being dead. It follows than the chances of life after death are umpteen to one.'

'When you come to think,' chimed in Captain Negodyaev, 'what can we know! If I trust my inspired moments I say, yes, death is not the end. If I trust my stock moods, I say, probably it is.'

'And you, George?' asked my aunt. 'How do you really *feel* about it?'

I sighed.

'As George Hamlet Alexander Diabologh, author, I shall bow my *adieux* and never emerge after death; but as rightful shareholder in *Life* I am immutable, and will go on till the Universe perish with me. Perhaps as one on the board of directors of *Cosmos, Unlimited.* Perhaps—since I'm a holder of preference shares—as some sort of joint chairman with God. But perish I shall not: since, like any another, I am a holder of shares in the cosmic concern.'

Aunt Teresa sighed with relief. 'Ah, if it were so!'

'It *is* so. You may take my word for it, *ma tante*.'

'No death?'

'Never.'

Captain Negodyaev shook his head.

My aunt looked at him. 'Why should we live so little,' she asked, 'and be dead such a time? Why?'

'No reason at all,' said my uncle.

'So perhaps Anatole is alive.'

'You bet he is! More alive than before.'

'But does he remember? Does he remember me?'

'He doesn't remember a damned thing.'

'Oh!'

'We are but vessels of past memories,' said Captain Negodyaev. 'When I think of the living things around me which are to me as something that has never been, I am conscious of the nature of obliteration, of the seeds of death I already carry in me. A little more—and death will be complete.'

'So you think,' I said. 'Unthinkingly. It is not the memory that lives on in you, it's that little voice, that little lamp which is immortal. You may lose your memory forthwith and be none the worse for it; you would still go on feeling your *I* to be you and none else, as you do through every dream and nightmare: because this *I* is lit at the immortal altar of all life, and so remains immortal, may it immerse in whatever worlds, it is *you*, a world in itself and for ever.'

'Well, well. It's time we went in to lunch.'

A British merchant from Harbin who travelled with us gave us a champagne lunch. 'You may think it a little extravagant of me,' said he. 'But on such occasions one lets oneself go a bit, don't you know. And I have come to believe that generosity repays itself.'

'Oh, I want the *Daily Mail*. Can we see the *Daily Mail* here?' Sylvia asked.

'Well, unfortunately you can.'

Then we drove back to the station.

How, after a champagne lunch on a sweet spring day, standing on the platform—the engine: puff-puff-puff—life is wonderful and miraculous with sweet expectancy.

At Mukden the last coach of our special train was unhooked, and we took on the ordinary train to Peking. In the early morning hours Sylvia and I rickshawed in the noisy languid din through the pagan gorgeousness of the Manchu capital, and having lost our way we were hard put to it to tell the rickshaw coolies to drive us back to the station. We imitated the sound of a railway engine with our lips, and the look of steam issuing forth from the funnel with our hands. The coolies grinned a ready comprehension, but after driving about for twenty minutes or so, stopped and scratched their heads dubiously, when we hastened to resume overtures, apparently all to no purpose. Till happily two Europeans hove in sight. We caught the train by a split second. Aunt Teresa was in hysterics. Early next morning we saw the Great Wall of China. And at midday the train steamed into Peking.

We saw what there was to see; climbed up the pagodas; visited the Summer Palace; a couple of Buddhist temples. Aunt Teresa lifted her feet high up to prevent horrible large ants from climbing up her legs.

'And what is that?' Berthe asked.

'That is Buddha.' I looked into her eyes with glee.

'H'm,' said she. 'H'm.—Well, well!'

We visited the cemeteries of rank, and Uncle Emmanuel even signed his name in the register as well as on the wall and on the painted wooden pillars. Whereupon we got into our rickshaws and drove back to the hotel.

I drove behind and thought: 'It would be nice to slip away from them all—to go off by myself.'

After the pony race there was a gala dinner and dance, and we danced in the crowded ball-room and then drove back to the hotel through the moist heavy spring night of Peking. It was as though I had been *given*, for ever given, life, as though the *I* was the effect of that particular gift, and that the whole world was not itself but through me. Why then was I asking questions? Why always was I asking questions? There was a meaning in it. But what meaning if black death obliterated all? Then a meaning in that, a hidden significance. And if death was silence eternal, there was a significance in that silence. It was as if all—death and all—were *in* life; and if I thrilled with emotion, feared, prayed, my nerves were somehow linked with the rest of the world: they were like strings of a musical instrument that reverberated to some faint, unknown music; and even now, as in the spidery vehicle, I drove past the palatial legations by the silent queer-smelling canals, the nocturnal foliage glancing in the mirror of black water, at its own sombre visage, the yellow lanterns bobbing on the water and the leaves, I was a traveller, I felt, to whom these lights and shadows were mysterious and strange, but no stranger than the shadows I had seen when, as a particle of light, I coursed my way through space, a planet, a fiery torch lighted at what altar? at what sun? before I fell.

Next day there was a treat for us: the Berlin Philharmonic Orchestra came and played extracts from Wagner. They received a tremendous ovation, and at the very end, as an extra, played the Overture to *Tannhäuser*. I thought I should burst. It was so rich, so mighty, so ineffably glorious and majestic. One felt one's soul standing on tiptoe! Music—I felt that music was life, that music understood what words and thoughts could never convey. There were echoes it wakened, heart-strings it touched. O Music, where have you learnt your secret?

Poor old Aunt Teresa, I thought. Poor old Uncle! Poor old everybody...

I ran into Uncle Emmanuel coming out, and he was red and bright-eyed with excitement. 'By God,' he said, 'that was wonderful. It takes Germans to play Wagner. I got so excited and stirred up I wanted to shout or cry.'

I felt he and I were brothers, in fact all men brothers, and all born to do great things!

The date of sailing of the *Rhinoceros* having again been postponed, we lingered in Peking for a few days. Siberia—so we read in the newspapers—was red and growing redder. Chita was the one white isle in a sea of red, and thither (and to China) had flocked all that there remained of the refuse of reaction. And Peking was absorbing more than its fair share. White generals, bankrupt ministers, experts in *coups d'état*, failures, nonentities of every kind had made this spot their headquarters. We found many an old friend. Suddenly, quite unexpectedly, we ran into General 'Pshe-Pshe'.

'Your Excellency!' I greeted him. 'We thought you had been hanged long ago!'

'Not till I have done a little myself,' he replied, smiling a little warily. 'And how are you?'—he turned to Aunt Teresa, and brushed her pale bejewelled hand against his prickly moustache. Things, it seemed, looked bad in Harbin. The red bandits had wrested the town from him—and now *anything* might happen to the population. Anything! He himself had deemed it wise to leave the town incognito, overnight. The anarchists and agents of destruction were hard at work all over the world. The only hope lay, he was bound to say, in Mr. Churchill. But that gallant statesman, he thought, had enemies even at home.

I looked at him as he spoke. How he had ever managed to become a General, God only knows! the most probable explanation is that he had appointed himself—in the interests of the fatherland. 'Pshe-Pshe', I learnt afterwards, had taken with him a few bars of solid gold from the national exchequer, deeming it to be well out of the hands of the miscreants who opposed him. He was living now with his wife and family at the best hotel in Peking. He was patronizing to the indigent. 'Money,' he said on more than one occasion, 'is no object.' Asked what were his plans for the future, he said that he was going on to Tsingtao for a cure and a rest, where he would wait till Mr. Churchill's political star was again in the ascendant, when 'The Day' would return, and he would decorate the lamp-posts of the city of Harbin with the corpses of the bandits; for in civilized society law and order came first. He was loyal to the past. But Russia would not mould to his bankrupt dreams. He was sad, taciturn, bitterly disappointed in fate; but the deaths he had occasioned he somehow overlooked. In the train—he left in our company—the General told us that shortly before leaving Harbin news had come through that Dr. Murgatroyd had been captured in Omsk by his enemies the Bolsheviks. And quite apart from the human factor, it was felt by all that the situation was not without humour. But we were sure that the old man in the *moujik* clothes would eventually stroll down to some place of safety, with a pencil between his teeth and a few sheets of written paper in his hands, perhaps a little wiser for his experience, and perhaps no wiser than before—and eventually produce a book.

'And how are you?'—the General turned to Mme Negodyaev.

'*Ach*!' she uttered—and sighed.

'What a life!' He looked out of the window.

'Yes, it's a life in name only. We wait. In the winter we wait for the spring. But spring has come, and I am pestered by flies and mosquitoes. In the spring we wait for the summer. But summer comes—and it rains like in autumn. *Ach*!' She waved an abject gesture, and grew silent.

'You're a pessimist,' said he, screwing up one end of his short crisp moustache. 'I am not entirely so.'

'I have always, all my life, been on the point of beginning to live, and I haven't lived. I haven't, I haven't, and I haven't. I had hoped so much, and nothing has come of it. Now I hope no more—so perhaps something may come of it.' The sun flashed through the glass and lit up her sunken face. 'I have great hopes,' she said.

She lived, and the life that should have been went beside her. I thought: hopeless natures, like hers, are easily let down by life, but on the other hand, just as easily consoled by hopes as shadowy and baseless as those which they had just discarded.

At Tientsin—he was going on to Tsingtao—the General got out together with the squinting Corporal Cripple, who now marched on with the kit on his back along to the depôt. The General pressed his prickly moustache against my aunt's pale fingers; but our train was about to go, and Aunt Teresa, as she waited for him to finish his embrace, looked troubled and impatient. 'Berthe! I do sincerely hope they haven't left my medicine-chest behind!' she wailed across her shoulder. He released her hand. She got in, and the train moved, and the saluting General, with the platform he was standing on, and the sandbank with the squatting Chinese child gaping at the train, and the country road that Corporal Cripple was traversing, moved backwards, and whirled out of sight.

I felt the wind rushing in through the open window, and saw the sun shining purple through the fretful yellow blinds, and the year was awakening and the day stubbornly dying.

Crossing the Yangtsekiang in a steam launch, I looked at the wide yellow river, and then at Aunt Teresa at my side. I loved my aunt—in moderation. But now seeing her, so pale and frail before me, I thought: 'Poor Aunt Teresa! How long will she survive?' And it seemed to me that now in this strong light I could see for once beyond her share of foibles. I could see—But, oh, what is there to see in the human soul stripped of outward ornament? Bewilderment, day-dreaming, and hope, unending hope…

Landed on the other side, we mounted the coach and sat mute as if bound by some mysterious sense of fraternity, while the train raced on to Shanghai. Suddenly, as though some huge bird had eclipsed the sun, it grew dark. And we felt as if a shadow had fallen on the clear still-water surface of our souls. Gloom. Rain; hail drummed at the pane. The world was a sorrowful place to live in!

I watched Beastly pull up the window, and I thought it was characteristic of us that he should be the first to be aroused to the necessity of action. It was of value. I meditated.

' "The one thing in the world of value," said Emerson,' said I, ' "is the active soul." '

'Very truly said,' rejoined Captain Negodyaev.

Natàsha sat facing me, and as I looked into her sparkling sea-green eyes I thought—I knew not why—I thought of death. Why, looking at her, should I think of death? This camping-ground that we call life: our turn, and we go forth into those bleak immensities. And behind us, at the port which growing distance separates us from, the church bells are tolling mournfully, solemnly, as out we sail into the boundless misty sea…Where? Why? Ah, now we know these questions do not arise. They are not; they were unreal.

It had stopped raining and the sun had come out.

'Look, my girls, it's a lovely day!' said Harry.

The sun had come out, and at once all had become radiant and gay. I closed my eyes and fell asleep in the sun.

47

The Paris of the Far East

When I woke it was past midnight, and the train was already nearing Shanghai. Berthe was busy packing the hand-luggage of my aunt, and we were hauling down our baggage from the rack and putting on our hats and coats, when the train rushed into the station. It was a station much like any other station. It might have been Victoria or Charing Cross for all the difference I noticed. Two motors—so we learnt from a chasseur—awaited us. It seemed we could choose between the Cephas Speaks and the Septimus Pecks—two merchant princes of Shanghai, who, imagining that we were heroes who had won the war, in fact competed for the opportunity of offering us their hospitality. We chose the Cephas Speaks, and stepped into a luxurious limousine, with the aid of a smartly arrayed chasseur, and drove off. I think we chose them on account of the imposing look of the chasseur, and drove in the luxurious motor through the dark shimmering city, which is called, with a degree of truth, the Paris of the Far East. I looked out at the nocturnal streets with their many lights, that curious blend of Europe and the Orient, so disquieting and enchanting as though just on account of that blend, as the great big car rolled magnificently through the warm, moist air of spring. Through beautiful well-kept lanes which in the moonlight looked as if covered with snow, between deep walls of dark foliage we moved. The big car rolled along swiftly, but its size and grandeur gave its very swiftness a look of leisure, as though it said, with a self-contented, patronizing air: 'That is nothing to me.'

And thinking of our curious destinies, I said: 'Life is a chance cross-section—with chance encounters happening to come our way. Events come casually, begin discordantly, and end abruptly: they hinge entirely on chance; but within each event which comes our way we develop our inner harmony wholly and coherently.'

'Darling, why don't you talk to me of something interesting instead?' Sylvia demurred.

Melancholily, the car rolled along, and then giving forth a small hoot of the horn, turned into another lane of deeper foliage and more moon. The car drove into a courtyard. Servants rushed to our feet. And, helped out on all sides, we alighted and mounted the steps into the palace of the hospitable merchant prince.

In the hall, despite the late hour, stood Mr. Cephas Speak, a crude but shy, diffident man, with extended hand (he would have liked to extend both, but he was too shy), and a hearty solicitude for our welfare and comfort. Having apparently done nothing in the war but fill his own pockets, he felt the more diffident with people like ourselves whom, on account of our heroic-looking uniforms, he imagined to be warriors without fear and without reproach. As I came down from my bedroom, Mr. Speak was already listening to Uncle Emmanuel's highly coloured accounts of our bleak experiences.

'You've had a pretty rough time, I can see, at the hands of the Bolsheviki,' observed Mr. Speak, and filled Uncle Emmanuel's glass and passed round the sandwiches.

'*Ah! mais je crois bien!*' agreed my uncle, swallowing a cocktail and pieces of a sandwich.

'The trials, the perpetual excitements and uncertainties, the tribulations of this life of my sad exile,' said Aunt Teresa, 'have completely wrecked my poor nerves.'

'*Ah, c'est terrible*,' echoed my uncle.

Our host surveyed us all with infinite compassion. 'Now you must have a thorough rest and pull up if you can. You must try and completely forget the Bolsheviki.' And he passed round the sandwiches. It was as though we had been shipwrecked and were now picked up, and Mr. Speak was administering first-aid. Aunt Teresa heaved a deep sigh, and Uncle Emmanuel said:

'I askèd dem, *Eh bien*, 'ow long is ze civil war goin' to las', and zey tellèd, "We know not 'ow long, doan ask us." *Voyons donc*, I say, you mus' know, *vous autres militaires*!'

'Are they pretty awful, the Bolsheviki?' asked Mr. Speak,

with an air as if he fully expected to hear that they *were* awful.

'*Ah! je crois bien!*' rejoined my uncle with some heat. 'A nation must protect its 'ome, the family, the sacred hearth. We want our girls to remain girls. If they—the Bolsheviks I mean—are allowed to go on the way they please, why, at that rate soon there won't be a virgin left in Russia! *Ah! c'est terrible!*'

Mr. Speak looked as though he wanted to hear more about the virgins, but Uncle Emmanuel looked grave, and so Mr. Speak too put on a look of gravity.

Unconsciously, our tales became heroic. We felt they *had* to be if we were to be equal to his hospitality. And that was very great. Great as it was, though, it seemed to grow in proportion to the magnitude of our tales, and these must needs keep pace with his growing hospitality. 'Oh, come,' I said at last, to check Uncle Emmanuel's extravagant imagination.

'Excuse to me,' he rejoined, 'I know of what I'm talking.'

Mr. Speak could only listen. He shook his head. It seemed incredible. Uncle Emmanuel went on.

'Very truly said,' Captain Negodyaev chimed in. 'I have myself two daughters, Mr. Speak: Màsha and Natàsha. Màsha, poor thing, is married, and she has to live in the most miserable conditions in South Russia, with her husband, Ippolit Sergèiech Blagovèschenski. And this—Natàsha!—this is Natàsha.'

Mr. Speak nodded approvingly, for he regarded Captain Negodyaev as a bulwark against Bolshevism. And he gave Natàsha a round box of chocolates tied with an orange ribbon.

'Oh, look! look! Harry, look! What a beauty thing! Oh, what a lovely!'

'A nice little girl!' commented Mr. Speak.

'Unfortunately, things being what they are, Mr. Speak, Natàsha's education is being completely neglected. We simply don't know what to do.'

'And now, I suppose, we had better all go to bed,' said my aunt. 'It's a quarter-past two.'

Mr. Speak wished us all a good night.

On the bedside-table were novels. The dear old thing had put them there for me to read. There they were—Gilbert Frankau, Compton Mackenzie, Stephen McKenna. The house, for all its luxurious magnificence, boasted no water-pipes, the water, cold or hot, having to be carried up by Chinese servants, of whom there was a host at our disposal. The reason for this idiosyncrasy was that nowadays water-pipes were by no means rare, being laid in every decent house, whereas Mr. Speak preferred to see his regiment of Chinese servants really earn their pay at some considerable exertion. During the night the roof, it seemed, had fallen in and burst through the ceilings. (These palaces were not of a substantial build.) And at breakfast Mr. Speak apologized for the disturbance caused during the night. 'I regret,' said he, 'that owing to the roof accident I shall have to put you and your wife into one room.'

'*A là guerre comme à la guerre*,' replied Uncle Emmanuel.

'How pale Natàsha looks!' Aunt Molly observed. Natàsha, according to Mme Negodyaev, had been crying in her sleep. And Natàsha related a dream that had frightened her in the night. A snow-covered hill somewhere in Russia. Tired of walking, she had sat down—and waited. Dusk was falling quickly. And as she waited, what she waited for appeared. Over the snow-clad mountains lost in twilight, in the dim blue distance a black mass was moving towards her. As it approached, her eye could discern that it was a procession of men. 'Awful mens coming along and not looking at me and carrying something—oh, like a coffin. Oh, I was so frightened. And they came nearer and nearer, not looking at me, and then stopped before me and laid down the coffin, saying nothing. And I saw it was open and empty. I said, "Oh, who have you come for?" And they said: "For you." Oh—it gave me such a—oh!' She shuddered, and then suddenly began to cry.

After lunch I strolled about in the garden. Magnificent trees. A bed of tulips all bending towards the sun, like a *corps de ballet*. Strange: the Shanghai house was like the house of my dreams. Its shape reminded me of our house in Petersburg, dreaming upon the bank of the wide Neva. I remembered so well how it stood there, a little worse for wear and tear, but infinitely near, as if saying with reproach: 'You have left me, but I have a soul of my own, and I shall live even when you will not.' The interior, to some extent, also seemed familiar. This is my sister's room, I thought. Here on the wide landing I used to wait for her on my tricycle car to come home from school, merely to convey her down this corridor to her room...Here at this window we would sit and wait for the carriage to return from the station with our parents, home from Nice.—All that is over...But *is* it over?

Natàsha came running across the path, her sea-green eyes sparkling in the sun. 'Oh, I have been to the pictures; Mr. Speak took us! Oh, what a lovely!' she cried. 'Mary Pickford. Oh, what a beauty boy little Lord Fountainpen! with long beauty hair like that. Oh, and so sad—I so cried! Oh, how I cried all the time! Oh, how beauty! Oh! oh!' She liked Mr. Speak, but wondered how it was that he who was so rich did not fill all his cupboards with chocolate.

While in Shanghai Natàsha attended the dentist, and Mr. Speak said that for each tooth she put under the door Mouse would bring her a dollar. Two teeth had been put by her there, and Mouse brought her two dollars. Natàsha's eyes sparkled with joy as she picked up the coins in the morning. 'Look, Harry, look!' she exclaimed. When the third tooth was extracted, Natàsha demurred. 'Poor Mouse, she can't get so many dollars,' she sighed.

At dinner there was sole dieppoise; saline of partridge with button mushrooms and an orange salad; roast shoulder of mutton with braised celery, potato fritters, red currant jelly, and brown gravy; Coup Jacques; and Angels on Horseback. The table had been set magnificently. The old Chinese butler stood behind our host, mute like a statue, the incarnation of duty and devotion, and saw to it that every whim of his master's was carried immediately into effect. A procession of servants, whom he marshalled, stole in and out without a sound and served us reverently, as though offering a sacrifice, while the high-priest looked on in awe. The ladies having left us, Uncle Emmanuel talked of the wrongs suffered by Belgium at the hands of the late enemy, as he puffed at a cigar. '*Ah, figurez-vous*,' he began in a confidential tone, buttonholing Mr. Speak, a tone which implied that he was going to impart something of value. '*Les crapauds*!' The message died in the cigar smoke as suddenly as it had come to life. Mr. Speak, withal a profiteer who felt a little awkward in the presence of such officers as had 'done their bit' in the war but at ease with the confidences of my uncle, told us eagerly of his own work in ousting German merchants from Shanghai and installing himself in their places. He had done *his* bit. Our host looked at us timidly expectant, anxious for approval of his patriotic work; which he received forthwith from Uncle Emmanuel, who said: '*Les crapauds*! In Belgium they tookèd Bourgmestre Max, they tookèd him and they takèd him, *les crapauds*!'

Mr. Speak sighed. 'A great war', he uttered.

'*Ah, nous autres militaires* we have cause to remember it!' said my uncle. 'Now we are sailing home *vers la patrie*.'

The patriotic business over, our host began telling us joke after joke. But I did not listen because, while he was telling his joke, my time was occupied in preparing my next (I had to be ready or he would go off with his next), and at the end of each of his jokes I laughed automatically with the others. For, as everyone knows, it is much more fun telling your own anecdotes (since anecdotes to be enjoyed must have sunk in, and that needs time) than listening to new ones.

Next morning Sylvia, in her new clothes and hat, went off without me and had a rattling good time with her new friends. But she returned for the Carlton dance, and I felt the silk glide on her smooth warm limbs as she pressed against me in the tango. And everybody asked: 'Who is that lovely girl with the dark-brown locks?' And I felt she was mine for all time. Now I should have been happy. Yet every hope fulfilled bears its own fatality. What we hoped for has come true; but not quite as we had hoped it. 'I have been to Confession this morning,' she said as we danced. 'To confess my love for Princie. A young priest,' she added. 'Quite good-looking.'

'And what did he say?'

'He said: "Everything?"

'I said "Yes."

' "But why?" said he.

' "Because," said I, "because I love him."

' "But who is he?" said he.

' "I do not know," said I. "I love him." '

Before leaving Shanghai, my uncle and aunt deemed it proper to drop cards on the Captains and Ward Room Officers of the Allied cruisers, and Uncle Emmanuel being laid up with indigestion, he requested me to take round his cards for him. I liked being 'piped'. The American Flag-Lieutenant, a friend of mine, used to pipe me as befits a colonel rather than a captain, and I went on board the U.S. Flagship pretty frequently. Philip Brown met me on the quarter-deck. 'I am right glad to see you, George,'—he held out his hand. 'Well, it's against the regulations of our country to keep any liquor on board, but if you will follow me to my cabin I'll see to it that you get some all the same.' And indeed! and indeed! From underneath his bunk he produced a bottle of whisky and a siphon, and Philip used the bottle rather more than the siphon. 'Come on, you old Cheese. Come, get it down your system! Pour it down your cavity!'

From the American Flagship I went on the British, from that on the French, the Italian, the Jap, and so forth. Everywhere I was duly 'piped' on and off. On the quarter-deck of the Chink ship I was met by a befuddled petty officer who could not comprehend the nature of my visit. 'What do you want?' he asked with startling directness.

'Commandant Vanderflint,' I began, 'who is ill——'

'Who ill? You ill?' asked the Chink.

'Great heavens, no! This is his card—for the Captain.'

'Ah—!——Nobody at home,' he said after a pause.

As I turned to go something struck a spark between his brows, but he stood there, still dubious and undecided, while I gained the gangway. Then, after some excogitation, he began to screech for a sailor, who, as I stepped ashore, piped after me a solitary miserable thin note.

On Friday Mr. Cephas Speak took leave of us, for he was due elsewhere over the week-end, and he left his huge palatial house with its retinue of servants, stables, the garage holding his four cars, entirely at our disposal. 'There,' he said, handing Nora a box of sweets. 'And give this to Harry.' Berthe had been dispatched to spend the night on board the boat to superintend the loading of our luggage in the early morning; and she had taken Harry with her. 'You had better take charge of my typewriter, Harry,' I had said to him. When next morning Aunt Molly came down in her new travelling dress which she had ordered locally—'Oh, mummy, you do look a sight!' Nora exclaimed. 'I want to——'

'I have no time, darling.'

'When will you have time to have time?' Nora persisted.

But she would not move, and when urged to put her hat on, she began to cry.

'What are you crying for, Norkins?'

'I want to stop for dinner—that's the trouble!' she whined. Natàsha, with her parasol in her gloved hands, walked like a little lady. Then we were sitting in the stately limousine, waiting for the chauffeur to move. The chauffeur had got out of his seat and was fiddling with the engine which was firing shots like a maxim. In the end, his efforts were rewarded. The machine obeyed. He switched in the gear, and the gigantic automobile leapt forward. The man put on speed. Aunt Molly, who was frightened of motor-cars when crossing a street, was no less frightened when sitting inside: lest the car should collide with another. Soon we were speeding down the Bund, hastening towards the docks. 'What is that boat there?' asked Aunt Teresa, pointing to a large three-funnelled liner.

'That is our boat, the *Rhinoceros*, I think.'

The car stopped. We were at the water's edge. Another ocean liner was receding steadily towards the sea, receding from the shore that hugged her towards the moody main, till she became a point on the horizon and then was lost to sight.

48

So soon as she saw Harry, Nora began to yelp from sheer joy. It was the first time in their lives that they had been parted for so long as a whole day. He stood on the deck and looked down at us—a little man in a big cap.

'Aunt Berthe hasn't touched your typewriter; it's all right, nobody's touched it,' he said to me first thing I came on board.

Harry and Nora, meeting again after this their first parting, stood face to face and laughed quietly for a whole two minutes. Then they tore off together all round the deck.

'And where's that sweet for Harry from Mr. Speak?' Aunt Molly asked Nora.

Nora had never once delivered a sweet to Harry since the time she was born.

'You've eaten my Easter egg,' she said lamely—though that was now over two years ago.

Harry said nothing. He now never smiled—he was so serious, as if the cares of the world were upon him; or if he did, it was more than ever the smile of a very old man—perfectly senile! Harry did not seem to grow, while Nora was fast catching up with him. He looked like a little old man—very wise, cynical, toothless.

Bubby approved of the ship, saying, 'Thank goodness there are no motor-cars here, mummy'; while Nora spoke of it as 'This slippery house'. She was blossoming out every day. 'I don't say any more "I 'hink"; I say "I *th-th*-think".' So pleased with herself.

It was a real long voyage—with children, with a shipload of luggage, a voyage destined to last many weeks; the ending of a life-period, a new beginning in time, of which the fate could not be foreseen. It made me think of that dreaded long voyage to America in *Les Malheurs de Sophie*. The children were delighted. They thought that they were setting out across the water, and that at the other end of the sea, called England, they would meet Daddy, who was waiting for them on the shore.

'I writed, writed, writed to him—and he never wroted,' said Nora.

Harry looked on demurely with his forget-me-not eyes. 'He'll come if we give him sumfink,' said he.

'Ah! little Norkin!' Natàsha exclaimed. And almost at once, as we stood there, there passed down the deck the inevitable old seaman in a dark-blue blouse; and as he passed us he winked at Natàsha so merrily that it called forth from her a lingering outburst of gurgling delight. I have no special insight into seamen's hearts—for that I must refer you to Joseph Conrad—but the old seaman struck me on the face of it—how shall I put it?—as 'a bit of all right'. Natàsha made friends with him. 'You just come from England?' she asked. 'Have you seen Princess Mary? Oh, how beauty! Oh, what a lovely!'

How she had blossomed out! She became a great favourite of his, and each time he passed her on deck he winked at her so merrily that she issued a gurgling sound of delight.

'And what is your name?' she asked.

'Tom.'

'And which is your cabin?'

He showed her.

She laughed. 'Ha-ha-ha-ha-ha! Uncle Tom's cabin!'

He winked.

'Oh! Oh! I so cried in *Uncle Tom's Cabin*! Eva—such—such—*such*—such a nice girl! Oh, such a lovely!'

From that moment on she called the old seaman in the dark-blue blouse 'Uncle Tom', and since to children everyone is either an uncle or aunt, they all called him now 'Uncle Tom'. And he liked it.

The *Rhinoceros* was a transport, and presently troops came on board in charge of a sergeant major, who detailed them in two parties. 'You fellows,' he said, 'go to the sharp end of the ship, and you here to the blunt end of the ship.'

The naval ratings looked sarcastic. Oh, they *did* look sarcastic! Even 'Uncle Tom' smiled into his chin. 'They are a hignorant lot, those army chaps,' he confided to me, shaking his head.

The sergeant major heard him. 'You hignorant hass!' he said. 'You bloody well mind your own bloody business!'

We were moving. From the bows came the regular impassive beat of the piston-rod. We were moving. The land slanted aside, and we were gliding farther and farther away on the green mirror of the sea towards the breeze.

'Oh, the green green sea!' Natàsha exclaimed, her sea-green eyes sparkling in the sun. Everywhere there were visible signs that the War Office had suddenly lost interest in us. The transport provided for us was definitely top-heavy, and as she went, lurched now on this side, now on that.

At lunch I found sitting next to me a Russian major general with wild pale eyes and long black fingernails, who said he had got back to Shanghai from Hong-Kong, but now, on reflection, was going back again to Hong-Kong without leaving the boat. I recognized his face: it was the man who had once called on me on New Year's Day and had sat in the waiting-room along with other lunatics. His eyes were almost mad, his conversation incoherent. At the outbreak of the Revolution he, a Tsarist general, had sided with the rebels, and assumed command of the revolutionary troops; then his nerves had given way, and now he was adrift in the wide world, without plan and without purpose. If he was mad, there was a little method in his madness. He lived, he said, by issuing I.O.U.s at every port of call. At one place, when nobody would take his I.O.U., he hired a grand piano and then sold it, using the money realized on getting out of mischief. In his view all means were justified by a great end. But after listening to him week after week it struck me that 'the end' with him was possibly the weakest portion of it all. Cross-examined by me, he admitted that he scorned programmes, but believed in living from day to day following the dictates of his complex personality. Asked how he reconciled this view with his declared ideal of public service, he answered that he scorned the public.

During lunch, Harry made audible remarks about the passengers: 'That boy over there has a fat head.'

'Harry!' uttered Aunt Teresa.

'S-s-s-sh!' Aunt Molly hissed.

The General's nails took away some of our appetite, and I tried, diplomatically, to propel the conversation into some such channels. 'The Chinese,' I remarked, 'have extraordinarily long nails.'

'It's a sign of aristocracy,' he replied complacently. 'To show that they do no work.'

'But they are black!'

'What matter? The colour is immaterial.'

The General confessed that he never took a bath, 'Because,' he said, 'once a bath, always a bath—it opens the pores.'

At dinner, the General with the mad eyes grew tearful and melancholy. Surveying his hands and his clothes—'I have sunk,' he said. 'God! how low I have sunk! My nerves have all gone to pieces. I am pursued from one end of the world to the other.' Tears were in his eyes.

A war—a pre-eminently stupid business—is run by stupid people (all the wise ones having set their minds on stopping it as soon as possible); and men who ordinarily would be in the shade rise to the surface and set to organize a 'Secret Service' whose agents spend their time in sending one another information about all sorts of lunatics and innocents, and Vice-Consuls and so-called M.C.O.s do their level best to impede the traffic of the world years after the war is over. And some such cuckoo—I think it was Philip Brown—reported our friend the General with the mad eyes, and another cuckoo apprised the Foreign Office, and the Foreign Office notified the Admiralty and the War Office, and zealous officers had begun to send each other slips of information about this 'dangerous revolutionary'.

The sea was a green mirror. All the way from Shanghai to Hong-Kong it was a green mirror. Not a sound reached our ears but the impassive beat of the piston-rod: proof of the unremitting toil of the engine. The infinite sea conduces to infinite thoughts about God and Man and the Universe. There is nothing to do, so one talks. Captain Negodyaev was philosophically inclined. I did not find that out till we fell into each other's company more intimately on board the *Rhinoceros*. He stood there, leaning back against the rail, a rat on its hind legs, a rat in khaki, philosophizing. 'If you go half the way of logic,' he said, 'and stop there, you have come as near the truth as you are likely to get this side of the grave. But describe the circle, and you are nowhere again. I— '

'You mean,' I said (as we are in the habit of saying when we interrupt to say what *we* mean), 'you mean it simply comes to this: you wander till you find a barrier. Then you allow your soul to grow mature, satiate within the barrier. (When the gruel begins to brew, make haste and set to work: write, paint, experiment.) Then, some time afterwards, the barrier will break down—and again you will begin to wander in the meadow until again you find your way to the high-road.' We talked unostentatiously, quietly, affecting, perhaps half-consciously, the pose of people of seasoned intellect that everything was understood between us, that we took for granted on the part of each all knowledge hitherto available about all things. His attitude to life was a dark smile—the smile of one who is pleased at the opportunity of recognizing a little additional evidence of the vileness which he had all along maintained pervaded life. Fundamentally, I believed in hope, he in despair. It was as if he said, '*Tant pis*!' 'You say it is impossible to despair. But it is possible to despair. I believe in despair. I live on it,' he said.

'You doubt the possibility of immortality, because———'

'Captain Diabologh,' he interrupted. 'Lend me £15. I'll pay it back to you—upon my word of honour—when we get to England.'

'You doubt it because you have a wrong idea of what is real.'

'I really will.'

'The external world seems real to you because you see and hear and smell and feel it. But it is because your senses are so focused and conditioned and attuned that you see and feel and hear and smell it as you do. Actually it consists merely of certain illusory vibrations marking time in nothing—a form of mathematics to sustain the figment of Time made flesh. It is merely a world of appearance in which your *I* has immersed, like a fallen star which has mistaken the clouds for reality and doubts its own light. As a drop of water from the ocean contains identical properties with those of the ocean itself, so that light in you—your real *I*—has the immortal faculties of a timeless sun.'

Beastly, hearing our arguments, butted in with: 'Jabbering like two old washerwomen!'

Captain Negodyaev smiled a propitiatory smile: 'We the philosophers of life are merely the naughty children, while the others are the good children. In the end, Mother Nature puts us all to bed.'

Beastly nodded his head heavily and guffawed loudly as he did so. While Captain Negodyaev talked philosophy, an English dame who read a Ouida novel looked at him disapprovingly through her *lorgnon*. 'You mustn't talk quite so loud and gesticulate quite so much,' I advised him. 'These people think it shocking bad form to get so excited about mere God and the Universe.'

'Well,' he rejoined, 'if it really comes to that, I never laughed so much as when I saw your English people playing cards last night. Not a sound, not a movement, as though they were in church. The monotony of it would be enough to kill any normal human being. In Russia somebody would long have jumped up, expostulated and called another a cheat and a liar. But these here—they sit like stones. Incorrigible people!'

At first I had to share a cabin with Beastly, but unable to stand his *stinks* any longer, I got Uncle Emmanuel to change places with me. But he got out, holding his nose. '*C'est assez*!' he said. 'How I understand you!' Nobody wanted to share a cabin with Beastly. So, in the end, the General with the mad eyes was induced to try his luck, and emerged successfully out of the experiment, remarking that to him *all stinks* were immaterial. But, anyhow, most of the voyage Percy Beastly was ill, and Berthe attended to him.

In the morning we entered the harbour of Hong-Kong. The clouds mixed with the mountains, so that one could hardly tell which were the clouds and which were the mountains. Two red-tabbed staff-officers in pale khaki drill came on a white steam launch flying the Union Jack and asked: 'Is there a General Pokhitonoff on board?' They were informed that there was one. And the General with the mad eyes, lest he should stir the native races into rebellion against the British Crown, was not allowed to land.

The General was a man who invariably agreed to everything —under protest; and so, having registered his protest in a letter to the Captain, he remained on board, while Sylvia and I went on shore. We took the Peak railway. And as we ascended the hill in it, 'You look upon the Other World,' I said, 'as a sort of furnished flat where everything has been prepared for our arrival. I believe that world is more like music seeking its rebirth in its own inspiration; and man like a composer who awakens life to make it echo to the cadence he has plucked out of its own deep sleep, to suggest to him new secrets and new melodies.'

'Darling, you speak so loud that everybody can hear you.'

'I don't care. I am speaking the truth.'

'Oh!'

'What?'

'Bother this fly,' she said.

'There is more impudence in a fly than in many a grown man or woman.'

'Do we get out here?'

'Yes. This is where all the snobby people live—up hill,' I said, stepping out. 'And all the plain folk (the Governor excepted) live down hill, being conveniently looked down upon (the Governor excepted) by their brethren up the hill.'

I walked arm-in-arm with Sylvia, and because I did not want the ants to climb up my trousers, I walked quicker and quicker, the ants, like all other creatures of God, having to take their level chance, some of them perishing under my heels. They ran along quickly, with a serious preoccupied air, over the stony ruins even as we humans climbed the hills—the rotting eruption of nature among which we had come to life. And, behold, a solitary beetle who, too, had come out for a walk this lovely spring day, traversed the path, seeking indolently whom he might devour.

'Darling, please don't run so fast, please don't pull me along—*please*!'

'Do you want these damned things to climb up your legs?' I slackened my pace, and at once one of the accursed creatures, who hurt out of all proportion to their size, climbed up my ankle and did his worst. I shook him off. If I could, I reflected aloud, I would come to an understanding with the ants, a *modur vivendi*, and let them live—while they work out their salvation, whatever it may be! But I cannot be bothered to—and so I crush them under foot rather than be incommoded. And so do we all one another. What a ludicrous world!

Then we found ourselves in a park, with the sea stretched at our feet. What a lordly feeling! A gust of wind stirred amidst the trees and shook some green leaves from their branches; for a moment they remained tremulous. The hot sun dipped its beams into the cool green waters below, and they sparkled with enjoyment. The sky, responsively playful, sent white downy clouds chasing each other across the azure. Sylvia looked at me with that infinitely tender look reserved for the only man who really matters in the world.

I looked at her.

She closed her eyes and sighed. 'Tired. I want to lie down.'

'Shall we go to the hotel?'

'Yes.'

We work, I reflected, but no one knows why. 'There,' I said, stopping and pointing down with my stick, 'ants also work.'

'Yes, darling, they do. But what they can do isn't worth anything, is it?' she said, looking at me with a sweet appeal of reasonableness as if she were sorry for the fated insignificance of the ants but could not overlook it since it was manifest to all.

'Isn't worth anything—you mean to the world?'

'Yes, darling.'

'It isn't a question of size. The universe in its aggregate has possibly not more, but less sense than the ants and is striving to speak through them, to realize its own soul in tangible work towards truth. The universe is awakening from sleep into life and is groping, building, that is, provisionally calculating, erecting outposts that will last for a time in order not to lapse back into the sleep where all is blurred as in a delirium. Our work here is merely the "over" which the world puts down in order not to get muddled in its calculations. But the auditor adds up, adds up without cease: He is trying to realize His full wealth, to get at last at the correct sum. For the Devil, I may tell you, is swindling Him of His possessions.'

'The devil he is!'

'And that is our work. That is what the ants are doing: registering the dream. But one must realize what that means and not register for registration's sake. You must have something to register, and for that you must continually dive back into the dream to bring out the pearls.'

'Darling,' she said, 'and you never bought me that little imitation pearl necklace after all.'

'The whole trouble is that we don't know whether the universe is directing us or we are directing the universe. Some hold that the universe is directing us to direct her. But the truth is probably that we all, the component parts of it, are propping up one another and cannot decide whither to go—as it really does not matter. The universe may not be going anywhere at all, but sensing the fatal barrenness of going anywhere in particular, for exactly the same reason is afraid of standing still. And so it is just restless. We are just restless. We do not know what it is we really want.'

'But, darling, you know very well what I want. You're only pretending you don't.'

'Perhaps when we get sick of wanting something in particular, and sick of wanting nothing in particular, we shall get sick of wanting anything at all, and then we shan't want anything. Sooner or later we shall get sick of not wanting anything. Till we get sick of being sick.'

'And then?'

'Then we shall have stepped into the shoes of God.'

'You are very naughty, darling,' she said.

In a long room that smelt of newly polished wood, with windows overlooking the sea front, we took our *siesta*, and then the waiter brought up tea.

'Tip him well, darling,' Sylvia said. 'He's been quite good to us.'

Leaving the hotel, she gave the lady-manager her hand.

'Thank you,' she said, 'my husband and I have enjoyed ourselves very much.'

As we descended the hill in the train, the sea stretched open before us. A big steamer was coming in, finding her way carefully into the harbour; while there was another steamer just sailing out to sea; and the image of it, coupled with the humming life of the sea front vibrating in the sunlight, portended of a peace—a peace uttered long before us. I thought: I shall perish: but the Universe is mine.

'If the whole world doesn't matter, then what matters? And what is the reason, anyhow, of this "not-mattering" existing at all? For if life were there for no intelligent reason and from no intelligent cause, it would be more than ever a mystery that it was there at all. And if there were no life at all, only death—it would be no less strange and mysterious that death was—a vast sleeping Nothing.'

'The world beyond—Darling, I know nothing of the world beyond, only what my little heart cries about and whines, like a baby,' she said, 'who is crying for milk. Will the mother turn up?'

'Oh, she will! Oh, she will!'

And when we descended into town, it swarmed with busy little people, like beetles—dark human beetles who rushed in all directions, and among the many dark ones there rushed a few white beetles, shouldering the white man's burthen. And I hated myself.

'But if we can hate ourselves and laugh at ourselves—whence this sense of humour in us? What is that in us which laughs, that will not stand solemnities, that will not be impressed by life? What portent is that safety-valve, that constant rise from certain fact into uncertain sublimation? Is that not the real God from which we cannot tire?'

'You are so naughty, darling,' she said.

It was nearing dinner-time, and the evening air was tinged by a faint breeze that made breathing tolerable. The sinuous music that reached us from some café or dancing hall stirred our thirst for life; the shaded table lights beckoned to us to partake of their seclusion.

'Let's dine here, darling.'

'No, no, *maman* will wonder where we are.'

We rickshawed about; got out at the square and looked at the statue of the Duke of Connaught. Then got back into our rickshaws and drove to the shore.

Life is wiser than reason, I thought. Life *is*, and so being, it has nothing to reason about: while reason is only a partial discovery of what *is*—incomplete and therefore inquisitive.

'Darling, she's waiting for you to step inside.'

We stepped into the sampan.

It was the old complaint which, when we are overworked, we put down to drudgery, or when we are lovesick we put down to love. It wasn't drudgery. It wasn't love. It was different. Sylvia, sitting close by my side, looked moved and gravely enchanted, and, by some mute agreement, we did not speak. Her large luminous hazel eyes gazed intently, in silent awe. Hong-Kong behind us, too, seemed in a spell of languor, stirring not, dreaming not: looking on, content just to be. There was no sound but that of the water lapping against the sides of the sampan; and the Chinese face of the woman who worked at the oar, fashioned no doubt in the image of God, was yet so different from ours. She either expected no miracles, or she took them for granted; she looked out to sea with a lethargic, expressionless stare, and worked dumbly and evenly at the oar. The *Rhinoceros*, with its white marble deck-house, looked like a sea-shell, translucent in the evening sunlight, wondrous and spellbound. The sturdy ship which was afraid neither of storms nor of space nor of darkness, looked moved and strangely tranquil as she lay out in midstream; like a hard-faced being melting to a cherished phrase of music, or a hardy seaman smiling at a child. And as you looked over the water at the wide expanse of sea and sky and back at the pearly city shimmering in the fading sunlight, you had a feeling then as if we were indeed immortal.

'*Jesus*!' she purled, 'how I want to go on living for ever!'

Tears welled up from her eyes and hung on them, which made them seem golden, like Salomé's. She smiled, and this shook them from her lashes.

But at dinner that night she was already laughing, drinking much wine and cooing gaily and, as always, half-audibly. Her teeth glittered as she held the glass, like a flower on a stem, and nearly spilt the wine, and because of this and her inherent gaiety, laughed more. Uncle Emmanuel and I had donned white flannels, and white almost transparent jackets—clean and crisp out of the wash—and Aunt Teresa and Aunt Molly, Berthe and Sylvia were also clad in gay white open lace; it was spring, almost summer now, and we were full of the joy of life. Aunt Molly with the children was at another table, and round the corner was Captain Negodyaev with his consort and Natàsha who kept looking round at us at intervals, laughing in her gurgling way. And suddenly she was crying softly.

'What is it, Natàsha?'

'What is it, dear?'

She cried very softly.

'Darling, what is it?'

'A wasp,' she sobbed.

Harry laughed.

During dinner Uncle Emmanuel drank much wine and talked of the Governor's ball that night and the mistake he had made in not calling on him. 'I would have liked to go, too.'

'*I*'m not going: I have no dress uniform.'

'It's a great pity.'

It transpired that Aunt Teresa, accompanied by Berthe, had also been on the Peak railway. 'It pulled,' she complained, 'before I had sat down.'

'That happens,' I rejoined, 'sometimes in sleep. One night I jumped clean out of bed.'

'Oh yes, I remember!' Sylvia cried happily.

'Excuse me'—my uncle turned to her, looking suddenly like a detective—'but how do you remember?'

'Sorry,' she said, lowering her lashes.

'That won't do at all.'

'Sorry,' she said. 'Sorry.'

'The point is that I jumped out clean on to the carpet.'

'That is very interesting, I am sure,' said he.

There was a stiff little pause. My uncle cleared his throat. 'I suspected something all along. I suspected it.'

'And I wish you joy of it!'

'I would have advised you to be more careful, though.'

'When I want your advice I shall cable for it.'

'If we were here alone I would give you a bit of my mind.'

'Then we should exchange our minds like visiting cards.'

'She has no brother,' he whimpered. 'Anatole——' And the tears came to his eyes.

'I loved Ophelia; forty thousand brothers could not, with all their quantity of love, make up my sum.'

'What has Ophelia got to do with it?'

'I had made her happy.'

'My poor daughter...'

Languidly I sipped my brandy. Wearily I raised my eyes at him. '*Must* I really blow your silly brains out?'

'This is scandalous! a scandalous affair!'

'The only equity for your existence that I can tentatively advance, *mon oncle*, is that you may be a blessing in disguise.'

I may be—intermittently—a cynic; but he is worse: he does not know he is a cynic. His daughter! His daughter! But the daughter wanted me to love her, and her father meantime loved other men's daughters. So why does he squeak and squeal, this future censor of films?

'I am the last man,' my tone was conciliatory, 'to want to give the matter a significance it does not possess.'

'Oh!'

'Emmanuel,' said Aunt Teresa in a tone which clearly implied that she was proud of his display of paternal authority but sought to show that much in life must be forgiven. She fumbled in her speech. What she meant, but found it difficult to convey in words, was that she had been unhappy all along at the thought of having done her daughter out of her birthright—which is love—but that I had somehow managed to restore that privilege. 'But Emmanuel, Sylvia was already married at the time.'

'On the eve of my departure, you old cuckoo of an uncle!'

'Married?' said Uncle Emmanuel, agreeably astonished at this extenuating circumstance. 'Of course, that puts a different complexion on it. Well, at that rate we shall presume that she knew what she was doing. Still—still——'

But he did not get beyond that 'still'—a protest put on record, but not pressed.

Dinner over, we lounged over coffee on deck. The big steamer had gone out into the open sea; the pier was discernible only by its string of lights. When the café orchestra subsided, in the intervals we could just catch the distant strains of the band playing in the illuminated gardens of Government House. On the bows a gramophone screamed shrilly, and some Cockney petty officers danced to it with one another in quick, vulgar movements.

This was China—the Far East! The moist heat of evening enveloped us, and standing at the rail, the ship in midstream, somehow one felt sorry for onself and all the lives that live.

49

Methinks it should be now a huge eclipse
Of sun and moon and that the affrighted globe
Should yawn at alteration.

OTHELLO.

When we had come back next day (the ship had broken down and was undergoing alterations and repairs) the General with the mad eyes was still on board, pacing the deck in his sweat-eaten canvas shoes, as a cat paces the roof of a house in flames. The General, who had come from Hong-Kong to Shanghai and had arrived again at Hong-Kong, decided to go on to Singapore, where the Russian Consul—so he hoped—would finance him and request and require that he be allowed forthwith to land on British soil. To this idea he clung with that ready hope of the faint-hearted who, because he dreads the prospect of despair—his sole alternative, clutches at each straw with the assurance of salvation. The General with the mad eyes looked on the British Empire as a huge joke, while Captain Negodyaev regarded it as a refuge for himself and for his family from the imagined persecutions which he so feared on Russian soil, and gravely saluted the Union Jack on every possible occasion; and the occasions, considering that every port we touched was unequivocally British, were not few. It is a truism that whenever Russians meet they quarrel. Captain Negodyaev was a monarchist at heart, and the General with the mad eyes a Bolshevik convert. When on board I played the magnificent old Russian national anthem, the General remarked that it was most improper, while Captain Negodyaev begged me to go on. Yet, it was the Captain who was socially despised by the General, who called his junior a vulgar time-server, and scoffed at his undistinguished unit and provincial upbringing. The Bolshevik General had been a guardsman and a military academician. He prided himself on his connexions in England, and spoke a great deal of the peers with whom he was intimate. 'I have only to write to Lord Curzon,' he would say, with a self-satisfied smile, 'and all the British ports will lie open before me.'

'But in spite of all your aristocratic friends,' rejoined Captain Negodyaev, 'they won't let you out to buy yourself a pack of postcards. Whereas I——'

'Of course not, because I am a big gun; but you—you're a nonentity, they don't notice you.'

The Captain of H.M.T. *Rhinoceros*, a stout little man with an unpleasant smile, and wearing the C.M.G. ribbon, implied in all he said and did that he was every bit as good as a regular Captain of the Royal Navy. But the R.N. Commodore, who travelled as a private passenger on board and wore plain clothes, was a constant eyesore to him; and during dinner the Captain dwelt at length on the service rendered in the war by the Mercantile Marine.

'Certainly!' Beastly nodded heavily as was his custom. 'What *I* always say is: one man's as good as another and a damned sight better!' And he guffawed loudly.

The Captain looked round at the company, and the Commodore. The Commodore made no comment.

Each morning at 10.30 the procession of inspection passed along the deck, headed by the Captain and the Officer Commanding Troops, and followed by the First Officer, the Adjutant, the Second Officer, the Officer of the Day, the Purser, the Chief Engineer, the Medical Officer, and the Ship's Surgeon. At the conclusion of one of these parades Captain Negodyaev stopped the Captain (who was on his way to do something) and, through me, conveyed:

'I have two daughters, Captain: Màsha and Natàsha. Tell the Captain that Màsha is away—married. And this is Natàsha.'

'This is Natàsha,' I translated, ignoring the preamble.

The Captain touched Natàsha kindly on the shoulder, not because he wanted to, but because she happened to be in his way. 'This is your daughter?' he asked, in a tone implying that she should not be allowed to block the passage. And he went his way.

After lunch there was deck-tennis. Beastly played, as you might expect him to, with cheery determination, nodding significantly, a look of evident satisfaction and a broad proud grin coming on his face as his opponents proved unequal to returning his stroke (not because he was so good but because they were so bad). But he looked round as if to say: 'There! this is me all over: to settle it by one stroke!' And he would look round to see if all had noticed it. And Mme Negodyaev played as though she quite expected (assuming a degree of justice in the universe) that her measure of exertion must also be her measure of success. And when it wasn't—well, then she looked as though there was no justice in the world, no reason, no goodness, no God!

'What a lovely, lovely sea!' Sylvia exclaimed, as she stood at the rail awaiting the dinner-gong.

'A stagnant pool reflecting a stray sunbeam may appear to a short-lived insect as evidence of the miraculous and divine. The sublime in nature does not depend on such simple answers as whether this glorious sea before us be the elixir of divine nature or merely a chance pool of slop spilt by some careless charwoman of another dimension: for the miracle might well be in the essence of its being all these things at once.'

'Darling, you are getting very dull,' she said.

Early in the morning we cast anchor off the shore of Singapore. A green-tabbed officer steamed up in a white launch flying the naval ensign, and stepping on board enquired, 'Is there a Russian General here—a General Pok-Pok-Pokhitonoff? A dangerous man.' There was. And the result of it was that the General with the mad eyes was not allowed ashore.

At Singapore, among other things, books were purchased for the education of Natàsha. Her parents had been worrying more and more about her education. 'She's already eight, she will be nine in a year, and she's not too attentive,' Mme Negodyaev complained. 'I always said that I would have my children educated to perfection. And I did not stint my last penny on Màsha. Poor Màsha! She's been so well educated, and yet she's not too happy. Ah, well. And now there is Natàsha.—Ah, here is my cherub.'

Natàsha stood at her side, with eyes bright as daylight. 'We have seen the bullocks,' she said. 'Oh, how many bullocks in the street!'

At Singapore an old dug-out of a British General came on board, and then we steamed up the straits between dark forests of malacca trees till once again we bulged into the ocean. The General with the mad eyes decided he would drift on to Ceylon. To the British General who said, 'What a nice little daughter you have', Captain Negodyaev replied through me: 'I have, your Excellency, two daughters: Màsha, the eldest, is away —married, your Excellency. And this, your Excellency, is Natàsha. She is only eight. Unfortunately, your Excellency, things being what they are, your Excellency, her education is being seriously neglected. Yes, very truly said: it is a long journey, your Excellency.'

Captain Negodyaev liked the British General for his apparent absence of snobbery, just as he disliked the Russian General for his arrogant superiority. But that was because he had not yet learnt to discriminate between the two traditions. The grander the Russian sire the more abrupt his manner with inferiors. Not so in England. English snobbery is a snobbery subdued, a snobbery in shade, in undertone. Your Russian Count will simply fire a volley of abuse at an intruding upstart; and all the other Counts will feel with satisfaction that he has vindicated the integrity of their exclusive caste. Not so in England. It is by an exaggerated deference, by an innuendo of reserve, that your English snob will show you that in the society of him and God you are *other* than his kind. The English General did not take well to the Russian General. 'You're a Bolshevist,' he said to him, as if with a deep concern for the Russian's welfare.

The Russian sniffed. 'Any man who doesn't smoke a pipe or play billiards is called a Bolshevik in your country nowadays. You might as well call me a chair or a carpet for what it conveys.'

The British General would not let the Russian General out of his sight, and followed perpetually on his heels. 'He's a dangerous man,' he confessed to me. 'I am sure he'll set the ship on fire if I don't keep an eye on him. Dreadful fellows, these Bolshevists.' And as you lounged in your deck-chair you would catch between one deck-house and the next a glimpse of the English General's immaculate white tennis shoes, and then shortly afterwards a glimpse of the Russian General's sweat-eaten brown canvas shoes making away, it seemed, from the white tennis shoes, round and round the deck.

For Sylvia and me the voyage was of pure unmitigated bliss from early morning until late at night—love all the way—till perhaps one tired of it just a little. I was content—indifferent. Bovril and biscuits, deck-tennis and quoits, concerts, dances, cocktails, conversations, bridge, and lemon-squash.

'The weather,' she remarked, 'is beautiful.'

'You and I together, love, never mind the weather, love. Look at these two generals chasing each other round the deck.'

It was hot and stifling in the cabin. We dragged our mattresses up on deck and slept at the water's edge to the sound of the lazy splash of the sea.

'What are you laughing at?'

'At our deceiving him.'

'Whom?' she asked, with a stir.

'The Captain.'

'This is not love.'

'Love and love and always love—I love you and you love me—bliss—contentment—perfect happiness everlasting. Still, why is it, darling, that sometimes one longs to hang oneself?'

'Alexander,' she said, 'you have changed.'

'I haven't changed, but it's...exasperating.'

In the midst of the Indian Ocean Captain Negodyaev had a relapse of persecution mania, and he bid his wife and daughter don their overcoats (it seemed to him that fleeing involved fleeing in overcoats) and sit down in the saloon lounge in their furs and muffs and overshoes, surrounded on all sides by the tropic water, till he declared 'All Clear' and sent them back to bed. When I asked Natàsha why her daddy made them don their overcoats and sit out in the lounge, she said, with a shrug, 'I don't know what's it means.' Her education now began in earnest. Her mother taught her Russian syntax. I undertook to teach her English, and three times a week I would dictate from *First Steps* to a distracted infant: 'Nat had a cat but no rat. Did the cat eat the rat of poor Nat?' And punctuating the lesson, sometimes there was the sound of shuffling steps portending the approach of the sweat-eaten canvas shoes; you caught a glimpse of the pale mad eyes, heard him sniff the air, snort a little, and pass by. Sylvia undertook to tutor the French side, and

Natàsha would be exercised in such pregnant conversation as: '*Avez-vous vu le pantalon de ma grand'tante qui est dans le jardin?*' Berthe undertook the piano, which meant that every day for a whole hour Natàsha's slender pink fingers travelled the keys in a dull series of Hannon's exercises, up, up, up the scale, and having reached the utmost top, down, down, down they came till they roared hoarsely (and somewhat unnaturally if you remembered the age and sex of the being who produced these desultory sounds), adding to the ordinary monotony of the sea-voyage, making you want to sleep and never to waken! And Beastly, while the sea was calm, undertook (since he could not affect the culture of a foreign tongue) to instruct Natàsha in arithmetic, to which class of his (since he was always eager to outshine us others) he invited Harry, who counted '1, 2, 3, 5, 7…' or when asked how much two and two made together usually relied on his considerable imagination and replied, after a dreamy spell: 'Eleven.' Uncle Emmanuel, a German scholar in his day—a language which he chose for special study from the General Staff aspect, foreseeing as he did a war between his country and the German Empire—made use of it for the first time by undertaking to propel Natàsha's steps; and when just after luncheon on the way to your cabin you passed the saloon, there was the spectacle of a distracted little girl with plaited hair revealing the tenderest of necks, biting at her pen that she wielded with her slender ink-stained fingers, swinging lazily her bare-kneed legs, and little Uncle Emmanuel, his hand stuck in the front of his waistcoat, strutting up and down with a serious professorial mien, dictating: '*Ist das ein Mensch? Nein, es ist ein Stuhl.*' And if you chose to wait a little longer, you would be rewarded by desultory steps and a pair of shabby canvas shoes emerging from behind the corner, a sniff, a snort, and a fade-out. Natàsha's belated education was thus accelerated to the last degree, even Aunt Teresa undertaking to supervise the infant's efforts at fancy needlework. And, indeed, Natàsha looked proud, sitting on a cushion at the feet of the grand grey-haired bejewelled dame, who occasionally corrected her in a deep drawling baritone.

Uncle Tom passed and winked. She gurgled in ecstatic delight. The lessons over, she would run after him and plead: 'Play with me; oh, *play* with me!' She told him all about Little Lord 'Fountainpen'. Uncle Tom's finger-joints cracked when he bent them, which, he said, was because he had rheumatism. 'Oh, Uncle Tom, you are so funny!' And she had a new name for him—'Uncle Romatism', because, she explained, 'his bones were all crackling'. Harry and Nora, too, were extremely interested in this 'crackling' on the part of 'Uncle Romatism'; and the children would listen in hushed awe to the cracking of the seaman's joints. He had to do it over and over again for their amusement.

The nearer west we moved, the duskier became the yellow, Chinky faces; the more regularly featured, Hindu-looking, more and more like my lean friends from India whom I had known at Oxford. It was a gradually changing panorama noticeable at each port of call, a stimulating subject for reflection, as the big ocean liner, rendered miniature in my imagination, struggled on the troubled ocean somewhere between the Malay coast and the island of Ceylon.

The sea had calmed down, the sun came out, radiant as a smile. I closed my eyes, and the breeze, full of that vigour of the sea, swept across my face; and I slumbered in the keen delight. I dreamt that Captain Negodyaev asked me for a loan of £50—and I woke up.

At Colombo, the General with the mad eyes was again confined on board as a dangerous revolutionary. The staff officer, who had come up in a cutter with the orders, placed his craft at the disposal of the English General, and in the morning we all went ashore. Ah, the Ceylon sea. Ah, the tropical night. The early morning rickshaw ride down to the green roaring ocean which rushed at one and receded, rushed and receded, sparkling in the sun. The dance at the Galle Face Hotel. Again the tropical night with the big pale moon, and the palm-tree forest leering at us from behind, and the lighted ship in midstream keeping watch, faithfully waiting. What were we waiting for? Death? Crouching on all fours, it will creep up and—snap—! take us away, one by one.

We were gathered on the upper deck of the *Rhinoceros*, as she steamed away carefully past the bright foam-washed breakwaters of Colombo's sun-lit coast, and bulged into the open sea. The ocean rose in green mountains, with glints of light on the crests; the gulls wheeling and crying now soared in the sun, now rocked on the waves. Sylvia stood at my side, looked at me. 'With that old, dilapidated bow of yours you look like a minor poet. Come, I'll tie it for you.' I felt the touch of her tender fingers on my neck; and I smelt the fragrance of her hair, and it reminded me of the dances I had danced with her the night before at the hotel, and that brought back to me a swarm of delicate sensations, of tropic nights, of thwarted rivalries, of love, which had transfigured for me, like nothing else, that strange journey round the world; and I felt that we should yet be long together, and that the flower of our happiness was still to come.

The boat began to roll.

The General with the mad eyes had no more plans.—Anyway, he would go on to Egypt—see what happened at Port Said. 'I think,' he confided to me, 'that Churchill and Lloyd George are conferring as to what is to become of me, and I think they will place a residence at my disposal—probably in London, in which case I would apply for your services as my A.D.C.'

On Thursday night there was to be a fancy-dress ball on board, and my idea was to appear as a scarecrow. Nora was mildly amused at my rehearsal of this part, Natàsha wildly so—she even clapped her hands. 'Ooh! Ooh! Look! Scarecrow! Look! Scarecrow!' she cried, while Harry disdained my whole performance. 'Silly,' he said. But on Tuesday Captain Negodyaev had another persecution scare, and he made his wife and daughter dress for flight at a moment's notice, and they sat all dressed up in their furs, in the saloon. Mme Negodyaev looked as though she were loyally performing a necessary act, the necessity of which she did not question, while Natàsha looked confused in our presence, a little ashamed that by virtue of belonging to her Daddy she was in honour bound to participate in this strange rite. The vast, green-coloured ocean was calm, without a ripple. The liner glided noiselessly between the foam. All the long day we lay in deck-chairs and looked out on the sea that stretched everywhere around us. We had not been in sight of land for days and days, and we would not be in sight of land for days and days to come. Natàsha and Nora played nicely together, while Bubby always played by herself. But Harry, who strode as if disdainfully aloof, his hands in his breeches-pockets and with no show of interest in their game, now and then made a sudden unprovoked attack on their hoardings and upset their belongings; and then anguished cries of 'Harry! Harry!' resounded on the quiet mirror of the Indian Ocean.

'Where's that sword?'—he came to me.

'What do you want it for?'

'I want to chop Nora's head off. I'm *sick* of her!'

'You can't have it.'

'Why?'

'I want it myself.'

'Yes, kill uncle with it. And Auntie Terry. And Nora. And Mummy. And Natàsha. And Aunt Berthe.'

'Uncle Romatism', old and toothless, came along the deck whistling 'I'm for ever blowing bubbles'. And passing Natàsha, he winked at her again so merrily that she gurgled with delight.

'Harry! Harry! What for you doing?'

'Harry, leave me alone! Shu*p* up!'

'Whatever is the matter?' Aunt Molly hastened on the scene.

'Harry kicked me,' Natàsha cried.

'No, s'e kicked me first.'

Natàsha was slapped by her father and put in the corner; she cried. And Harry, out of courtesy to the foreigner, was slapped on the head by Aunt Molly: 'Oh, you naughty boy!'—she slapped him.

'Why are you slapping me?' And he cried out of the bitterness of his heart. But presently he ran away round the deck as though all was well and nothing was the matter. The hatch opened, and Natàsha, stealing up from behind, covered my eyes with her cool slender hands; and though by her tender touch, her peculiar breathing, by the rustle of her frock you knew it could only be Natàsha, she said in her ecstatic way: 'Guess! Guess, who is it!' And there followed upon the correct recognition her bubbling, gurgling laugh. 'Shut your eyes and open your mouth!'

Natàsha had grown very tall, slender, a little bashful and reserved. I gave the children some nuts; the rebels took them greedily and asked for more. But Natàsha said each time she had some—'Thank you.'

What a nice young girl was growing up, what an observant, graceful little girl, what a sensitive plant. And we were educating her crescendo, forte, fortissimo! Her hair, plaited on account of the extreme heat, exposed the tenderest of white necks. In all creation there is not a more tender, more responsive, soulful, exquisitely graceful thing than a girl-child of nine!

'Tomorrow,' she said, 'there will be fancy-dress ball. I am "Night".'

Next morning, however, Natàsha had a headache. Whether it was from the excessive heat, or whether because we were educating her at top speed, but already since breakfast she drooped; she sat still. 'Headache,' she said. 'Headache.'

I was standing with Sylvia at the stern, watching the foam trail behind us and loose itself asunder.

'Look!'

I looked. At first I saw a black surface emerging from the waves. It rose and vanished. The beast emerged once more and flashed its white belly in the sun, and then was gone.

In the afternoon we saw him again. A black head emerging and submerging at intervals—a shark, like an enormous black dog in the water, with a pair of wicked black eyes, coursing his way in our trail. Then he was gone.

'There!' she cried. 'There he is again—abreast with us. He is following the boat.'

He vanished in the waves. We waited to see if he had gone. But there he was again, coursing his way in our trail. Now and then you could catch a glimpse of his glittering white belly as he half rose from the waves. Now he was to starboard, now to port, but always about fifty yards from our stern, following us as if with a secret resolution.

Natàsha sat still in the deck-chair and frowned. Uncle Tom passed and winked. 'G-g-g-g-g,' gurgled Natàsha. But she did not ask him to play with her.

'What is it, Natàsha?'

'Headache,' she said.

Suddenly, towards evening, Natàsha felt worse, and she was put to bed, where she lay with red spots on her cheeks, writhing in fever. After dinner, since her condition was reported to be grave, the fancy-dress ball was put off, and the passengers who had looked forward to it and slept all day so as to be up all night lounged upon deck in ennui. Captain Negodyaev had just come back from his daughter's cabin.

'The doctor says she'll be all right in a few days, after a complete rest in bed. She's had too much excitement, she's been running about too much in the sun.'

'And the cause?'

'He supposes it to be a mild sort of sunstroke. Who knows?'

'He isn't a doctor for nothing; he ought to know.'

'He doesn't know.'

We stood at the rail in the moonlight.

'Tonight I am bored. I don't think I have ever been so excruciatingly, so overwhelmingly, so outrageously bored as tonight.'

'Why don't you,' he laughed, 'commit suicide?'

'It would not be enough. What I'd like to do tonight is to blow up the whole earth, commit suicide for and on behalf of everybody. A short cut to the Kingdom of Heaven on earth is to do away with earth.' He smiled indulgently.

'Think what a subject for a painter—what a plot for a story—a scientist secretly at night steals the glowing globe and sends it, lock, stock and barrel, judge, jury and all, to Kingdom Pot. And there is no more sea. What a sublime crime. See his expression. Some lunatic like Balzac could have written it.'

'Why confine yourself to the earth? Why not the whole universe, the entire cosmos?'

I paused, thinking. 'I am for it.'

He looked at me. 'But where would it all go to? All the souls, and so on?'

'Where? To Glory.'

'What would God do?' he asked.

'Oh, God and all.'

'It can't be done,' he said, on reflection.

'Ah!'

'Ah!'

I like the man, he is of the intellectual sort, but for one reason or another our intellectual conversations have a way of ending in the most distressingly practical way, as now when he followed me, all wreathes and smiles, to my cabin and came out crumpling a £5 note and saying nonchalantly, 'We'll settle it next week, I promise faithfully,' having previously given me an I.O.U., signed 'Peter Negodyaev'. I hate generalities, and I would be the last man to want to create the mistaken impression that all Russians are necessarily impractical; but, speaking broadly, I would give this general advice: let no Scotsman lend money to a Russian if he can help it.

This piece of business over, we returned on deck and continued our conversation on the higher plane. 'If there is no eternity now,' he said, 'mankind may create it after our time. Who knows?'

'Yes, those who have suffered and loved and found their way back to the founthead may one day redeem us. The trumpet that will call us back to life might be a trumpet made in Birmingham or Massachusetts: what matter? The last trump will sound; but we shan't appear before God: we shall be God.'

Sylvia came up. 'Didn't I tell you, darling, about the Massachusetts trumpet?'

'You told me of some trumpet, but I understood nothing. It makes me sick to listen to you nowadays. Darling, you're getting *fearfully* boring.'

Berthe came to tell Captain Negodyaev that his wife wanted him below, that Natàsha was worse again. He went off hastily. The General with the mad eyes who had been watching us from afar (he was not on speaking terms with Captain Negodyaev) now came up to enquire what was the matter. 'Cramming a child's mind with rubbish,' I replied. 'That's what has done it. And now a nervous breakdown, I expect.'

'But you've been teaching her yourself.'

'I only pretended it was a lesson to set the parents' mind at rest, but told her funny things instead. She already talks English delightfully. I don't know what they want.'

'They don't know themselves,' he answered gladly.

'Here you have a child with the most delicate intuitions, and you are cramming her head with arithmetic! And now she's gravely ill.'

'Not from that.'

'Very likely from that.'

'Nonsense.'

'There's no nonsense about it.'

Suddenly lapsing into English: 'This is sheer infantry to talk like that!' he cried.

The General had learnt his English without extraneous aid, relying exclusively on his own deductions—a process that was not without danger. So coming in the dictionary across the word *infant* and rightly deducing from the well-known Spanish word *infanta* that *infant* stood for *child*, he further deduced (not correctly this time) that what he meant by *infancy* was *infantry* in English. So he would often observe, 'Socialism is as yet only in its infantry.' I tried to correct him; it was useless: he knew better. Incidentally, himself an infantryman, one would think that he had reserved a word for it in English. He had: he called it, as in Russian, *infanteria*. Now being angry with me, and wishing to imply that I was childish, he said : 'It is sheer infantry to talk like this.'

'General!' I cried. 'General! will you please believe me when I tell you that you can't——'

'Sheer infantry!' he shouted, 'infantry and nothing else!'

'Well, I ought to know better than you.'

'You—you,' he said, 'you're no more English than…you polyglot.'

I confess I don't like this. International as are my sympathies—I do not like this. If you had been born in Japan and brought up in Russia and called Diabologh into the bargain, you would want to be English. When in the war I rode with my troop in Ireland and an old woman called out, 'The English swine!' I felt elated, flattered, exhilarated, secretly proud.

'You cuckoo,' I said, 'my father was born in Manchester, and my mother in York.'

'I thought as much. You Yorkshire pig,' said he.

There was a pause. The British General, with his eye fixed on the Russian General, passed by in his white tennis shoes and stood off, watching.

'That idiot of a General!' the Russian said. 'Imagine him commanding an army corps!'

'All generals are mugs.'

The General suddenly looked at me with fierce insight, as if considering his own position and deciding whether to be offended or not. He strolled off a few paces, and returned, deciding to be offended.

'Get out!' he shouted suddenly, and stamped his foot.

'Get out yourself.'

He waited a moment, foaming with fury, and then said, 'In that case I'll go myself, Yorkshire pig that you are.'

'Good riddance to bad rubbish.'

I went away with a heavy heart: why had I offended him? The poor devil was not too happy as it was in our midst. Suffering from qualms of conscience, I went in search of him in order to apologize to him, when, rounding the deck-house, I saw him shuffling along in his sweat-eaten canvas shoes towards me.

'Oh, forgive me, forgive my rudeness,' he began, ignoring my apologies. 'But I feel I am here like a beast in a trap—alone amidst a crowd of enemies. All look at me with suspicion. That idiot of a General of yours is on my heels all day long. I can't go down to my cabin without his coming down behind me. All talk, whisper about me, point at me. I'm not allowed to go ashore to buy myself a picture postcard; all the secret service agents in the world have been set on my heels. I—I—I—my nerves have all gone to pieces. Forgive me, my friend, do.' He held out his hand.

I hastened with counter apologies, and we were friends once more.

'I hear,' he said, 'Natàsha isn't at all well. I've just met Nurse. She seemed worried. And we are likely to run out of coal, in which case we might have to drift to Bombay. I think the Captain will have a meeting to decide the question tonight.'

Next morning Natàsha was better. Directly after lunch I went to see her. As I entered the hospital ward I saw the ship's surgeon—a darkish Argentine—making up to the pretty nurse. He had had his eye on her ever since we left Shanghai. And here at last was the opportunity. 'Well, Nurse,' he said, 'let's put our heads together.' Which they immediately did, as he shot his hand under her arm, and sitting thus, arm in arm and brow to brow, across Natàsha's bunk, 'Well, what the devil d'you think's the matter with her, Nurse?' he asked her cheerily.

Nurse looked very thoughtful, and answered: 'I wonder.'

They had not heard my steps, and blushed a little as I came up. The air was stifling: it smelt of disinfectant. Natàsha, looking small in her striped flannel chemise, looked up at me and raised her delicate faint brow. 'Ah! Mr. Georg*es*!'

The ship's surgeon had diagnosed her illness as being due to a mild sunstroke, the remedy being complete rest and special diet, for the little girl was very sick and could not eat.

'Well, Natàsha, what is the matter, dear?'

'It is romatism,' she said—and sighed.

I stood watching her, at a loss for what to say. When we were left alone, she motioned me to her side. 'Sit on my bed.'

I took her warm, perspiring hand, touched her slender fingers.

'No fancy-dress,' she said. 'No fancy-dress because of me!'

'Yes. No one wants to have one without you. It's been put off for a week till you get better again.'

'Oh, goodness gracious! A week! I'll be up tomorrow——' And she sighed.

'What is it?'

'Headache,' she said. 'Headache,' wrinkling her brow.

'Is Harry not breaking my doll?' she suddenly asked.

'No, I'm keeping an eye on it.'

'Norkins can play with my doll. But tell Harry he mustn't touch it; he'll break it—and s'mine.'

'I'll touch him if he touches it.'

'Gug-g-g-g-g——' she laughed her gurgling laughter, and then said:

'Have you seen Princess Mary?'

I had to confess that I had not.

'Give me that paper, please.'

I stretched across to the opposite bunk and got it for her.

'What are you looking for?'

'Wait.'

She had seen Princess Mary's photograph in the *Graphic*, and had fallen in love with her. Now she found the page. 'Look! Oh, how beauty!' she said. 'Oh, what a lovely—Princess Mary!'

'When we get to London,' I said, 'you shall see her.'

'London. What's it means London? How do you get at London?'

'We shall get at it all right. It's a big place with lots of buses and underground trains and moving staircases and things, on which you have only to stand still while up—up—up they take you, straight into the streets.'

'Is that how you get to the King and—his wife?' she enquired.

'Oh yes. I will take you when we get there.'

'Oh, goodness gracious!' she said, bubbling all over. She sat up in bed, and pulling me over to her side nestled to me in her warm striped flannel chemise. 'Oh, you are my uncle, I love you. You are my daddy, when daddy is away...you are my daddy.

Headache,' she said, wrinkling her brow. 'Headache—headache.'

I touched her forehead with my own; it was hard, warm, hot, moist. As I got up to go, she held me by the hand: 'Stay with me.'

'Lie down, Natàsha. You must lie down. Lie down, that's right.'

'Oh, you are my uncle. Oh, stay with me. Uncle Georgie: I love you. I love you, Uncle Georgie. Uncle Georgie: I love you. Stay with me.'

I was loth to leave her, and she was loth to let me go; but when her mother came I went away, and smoking, pondered on the nature of her illness. What was it? No one knew. The doctor didn't really seem to know himself.

But the third day she only said: 'Drink Drink Drink...' The skin was very tight on her face. When in good health she was very pale, had scarcely ever any colour. But now, writhing in fever, her cheeks were like ripe cherries in their warm gloss; she was flushed and more beautiful than I had ever seen her. In her delirium she muttered: 'These awful mens—take away these awful mens.' When she came to, she only muttered: 'Drink. Drink. Drink...'

Berthe dashed past me as I came up the steps of the saloon. 'What is it, Berthe?'

'The little one,' she said, 'is very bad.'

I dreamt that what I dreaded most—Natàsha's death—had come true, and then I dreamt that my fears were false: that I had only dreamt it, and I felt at ease. Later I woke. I woke—and she was dead; and it was unreal like a bad dream.

In the morning, before I knew the worst, I slipped up in my dressing-gown and slippers. It was very early still, and the decks were being scrubbed; the water rushed out of the hose and streamed in broad floods down the sloping deck. In the saloon doorway stood the ship's surgeon, looking out to sea, and puffed at the end of his cigarette. His tired eyes twitched in the smoke, and the way he held the cigarette, between forefinger and thumb, spoke of relaxation after extreme strain.

I dared not ask. I dared not look. He greeted me with a nod, and looked out to sea.

I waited. 'How is she?'

The surgeon first puffed at his cigarette.

'Just died, poor little girl.' And he looked out to sea.

'We shall drift into a monsoon by tonight. See those two cursed sharks—see them? Been following us these last three days. We shall drift into a monsoon. But the Captain wants to go on and coal at Aden. First Officer thinks we ought to go to Bombay before we run out of coal. Never been on such a ship before! Yes, she's dead, poor little girl.'

I did not understand. It was devoid of meaning. I went down into the ward to have a look at her. Natàsha lay perfectly still, and her closed lids made her faint brows look the more naïve, tender and touching. She looked like a wax doll.

Perhaps all life is but a dream within a dream, and what we call reality is but our dream of waking, of having woken; that presently we shall awake again and find that what we thought to be 'reality' is all without existence. Natàsha's death… I'm dreaming? The sea breeze touches my hair perceptibly: all the same, I may be dreaming that. And if not, what matter? For even as she died she may have woken—wide awake—and smiled, and smiled, over the erstwhile burthen.

I went back into my cabin, shaved, bathed, and dressed as usual. And all the time it seemed as if all this sudden meaningless disaster was but a bad dream, that in a little while I would *really* wake and smile at having dreamt of so intolerable, so hideous, a bereavement.

Yet she was dead. Strange as it was, she was dead. Came a time when it no longer seemed strange. A sharp fact, it had to be faced; and faced, it became a blunt fact. She had gone unharmed through two revolutions, five sieges, two seasons of famine and pestilence. She died on the tropical water, in plenty and comfort and quietude, no one ever knew why.

The parents felt anxious to postpone the moment of burial; but the Captain's attitude in the matter was that he would brook no interference with the ship's routine. At 8 a.m. a procession of men carrying a plank walked down imperturbably to the hospital ward below. Natàsha, sewn up in sail cloth, with weights put inside to prevent her from floating, was placed on the plank, and the Russian tricolour—the obsolete flag of white, blue and red, hurriedly stitched together—was laid on the little body. The same men took up the burthen and carried it out on to the forecastle, followed by the procession of the ship's officers, who had donned their full-dress uniforms, which looked like glorified frock coats. Here the procession of men halted, the burthen was laid down on two stools. In front stood the Anglican Chaplain, in surplice and hood (for want of an Orthodox priest). Behind stood the taciturn Captain, his staff drawn up at his back: the silent First Officer, shabby and long-legged in his moth-eaten full dress, the Second Officer with black whiskers, the tall Chief-Engineer, the darkish Ship's Surgeon, the fat little Purser, and others. The Captain looked unpleasant, but yet as though pleased at the opportunity of shining in his gala dress. His look, ominously triumphant, seemed to say: 'I am the smallest of the bunch, but the boss of you tall ones for all that.' There was a subtle distinction about it, of which he seemed conscious. He reminded me of little Lloyd George as head of his tall Cabinet. His eyesore, the Commodore, on the contrary, stood gazing down nonchalantly from the upper deck, in a blue river jacket, his hands in his white flannels, and watched dispassionately at what we were 'up to'. Captain Negodyaev seemed to have shrunken in stature, as he stood there with the inexorable rays of the morning sun beating down on his scantily covered temples and nape of the neck. He was very nervous, and his scraggy longish yellow moustache twitched without cease. Next him stood his wife, a crumpled swooning figure, as though Fate itself this time had stepped on her. Obstinately my mind refused to believe in the reality and the finality of death, until I mocked my own mind, refused to believe she was dead despite the body at my feet. Such things may happen in books, or in nightmares, or in other people's lives, but not in mine. It was a cloudless morning of extreme heat and stuffiness and damp, and the decks were crowded, noisy and indifferent, and I thought that suffering and death should be in the wind and cold of winter, in the slough and drowsiness of autumn, but not in summer—oh, not in summer. Some curious passengers looked down from the upper decks. I noticed the General with the mad eyes. His own tragedy swept aside to naught, he stood there, his legs considerably apart, his head unkempt, a gaping figure, dirty and uncouth, whose only feeling seemed curiosity.

The Anglican Chaplain (who looked like a horse) read the service, commending the body to the deep, when Harry whispered loudly in his mother's ear: 'The flag is hanging crooked.'

'S—s—sh! You must be quiet,' Aunt Molly reproved him.

'Why must I?' he asked.

'Because we're all sorry.'

'No! I'm glad,' he said.

'Harry!' And she slapped his head.

'S'e kicked me,' he cried grievously.

'But Harry!'

'*But s'e kicked me.*'

Slap! came another—nasty one—on the head. (Why always on the head?)

'Ow—a—o—ow—o!' wailed Harry, issuing a yell disproportionate to the whack—to impress the onlookers and enlist their sympathy on his behalf. And Captain Negodyaev's face winced as he turned back. As if there were not enough anguish in the air to have to bear this little shrill discordant cry as well!

'Harry, stop it! Stop it at once!'

'Oh, children should never have been brought to see this,' Berthe wailed aloud. 'They don't understand it! They shouldn't understand it!'

Our thoughts went out to the parents as they stood beneath the tropic sun, their eyes fixed on their little daughter for ever hidden from them. The sea went out in large ripples. The gulls flew screaming and wheeling above them. And I thought that if at this moment they craved for another last sight of her the Captain would not allow it. Their child had ceased to be theirs, had suddenly become inaccessible. And they deplored that the things they had to say to her they could no longer say, unconscious of the truth that she had now forgotten even all that they had ever said to her. Berthe had tears in her eyes, and murmured:

'*Pauvre petite.*'

I have no insight into seamen's hearts; but Uncle Tom looked grave, stern, dignified, conscious of his duty as with, head uncovered, he stood at the side of the plank, with that curious haughty servility peculiar to the old English servant class. Oxford scouts look like that when of a Sunday evening they serve in hall at the 'high table'. A piece of rail had been displaced. The ship had been brought to as near a standstill as possible; barely perceptibly she slid along on the deep, deep, flapping sea. The plank was on ropes, like a swing: a seaman at each side—Uncle Tom and a young one. Below loomed the Indian Ocean, stretching its white paws of froth—like a big cat. A sleek pussy cat with green eyes, purring—but treacherous, unreliable.

They got hold of the ropes—Uncle Tom and the young one. The mother was held up by her husband and Berthe. She looked pale, pasty, she looked awful. Swiftly the flag was pulled off. Then they swung it—once our way, once to the sea. Natàsha slid off, and describing a curve in the air splashed into the water. A few seconds—and she disappeared beneath the foam.

The mother reeled in a swoon. They took her away down the hatchway, a crushed, crumpled thing, whom fate had struck a blow in addition to her level of burthens. The rail was replaced. Slowly the gathering dispersed.

It was mournful in the sky and the still air and on the sunny water, while the liner, stealthily, relentlessly, like life itself, went on. And as we stood there at the rail, involuntarily we gazed back at that lonely far-off spot where the sea sighed in green waves, and the mind went out in that desolate journey in the water, two, three miles, perhaps, to somewhere near the bottom of the sea, where she would sway and bounce and tremble in the current. A little Russian girl in the deep vastness of the Indian Ocean.

Once more we looked back at the sea, and went down to breakfast. But the table where the girl with the sea-green eyes had sat showed empty, and we avoided looking at it as we ate. They talked of a mishap to one of the boilers, of the ensuing delay in our voyage, and that we might have to drift to Bombay to replenish our vanishing coal supply; but I did not care whither we steamed or whither we drifted, and if we were destined to drift for the rest of our lives and never reach England, or stop drifting, or drift straight into hell, it was to me, in my mood of acute resignation, a matter of welcome indifference. After breakfast Aunt Molly came out on deck with a bottle and tablespoon, and gave Nora her cod-liver oil. Perhaps the burial had wrecked her nerves a little, but she said impatiently, 'Get on, Nora, don't waste half an hour over it.'

'Wait—but I like to *taste* it,' Nora pleaded, as she licked the spoon.

'Now go and fetch Harry.'

'Harry: your wi*me*!' came Nora's voice as she ran off down the slippery deck.

He frowned. 'Sickening Mummy,' he said.

Clapping her hands she exclaimed: 'Natàsha has gone to the fishes.' And bored at playing alone, after luncheon, she asked: 'Where is Natàsha? Is she still in the sea playing with the fishes?'

The sharks had gone.

I lay back in the deck-chair, and stared at the motionless clouds, which looked like huge mountains. And the blue sky was like the sea, and the mountainous clouds like the rocks that loom at the bottom of the deep. And behold, there sailed a small cloud like a grinning monkey—inhabitant of the deep!—it stretched out two muscular arms, and became like the bare back of an athlete, and then changed into—yes, *two* grinning monkeys with their heads close together, one of them pointing a hand to the sun. Then they lost shape, turned into a vague translucent mass —and behold, it developed fins, changed into a fish, an enormous white shark which swam ever so slowly and cautiously, staring towards me. I watched it, fascinated like a rabbit; like a pedestrian, glued to the spot by the closeness of a vehicle (because, to him, the calamity is already over and beyond repair: fear has done it). And I fancied that if one were to be confronted by a beast so dreadful, the self-same trance would suddenly come over one in the last few fateful seconds, causing one to feel detached from one's own fate; one would see oneself as some third person, recall in a single moment one's whole life, regard it over, a closed book, one's soul returned to whence it came. I have perished: but the Universe is mine.—Then, gazing at the sky, I fancied I saw Natàsha's little body sewn up in sail cloth coming down out of the blue, swaying lightly. Now she reached the top of the rocks; downward she came into the valley. Today the sea is calm—a dark-green mirror, and the celestial sea, a deep-blue mirror. But when the sea is perturbed, what a hole the waves make, and if they moved asunder—it's only water—there would be a pit of many miles. What a distance to fall. What a journey to make. Now she lies, maybe, in a valley between high hills, and higher than the hills is the sea, and on the sea sail we…

The children played on. Aunt Molly knitted a jersey. Aunt Teresa suffered from headache. I basked and dreamt in the sun.

We were a raft drifting on the sea of eternity. Long, long ago, having seen it face to face, we had fought shy of it. We saw a raft, and made for it. But even safe on the raft we are on the sea of eternity. Three had now been washed off by the sea, but we others still clung to that raft. A crowd of bewildered spirits caught upon a planet. We merely brush against each other's surfaces, and something deep down, unexplored, is ignored or dismissed. Uncle Emmanuel lit a cigar in the sunset; there was a pink gleam of light in his eye. I wondered if he had a soul. We caught a glimpse of Captain Negodyaev gazing steadfastly to sea, puffing hungrily at the remainder of his cigarette. I looked up at the sky: what shall we take from *you* for taking this life from us? There was no answer, save a blighting sense of our impotence. 'Poor man,' said Aunt Teresa. 'We must do something for him.' And looking at this red-eyed creature gazing at a world of red despair, Uncle Emmanuel took the cigar out of his mouth and sighed. 'Yes, he is a good fellow, *le capitaine*. I will recommend him to the Ministry of War for the *Ordre de Léopold 1er* when I get back to Brussels. I am really sorry for him.' The sky was a pellucid mother-of-pearl—as though through all the shadows and clouds, the suffering, confusion and doubts, God smiled: I still knew what I was doing. And curling up into vistas of space, it spoke of what *is* beyond time, beyond loss, and the need of redemption.

The sun had set, and at once the ocean looked dark, the sky was unfriendly: God had gone back to His bunk. Then, strolling about, I came across Captain Negodyaev. He sat very still on a bench at the stern, gazing at the dark trail running away from us, as if asking a meaning from it of a death that had no meaning. In the day-time, half dazed by the sun and the heat, he had braved it somehow, pacing about, avoiding condolences, unable to find a place for himself. But now with the twilight, his grief, like a vulture, descended upon him, and cringing in the corner of the bench he began to cry. I touched him on the shoulder: his face convulsed, he covered it with his hands.

'Trust your feeling. Remember Turgenev: "Can it be that their prayers, their tears are fruitless? Can it be that love, holy, devoted love, is not all-potent? O no! However passionate, sinful, rebellious, may be the heart that has taken refuge in the grave, the flowers which grow upon it gaze tranquilly at us with their innocent eyes: not alone of eternal repose do they speak to us, of that mighty repose of 'indifferent' nature; they speak also of eternal reconciliation and of life everlasting." '

'Flowers,' he said, after a moment's pensive silence, and looked at the dark burrows that eluded our steady course into the loneliness of the ocean, unafraid. 'Innocent eyes…' He choked.

'It didn't need the war. It didn't need the revolution.'

He rose and stalked away. He went back to his wife, who henceforth lay in her cabin, a wounded thing, and was never seen to emerge. Whether he was kind to her, we did not know. I passed the half-open door of Aunt Teresa's cabin. Aunt Teresa's going to bed was always rather an event. She took pyramidon for her head, and aspirin for her cold, and pills to counteract the effect of pyramidon on her stomach, and a remedy to counteract the effect of aspirin on her heart, besides which she used lotions: a tooth lotion, a gum lotion, a jaw lotion (to prevent dislocation), and sunflower seed oil as a general lubricant, and of late a lotion to rub into the roots of her hair. She was sitting now in her chemise upon the bunk in an attitude of great distress and, with the help of Berthe, was rubbing coconut oil into the nape of her neck. In the last few days she had suddenly begun to lose her hair at a terrific rate; there was a bare space on the nape as large as the size of an average saucer. '*C'est terrible*,' she was saying to Berthe, 'there will be nothing left.'

I went out on deck. The nocturnal sky, vigilant, soared above me. The stars looked at me kindly, good-humouredly. The ship's lights twinkled demurely in the dark. I stood very still, following the dark phosphorescent trail that now and then gave a glint of light in the moon. When I was alone I whispered: 'Can you hear me——?' But only the wind that ruffled the topmost flag on the mast answered me. The wind and the lazy splash of the waves.

50

The day we came to Perim I was Orderly Officer, and had to take a party of soldiers, bluejackets and marines to bathe off the island. Aunt Teresa, Sylvia, Uncle Emmanuel, and Berthe (very meagre in her bathing-dress) also came on our launch. There were naked black men and women on the beach, and Aunt Teresa and Berthe cleverly pretended that they did not see them. They did not look aside; they looked at them as though they were so much air. And a black beauty had taken Uncle Emmanuel's fancy. We were back on the launch, and nearly alongside the boat, but he was still standing inert, his binocular gaze fixed on the shore, till Aunt Teresa saw fit to interrupt him: '*Emmanuel! Eh alors!*'

'*Ah, c'est curieux*!' he said genially, looking round at us, as though inviting assent. 'There are no trees, not a single one! Extraordinary country!'

'Mind the steps, dear,' I said tenderly, as we were alongside and climbing the slippery ladder to the quarter-deck.

I know I felt that there was something ineffably pathetic about our anchoring in the fading sunlight of a scorching afternoon—gliding noiselessly into the silent harbour, still as doom. What spots there were in the world. What places! Aden, the back-stairs of the globe. Sylvia leaned on the rail and looked, and I beside her. It made her want to weep softly and woefully, she could not say why. And when the boat, gliding noiselessly, halted still in this uncanny stillness of moist air and yellow water, she looked at me as though expecting that I too must be aware of her emotion. Beastly looked too. He shook his head slowly. 'What a black hole to live in!'

We dined on board, and after dinner stepped into the launch and crossed the tepid shark-infested strip of water to the cheerless shore. Not a tree, not a patch of grass. The sun had sunk into the sea, but the baked desert earth still glowed with heat, and when, driving through the dark of night in a car dashing at full speed, I held out my hand, it was like putting it into an oven. The Sahara was breathing on us from behind. The moon in heaven seemed stifled by the night. The General with the mad eyes who was not allowed to come with us (lest he detract the Arabs from the line of duty to iniquity) asked me to buy a packet of tobacco for him. This done, we visited the famous cisterns deemed to have been built by King Solomon, passed down the many flights of stairs into the hollow depths wherein our steps and even whisper resounded magnified a hundredfold. The night was black, and Aden a dark pit. The car put on speed. We were back at the coast—back on the boat.

In the midst of the Red Sea, Sylvia dreamt of how nice it would be to go on a beautiful voyage together.

'Darling, even in dreams one should observe a certain measure of reality. What is the use of dreaming of future voyages now? We're in the midst of one and—and it isn't that we like it awfully.'

'You're only making a convenience of me.'

'An inconvenience.'

'Kiss me; you never kiss me now.'

'A kiss today, a kiss tomorrow. How it doesn't tire you!'

'You have got up with the wrong leg this morning, darling.'

'Very likely. Very likely. Captain Negodyaev has borrowed £7 from me this morning.' I looked into my pocket-book to see what was still there, and suddenly I came across a card with—

Some day our eyes shall see
The face we love so well,
Some day our hands shall clasp,
And never say 'Farewell.'

'What is it, darling, let me see?'

'Ah, that was a beautiful evening.'

'It was. Better than any we have had since.'

'It was.'

'But, darling, what will happen to us next when we get back to Europe? Have you thought of it?'

I sighed. 'There are in life such concatenations of circumstances when you neither know nor care what happens next or next after.'

'But I want to know.'

'Exactly. I notice, with regret, the same morbid and unhealthy appetite in the readers of novels. How do *I* know? There is no end to life except death—and so when this boat of ours reaches the shores of England it will merely mark the end of a particular group phase in our individual existence.'

'You speak to me like a teacher,' she complained.

'I favour a mild measure of uncertainty as regards the future.'

'Gustave,' she said—and was silent.

'The extradition of Gustave may prove to be a costly business.'

'No. When I get to London I shall go to see my solicitor,' she said, 'to arrange a divorce immediately.'

'On what grounds?'

She thought a while. 'Desertion.'

'Oh!'

'Restitution of conjugal rights,' she said knowingly.

'Why divorce? He's a good man.'

'But I want to marry you.'

'He might die,' I said, 'of hydrophobia. Wait and see.'

'How long?'

'Perhaps not very long. All is in the hands of God—and Aunt Teresa.'

She paused, thoughtful.

'If you go on loving me, and I go on loving you—what else do we want?'

'Oh, that's all right, we shall go on and on and on!'

She cooed like a dove.

From Port Said, Sylvia, Uncle Emmanuel and I set out for Cairo. On the platform at the station I saw Wells's *First and Last Things* and bought it.

'Buy me a *Daily Mail*, darling,' said Sylvia.

The hot, weary journey. Restaurant-car like anywhere else, but Arab waiters in red fezes. The head waiter, whose conception of the lunch seemed to be to get it over in order to begin the second lunch, and to get that over in order to get over the third lunch, exhorted us to take our places, and the waiters, urged on by the head waiter, rushed us through our meal. The man next to me winked one eye at me. 'They don't 'arf chuck it at yer!' he remarked; thus, in a second, wafting us to the Thames-side from where he sprang. But we looked out of the window at the whirling fields of Egypt: a white-robed Arab leading a donkey, a dusky young woman flashed by. On, on, and on.

Cairo at last. We stepped into the victoria and drove off, my knees touching Sylvia's as I sat on the little seat, facing her. Why had she bought that hideous hat, which was like a helmet, covering wholly the upper portion of her face which was entirely lovely, and revealing but the lower part which was less lovely? And sitting there, I thought, as the carriage wafted us out of the station confines into the splendours of the city, that I shouldn't have overtipped the Arab porter as I did. But then I could not very well have asked for change with Sylvia and Uncle waiting for me in the carriage. So there you are, and as we drove along I had to make the best of it. Still, why that hat?

'Darling, why that hat?'

'Eighty-seven rupees,' she said. 'Besides, it protects against sunstroke.'

There was a pause. The still angel winged by.

'Poor Natàsha.'

'Yes.'

'Why didn't I bring my uniform? We ought to have called on Lord Allenby,' observed Uncle Emmanuel.

Sun-scorched houses, shuttered windows, elegant victorias, red-fezed coachmen. But, withal, distrust verging on hostility. And when we set out, on camels and dromedaries, to see the Sphinx and the pyramids, the look upon my driver's face was a dark leer, foreboding the rebellion of the Moslem world, and Uncle Emmanuel, balancing himself upon the dromedary's hump, looked small and frightened, while the white-robed Arabs all the way along kept yelling for 'Backshish! Backshish!' or selling us, at intervals, Egyptian coins dating back to 2,000 years B.C. (actually manufactured by an enterprising firm in Sheffield for the benefit of unsuspecting tourists).

But the failure to fall in with the driver's offer to backshish him or to buy his coins always meant his giving the dromedary a vicious whack with his big stick which sent the animal a-cantering in a most unpleasant fashion, so that Uncle Emmanuel from the uneasy vantage of the hump, exclaimed: '*Cessez! Ah! Voyons donc!*' in anguished protest.

'Backshish!' cried the Arab.

'No!'

And he whacked the animal again, so that my uncle found it difficult to keep his balance on the hump, which pitched and tossed like the mast of a small schooner in a heavy sea. Arrived at the foot of the pyramids, two Arabs climbed to the top in less than three minutes, and then demanded a backshish. Backshished, they offered to repeat the feat provided we backshished them all over again.

The Sphinx—what did he think of it all? For, contrary to tradition, the Sphinx, I insist, is male. He was right: life *was* terrible. *He* knew that talking, writing, even at its best, was prating. To make a statement, unless it be safeguarded by a thousand definitions (when it were better it had not been made at all), is to prate. To state is to ignore. To maintain a position is to maintain a false position. To maintain no position is to negate existence. To assert is to give oneself the lie. To cease asserting is to give the lie to other men's assertions—the sanction to that lie. To know, to know all, would mean to be silent; indeed, what is there in the world to do for such as he? Will you have him explain that things are and are not; that we have a will and have not; that we change and change not? There are moments when one feels uncertain about everything, even the essential, fundamental things of life; when one gropes in the darkness waiting for the light to return; when all is transient, vague, unfounded, casual, one's soul not worth expressing; when every phrase seems arbitrary, every page a string of sentences beginning with 'perhaps'. It is as if one trod upon an empty world, an atmosphere of void, a universe of nothing. Hush! if the whole world be unreal, by what standard, what undying reality is it so? If we are to be dead for all time, by what living truth is it to be?

Arrived back from where we had started, the Arab drivers demanded more backshish. We refused—and they cursed our children and our children's children into the seventh generation.

Next day we went by motor to the splendid Cairo suburb Heliopolis—the Monte Carlo of the East. How luxurious and for the most part how vain. A faint melancholy summer day was nearing to its close, and there was that other feeling that…a little more, and it would all be over. In the evening we sat in the park, along with others, round in a circle. The flower beds are so symmetrical, so neatly laid out. We watch the flower beds, we watch our sticks and parasols. How dull and how senseless. Among other things, the mosquitoes are biting through the socks atrociously. I think: as days gone by have crumbled into dust beneath my feet, so my future days will crumble—give them time; and the unmeaning present, poising, pale, in the abyss, shall fall—and be no more. I felt sorry for Sylvia and for myself, and for the Arabs, over whom we had come—God knows why—to exercise a perennial fatherly control, and even for the simple-minded, cheerful, military brass-hats who were making asses of themselves. Their band played absurd music in the hot, stifling, melancholy air. One sat and drank against the all-invading heat. And life passed, and one hardly minded its passing.

At night, when we walked down the dormant Cairo streets, harlots called after us from the balconies, enticing us to come up, and Uncle Emmanuel waved his hand to them. Sylvia in bed, my uncle insisted on my seeing the *kan-kan*, the *danse du ventre*, the big black man, and the rest of it. Perhaps I am too much of a puritan, but the sight of the nude Arab woman kan-kaning was enough for me.

'Let us go home.'

'*Ah, c'est la vie*!'

And walking home, through the stifling night, all the time there was that feeling that…a little more of this, and we shall go forth into more bleak, more real experiences.

When we came back from Cairo we found the General with the mad eyes, who had not been allowed on shore, wearily strolling about the deck in his sweat-eaten canvas shoes, like a cat on a deserted raft. He would, he decided, go on to Gibraltar and thence, through Spain, to Italy. We found a cable for us from Gustave, who confirmed Uncle Emmanuel's appointment as Member of the Dixmude Municipal Films Censorship Committee, with a salary of 300 francs *per mensem*.

On Friday morning we left Port Said—the gate into Europe—and passed into the astounding deep blue of the Mediterranean Sea. In the quiet blue waters Beastly had risen, and Berthe and he were standing a good deal together at the rail. But I do not think that anything came of it. At Gibraltar a white motor-boat flying the naval ensign came up cutting the water, with two white-capped sailors standing up at the stern and three naval officers inside in white flannels and white-topped caps. They asked for 'General Pokhitonoff', and left word that he should not be allowed on shore.

Henceforth the General could not make up his mind whether

he should go on to Sicily, France, Czecho-Slovakia, Germany, or England. With Gibraltar—across was scorching Africa—the Mediterranean blue was left behind, and the tropical green of the Indian Ocean with Natàsha in it was long out of sight, out of call. No sooner had we turned the 'corner' and plunged into the Bay of Biscay than we began to feel the difference. Suddenly it had become cold. We paced the deck in our overcoats. There was the drizzling rain. Then Percy Beastly, as though nothing was the matter with him, walked quickly to his bunk.

'Sylvia wants to have the fancy-dress ball tonight,' Aunt Teresa observed to me. 'But I hear the Captain is against it—it being Sunday.'

'That is no reason.

'Of course, it's too rough.'

'That too is no reason.' Had they forgotten, so soon forgotten, my little friend?

'The Chaplain is also against having it on a Sunday.'

'If there is a reasonable God in heaven'—and I already felt her shrinking from what she felt to be a coming piece of blasphemy —'if there is a reasonable God in heaven, He won't care tuppence if you dance on Sunday or if you don't.'

'That is so,' she agreed; and suddenly a cynical look came into her eyes. 'But if He is unreasonable?' Her face twitched, her charming powdered nose wrinkled with a touch of devilry; she seemed both frightened lest she should be blaspheming and proud of her original cynicism, as if to say, 'I can do as well as any, if I want to.' But the next moment the fear of blaspheming outweighed the other impulse. 'We ought not to say these things'; adding, after a pause of reflection, 'And particularly now we're at sea.'

Instinctively we both looked at the gathering clouds. The sun had sunk; the waves were getting very black. Twilight at sea! What sadness. I remembered that these things come like bolts from the sky. You come home and find your uncle hanging in the dark-room. Or you wake up to find a child had died at sea. 'We ought to be at the service, instead of talking like that.' Away in the saloon, they paid homage and thanks to their Lord. The evening service was nearing to its end, and the hymn resounded, dim and melancholy, through closed doors.

Abide with me; fast falls the eventide;
The darkness deepens; Lord, with me abide.

It was dusk. The sea raged without abating. What was intolerable was that it would evidently go on raging as long as it pleased. It showed no sign of abating with the second, the third, or tenth surge. The waves began, not at the shore, but somewhere in the middle of the Bay, gathering momentum, till they rose in mountains and broke over us, leaving deep yawning gaps that threatened to swallow us. This fury of inanimate nature let loose is awful because it behaves with an unmeaning mercilessness just as if *we* were not there—as it did before man had stepped out of the slime to try and bridle it. So the waves must have raged when this earth was one ocean. Why this wrath? The inanimate taking on the mood of an animate being; the ocean crouching at you like a tiger. What did it want from us? 'Ah, he is *terrible*, the ocean!' Uncle Emmanuel said, as, after dinner, in the falling dusk, we stood in our overcoats, clenching at the rail and watching the approach of the surges. The waves, like fierce white-maned horses, galloping from afar, crashed down upon us and rushed past without cease, and their flying manes sent a chill through our hearts as, tearing, swelling with rage, they came on.

I turned in. Aunt Molly sick, Sylvia sick, Berthe sick, Harry sick, Nora sick. Nor was my commission, be it remembered, a naval one. The dark turbulent mass will not rest in the night; the spray splashed at the glass, as I sat on the rocking seat at the rocking desk in the writing-room and coped with my diary.

I wrote:

Her prime young loveliness, swift grace, her springtide brightness—it was not for long.—No matter. Her true being was not in that but in her shining star, a light for ever, now dipped into new worlds.

My thoughts drifted. In years to come she would have been an exquisite young girl. The answer, it may be, to my yearning being. Perhaps—I saw it half-foreshadowed across the cheated years—my one true love. Dreams! Life itself has died with her, and beauty with it, and all the promise of all beings yet to be born.

The sea swept on heedless of everything. I wrote—I dozed off. I dreamt that I was at Liverpool Street Station, just stepping on the moving stairs and going up to the street level—the way out. The stairs of transcendence; the unchanging spirit of movement and change: if we can get a foot on to this moving staircase, we go towards new wonders without end. And suddenly I saw Natàsha sitting on the step holding fast with both hands, wonder and delight writ in her shining eyes. And a few steps behind sat Anatole, in Belgian uniform, with boots soiled by the mud of Flanders, happy, debonair, waving the national colours, and shouting: '*Vive la Belgique*!' And then behind him, at a little distance, Uncle Lucy, taciturn and unresponding, in the knickers and the boudoir cap. All racing up—up—up to heaven. Past and past they went, past the street level, past the 'way out'. For there is no way out as there is no way in: for all is life and there is nothing to get out into.

'Time, sir!'

I opened my eyes. The steward had come to put out the lights in the writing-room. 'Of course. Of course.' I rubbed my eyes. From outside came the melancholy chant of the surges, and the uneven beat—as though of a contrite heart—of the piston rod. Here they still push and shuffle, I thought, and get into one another's way in the corridors, or some try to run up the stairs, press forward, fall off—irreligious dullards!—when all they need do is to get on and keep still. To escape from this sheer restlessness, to get an abiding place in the eternal newness of the world!

As the saloon doors leading out on deck were always shut before this hour I was surprised to see them open. But when I spied my aunt crouching in a deck-chair I was not astonished. For one who had carried clean off her officer-husband in the midst of a great war; who had induced her daughter to break with her lover and marry clean against her will; who on the bridal night had sent the bridegroom home to his solitary bed, and sailed away with his young wife: for a woman who had done these things without forfeiting the least good will, to break the routine regulations of a ship was, I suppose, little more than a routine. I looked at her sitting there, all shrivelled up, crouching, gasping for air. But I was not a little frightened lest she be sick, and the pretty sight of it provoke my own sensitive entrails; so I had no sympathy to waste on her condition.

She looked at me darkly. 'Where is Berthe? Here am I, ill and faint and quite alone! Oh, my God! where *is* she?'

'She's with Percy. He is indisposed. It's the sea.'

'Ah! but this is extraordinary! He is a man! and I am a woman, a poor invalid! and I have no one to attend on me!'

With expiatory gestures I mimicked back at her thus: '*!!! Que voulez-vous?*'

The ocean still rolled its angry surges. As far as the eye could see it was black night. I paced up and down like a captain on the bridge, on guard—against what? These lines from Goethe:

Was, von Menschen nicht gewusst
Oder nicht bedacht,
Durch das Labyrinth der Brust
Wandelt in der Nacht

came into my mind.

I do not want to sadden you with pessimism; nevertheless it looks—it very much looks, Uncle Emmanuel's salary as Member of the Dixmude Municipal Films Censorship Committee being a paltry one—as though my royalties on this forthcoming book would be the sole support of Aunt Teresa and her retinue. A sad look-out for an intellectual! Before I left Harbin in the sunshine, my pocket-book was bulging with bank-notes of a high denomination; now after being fleeced and drained by my relations I am again as poor as a curate. I have an insane desire to sneak down the gangway as the boat touches the quay of Southampton, and only let them see my heels.

Reason for yourself. Yesterday again Captain Negodyaev borrowed money. As usual we spoke of religion and the hereafter; he listened amiably, only to ask me at the end of it to lend him £7. Of course he assured me that he would pay me back the money. The sincerity of his intention, in the face of the clean impossibility of his ever doing so, is formidable indeed, and does him credit. But Russians never pay their debts; they don't consider it good fellowship. Aunt Molly had drawn to date the sum of £14 12*s*. Uncle Emmanuel this morning asked me for £2. Captain Negodyaev's debt was £19. Berthe had had £4. Sylvia £30. A total of £69 12*s*.

	£	s.	d.
At Singapore I spent on rickshaw drives alone	1	10	0
At Colombo	1	4	0
Camel ride for Uncle, Sylvia and myself, including backshish and purchase of old Egyptian coins	3	14	7
Motor drive to Heliopolis	2	5	0
Danse du ventre	0	7	0
Kan-kan	0	8	6
To the big black man	0	10	0
Total	£9	19	1

Grand Total: Seventy-nine pounds eleven shillings and a penny.

'Hell! Hell! Perfect hell!'

'What is it, darling?'

'Oh, not you.'

'Alexander—please give me £15. Do you mind?'

'I don't mind. But where am I to take it? Honestly and truly—*where*? Unless I really go and borrow some!'

'Yes, borrow some.'

My grandfather rose in the grave.

So far Aunt Teresa had not drawn on me. But I knew she had almost exhausted the advance from Gustave's bank.

'What shall we do,' she asked, 'when we have no more money?'

'Of course, there is the International Red Cross.'

She meditated. 'I hardly think——' she said. There was a pause.

'Can't you, George, do something?'

'I can.'

'What?'

'I have begun a novel. I have already written the title-page.'

My aunt looked at me with that strange look an English public school boy may cast upon a boy he secretly respects for being 'clever' but nevertheless regards as 'queer', and is a little sorry for him, for all that.

'Is it going to sell well?' she asked.

The exorbitant demands of my aristocratic aunt would tax the circulation of a best-seller. You will see the force of this my writing.

'I hope you'll make money,' she said.

I was silent.

'Anatole would have helped me if he were alive, I know. He was so generous.'

I was silent.

'Is there a lot of action in it? People nowadays want something with lots of action and suspense.'

'Oh, lots and lots!' I answered savagely. 'Gun play in every chapter. Fireworks! People chasing each other round and round and round till they drop from exhaustion.'

Aunt Teresa looked at me uncertainly, not knowing whether I was serious or laughing, and if laughing whether I was laughing at herself. 'I wonder,' she said, 'whom you could write about?'

'Well, *ma tante*, you seem to me a fruitful subject.'

'H'm. *C'est curieux*. But you don't know me. You don't know human nature. What could you write about me?'

'A comedy.'

'Under what title?'

'Well, perhaps—*À tout venant je crache*!'

'You want to laugh at me then?'

'No, that is not humour. Humour is when I laugh at you and laugh at myself in the doing (for laughing at you), and laugh at myself for laughing at myself, and thus to the tenth degree. It's unbiased, free like a bird. The inestimable advantage of comedy over any other literary method of depicting life is that here you rise superior, unobtrusively, to every notion, attitude, and situation so depicted. We laugh—we laugh because we cannot be destroyed, because we do not recognize our destiny in any one achievement, because we are immortal, because there is not this or that world; but endless worlds: eternally we pass from one into another. In this lies the hilarity, futility, the insurmountable greatness of all life.' I felt jolly, having gained my balance with one *coup*. And suddenly I thought of Uncle Lucy's death; and I realized it was in line with the general hilarity of things!

'I suppose,' she said, 'we shall have to put up at an hotel in London.'

I sighed.

'To live at a London hotel is like living in a taxicab with the taximeter leaping all the time—2*s*. 6*d*.—3*s*. 3*d*.—4*s*. 9*d*.—while you breathe. It's awful.'

There was a pause.

'The book,' said my aunt.

'The book,' said my uncle.

The sea had calmed down a little, the surges rolled more steadily and more sensibly, as if ashamed of their drunken excesses of the night before.

'It seems to me I have a soul for music, that possibly I had better chuck the book and start on a sonata, but the thought of crochets, quavers, demi-semi-quavers and what not, necessitates my keeping all my musical emotion to myself.'

'There is no money in music,' she said coldly.

'Or I may conceivably become a psycho-analyst, an architect, a boxer, or a furniture-designer.'

'No, no,' she said. 'The book. The book.'

'The book,' said my uncle.

Well, writing has its compensations. For if you cannot put the fire into your manuscript, you can always put your manuscript into the fire. You have written one novel, and you are writing another. Your own particular publisher writes to you at intervals: 'How goes it? How is the spirit moving you?' And you reply, with the expression of a hen hatching a rare egg: 'I think it is all right...I think it is coming out all right. I think we are saved.' And he retires on tiptoe, frightened, frightened lest he frighten you off this precious gold egg. And then he comes again: 'How goes it? Nearly ready?'

'Not yet.'

And he goes and buys the paper and the cardboard and the necessary implements in anticipation of your work which is now 'in preparation'.

Writing has its compensations. The misguided reviewers who have damned my last book, and who will damn this one, I damn in advance. My last one was a *macédoine* of vegetables. The critics —big dogs, small dogs, hounds and pekingese, came up and sniffed at an unfamiliar vegetable dish, and went away, wagging their tails confusedly. But this should be more beefy. Shall I write it as a moral story with a lesson: pointing out what happens when a selfish aunt is allowed to have it all her own evil way? Or shall I——? No matter. I am not—you won't misunderstand me—writing a novel: I am asking: will this *do* for a novel?

Suddenly I was seized with energy, filled with dread lest I should lose another moment. After all these months of indolence I suddenly conceived that I was in a hurry. It was as if these wasted months had tumbled over me and were pressing me down with their weight. I longed to see it finished, printed, an accomplished task embodied in between two cardboard sheets of binding, wrapped in a striking yellow jacket, and sold at so much net. This old decrepit ship was so intolerably slow. She literally went to sleep. I wanted to *do* things, to live, to work, to build, to shout. To promote companies, conduct a symphony orchestra, organize open-air meetings, paint pictures, preach sermons, act Hamlet, work in a coal mine, write to the Press. And then Sylvia comes and tells me that my aunt is again as sick as a cat. Gustave—the lucky dog. How I envied him, and how stupid it was that at this very moment, perhaps, he might be envying me.

Bah!

I am mortally sick of them, of immoral old uncles, insatiable women, Belgian duds, impecunious captains, insane generals, *stink*-making majors, pyramidon-taking aunts! Of aspirin, *tisane*, eau-de-Cologne. Of the scent of powder, of *Mon Boudoir* aroma. And when Sylvia steals at night into my cabin and talks of divorce in order that we may consolidate our union, I visualize the camisole and knickers, my head goes round from her scent *Cœur de Jeanette*, and though I still feel she is very beautiful I say 'What of it?' and my thoughts go out to my unfortunate Uncle Lucy with a dawning understanding.

And the end? you will ask. For you may have a morbid taste for a strong dramatic ending which may seem to you appropriate to any kind of book. I say to you: 'Bunkum!' The end? I don't know and I don't care. The end depends on what you choose to make it. And I invite the reader to co-operate with me in a spirit of good will to make the end a happy one for all concerned: buy this book. If you have already bought it, buy it again, and get your brother and mother to buy it. And the end, for Aunt Teresa and Aunt Molly and the Negodyaev family, will be different—very different—from what it might otherwise become. So tell your friends, tell all your friends—my aunt wants you to.

'By tomorrow evening we shall see the English coast lights.' I was thrilled at the prospect, and Aunt Teresa—after all, my aunt was born in Manchester—was also thrilled. She had begun a Russian novel about a woman with six husbands, all living. Three husbands, or even four—she could have stood, perhaps. But *six*!—It was too much. 'I can't read this,' she said.

'*Ma tante*, your attitude to literature is as though you were doing it a favour by touching it at all.'

'Talking of literature, have you read in yesterday's *Daily Mail*,' Sylvia said—'*Is Woman's Love Selfish*?'

I looked at the horizon. 'No land in sight?' she questioned.

The Spanish Fleet thou canst not see, because
It is not yet in sight.

'What Spanish Fleet are you talking of?' said Aunt Teresa. My familiarity with quotable literature seems to constrain my family.

'Ah, *ma tante*, your distinction lies outside the sphere of letters!'

That night we dallied, played bridge, and noted the addresses of our fellow-passengers, earnestly assuring and assured that we would call, or at least write—when early in the morning on the dim horizon we perceived the shore of England.

The approach of England, as if of a sudden, had precipitated the crystallization of our plans. The General with the mad eyes resigned himself to go to London. There must have been a Cabinet meeting, he thought, perhaps a debate in the House of Commons as to what might be the proper thing to do by him in his exile.

'Why not see Krassin and go back to Russia and serve under the new régime?'

'Too much honour for Krassin. Let him come to me. If they all come I might consider the invitation.' The General said he thought the British Government, in concert with their Allies, would accord him the freedom of their countries and place a suite of officers at his disposal, one from each Ally, to accompany him on his travels through Europe; and he repeated his advice to me to apply for the highly enviable post of A.D.C. to him. 'The war is over,' said he, 'and you cannot do better for yourself. I would treat you with all courtesy.' Failing this, the General thought that he might eke out a handsome living in the British Isles by telling fortunes—disguise himself as the Black Monk of Russia, with long black fingernails and pale, terrible eyes. 'I only thought of it last night. I'd make my headquarters in Bond Street. All the society women would come in swarms. They would think I was Rasputin. I'd make tons and tons of money. What do you think of it?'

'Not much.'

'I go by what Carlyle said of the population of England.'

'That applies to any population. If your recent utterance is to be regarded as at all characteristic it would prove it.'

'Why, there are so many idiots in England that I would have a royal time!'

'And the police, of course, are no exception: they would be silly enough to arrest you.'

'H'm,' said he, scraping his bristling chin with the black fingernails. There was silence. His spirits drooped. His usual optimism had deserted him. For a moment he was downcast, without plan, without hope. 'I don't know what to do,' he said, looking at me with pale, desperate eyes.

'Have you no relations?'

'I have a wife somewhere, a sister.'

'Where are they?'

'Heaven only knows!'

As I strolled off I saw Mme Negodyaev leaning on the rails. It was her first appearance since Colombo.

'Do you see those white cliffs? This is England,' I said with a secret sense of proprietorship.

'Yes. But to us,' she said, 'it makes little difference now whether it's England or Belgium or what. Do we get off tonight?'

'We shall anchor tonight, very late, but shan't be allowed on shore till the morning on account of passports and things.'

We were silent; then she said:

'Now there are only the two of us—and, of course, Màsha. Poor Màsha! Your aunt told me she would see us through. She commands such influence and authority, so we don't worry. We two don't need much. We have no one to educate now.' The tears came to her eyes.

I looked on.

England, my England!

Though we had all looked for it with impatience, it seemed as if nevertheless it had been sprung on us unawares. Passengers suddenly transferred their interest from one another to their luggage. All had found their way into the hold and were opening and shutting up boxes and generally interfering with their fellow-men. (And when I say 'men' I also mean women.) People were busy and aloof and not a little irritable, while stewards became conspicuously courteous and obliging. Everyone thought of what he would do next: and that 'next' seemed to have little or nothing to do with the man standing next to him. Towards lunch-time the sun came out, but vanished again after lunch.

By four o'clock, while the boat was still moving, passport and quarantine officials came up on a cutter, and, like pirates, climbed up our ship long before the port hove in sight. The white cliffs were now more than ever clearly visible in the distance.

'We shall probably land tonight.'

'More probably tomorrow morning,' said Beastly. 'When a boat comes into port she always begins hooting and messing about for the best part of six hours. High Navigation, I expect! Ha-ha!' He guffawed loudly. 'Eye-wash, that's all it is! Done on purpose to bluff you. They don't want you to run away with the idea that navigation is as blessedly simple a matter as it really is—that's about the truth of it! Same with applying for a passport and that sort of silly thing. All done to impress you. So here. You bet we'll mess about till the morning instead of driving up like in a cab.'

'And in Russia,' I observed, 'the coachman whips up the horse and drives up at the greatest possible speed, pulling up, abruptly, at the porch. It's supposed to look grand.'

'I know. Of course, this cannot be done with a car.'

'Well, I knew a French lieutenant in Russia who did it.'

'The ass, ruining the tyres!'

'Therein,' I observed, 'lay the whole piquancy of the thing.'

Beastly nodded his head heavily, as if wondering what the world indeed was coming to! *He* knew *what was what*. There was no pessimism, no doubt, no inaction about *him*. He would go back to the Argentine to his railroads; he would go and dig a gold mine in Canada; he would start a company for the developing of the port of Vladivostok and make bags of money, and then go into politics abroad and at home, shout at open-air meetings, build bridges, dig oil wells, exploit forests and coal-fields, and raze the whole earth to the ground; he would—he would turn the world upside down and stand on it, gesticulating and holding forth with authority. He would—But as I listened to him I was certain that, whatever he did, he would miss the essential.

The dismal afternoon was nearing to its close, and still the mild waves ran past us, and the *Rhinoceros* held towards one point in England like the needle of a compass to the Pole. Already we could see the faint flickering lights of the English coast-line. And still the *Rhinoceros* heaved.

Towards six, when the coast seemed at arm's length but the boat still moved unabated, and the steward was strapping up my hold-alls in the cabin, I went up on deck. In the marble saloon at the 'blunt end' of the ship sat the passport and quarantine officials holding judgment, like inquisitors, on the 'aliens'. The General with the mad eyes, Captain and Mme Negodyaev looked like helpless buzzing flies fallen a prey to the tentacles of a spider. We—the Commodore among us—had donned uniforms, and otherwise, as British subjects, took up privileged positions at the front of the saloon, at the back of which the 'aliens' were rounded up and herded, like hostages in a siege, and pressed to answer hypothetical questions, in shame and iniquity, before they too could be admitted to the promised land.

We had come up. England hove in sight quite plainly now as a green island with houses and people and parks. We were outside the harbour, just going in; the ship listed heavily now on this side, now on that, clumsily turning round, finding her way into the harbour and hooting hoarsely and hideously; while from the funnels columns of black smoke broke into the drizzling sky. The man at the wheel told the man down below to back engines; then the ship stopped; then the engines resumed. And, true to prophecy, we were 'messing about' just outside the harbour. All the ship's officers were at their posts; only the surgeon, his job over, stood idle at the hatch, puffing at a cigarette. A very long time yet she lolled there, hooting and turning about, it seemed aimlessly, while we stood at the rail balancing on our heels, as at last, pitching heavily, she entered the harbour. We went, past the breakwaters, up the long, wide enclosure of Southampton Water, between two rows of green lawn, when the engines, as if tired, gave way and stopped, the big boat drifting on noiselessly of her own momentum, till she cast anchor—lying-to in midstream.

Arrived. The *Rhinoceros* had become very still, her task done, her strength spent, listless and drooping. Sylvia stood at my side by the rail and cooed a lot of divorcing Gustave and marrying me on the strength of it. But I had long since got used to it and did not listen, but looked out on the handsome trimmed lawns of the banks. She put a sweet in her mouth and looked on, munching. 'Dinner on board before landing,' she said.

'Oh, we shan't land till the morning.'

'Oh! Really? Oh! Oh!—Darling,' she said; 'I love you. Oh, I love you! I love you! I love you!'

'And I too.'

A passport official came up to me. 'Will you kindly interpret for this gentleman; he can't speak a word of English?'

As I went up, he said, 'There is the question of his daughter——'

'I have two daughters,' Captain Negodyaev was saying, 'Màsha and Natàsha——'

'There's only one on the passport,' rejoined the official.

'Quite so,' flustered the other. 'Màsha does not appear on the passport because she is grown up, is married, and lives with her husband, Ippolit Sergèiech Blagovèschenski, away in South Russia. And Natàsha——'

His eyes filled. His face twitched. He gulped. 'The gong has—hasn't sounded yet?' he asked nervously.

'Not yet.'

Red-eyed, he looked at his wife. A tiny tear glittered on her lashes. 'Our cherub,' she lisped, 'is gone—gone from us—to the cherubim.'

I told the passport official.

'I see,' said the man.

And while we stood there and waited, and while we paced on in silence I heard no stealthy steps; no cool covert hands hid my sight. There was no gurgling laughter, no shrug, no ecstatic delight. It was doleful in the gathering twilight, and the lights of England blinked at us ruefully, sadly. The gong echoed to the sound of the sea, and the gulls, the wind, and the drizzling rain.

THE END